EROTIC STORIES FOR PUNJABI WIDOWS

Also by Balli Kaur Jaswal

Inheritance
Sugarbread

BALLI
KAUR JASWAL

EROTIC STORIES FOR PUNJABI WIDOWS

wm
WILLIAM MORROW
An Imprint of HarperCollins*Publishers*

This is a work of fiction. Names, characters, places, and incidents are products of the author's imagination or are used fictitiously and are not to be construed as real. Any resemblance to actual events, locales, organizations, or persons, living or dead, is entirely coincidental.

HarperCollins books may be purchased for educational, business, or sales promotional use. For information, please email the Special Markets Department at SPsales@harpercollins.com.

A hardcover edition of this book was published in 2017 by William Morrow, an imprint of HarperCollins Publishers.

FIRST WILLIAM MORROW PAPERBACK EDITION PUBLISHED 2018.

Library of Congress Cataloging-in-Publication Data has been applied for.

ISBN 978-0-06-264511-1

18 19 20 21 22 LSC 10 9 8

For Paul

Chapter One

Why did Mindi *want* an arranged marriage?

Nikki stared at the profile her sister had attached to the email. There was a list of relevant biographical details: name, age, height, religion, diet (vegetarian except for the occasional fish and chips). General preferences for a husband: intelligent, compassionate and kind, with strong values and a nice smile. Both clean-shaven and turban-wearing men were acceptable, provided beards and moustaches were neatly maintained. The ideal husband had a stable job and up to three hobbies which extended him mentally and physically. *In some ways*, she had written, *he should be just like me*: *modest* (a prude in Nikki's opinion), *practical with finances* (downright stingy) and *family-oriented* (wants babies immediately). Worst of all, the title of her blurb made her sound like a supermarket seasoning spice: Mindi Grewal, East-West Mix.

The narrow corridor connecting Nikki's bedroom to the kitchenette was not suitable for pacing, with uneven floorboards that creaked in various pitches under the slightest contact. She travelled up and down the corridor nonetheless, gathering her thoughts in tiny steps. What was her sister thinking? Sure, Mindi had always been more traditional – once, Nikki had caught her watching an internet video on how to roll perfectly round rotis – but advertising for a groom? It was so *extreme*.

Nikki called Mindi repeatedly and was connected to voicemail each time. By the time she got through, the sunlight had leaked away into the dense evening fog and it was nearly time to leave for her shift at O'Reilly's.

'I know what you're going to say,' Mindi said.

'Can you see it, Mindi?' Nikki asked. 'Can you actually picture this happening?'

'Yes.'

'You're insane, then.'

'I've made this decision on my own. I want to find a husband the traditional way.'

'Why?'

'It's what I want.'

'Why?'

'It just is.'

'You need to come up with a better reason than that if you want me to edit your profile.'

'That's unfair. I supported you when you moved out.'

'You called me a selfish cow.'

'But then when you left, and when Mum wanted to go to your place and demand that you come home, who convinced her to let it go? If not for me, she would never have accepted your decision. She's over it now.'

'*Almost* over it,' Nikki reminded her. Time had worn on Mum's initial sense of outrage and stretched it threadbare. These days Mum was still deeply dissatisfied with Nikki's lifestyle, but she had given up lecturing Nikki about the perils of living on her own. 'My own mother would not have dreamt of allowing this,' Mum always said to prove her progressiveness, a balance of boastfulness and lament in her tone. *East-West Mix*.

'I'm embracing our culture,' Mindi said. 'I see my English friends meeting men online and in nightclubs and they don't seem to be finding anyone suitable. Why not try an arranged marriage? It worked for our parents.'

'Those were different times,' Nikki argued. 'You've got more opportunities than Mum had at the same age.'

'I'm educated, I've done my nursing degree, I've got a job – this is the next step.'

'It shouldn't be a step. Acquiring a husband, that's what you're doing.'

'It's not going to be like that. I just want a bit of help to find him, but it's not like we're going to meet for the first time on our wedding day. Couples are allowed more time to get to know each other these days.'

Nikki balked at the word 'allowed.' Why did Mindi need permission from anyone to take liberties with dating? 'Don't just settle. Do some travelling. See the world.'

'I've seen enough,' Mindi sniffed – a girls' trip to Tenerife last summer during which she had discovered her allergy to shellfish. 'Besides, Kirti is looking for a suitable boy as well. It's time for both of us to settle down.'

'Kirti couldn't spot a suitable boy if he came flying through her window,' Nikki said. 'I'd hardly consider her a serious competitor.' There was no love lost between Nikki and her sister's best friend, a make-up artist, or Facial Enhancing Practitioner, according to her name card. At Mindi's twenty-fifth birthday party last year, Kirti had scrutinized Nikki's outfit and concluded, 'Being pretty is about making an effort though, innit?'

'Mindi, maybe you're bored.'

'Is boredom not a valid reason to try to find a partner? You moved out because you wanted independence. I'm looking to marry someone because I want to be a *part* of something. I want a family. You don't know it now, because you're still young. I get home after a long day at work and it's just Mum and me. I want to come home to *somebody*. I want to talk about my day and eat dinner and plan a life together.'

Nikki clicked open the email attachments. There were two close-ups of Mindi, her smile like a greeting, thick straight hair spilling past her shoulders. Another photo featured the whole family: Mum, Dad, Mindi and Nikki on their last holiday together. It wasn't their best shot; they were all squinting and tiny against a wide landscape. Dad had died later that year, a heart attack snatching his breath at night like a thief. A pang of guilt seized Nikki's stomach. She closed the window.

'Don't use any family photos,' Nikki said. 'I don't want my image in any matchmaker's files.'

'So you'll help me?'

'It's against my principles.' Nikki typed: 'arguments against arranged marriage' into a search engine and clicked on the first result.

'You'll help me, though?'

'The arranged marriage is a flawed system which undermines a woman's right to choose her destiny,' Nikki read aloud.

'Just make the profile sound better. I'm not good with that sort of thing,' Mindi said.

'Did you hear what I said?'

'Some radical rubbish. I stopped listening after "undermines".'

Nikki clicked back to the profile and spotted a grammatical error: *I'm looking for my soulmate. Whose it going to be?* She sighed. Clearly, Mindi's mind was made up – it was a matter of whether Nikki wanted to be involved or not.

'Fine,' she said. 'But only because you're at risk of attracting idiots with this profile. Why have you described yourself as "fun-loving"? Who doesn't love fun?'

'And then could you post it on the marriage board for me?'

'What marriage board?'

'At the big temple in Southall. I'll text you the details.'

'Southall? You're joking.'

'It's much closer to where you live. I've got double shifts at the hospital all week.'

'I thought they had matrimonial websites for this sort of thing,' Nikki said.

'I considered SikhMate.com and PunjabPyaar.com. There are too many men from India looking for an easy visa. If a man sees my profile on the temple board, at least I know he's in London. Southall's got the largest gurdwara in Europe. Better chances than posting on the noticeboard in Enfield,' Mindi explained.

'I'm very busy, you know.'

'Oh please, Nikki. You've got plenty more time than the rest of us.'

Nikki dismissed the hint of judgment. Mum and Mindi didn't consider her bartending work at O'Reilly's a full-time job. It was not worth explaining that she was still searching for her calling – a job where she could make a difference, stimulate her mind, be challenged, valued and rewarded. Such positions were disappointingly scarce and the recession had made things worse. Nikki had even been rejected from volunteer positions with three different women's non-profits, all apologetically explaining how overwhelmed they were a record number of applications. What else was out there for a twenty-two-year-old with half a law degree? In the current economic climate (and possibly all other economic climates): nothing.

'I'll pay you for your time,' Mindi said.

'I'm not taking money from you,' Nikki said reflexively.

'Hang on. Mum wants to say something.' There were muffled instructions in the background. 'She says "remember to lock your windows." There was something on the news last night about break-ins.'

'Tell Mum that I've got nothing valuable to steal,' Nikki said.

'She'll say you have your decency to protect.'

'Too late. Already taken. Andrew Forrest's party after the year eleven prom.' Mindi said nothing in response but her disapproval crackled like static over the line.

Getting ready for work afterwards, Nikki considered Mindi's offer to pay her. A charitable gesture, but Nikki's burdens were not financial. Her flat was above the pub and the rental rate was subsidized by her availability to work extra shifts at the last minute. But bartending was meant to be temporary – she was supposed to be *doing something* with her life by now. Each day brought a new reminder that she was sitting still while her peers moved forward. On a train platform last week, she had spotted a former classmate. How busy and purposeful she looked as she marched toward the station exit, briefcase in one hand and coffee cup in another. Nikki had begun to dread the daytime, the hours when she was most aware of London outside, ticking and clicking into place.

The year before Nikki took her GCSEs, she had accompanied her parents on a trip to India where they made a point of visiting temples and consulting pundits to bestow upon Nikki the necessary guidance to excel. One pundit had asked her to visualize herself in the career she wanted while he chanted prayers to make her visions a reality. Her mind had gone blank, and this canvas of nothingness was the image sent up to the Gods. As with all trips to the motherland, she had been given strict guidelines about what not to say in front of Dad's older brother who hosted them: no swearing; no mention of male friends; no talking back; speak Punjabi to show gratitude for all those summer lessons here that we hoped would nurture your cultural roots. Over dinner, when her uncle asked about the pundit visits, Nikki bit her tongue to keep from replying, 'Fraudulent bastards. I'd be better off asking my mates Mitch and Bazza to read my palm.'

Dad spoke up for her. 'Nikki will probably get into law.'

Her future was sealed then. Dad dismissed her uncertainties with reminders that she would enter a secure and respectable profession. These were only temporary assurances. The fluttering anxiety of sitting in the wrong lecture on her first day of university only multiplied throughout the year. After nearly failing a class in her second year, Nikki was summoned by a tutor who remarked, 'Perhaps this isn't for you.' He was referring to his subject, but she saw how the comment applied to everything: the tedium of lectures and tutorials, the exams and group projects and deadlines. They just weren't for her. She withdrew from university that afternoon.

Unable to tell her parents that she had dropped out, Nikki still left home each morning with her Camden Market vintage leather satchel. She walked through London, which provided the perfect backdrop to her misery with its soot-filled skies and ancient towers. Quitting university provided some relief but Nikki became plagued with anxieties about what she should be doing instead. After a week of aimless wandering, Nikki began filling her afternoons by attending protests with her best friend Olive, who volunteered for an organization called UK Fem Fighters. There was much to be indignant about. Topless models were still appearing on Page Three of the *Sun*. Government funding to women's crisis centres was being halved as part of new austerity measures. Female journalists were in danger of being harassed and assaulted while reporting in war zones overseas. Whales were being senselessly slaughtered in Japan (this was not a women's issue but Nikki felt sorry for the whales nonetheless and accosted strangers to sign her Greenpeace petition).

It was after Dad's friend tried to offer Nikki an internship that she had to admit that she had withdrawn from university. Yelling had never been Dad's style. Distance was his method of expressing disappointment. In the long argument that followed her confession, he and Nikki were rooted to separate rooms, territories that they had unwittingly staked out, while Mum and Mindi orbited in between. The closest they came to a shouting match was after Dad made a list of Nikki's suitable attributes for a law career. 'All of that potential, all of those opportunities, and you're wasting it on what? You were nearly halfway through. What's your plan now?'

'I don't know.'

'You don't know?'

'I'm just not that passionate about law.'

'Not that passionate?'

'You're not even trying to understand. You're just repeating everything I say.'

'REPEATING EVERYTHING YOU SAY?'

'Dad,' Mindi said. 'Calm down. Please.'

'I will not—'

'Mohan, your heart,' Mum warned.

'What's wrong with his heart?' Nikki asked. She looked at Dad with concern but he wouldn't meet her eyes.

'Dad's been having some irregularities. Nothing serious, his EKGs are fine but the blood pressure reading was 140 over 90, which is a little alarming. Then again, there's a family history of DVT so there are concerns . . .' Mindi prattled on. One year into her nursing career and the novelty of using medical jargon at home still hadn't worn off.

'What does it mean?' Nikki asked impatiently.

'Nothing conclusive. He needs to go in for more tests next week,' Mindi said.

'Dad!' Nikki rushed towards him but he held up his hand, stopping her mid-step.

'You are ruining everything,' he said. They were the last words Dad spoke to her. Days later, he and Mum had booked a trip to India even though they had visited only months before. Dad wanted to be with his family, Mum explained.

Gone were the days when Nikki's parents threatened to send her back to India when she misbehaved; now they exiled themselves. 'By the time we return, maybe you will have come to your senses,' Mum said. The comment stung but Nikki was determined not to pick another fight. Her own bags were being discreetly packed. A pub near Olive's flat in Shepherd's Bush was looking for a bartender. By the time her parents returned, Nikki would be gone.

Then Dad died in India. The heart condition had been worse than anything the doctors had detected. In traditional Indian morality tales, wayward children were the primary cause of heart conditions, cancerous lumps, hair loss and other ailments in their aggrieved parents. While Nikki wasn't naïve enough to be convinced that she had given Dad a heart attack, she believed he might have been saved by the follow-up visit in London, which he had postponed to take this hurried trip to India. The guilt gnawed at her insides and made it impossible for Nikki to grieve. At the funeral, she willed for tears to arrive and provide some release but they never did.

Two years on, Nikki still wondered if she had made the right decision. Sometimes she secretly considered returning to her degree even though she couldn't bear the thought of poring through more case studies or sitting through another droning series of lectures. Perhaps passion and excitement were meant to be secondary to a stable adult life. After all, if arranged marriages could work out, maybe Nikki could muster enthusiasm for something she didn't love immediately, and then wait for that love to arrive.

In the morning, Nikki emerged from her building to receive a punishing spray of rain across her face. She pulled the faux fur-lined hood of her jacket over her head and made the grim fifteen-minute march to the train station. Her beloved satchel thumped against her hip. While she was buying a pack of cigarettes at the newsagents, her phone buzzed in her pocket; a message from Olive.

Job at a children's bookshop. Perfect for you! Saw in yesterday's paper.

Nikki was touched. Olive had been scanning the job ads ever since Nikki confided that she wasn't sure if O'Reilly's would stay in business much longer. The pub already seemed to be on its last legs, its old décor too dingy to be considered hip and its menu no competitor for the trendy café that had opened up next door. Sam O'Reilly spent more time than ever in his small back office, surrounded by reams of receipts and invoices.

Nikki replied.

I saw it too. They want min five yrs sales experience. Need a job to get experience, need experience to get a job – madness!

Olive didn't reply. A trainee secondary teacher, her weekday communication was sporadic. Nikki had considered studying to be a teacher but each time she heard Olive talk about her rowdy students, she was thankful that she only had to manage the occasional swaying drunkard at O'Reilly's.

Nikki typed another message.

Will see you at the pub tonight? You wouldn't believe where I'm off to – Southall!!

She stubbed out her cigarette and joined the rush hour crowd to board the train.

During the journey, Nikki watched as London fell away, brick buildings replaced by stretches of scrapyards and industrial lots as the train rushed westwards. One of the final stations on the line, Southall's welcome sign was printed in both English and Punjabi. She was drawn to the Punjabi one first, surprised by the familiarity of those curls and twists. Those summer lessons in India had included learning to read and write Gurmukhi script, a useful party trick later in life when she wrote her English friends' names in Punjabi on bar napkins in exchange for free drinks.

Through the windows of the connecting bus to the temple, the sight of more bilingual signs on shop fronts gave Nikki a slight headache and the sensation of being split in two parts. British, Indian. There had been family day trips here in her early childhood – a wedding at the temple, or a shopping trip dedicated to finding fresh curry spices. Nikki recalled the confused conversations of these trips as Mum and Dad seemed to both love and loathe being amongst their country folk: wouldn't it be nice to have Punjabi neighbours? But what was the point of moving to England then? As North London had taken the shape of home to her parents, there were fewer reasons to visit Southall, which faded to their pasts along with India itself. Now a bhangra bass beat throbbed from the car in the next lane. In a textile merchant's window, a row of glittering sari-clad mannequins smiled demurely at passers-by. Vegetable markets spilled out onto the pavement and hot steam rose from a samosa vendor's cart on the street corner. Nothing had changed.

At one stop, a group of secondary school girls boarded. They giggled and spoke over each other and when the bus lurched suddenly, they flew forwards with a collective shriek. 'Fuckin' hell!' one girl yelped. The other girls laughed but their noise faded quickly when they noticed the glares of two turbaned men sitting across from Nikki. The girls nudged each other to be quiet.

'Have some respect,' somebody hissed. Nikki turned to see an elderly woman giving the girls a withering look as they ducked past.

Most passengers alighted the bus with Nikki at the gurdwara. Its golden dome glinted against the stone-grey clouds and brilliant sapphire and orange curlicues filled the stained-glass windows on the second floor. The Victorian terraces that surrounded the temple looked like toys in comparison to this majestic white building. Nikki itched for a cigarette, but there were too many eyes here. She felt them on her back as she overtook a pack of white-haired women who slowly made their way from the bus stop to the temple's arched entrance. The ceilings in this vast building had seemed infinite when she was a child and they were still dizzyingly high. A faint echo of chanting floated from the prayer hall. Nikki took the scarf out of her bag and draped it over her head. This temple's foyer had been renovated since her last visit years ago and the location of the noticeboards was not immediately obvious. She wandered around for a while but avoided asking for directions. She had once entered a church in Islington looking for directions and made the mistake of telling the minister that she had lost her way. The ensuing conversation about locating her inner spirituality took forty-five minutes and did nothing to point her towards the Victoria line.

Finally, Nikki spotted the noticeboards near the entrance to the langar hall. There were two large boards taking up most of the wall: MARRIAGE and COMMUNITY SERVICE. Whilst the community service board was woefully scant, the marriage board overflowed with flyers.

HEy thEre, HoW U DoIN'? JUST KiDDInG! I'm A PrEtTy LAid BAcK GuY bUT I CAn AsSuRE U, I AiN't The PlAya tYpE. My GOAL IN LIFE is tO EnJoY iT, TaKE OnE DaY At A TiME and DoNT sweAT tHe SMALL StUfF. MoST ImpOrTantLY I WanT 2 FiND My PRINCESS aNd TrEAt hEr THE wAy sHe DeSeRves.

Sikh boy from Jat family of good lineage seeking Sikh girl from same background. Must have compatible likes and dislikes and same family values. We are open-minded about many things but will not accept non-vegetarians.

Bride for Sikh professional.
Amardeep has finished his BA in Accounting and is looking for the girl of his dreams to complete him. First in his graduating class to secure a top position at

a top London accounting firm. Bride must be a professional as well, with BA preferably in one of the following areas: Finance, Marketing, Business Administration or Management. We are in the textile business.

My brother doesn't know I'm posting this here but I thought I'd give it a go! He's single, age 27, and available. He is clever (two Masters degress!!!), funny, kind and respectful. And best of all, he's HOTTT. I know it's a little weird to say this because I'm his sister but its true, promise! If you want to see his pic, send me an email.

Name: Sandeep Singh
Age: 24
Blood Type: O Positive
Education: Bachelor of Mechanical Engineering
Occupation: Mechanical Engineer
Hobbies: Some sports and games
Physical Appearance: Wheatish complexion, 5'8", easy-going smile. Also see picture.

'No way,' Nikki muttered, turning away from the board. Mindi might be going the traditional route but she was too good for any of these men. Nikki's modified version of the profile advertised a compassionate and confident single woman who struck the right balance between tradition and modernity.

I am just as comfortable in a sari as in a pair of jeans. My ideal mate enjoys fine dining and can laugh out loud at himself. I'm a nurse by profession because I find true pleasure in caring for others, but I also want a husband who is self-reliant because I value my independence. I like the occasional

Bollywood film but usually watch romantic comedies and action films. I've done a bit of travelling but I've put off seeing more of the world until I find The One to accompany me on the most important journey: life.

Nikki cringed at the last line but it was the sort of thing her sister would consider profound. She surveyed the board again. If she walked away without posting this profile, Mindi would find out and pester her until she returned to finish the job. If she posted it, Mindi might end up settling for one of these men. Longing for a cigarette, Nikki chewed on her thumbnail. Finally she tacked the profile on the marriage board but on its farthest corner where it was virtually invisible, overlapping with the scant flyers on the Community Notices board. Technically, she had carried out her task as instructed.

There was the sound of throat clearing. Nikki turned to find herself facing a wispy man. He shrugged awkwardly as if responding to a question. Nikki gave a polite nod and looked away but then he spoke.

'So you're looking for . . .' He waved bashfully in the direction of the board. 'A husband?'

'No,' Nikki said quickly. 'Not me.' She didn't want to draw his attention to Mindi's flyer. His arms were like toothpicks.

'Oh,' he said. He looked embarrassed.

'I was just looking at the Community board,' Nikki said. 'Volunteer opportunities, that sort of thing.' She turned her back on him and pretended for a moment to scan the board, nodding as she took in each advertisement. There were cars for sale and flat shares for rent. A few marriage notices had sneaked their way here as well, but these prospects were no better than the ones Nikki had already screened.

'You're into community service then,' he ventured.

'I really must be going,' Nikki said. She rustled through her bag busily to avoid further conversation and turned towards the entrance. Then a flyer caught her eye. She stopped and read it quietly to herself, her eyes moving slowly over the words.

Writing Classes: Register Now!
Ever wanted to write? A new workshop on narrative techniques, character and voice. Tell your story!
Workshops will culminate in an anthology of best work.

A handwritten scrawl below the print read: *Class open to women only. Instructor needed. Paid position, two days weekly. Please contact Kulwinder Kaur at the Sikh Community Association.*

There was no mention of qualifications or prior experience, which was an encouraging sign. Nikki pulled out her phone and typed in the phone number to save it. She noticed the man's curious gaze but she ignored him and fell in step with a current of worshippers who had emerged from the langar hall.

Could she run a writing workshop? She had contributed a piece to the UK Fem Fighters' blog, comparing her experiences with catcalling in Delhi and London, which had enjoyed three days on the Most Read Posts list. Surely she could give writing tips to some temple women? Perhaps publish *An Anthology of Best Work*. Editorial credentials would sit well on her bare résumé. Hope flittered in her chest. This could be a job she could actually enjoy and take pride in.

Light streamed into the temple through its wide windows, splashing the tiled floor with brief warmth before a patch of clouds rushed to conceal the sun. Just as Nikki was about to leave the building, she finally received a reply to her earlier message to Olive.

Where's Southall?

The question surprised Nikki. Surely in their years of friendship, Nikki had mentioned Southall to Olive? Then again, she and Olive had met in secondary school, years after Nikki's parents had deemed these Punjabi day trips too much trouble, so Olive was spared Nikki's complaints about wasting a perfectly good Saturday on the hunt for high quality coriander powder and mustard seeds.

Nikki stopped and looked around. She was surrounded by women with their heads covered – women hurrying after their toddlers, women giving each other sideways glances, women hunched over walking frames. Each one had a story. She could see herself addressing a room full of these Punjabi women. Her senses became overwhelmed with the colour of their kameezes, the sound of fabric rustling and pencils tapping, the smell of perfume and turmeric. Her purpose came into sharp focus. 'Some people don't even know about this place,' she would say. 'Let's change that.' Fiery-eyed and indignant, they would pen their stories for the whole world to read.

Chapter Two

Twenty years ago, in her first and last attempt to be British, Kulwinder Kaur bought a bar of Yardley English Lavender Soap. It was a purchase she justified by noting that the family's regular bar of Neem soap had shrunk to a sliver from frequent use. When Sarab reminded her that they had a closet stocked with necessities from India (toothpaste, soap, hair oil, Brylcreem, turban starch and several bottles of feminine wash that he had mistaken for shampoo) Kulwinder reasoned that, eventually, their toiletries from the motherland would run out. She was only preparing for the inevitable.

The next morning she woke early and dressed Maya in woolly tights, a plaid skirt and a jumper. At breakfast, she anxiously reminded Maya to keep still, lest she spill food on her very first school uniform. Kulwinder's own roti was dipped in achar, a mango pickle that stained her fingers and left a lingering smell on her hands. She offered the achar to Maya whose nose crinkled at the sourness. After eating, Kulwinder used the new soap to scrub both her and Maya's hands – between fingers, under the nails, and especially in those fine palm lines that spelled out their futures. Scented like an English garden, the pair arrived at the primary school registration desk.

A young blonde woman introduced herself as Miss Teal and crouched so her gaze could meet Maya's. 'Good morning,' she said with a smile, and

Maya shyly smiled back. 'What's your name?'

'Maya Kaur,' Maya said.

'Oh, you must be Charanpreet Kaur's cousin. We've been expecting you,' Miss Teal said. Kulwinder felt a familiar tension. This was a common misunderstanding – that all people with the surname Kaur were related – and one that she could usually explain, but today the English words escaped her. She was already overwhelmed by this new world that Maya was about to enter. 'Tell her,' Kulwinder urged Maya in Punjabi, 'or she'll think I'm responsible for all the other Punjabi kids here.' She had a frightening image of dropping off Maya and returning home with a gaggle of new children.

'Charanpreet's not my cousin,' Maya said with a small sigh for her reluctant mother. 'In my religion, all girls are Kaurs and all boys are Singhs.'

'All one big family, God's children,' Kulwinder added. 'Sikh religion.' For some stupid reason, she gave a thumbs-up, like she was recommending a brand of detergent.

'How interesting,' Miss Teal said. 'Maya, would you like to meet Miss Carney? She's the other teacher here.' Miss Carney walked over. 'Look at those lovely eyes,' she cooed. Kulwinder relaxed her grip on Maya's hand. These were kind people who would take care of her daughter. In the weeks leading up to this day, she had fretted over sending Maya to school. What if the other children teased Maya about her accent? What if somebody had to call Kulwinder about an emergency and she was unable to understand?

Miss Carney handed Kulwinder a folder of forms to fill out. Kulwinder drew a stack of forms from her bag. 'The same,' she explained. Sarab had filled them in the night before. His command of English was better than hers but it had still taken a long time. Watching him point to each word as he read, Kulwinder felt the smallness of being in this new country, learning the alphabet like children. 'Soon Maya will be translating everything for us,' Sarab had remarked. Kulwinder wished he hadn't said this. Children shouldn't know more than their parents.

'You're very prepared,' Miss Teal said. Kulwinder was pleased to have impressed the teacher. Miss Teal flipped through the forms and then stopped.

'Now, over here, you forgot to write your home telephone number. Can you just tell me what it is?'

Kulwinder had memorized the digits in English so she could recite this combination of words whenever she was called to. 'Eight nine six . . .' She paused and grimaced. There was a tightness in her stomach. She started over. 'Eight nine six five . . .' She froze. The achar from that morning was bubbling in her chest.

'Eight nine six eight nine six five?' Miss Teal asked.

'No.' Kulwinder waved as if to wipe the woman's memory clean. 'Again.' Her throat felt full and hot. 'Eight nine six eight five five five five five five five.' There were fewer fives than this but she became a broken record as her concentration moved towards suppressing the rising burp.

Miss Teal frowned. 'There are too many numbers.'

'Again,' Kulwinder squeaked. She managed the first three digits before a fierce eruption rose from her throat, blaring a trumpet note across the registration table. The air smelled fetid and – at least to Kulwinder's exaggerated recollection – filled with warty brown bubbles.

After the air filled her lungs again, Kulwinder hastily rattled off the remaining digits. The teachers' eyes bulged with suppressed laughter (This, she did not imagine). 'Thank you,' Miss Teal said. She wrinkled her nose and tipped her face slightly above Kulwinder's. 'That will be all.'

Mortified, Kulwinder hurried away from the women. She reached for Maya's hand but then spotted her in the distance being pushed gently on the swings by a little girl wearing her curly red hair in pigtails.

A few years later, upon Kulwinder's announcement that they would be moving to Southall, Maya protested. 'What about all my friends?' she wailed, meaning the red-haired girl, the blonde girl, the girl who wore overalls and cut her own hair ('Isn't it just awful' her mother said in that adoring way that made one word have two meanings). 'You'll make better friends in our new area,' Kulwinder said. 'They will be more like us.'

These days, Kulwinder took medication to control her gastric reflux condition. Her English had improved somewhat, although she did not need to use it in Southall. As the recently appointed Community Development

Director of the Sikh Community Association, she had her own office space in the Recreation Centre. It was dusty and full of neglected files that she had intended to throw out but kept because they gave the room an air of officiousness, with labels such as BUILDING REGULATIONS and MEETING MINUTES – COPIES. Such appearances were important for the occasional visitor, like the President of the Sikh Community Association, Mr Gurtaj Singh, who was standing in her office now, interrogating her about her flyers.

'Where did you post these?'

'On the temple noticeboard.'

'What sorts of classes are they?'

'Writing classes,' Kulwinder replied. 'For the women.'

She reminded herself to be patient. During their last budget meeting, Gurtaj Singh had rejected her funding requests. 'We have nothing in the budget for that,' he said. It wasn't like Kulwinder to put up a fight in the presence of so many respected Sikh men but Gurtaj Singh always took a certain pleasure in dismissing her. She had to remind Gurtaj Singh that the Sikh Community Association Centre was within temple property and a lie here bore the same weight as a lie in the temple. For that matter, both their heads were covered by turban and dupatta respectively, signifying God's hallowed presence. Gurtaj Singh had to relent. He slashed his pen across his written notes and muttered some figures and it occurred to Kulwinder that finding money for women was not so difficult in the first place.

Yet here he was, asking questions as if this was the first he ever heard of it. He hadn't expected her to go out right away and begin advertising for instructors. Kulwinder presented a flyer. Gurtaj took time putting on his bifocals and clearing his throat. Between lines, he gave Kulwinder a sideways glance that made him resemble a crook in an old Hindi movie. 'Do you have any instructors?'

'I'm interviewing someone. She'll be here soon,' Kulwinder said. A girl named Nikki had called yesterday. She was supposed to have arrived fifteen minutes ago. If Kulwinder had other applicants she wouldn't be worried, but after a week of the flyer being posted, this Nikki had been the only one to respond.

Gurtaj assessed the flyer again. Kulwinder hoped he wouldn't ask her what all of the words meant. She had copied this flyer from another one she saw pinned up at a recreation centre off Queen Mary Road. The flyer had looked professional so she had taken it down, added a note below, and taken it to the photocopying shop where Munna Kaur's son worked. 'Make me a few of these,' she instructed the pimply boy. She thought to ask him to translate some words she didn't understand but if he was anything like that calculating Munna, he would not do a favour for free. Besides, the point was not to be accurate; she just wanted to get the class – any class – running immediately.

'Are there any interested students?' Gurtaj Singh asked.

'Yes,' Kulwinder said. She had gone around personally, informing women of these classes, telling them that they were twice a week and free, and therefore their attendance was expected. Her main targets: elderly widows who could use a more worthwhile pastime than gossiping in the langar hall. They were the most likely to turn up and make the classes appear successful. Then there would be more initiatives to occupy Kulwinder's time. 'Eventually, I hope we can offer much more to the women,' she couldn't resist saying.

Gurtaj Singh replaced the flyer on her desk. He was a short man who wore his khaki pants high on his waist as if altering their hems would be conceding to his lack of height. 'Kulwinder, everybody feels bad about what happened to Maya,' he said.

Kulwinder felt a stab that took her breath away. She recovered quickly and fixed Gurtaj Singh with a stare. *Nobody knows what really happened. Nobody will help me find out.* She wondered how he would react if she said those words aloud. 'I appreciate it,' she said. 'But this has nothing to do with my daughter. The women in this community want to learn – and as the only woman on the board, I should be representing them.' She began stacking the papers on her desk. 'If you'll excuse me, I have a very busy afternoon planned.'

Gurtaj Singh picked up the hint and left. His office, like the offices of the other men on the Board, was in the newly renovated wing of the temple. It had hardwood floors and wide windows that looked out onto the gardens of surrounding homes. Kulwinder was the only Board member who worked in this old two storey building, and as she listened to Gurtaj Singh's fading footsteps, she wondered why men needed all that space when their answers to everything were always 'no'.

A draft passed through the cracked window and blew Kulwinder's papers askew. Searching her top drawer for a proper paperweight, she came across her old complimentary Barclays Bank diary. In the Notes section, she had a list of names and numbers – the local police precinct, the lawyers, even a private investigator that she never ended up calling. It had been nearly ten months and sometimes she still felt as breathlessly desperate as the moment she was told her daughter was dead. She shut the diary and pressed her hands to her teacup. The warmth radiated in her palms. Kulwinder maintained her grip. The burn burrowed through her layers of skin. *Maya.*

'*Sat sri akal.* Sorry I'm late.'

Kulwinder dropped her cup on the desk. A thick stream of spilled chai ran across the table and soaked her papers. In the doorway stood a young woman. 'You said 2 p.m.,' Kulwinder said as she rescued the papers.

'I meant to get here on time but there was a train delay.' She retrieved a serviette from her bag and helped Kulwinder to blot the tea from the papers. Kulwinder stepped back and observed. Although she did not have a son, habit prompted a quick assessment of this girl for her suitability as a wife. Nikki had shoulder-length hair pulled back in a ponytail, revealing a wide forehead. Her beaky face was striking in its own way but she certainly could not afford to forgo wearing make-up like this. Her nails were bitten down, a disgusting habit, and hanging off her waist was a square bag that clearly belonged to a postal worker.

Nikki caught her looking. Kulwinder cleared her throat imperiously and began shuffling and stacking the dry papers on the other end of her desk. She expected Nikki to watch her. Instead she noticed the girl throwing a disdainful look at the crowded shelves and the cracked window.

'Do you have your résumé?' Kulwinder asked.

Nikki produced a sheet from her postal worker bag. Kulwinder skimmed it. She could not afford to be fussy – at this point as long as the instructor was literate in English, she would be hired. But the sting of the girl's look lingered and made Kulwinder feel less generous.

'What teaching experience do you have?' she asked in Punjabi.

The girl responded in hurried English. 'I'll admit, I don't have much teaching experience but I'm really interested in—'

Kulwinder held up her hand. 'Please answer me in Punjabi,' she said. 'Have you ever taught?'

'No.'

'Why do you want to teach this class then?'

'I have a . . . umm . . . how do you say it? A passion for help the women,' Nikki said.

'Hmm,' Kulwinder acknowledged coolly. On the résumé, the longest list was under a header called Activism. Greenpeace Petitioner, Women's Aid Volunteer, UK Fem Fighters Volunteer. Kulwinder did not know what all of it meant, but the last title – UK Fem Fighters – was familiar. A magnet bearing the same title had found its way into her home, courtesy of Maya. Kulwinder was vaguely aware that it had to do with the rights of women. *Just my luck*, she thought. It was one thing to battle for funding against the likes of Gurtaj Singh behind closed doors but these British-born Indian girls who hollered publicly about women's rights were such a self-indulgent lot. Didn't they realize that they were only looking for trouble with that crass and demanding attitude? She felt a flash of anger at Maya, followed by a bewildering grief that momentarily shut out her senses. When she snapped back to reality, Nikki was still talking. She spoke Punjabi with less confidence, peppering her sentences with English words.

'. . . and it's my belief that everyone has the stories to telling. It would be such a *rewarding* experience to help Punjabi women to crafting their stories and *compile* them into a book.'

Kulwinder must have been nodding the girl along because now her rambling made little sense. 'You want to write a book?' she asked cautiously.

'The women's stories will forming a collection,' Nikki said. 'I don't have much experiencing in the arts but I do like to writing and I'm an avid reader. I think I'm to be able to help them *cultivate* their creativity. I'll have some hand in *guiding* the process, of course, and then perhaps do some editing as well.'

It dawned on Kulwinder that she had advertised for something she did not understand. She took another look at the flyer. *Anthology, narrative techniques.* Whatever these words meant, Nikki seemed to be counting on them. Kulwinder rustled through her drawer and took out a receipt of confirmed registrations. Scanning the list of names, Kulwinder thought she should warn Nikki. She looked up. 'The students will not be very advanced writers,' she said.

'Of course,' Nikki assured. 'That's understandable. I'll be there to help them.'

Her patronising tone dissolved Kulwinder's sympathies. This girl was a child. She smiled but her eyes had a squinting quality, as if she was sizing up Kulwinder and her importance here. But was there a chance that a more traditional woman – not this haughty girl who might as well be a *gori* with her jeans and her halting Punjabi – would walk in and ask for the job? It was unlikely. Never mind what Nikki expected to teach, the class had to start right away, or else Gurtaj Singh would strike it off his register and with it any future opportunity for Kulwinder to have a say in women's matters.

'The classes start on Thursday.'

'This Thursday?'

'Thursday evening, yes,' Kulwinder said.

'Sure,' Nikki said. 'What time do the classes starting?'

'Whatever time works best for you,' Kulwinder chirped in the crispest English she could manage, and when Nikki cocked her head in surprise, Kulwinder pretended not to notice.

Chapter Three

The path leading to Nikki's childhood home in Enfield smelled richly of spices. Nikki followed the scent to the door and opened it with her own key. In the living room, *Minute to Win It* was on while Mum and Mindi bustled around the kitchen, calling out to each other. Dad had always watched the news while dinner was being cooked. In his chair, somebody had placed a quilted blanket and the side table where he used to rest his whisky glass had been removed. These shifts in details were little and mundane but they pronounced his absence loudly. She switched the channel to BBC. Immediately, both Mum's and Mindi's heads poked through the kitchen entrance.

'We were watching that,' Mum said.

'Sorry,' Nikki said, but she was reluctant to change the channel back. The presenter's voice brought a wave of nostalgia: she was eleven again and watching the news with Dad before dinner. 'What do you think about that?' Dad would ask. 'Do you think it's fair? What do you think that word means?' Sometimes when Mum used to call her to help set the table, Dad would give Nikki a wink and reply loudly, 'She's busy out here.'

'Can I help with anything?' Nikki asked Mum.

'You can heat up the dal. It's in the fridge,' Mum said. Nikki opened the fridge to find no obvious signs of dal, just a stack of ice-cream containers with faded labels.

'It's in the Vanilla Pecan Delight tub,' Mindi said.

Nikki picked out the container and put it in the microwave. She then watched in horror through the window as the container's edges melted into the dal. 'Dal's going to be a while,' she said, opening the door and removing the container. The noxious smell of burning plastic permeated the kitchen.

'*Hai*, you idiot,' Mum said. 'Why didn't you put it in a microwaveable container first?'

'Why didn't you store it in one?' Nikki asked. 'Ice-cream tubs are misleading.' It was a suggestion stirred from years of crushed hopes from searching Mum's fridge for dessert and instead discovering blocks of frozen curry.

'The containers work just fine,' Mum said. 'They're free.'

There was no rescuing the dal or the container, so Nikki disposed of both and stepped back to the edge of the kitchen. She remembered lingering here the evening after Dad's funeral. Mum was weary – travelling back to London with Dad's body had been a bureaucratic and logistical nightmare – but she refused Nikki's offers to help and ordered her to the sidelines. Nikki asked Mum about Dad's final hours. She needed to know that he hadn't died still angry with her.

'He didn't say anything. He was asleep,' Mum said.

'But before he went to sleep?' Perhaps his last words contained some hint at forgiveness.

'I don't remember,' Mum said. Her cheeks were high with colour.

'Mum, surely you can try—'

'Don't ask me these things,' Mum snapped.

Seeing that forgiveness was a long way off, Nikki had returned to her bedroom and continued her packing. 'You aren't still going to leave are you?' Mindi asked, standing in the doorway.

Nikki looked at the corners of boxes jutting out from under her bed. Piles of books had been pushed into Tesco recyclable bags, and her hooded jacket had been taken off the hook behind the door and rolled up to fit her suitcase.

'I can't live here any more. The minute Mum finds out I'm working in a pub, I'll never hear the end of it. It'll be that same argument all over again. I dealt with Dad ignoring me. I'm not going to stay here while Mum gives me the cold shoulder as well.'

'You're being a selfish cow.'

'I'm being realistic.'

Mindi sighed. 'Think of what Mum's going through. Sometimes it's worthwhile to consider what's best for everyone, not just yourself.'

On this advice, Nikki stayed for another week. But upon returning from errands one day, Mum would find Nikki's room bare and a note on her bed. *I'm sorry, Mum. I had to move out.* Her new address was listed below. She trusted that Mindi would fill Mum in on everything else. Two weeks later, Nikki gathered up the nerve to call Mum and to her surprise, Mum answered. She spoke stiffly to Nikki and gave minimal responses ('How are you, Mum?' 'Alive') but that she responded at all was a positive sign. During their next phone conversation, Mum had an outburst. 'You're a selfish, stupid, idiot girl,' she sobbed. 'You have no heart.' Each word made Nikki flinch and she wanted to defend herself but wasn't it true? She had left them at the worst possible time. Stupid, selfish, heartless. Words that Dad had never used to describe her. Afterwards, purged of her anger, Mum began to speak to her in sentences again.

The kitchen was thick with a spice-filled smog now. Dinner was ready. Nikki helped to bring out a serving dish brimming with chickpea and spinach curry. 'So,' Mindi said once they settled into their seats. 'Tell us about this job.'

'I'll be mentoring women to write their stories. The workshops are twice a week. At the end of the term, we'll have a collection of stories to put together.'

'Mentoring. That's the same as teaching?' Mindi asked.

Nikki shook her head. 'It's not so much teaching as facilitating them.'

Mum looked confused. 'So there is another teacher there that you're assisting?'

'No,' Nikki said. The impatience crept into her voice. 'Finding your voice isn't something which can be taught, at least not in the traditional sense. People write and then you guide them.' She looked up to catch a smirk passing between Mum and Mindi. 'It's hard work,' she added.

'Good, good,' Mum murmured. She folded a roti and drove it across the plate, scooping up the chickpeas.

'It's a great opportunity,' Nikki insisted. 'I'll have a chance to do some editing as well, which I can add to my résumé.'

'So do you think you want to be a teacher or an editor?' Mindi asked.

Nikki shrugged.

'They just sound like two very different things, being a teacher or working in publishing. You like writing as well. Are you going to contribute to these stories as a writer?'

'Why does it have to be defined?' Nikki asked. 'I don't know what I want to be, but I'm getting there. Is that all right with you?'

Mindi held up her hands in a gesture of surrender. 'It's fine with me. I'm just trying to find out more about what you're doing, that's all. You don't have to get so defensive.'

'I'm doing something to help empower women.'

Now Mum looked up and she and Mindi exchanged a look of worry. 'I saw that,' Nikki said. 'What's wrong?'

'Aren't the majority of your students going to be temple ladies?' Mindi said.

'So?'

'So be careful,' Mindi said. 'It sounds like a class for beginning storytellers but if you think you're going to change their lives by tapping into their personal experiences . . .' Mindi shook her head.

'The problem with you, Mindi—' Nikki began.

'That's enough,' Mum said. Her stern stare quieted Nikki's protests. 'You hardly ever come over for dinner, and then every time there's an argument. If you're happy with this job, then we're happy. At least it means you don't have to work in the disco any more.'

'It's a pub,' Nikki said and this was as far as she went towards correcting Mum. She had neglected to mention that she would still be working at

O'Reilly's. The pay for empowering women through narrative would not fully cover her living expenses.

'Just make sure you're travelling safely. Are these night classes? What time do they finish?'

'Mum, I'll be fine. It's Southall.'

'Crimes don't happen in Southall? I must be the only one who remembers Karina Kaur. You've seen the ads for *Britain's Unsolved Murders*, no?'

Nikki sighed. Trust Mum to bring up a murder case from fourteen years ago to prove a point.

'They never found out who did it,' Mum continued. 'The killer could still be on the loose, preying on Punjabi girls walking alone at night.'

Even Mindi rolled her eyes at Mum's theatrics. 'You're being a bit dramatic,' Mindi informed her.

'Yeah, Mum. All kinds of girls get murdered in London, not just the Punjabi ones,' Nikki said.

'It's not funny,' Mum said. 'It's the parents left behind who suffer with worry when the children leave.'

After dinner, Mindi and Nikki took over the washing up in the kitchen while Mum retired to the living room to watch television. They scrubbed the pots and plates in silence until Mindi spoke up. 'So Auntie Geeta's recommended a few eligible bachelors. She gave me the email addresses of three guys that she shortlisted.'

'Ugh.' Nikki could think of no other response to Mindi's mention of Auntie Geeta. She was a friend of Mum's who lived up the road and often dropped in unannounced, her eyebrows wiggling with all the secrets she struggled to contain. 'Not gossiping, just sharing,' she always claimed before unpacking the ruins of other people's private lives.

'I emailed a few times with one guy who seemed okay,' Mindi continued.

'Lovely,' Nikki said. 'By this time next year you'll be washing up in his kitchen instead of this one.'

'Shut up.' After a beat Mindi added, 'His name is Pravin. Does that sound like an all right name to you?'

'It sounds like a name.'

'He works in finance. We've chatted on the phone once.'

'So I go through all the trouble to post your profile on a noticeboard and you've enlisted Auntie Geeta as your matchmaker anyway?'

'I didn't receive any responses from the temple profile,' Mindi said. 'You're sure you put it on the Marriage Board?'

'Yes.'

Mindi studied her. 'Liar.'

'I did just as you asked,' Nikki insisted.

'What did you do?'

'I put it on the Marriage Board. It just might not be the most prominent flyer there. There are lots of flyers and—'

'Typical,' Mindi muttered.

'What?'

'Of course you'd put the least amount of effort into helping me with this.'

'I went all the way to a temple in Southall. That's no small effort,' Nikki shot back.

'Yet you've signed on for a job which means you'll be travelling there regularly. How does that work? You're all right with going to Southall as long as it benefits *your* needs.'

'It's not all about me. I'm helping women.'

Mindi snorted. 'Helping? Nikki, this sounds like another one of your . . .' she waved as if trying to stir up the word from thin air. 'Your causes.'

'What's wrong with having a cause?' Nikki demanded. 'I care about helping women tell their stories. It's a much more worthwhile pastime than advertising for a husband.'

'This is what you do,' Mindi said. 'You follow your so-called passions and don't consider the consequences for other people.'

This charge again. It would be easier to be a criminal fairly prosecuted by the law than an Indian daughter who wronged her family. A crime would be punishable by a jail sentence of definite duration rather than this uncertain length of family guilt trips.

'How exactly did my leaving university have consequences for other people? It was my decision. Sure, Dad could no longer tell his family in India I was becoming a lawyer. Big deal. It wasn't worth being unhappy just so he could have bragging rights.'

'It wasn't about bragging rights,' Mindi said. 'It was about duty.'

'You sound like an Indian housewife already.'

'You had a duty to Dad. He had been so devoted to championing you – all those school debates, all those speech contests. He included you in political conversations with his friends and he didn't stop you from arguing with Mum if he thought you had a point. He put such faith in you.' There was a note of hurt in Mindi's voice. Dad and Mum had taken Mindi on a trip to India before her exams as well, taking all spiritual steps to ensure that she got into medical school. After the results indicated nursing – not medical school – as her best option, Dad's disappointment had been obvious and, with renewed enthusiasm, he shifted his focus to Nikki.

'He was proud of you too, you know,' Nikki said. 'He wished I were more practical like you.' Having been measured up against his brother his whole life, Dad had been careful to avoid comparing his daughters but after Nikki dropped out of university, all fair play went out the window. 'Look at Mindi. She works hard. She wants a stable future. Why can't you be like that?' he'd said.

Nikki felt a sudden rush of irritation with Dad. 'You know, Dad contradicted himself all the time. One minute he was saying, "follow your dreams, that's why we came to England" and the next he was dictating what I should do for a living. He assumed that my dreams were identical to his.'

'He saw a potential career for you in law. You had the chance to succeed professionally. What are you doing now?'

'I'm exploring my options,' Nikki said.

'By this time, you could have been earning a salary,' Mindi reminded her.

'I'm not as concerned with money and material things as you are, Mindi. That's really what this whole arranged marriage thing is about, isn't it? You're not confident that you'll meet a professional with a fat salary in a pub but if you screen the profiles of a few Indian doctors and engineers, you can zero in right away on their earnings and filter them accordingly.'

Mindi turned off the tap and stared angrily at her. 'Don't you make me feel like a gold digger for wanting to support Mum! There are expenses to think about. You left, so you have no idea.'

'I moved across London. It's hardly as if I abandoned my family. This is what young women do in Britain! We move out. We become independent. This is our culture.'

'You think Mum isn't concerned about finances? You think she doesn't want to retire early from working for the council and enjoy her life? I'm the only one contributing here. Things need to be repaired, unexpected bills arrive, and the car servicing is overdue. Think about that the next time you spout out your lines about independence.'

Nikki felt a pinch of guilt in her gut. 'I thought Dad had savings.'

'He did, but some of his savings were tied up in his company's stock options. They haven't really recovered since the financial crisis. And he took out that loan to renovate the guest bathroom, remember? Mum had to defer payments and now the interest has nearly doubled. It means Mum has had to put off all these other home improvements she thought would be done by now. The curtains, the built-in shoe cupboard, the kitchen counters. She's already starting to worry about losing face. She's concerned about how our home would look to my prospective husband's family, not to mention what they might say if she couldn't afford a dowry or a lavish celebration.'

'Min, I had no idea.'

'I told her I wouldn't marry someone from a superficial family and she said, "There might not be any Punjabi boys for you to marry then." She was joking of course.' Mindi smiled but her eyes were tight with worry.

'I could help,' Nikki said.

'You've got your own expenses to think about.'

'I'll have some extra income from this new job. I could send some money once a fortnight.' Nikki hesitated, realising what she had just committed to. The extra income was supposed to go into her savings so she'd have something to fall back on when O'Reilly's went bust. She would need money to rent a place then because moving back home would be far too humiliating. 'It won't be much,' Nikki added.

Mindi looked pleased. 'It's the gesture that counts,' she said. 'I have to say, I didn't expect this of you. It's very responsible. Thank you.'

In the other room, Mum had turned up the volume of her television series and the shrill violin notes of a Hindi song poured through the house. Mindi turned the tap back on. Nikki stood by while Mindi scrubbed the dishes, her vigorous motions sending soap suds flying into the air. As they landed on the counter, Nikki wiped them off with her fingers.

'Use a towel,' Mindi said. 'You're leaving streaks.' Nikki did as she was told.

'So when are you meeting Pravin?'

'Friday,' Mindi said.

'Mum's excited about it, I guess?'

Mindi shrugged. She peered at Mum through the kitchen entrance and lowered her voice. 'She is, but I talked to him on the phone last night.'

'And?'

'He asked me if I wanted to work after marriage.'

'For fuck's sakes,' Nikki said, dropping a dishtowel on the counter and turning to stare at Mindi. 'What did you say?'

'I said yes. He didn't sound thrilled about it.'

'You're still meeting him?'

'You don't know until you meet someone face to face, do you?'

'Judging from the temple profiles alone, I wouldn't give any of those men the time of day,' Nikki said.

'But that's you,' Mindi said. 'You and your feminism.' With a flick of her wrist, she dismissed Nikki and everything she stood for.

Rather than enter another argument, Nikki finished her share of the dishes without saying another word. As she slipped out into the back garden to sneak an after-dinner cigarette, she felt as if she could breathe again.

The next day Nikki arrived at the community centre early to set up her classroom. The room was as modest as Kulwinder Kaur's office. Two rows of desks and chairs faced a blank whiteboard. Nikki moved the seats around – according to Olive, a horseshoe shape would help promote more discussion. A thrill shot through Nikki as she pictured the classroom full of women writing the stories of their lives.

For the first lesson, Nikki had prepared an introductory task. Everybody was to write a complete scene in ten simple sentences. Then, returning to each sentence, they had to add a detail – dialogue or description for example.

By 7.15 p.m., Nikki had paced the classroom and wandered out twice into the deserted hallway. She stepped back inside and wiped the board for the fifth time. She stared at the empty chairs. Perhaps this was all some elaborate prank.

As she began to pull the desks back to where she'd found them, Nikki heard footsteps. The loud, slow thumps made Nikki aware of her own heartbeat. She was in this rundown building all alone. She pulled a chair out in front of her, preparing to use it should she need to.

There was a knock on the door. Through the window, Nikki saw a woman wearing a scarf on her head. It was just a lost granny. It did not occur to Nikki that she was one of her students until the woman entered and took a seat.

'Are you here for the writing class?' Nikki asked in Punjabi.

'Yes,' the old lady nodded.

Do you speak English? Nikki thought it would be rude to ask.

'I guess you're my only student tonight,' Nikki said. 'We'll begin.' She turned to the board but the woman said, 'No, the others are coming.'

The women streamed in together at twenty-five past. One by one they took their seats and made no apologies for their tardiness. Nikki cleared her throat. 'Class begins at 7 p.m. sharp,' she said. The women looked up in surprise. Nikki saw that they were mostly elders who weren't used to being reprimanded by a young woman. She backtracked slightly. 'If this time doesn't work with the bus schedule, I'm sure we can arrange to begin at half-past instead.' There were some nods and a general murmur of approval.

'Let's quickly introduce ourselves,' Nikki said. 'I'll start. My name is Nikki. I like to write and I'm looking forward to teaching you all to write as well.' She gave the first woman a nod.

'Preetam Kaur.' Like some of the other women, she wore a white salwaar kameez, which indicated her widow's status. A scarf hemmed with white lace hid her hair and a walking stick printed with lavender floral patterns lay at her feet.

'And why have you joined this class, Preetam?' Nikki asked.

Preetam winced at the sound of her name. The other women looked startled as well. 'That's Bibi Preetam to you, young lady,' she said stiffly. 'Or Aunty. Or Preetam-ji.'

'Of course. I'm sorry,' Nikki said. These were her students but they were also Punjabi elders and she would have to address them appropriately.

Preetam accepted her apology with a nod. 'I want to learn writing,' she said. 'I'd like to be able to send letters on the internet to my grandchildren in Canada.'

Strange. She seemed to think the course would cover letter writing and emailing. Nikki nodded to the next woman.

'Tarampal Kaur. I want to write,' the woman said simply. She had small lips, which pinched tightly together as if she wasn't meant to speak at all. Nikki couldn't help her gaze lingering on Tarampal Kaur – like the older women, she was shrouded in white but there was hardly a wrinkle on her face. Nikki placed her in her early forties.

The woman next to Tarampal also appeared much younger than the rest, with reddish brown streaks dyed in her hair and pink lipstick that matched her purse. The colours stood out against the plain cream of her kameez. She introduced herself in English, with just the slightest hint of an Indian accent. 'I'm Sheena Kaur. I can read and write in Punjabi and English but I want to learn to be a better writer. And if you call me Bibi or Aunty, I'll just die because I must only be ten or fifteen years older than you.'

Nikki smiled. 'Very nice to meet you, Sheena,' she said.

The next elderly woman was tall and thin and had a distinct mole on her chin from which fine hairs poked out. 'Arvinder Kaur. I want to learn to write everything. Stories, letters, everything.'

'Manjeet Kaur,' said another woman without being prompted. She smiled brightly at Nikki. 'Do you also teach us how to do some basic accounting?'

'No.'

'I'd like to write and also learn how to do the bills. There are so many.' The other woman murmured in agreement. So many bills!

Nikki put her hand up to silence them. 'I wouldn't know the first thing about accounting. I'm here to run a creative writing workshop, to collect a collaboration of voices.' The women stared blankly at her. She cleared her throat. 'It's occurring to me that some of you might not be proficient enough in English to write confidently. Who is in this category? Not confident in English?' She raised her hand to indicate that they should do the same. All of the widows except Sheena raised their hands.

'That's okay,' Nikki said. 'In fact, if you'd prefer to write your stories in Punjabi, I can adjust to that. Some things are just lost in translation anyway.' The women's prolonged staring made Nikki uneasy. Finally, Arvinder raised her hand.

'Excuse me Nikki – how are we meant to write stories?'

'Good question.' She turned to the desk and picked up her stack of loose-leaf paper. 'Now I know we lost some time today but this is great place to start.' She passed the papers around and explained the instructions. The women reached into their bags and took out their pens and pencils.

Nikki turned to the board to write down a few essential notes for the next lesson. 'Next class is on Tuesday, 7.30–9.00 p.m. Be punctual.' She wrote this in Punjabi as well, thinking herself quite considerate and adaptable. When she turned back around, she expected to see the women hunched over their papers, scribbling away but they remained still. Manjeet and Preetam tapped their pens against their desks and looked at each other. Tarampal looked positively irritated.

'What's wrong?' Nikki asked.

Silence.

'Why isn't anybody writing?' she asked.

More silence and then Tarampal spoke. 'How are we supposed to write?'

'What do you mean?'

'How are we supposed to write,' Tarampal repeated, 'when you haven't taught us yet?'

'I am trying to teach you to write, but we have to start somewhere, don't we? I know it's difficult, but if I'm to help you with your stories then you need to actually start writing them. Just a few sentences . . .' She trailed off when she noticed Preetam. The way she clutched the pencil reminded Nikki of being in nursery school. It dawned on her then, just as Arvinder began to pack away her things.

'You knew,' Nikki said as soon as Kulwinder answered the phone. She didn't bother saying *sat sri akal* first – she wasn't going to pay respects to this conniving elder.

'Knew what?' Kulwinder asked.

'Those woman can't write.'

'Of course. You're meant to teach them.'

'They. Can't. Write.' Nikki wanted the words to burn past Kulwinder's calm exterior. 'You tricked me into it. I thought I'd be teaching a creative writing workshop, not an adult literacy class. They can't even spell their own names.'

'You're meant to teach them,' Kulwinder repeated. 'You said you wanted to teach writing.'

'*Creative* writing. Stories. Not the alphabet!'

'So teach them how to write and then they can write all the stories they want.'

'Do you have any idea how long that will take?'

'The classes are twice a week.'

'It will take more than twice-weekly classes. You know that.'

'These are very capable women,' Kulwinder said.

'You're joking.'

'You weren't born writing stories, were you? Didn't you have to learn your ABC first? Wasn't it the simplest thing you had to learn?'

Nikki caught the contempt in Kulwinder's voice. 'Look. You're trying to prove a point – I get it. I'm modern and I think I can do anything I want. Well, I can.'

She was about to tell Kulwinder that she quit but the words got caught in her throat. She considered it, a familiar sense of anxiety seizing her stomach. Leaving this job would mean having nothing to contribute to Mum and Mindi. Worse yet, they would know that she had given up after just one class and they would be proven right – that Nikki didn't follow through on anything, that she was just a drifter who avoided responsibilities. She thought of the crumbling pub and pictured Sam wrapped in ribbons of receipts apologetically telling her that she was being let go.

'This job was falsely advertised. I could report you for that,' Nikki said finally.

Kulwinder responded with a snort, as if she knew the emptiness of Nikki's threat. 'Report me to whom?' she challenged. She waited for a response but Nikki had none. Kulwinder's message was clear: Nikki had stumbled into her territory and now must play by her rules.

In winter, the days lost their shape early. The streets were blurry with shadows and traffic lights as Kulwinder walked home and thought about her day. She wasn't proud of deceiving Nikki but the more she thought about their conversation, the more she remembered how Nikki had incensed her. It was that demanding attitude that got under her skin. *How dare you ask me to teach these idiots,* she might as well have said.

Kulwinder's two-storey brick home was on the end of Ansell Road. From her bedroom window the golden tip of gurdwara's magnificent dome was visible on clear afternoons. The neighbours on the right were a young couple with two small children who sat in the porch and giggled together until their father came home. The neighbours on the left were a couple with a teenage son who had a big dog who howled for hours after they left each morning. Kulwinder was used to running through all of these details about her neighbours, anything to avoid thinking of *that* house across the street.

'I'm home,' she announced. She paused and waited for Sarab's acknowledgment. It pained her on the occasions when she found him deep in silence, staring at the unturned pages of his Punjabi newspaper. 'Sarab?' she called from the foot of the stairs. He grunted a reply. She put down her things, and went to the kitchen to make a start on dinner. From the corner of her eye, she checked to see if Sarab had moved the living room curtains. This morning, he had suggested opening them to let in a bit of light so he could read the paper. 'Don't,' Kulwinder had insisted. 'The glare from the sun gives me a headache.' Both of them knew it was Number 16 and not the pale English sunlight that bothered Kulwinder.

Kulwinder set out the plates and the bowl of dal and took the achar out of the fridge and set the table. There was nothing more comforting in all her years in England than the simplicity of a Punjabi meal. Sarab sat down and they ate quietly, and then he turned on the television and she cleaned the dishes. Maya used to help her with this, but one day she asked, 'Why can't Dad pitch in with the cooking and cleaning?' Such questions had crossed Kulwinder's mind in her younger days, but she would have been beaten for suggesting that her father or brothers did the housework. She had taken Maya roughly by the arm and steered her into the kitchen.

After completing her chores, Kulwinder went to the living room and sat next to Sarab. The television was on at a low volume. There was an English show on so it didn't matter that they couldn't hear it because the things the English laughed about were no laughing matter to Kulwinder.

She turned to Sarab and started a conversation. 'An odd thing happened today,' she said. 'A mix-up with one of my community classes.' She paused for a moment. *My community classes.* It was nice hearing it aloud. 'The girl I hired to teach it thought she was teaching women to write their memoirs, but the women who signed up can't even write. I had advertised creative writing classes and once the women started registering, I knew they were the types who couldn't even spell their own names, but what could I do? Turn them away? That wouldn't be right. I'm there to help the women of our community after all.' It was partially true. She had been vague with the women about what exactly they would learn in these classes. 'Writing, reading, that sort of thing,' she had told them while passing around the registration form.

Sarab nodded but his eyes were blank. He was staring at the screen now. Kulwinder glanced at the clock and saw that there were many hours to kill before she felt like going to bed, like most nights. The drizzle had cleared. 'Would you like to go for a walk?' she asked Sarab. How unnatural it felt to ask him like this, when evening walks used to be their after dinner routine. 'It's good for digestion,' she added. She instantly felt silly trying to persuade him but today she really wanted his company. Her conflict with Nikki had reminded her of the way she and Maya used to argue.

Without even looking at her, Sarab said, 'You go ahead.'

Kulwinder walked up Ansell Road and turned onto a main road where a small strip of shops were illuminated by long fluorescent ceiling bulbs. In Shanti's Wedding Boutique, a group of young women tried on bangles and held up their wrists, letting the sequins catch the light. The owner of the masala shop next door was patiently ushering out his customers, an English couple, looking very pleased with their bottles of red and yellow powders. Teenagers in puffy black jackets milled in the empty lots outside, stray words and laughter darting into the air. *Yeah. Hah! You dickhead.*

Kulwinder offered a few hellos to passing Punjabi women but mostly she looked past them. Before Maya died, she used to chat to ladies, turning these walks into lengthy social outings. If their husbands were there, they'd break off into another group with Sarab. On the way home, comparing stories, she often noticed that men and women shared the same information – who was marrying whom, the rising cost of food and petrol, the occasional community scandal. Now she preferred not to stop. There was no need these days – only occasionally did people approach to offer their condolences. Most people just averted their gazes. She and Sarab were outsiders now, like the widows and divorced women and all those shamed parents they had feared becoming.

At a traffic light she paused, turned the corner and found a bench to sit on. The smell of sweet fried jalebi rose from a cart nearby. Her feet were rough like sandpaper against her hands as she massaged her heels and considered Nikki. Clearly, the girl was not from here, or she wouldn't have been so disrespectful. Her parents were probably city types – Delhi or Bombay, and they probably turned their noses up at the Punjabis who washed up in Southall. She knew what the rest of London thought of Southall – she'd heard all of their comments when she and Sarab decided to move here from Croydon. *Village people who built another Punjab in London – they're letting all types of people into this country these days.* 'Best choice we ever made,' Sarab had declared when they unpacked their last box. Kulwinder agreed, her heart almost bursting with happiness from the comforts of their surrounds – the spice markets, the Bollywood cinema, the gurdwaras, the samosa carts on the Broadway. Maya eyed all of it with suspicion but she would adjust, they assured themselves. One day she would want to raise her children here too.

Tears welled up in her eyes and blurred her vision, as a bus rolled to a slow stop in front of her and the door opened. The driver looked at Kulwinder expectantly. She shook her head and waved him along. A sob escaped her throat but the sound of the engine rumbling drowned it out. Why did she always torture herself like this? Sometimes she got carried away and imagined little moments of Maya's life as it would be – mundane things like paying for groceries or replacing the batteries in her television remote control. The smaller the details, the harder it hit that Maya would never do these things. Her story was over.

The air felt colder now that Kulwinder was still. She wiped her eyes and took a few deep breaths. When she felt strong enough again, she stood up and headed in the direction of her home. Halfway across Queen Mary Road, Kulwinder spotted a police officer. She froze. What to do? Turn around and walk back? Keep going? She stood in middle of the road until the light turned red and cars started honking their horns, and this was worse because people began to stop and stare. The policeman began searching for the cause of the trouble until his gaze landed on her. 'Nothing. No problem,' she called out feebly. He rushed into the street and with a firm hand signal, ordered all the cars stay in place. Then he beckoned her to cross the road towards him.

'Is everything all right?' he asked.

'Yes,' she replied. She kept her distance and avoided looking him in the eye. A small crowd had emerged from the shops and gathered on the pavement to watch. She felt the urge to shoo them away. *Mind your own business!*

'You're just out taking a walk?'

'Just walking, yes.'

'Good exercise.'

She nodded, still aware of the stares. She tried to do a quick scan of who was watching. Unlike Maya, Kulwinder never considered Southall a hotbed of gossip. Most people just shared harmless observations. The problem was that Kulwinder could not afford to be observed talking to the police. Somebody might casually mention this scene to friend or a spouse, and then they might tell somebody else and—

'Are you sure you're all right?' the policeman asked. He peered into her eyes.

'I'm very good thank you,' she replied. She found an English word. 'Splendid.'

'Then take care when crossing the road in the future. The youngsters like to speed down the Broadway and they turn onto these main roads sometimes.'

'I will. Thank you.' Kulwinder spotted a middle-aged couple approaching. She could not recognize them from this distance but they were sure to notice her chatting with the police in the middle of the street, and if they knew her, they would ask each other, *'What trouble is she causing now?'*

'Stay safe,' the policeman called after her as she hurried home.

* * *

Sarab was upstairs when she returned. Kulwinder quietly tidied up the shoes in the small circle of light he had left on for her in the foyer. Then she looked for other things to tidy – the couch cushions surely needed plumping and maybe Sarab had left a glass in the sink. These tasks calmed her. By the time she was finished, she realized how paranoid she had been. What were the chances of being noticed? Southall wasn't that small, it just felt that way sometimes. There was no predicting whom she'd run into. She already avoided another major road because she had been spotted visiting a law office there (although she needn't have bothered because everything the fast-talking lawyer had said involved fees and no guarantees). If she started changing directions every time she saw somebody she would rather not see, she might as well spend all her time in this living room, with the curtains drawn.

But later that night, while Sarab snored lightly and Kulwinder eyes were wide open, she saw her mobile phone flashing. Unknown Number. On the other side, a voice that she recognized all too well. 'You were seen talking to the police today. Try it again and you will be in a lot of trouble.' Kulwinder tried to defend herself but, as always, her caller hung up before she had a chance to speak.

Chapter Four

'There are no good men left in London,' Olive remarked. 'None.' She surveyed the crowd from her perch at the bar while Nikki wiped down the counter, cursing the noisy blokes who had spent the past hour singing off-key rounds of football songs and winking sloppily at her.

'There are plenty,' Nikki assured her.

'Plenty of duds,' Olive said. 'Unless you want me to date Steve with the Racist Grandfather.'

'I would rather see you single for the rest of your life,' Nikki said. Steve with the Racist Grandfather was a regular at the pub who prefaced his bigoted comments with, 'as my grandfather would say . . .' He considered this a foolproof way to absolve himself of being racist. 'As my grandfather would say,' he once told Nikki, 'is your skin naturally that colour, or are you rusting? Of course, I would never say that. But my grandfather used to call khaki pants "Paki Pants" because he honestly thought the colour was named after their skin tone. He's terrible, my grandfather.'

'That guy's all right,' Nikki said, nodding at a tall man joining a group at a corner table. He took a seat and clapped one of his mates on the shoulder. Olive craned her neck to look. 'Not too bad,' Olive said. 'He looks a bit like Lars. Remember him?'

'You mean Laaawsh? He only told us a hundred times how to pronounce it correctly,' Nikki said. He was a Swedish exchange student that Olive's family had hosted when they were in Year Twelve. 'That was the year I spent more time claiming to study at your house than ever.' It was the only way she could get her parents' permission to spend so many evenings at Olive's house.

'With my luck, that guy's already taken,' Olive said.

'I'll go do some investigative work,' Nikki said. She made her rounds at the tables and floated towards him. 'Can I get you anything?' she asked.

'Sure.' As he gave his order she noticed the wedding ring shining on his finger.

'Sorry,' Nikki said when returned to Olive. She poured her friend a drink on the house and joined Olive on the other side of the bar once her shift was over. Olive sighed. 'Maybe *I* should go for an arranged marriage. How was your sister's date the other night?'

'Disastrous,' Nikki said. 'The guy talked about himself the whole time and then made a fuss because they were served water without lemon slices. I think he was trying to prove to Mindi that he was accustomed to a certain type of service.'

'That's a shame.'

'It's a relief, actually. I was worried that she'd settle for the first eligible Punjabi bachelor who came along but she told me she gave him a polite and firm "no, thank you" at the end of the night.'

'Maybe Mindi's more influenced by you than she realizes,' Olive said.

'I thought so too but Aunty Geeta who suggested this fine young man gave Mum the cold shoulder at the shops the other day. Mindi felt terrible and called her up to apologize. Aunty Geeta guilted her into signing up for Punjabi Speed Dating. It's really not Mindi's thing but she's going along with it.'

'Oh, you never know who Mindi might meet or where. The odds are in her favour at speed dating. Fifteen men in one night? Sign me up. It could be really fun. If nothing else, she comes out of it having put herself out there. That's more than I'm doing.'

'It sounds like a nightmare to me. These are fifteen Punjabi men looking for a wife. When Mindi registered, she had to tell the organizers her caste, dietary preferences and rate her religiousness on a scale of one to ten.'

Olive laughed. 'I'd be a minus three in any religion,' she said. 'I'd be a terrible candidate.'

'Me too,' Nikki said. 'Mindi's about a six or seven, although I think she'd claim to be more religious if it pleased the right man. I worry that she's only doing this for people like Auntie Geeta.'

'Well, she should be the least of your problems right now,' Olive said. 'You have to teach grannies the alphabet tomorrow.'

Nikki groaned. 'Where do I start?'

'I told you I have lots of books on literacy that you could borrow.'

'For Year Seven students. These women are starting from scratch.'

'You're telling me they can't read road signs? They can't read the headline scrolling by when the news is on? How have they managed living in England all this time?'

'I suppose they were always able to get by with their husbands' help. For anything else, they could just speak in Punjabi.'

'But your Mum was never so dependent on your dad.'

'My parents met at university in Delhi and Mum has her own livelihood. These women grew up in villages. Most couldn't spell their own names in Punjabi, let alone English.'

'I can't imagine living my whole life like that,' Olive said, taking a swig of her pint.

'Do you remember those writing books we used to have when we were kids? How to do capital letters and cursive?' Nikki asked.

'The ones where you practise writing in the lines – penmanship books?'

'Yes. Those would be useful.'

'You can find them online,' Olive said. 'The school textbook publishers have a good catalogue. I can look out for them for you.'

'I need something for tomorrow's lesson though.'

'Try one of the charity shops on King Street.'

After locking up, Nikki stayed back for drinks and then she and Olive stumbled out onto the glistening road, arms linked together like schoolgirls. Nikki took her phone from her pocket and typed a message to Mindi.

Hey sis! Found the man of your dreams yet? Does he starch his own turban and comb his own moustache or will that be one of your DUTIES?

She giggled and pressed Send.

Nikki woke in the afternoon, her head still spinning from the night before. She reached for her phone. There was a message from Mindi.

Drinking on a weeknight, Nik? Obviously if sending stupid messages at that hour.

Nikki wiped the blur from her eyes and wrote Mindi a reply.

U have such a huge stick up your bum

Mindi wrote back within seconds.

And u probably just woke up. Talk about bums. Grow up Nikki.

Nikki tossed the phone into her bag. It took her twice as long as usual to just get out of bed because her head felt so heavy. She winced at the squeaky sound of the shower tap and the sting of water on her skin. After getting dressed, she walked up the street to the Oxfam shop. The musty smell of ancient wool coats tickled her nose. Old school textbooks and worksheets sat on a bottom shelf, under the rows of popular novels that Nikki often browsed and bought. Here, Nikki finally woke up. The familiar comfort of books helped to dissolve her hangover.

Searching the shop, Nikki found a Scrabble game as well. A few tiles were missing but it would still be useful for teaching the alphabet. She went back to the shelf to see if there was anything there for her and while browsing, a title caught her eye. *Beatrix Potter: Letters.* She had a copy of this book at home but its accompanying book, *The Journals and Sketches of*

Beatrix Potter, was hard to find. She had seen it in a used bookshop in Delhi on her pre-exams trip with Dad and Mum but her wanting it had sparked an argument. She distracted herself from the memory by turning her attention to the adjacent shelf. Another title leaped out at her. *Red Velvet: Pleasurable Stories for Women*. She picked up the book and flipped through the pages and some of the phrases that jumped out at her were:

He undressed her slowly with his eyes, and then deftly with his fingers.

Delia was basking naked in the summer sun in the privacy of her own garden but somewhere, Hunter was watching.

'I didn't come here to see you,' she said haughtily. She spun on her heels to leave the office and she saw his manhood bulging through his trousers. He wanted to see her.

Nikki grinned and took the books to the cashier. Leaving the shop, she thought of the inscription she would pen in the *Red Velvet* book. *Dear Mindi, I might not be as grown-up as you but I do know a bit more about certain adult rituals. Here's a guide for you and your Dream Husband.*

Nikki hauled the bag of books to the classroom and heaved them onto the desk. A sheet of paper had been taped onto it: *Nikki do not move desks and chairs in this room – Kulwinder.* The desks had all been rearranged into their original neat rows. A low growl in Nikki's stomach reminded her that she hadn't yet eaten, but before she left for the langar hall, she shifted the desks into a circle again.

The smell of dal and sweet jalebis mixed in the air with the clatter of utensils and voices. She took her tray through the line and was served roti, rice, dal and yoghurt. Finding an open space on the floor near a row of older women, Nikki recalled being about thirteen and attending prayers with her parents at the smaller Enfield gurdwara. She had needed something from the car and approached Dad – who was sitting with some men – to ask for the keys. People had turned and stared as she crossed the invisible divide that segregated the sexes even though there were no such rules in the langar hall. What did Mindi see in this world that she didn't? All of the women seemed to end up the same – weary and shuffling their feet.

Nikki watched as they trailed into the hall, adjusting their scarves, pausing every few moments to give an obligatory greeting to another community member. The group of ladies sitting next to her chattered away about each woman who walked in. They knew entire histories:

'Chacko's wife – she's just had an operation, poor thing. She won't be walking for a while. Her eldest son is taking care of her. You know the one I mean? She has two sons. This is the one who bought the electronics shop from his uncle. Doing very well. I saw him pushing her around the park in a wheelchair the other day.'

'That woman over there is Nishu's youngest sister isn't it? They all have that same high forehead. I heard they had a terrible case of flooding in their house last year. They had to re-carpet the place and throw out a lot of furniture. Such a waste! They'd bought a new lounge set only six weeks before.'

'Is that Dalvinder? I thought she was in Bristol visiting her cousin.'

Nikki's eyes followed each woman as the commentary ran. She could barely keep up with this rapid stream of information and details. Then a woman that she recognized strode into the hall. Kulwinder. She noticed a drawing of breath from the little group next to her and their voices lowered to a hush.

'Look at that one, marching in here like she's a big boss. She's been so stuck-up lately,' said a middle-aged woman whose stiff green dupatta was pulled so low that it nearly concealed her face.

'Lately? She's always been Miss High and Mighty. I don't know what gives her the right to be like that now.'

It didn't surprise Nikki that they didn't like Kulwinder. She listened closely.

'Oh, don't,' a wrinkly older woman said. She pushed her wire-rimmed frames further up the bridge of her nose. 'She's had a rough time. We should be sympathetic.'

'I tried that approach but she didn't want my sympathy. She was downright rude to me,' said Green Dupatta.

'Buppy Kaur went through the same problems, but at least she still acknowledges us when we say "We're sorry for your loss". Kulwinder's different. I saw her walking around the neighbourhood the other day. I waved at her and she just looked in the other direction and kept walking. How am I supposed to be kind to somebody like that?'

'Buppy Kaur's problems were similar, not the *same*,' the woman with the glasses said. 'Her daughter ran away with that boy from Trinidad. She's still living; Kulwinder's girl is dead.'

Nikki looked up in surprise. The women noticed her abrupt movement but they kept on talking.

'Death is death,' somebody else agreed. 'It's far worse.'

'Nonsense,' Green Dupatta scoffed. 'Death is better than life if a girl doesn't have her honour. Sometimes the younger generation needs this reminder.'

Somehow, Nikki felt that these words were directed at her. She looked up at the woman who said it and met an even, challenging gaze. The other women murmured their acknowledgement. Nikki found her food harder to swallow. She took a gulp of water and kept her head down.

The woman with the wire-rimmed glasses made eye contact with Nikki. '*Hai*, they're not all terrible. There are plenty of respectable girls in Southall. It depends on how they're raised, isn't it?' she said. She gave Nikki an almost imperceptible nod.

'This generation is selfish. If Maya had just considered what she was doing to her family, none of this would have happened,' Green Dupatta continued. 'And don't forget about the damage she did to Tarampal's property as well. She could have destroyed the whole place.'

The other women looked uncomfortable now. Like Nikki, they lowered their heads and focused on their dinners. In the sudden silence, Nikki could hear her own heart beating faster. Tarampal? Nikki wondered if they were referring to the same Tarampal from her writing classes. Nikki silently urged Green Dupatta to say more but without an attentive audience, she grew quiet as well.

Entering the community centre building afterwards, Nikki was lost in thought. The woman in the langar hall had appeared so certain when she spoke of death and honour. Nikki couldn't imagine any offspring of Kulwinder's getting caught up in some act of dangerous resistance as the women had implied. Then again, Kulwinder was so unyielding that perhaps her daughter had rebelled.

Laughter rang down the corridor, breaking her thoughts. Strange, she thought. There were no other classes on at the same time. As she made her way to the room, the noise became louder and she could hear a voice clearly speaking.

'He puts his hand on her thigh as she's driving the car and, as she's driving, he moves his hand closer between her legs. She can't concentrate on driving, so she tells him, "let me just get to a small side street". He tells her – why do we have to wait?'

Nikki froze outside the door. It was Sheena's voice. Another woman called out.

'Chee, why is he so impatient? Can't keep it in his pants until they get to a side street? She should punish him by driving him around the car park until his little balloon deflates.'

Another wave of laughter. Nikki threw open the door.

Sheena was sitting on the front desk with the book open in her hands and all the women were crowded around her. When they saw Nikki, they scurried back to their seats. The colour drained from Sheena's face. 'So sorry,' she said to Nikki. 'We saw that you had bought us books. I was just translating a story . . .' She slid off the desk and went to join the ladies at their seats.

'That book is mine. It's private. It's obviously not for any of you,' Nikki said when she felt that she could speak. She reached into the bag and pulled out the workbooks. '*These* are for you.' She tossed them onto the desk and put her head in her hands. The women were silent.

'Why were you all here so early?'

'You said seven o'clock,' said Arvinder.

'I said seven thirty, since that was the time you all preferred,' Nikki said.

The women turned to look accusingly at Manjeet.

'I remember her saying seven o'clock last week,' Manjeet insisted. 'I remember it.'

'Turn up your hearing aid next time,' Arvinder said.

'I don't need to,' Manjeet said. She tucked her scarf behind her ear to reveal the hearing aid to the class. 'This has never had a battery in it.'

'Why would you wear a hearing aid if you didn't need one?' Nikki asked.

Manjeet dropped her head in embarrassment. 'Completes the whole widow look,' Sheena explained.

'Oh,' Nikki said. She waited for a further explanation from Manjeet but she simply nodded and stared at her hands.

Preetam raised her hand. 'Excuse me, Nikki. Can we change the start time back to 7 p.m.?'

Nikki sighed. 'I thought 7.30 worked better with your bus schedule.'

'It does, but if we finish earlier, it means we can get home at a decent hour.'

'Thirty minutes doesn't make that much difference does it?' Sheena asked.

'It does for Anya and Kapil,' Preetam said. 'And what about Rajiv and Priyaani?'

Nikki guessed these were her grandchildren but then the other women let out a collective groan. 'Those bloody idiots. One day they're in love, the next day she is confiding to the servants that she wants to marry someone else,' Sheena said. 'Don't change the time, Nikki. Preetam's just wasting her time following a television series.'

'I am not,' Preetam said.

'Then you're wasting electricity,' Arvinder chided. 'Do you know how much our bill was last month?' Preetam shrugged. 'Of course you don't,' Arvinder muttered. 'You waste everything because you've always had everything.'

'Do you two share a home?' Nikki asked. She noticed a resemblance. Both women were light-skinned, with the same thin lips and striking greyish brown eyes. 'Sisters?'

'Mother and daughter,' Arvinder said, pointing to herself and then Preetam. 'Seventeen years apart, but thank you for thinking that I'm that young.'

'Or that Preetam's that old,' Sheena teased.

'Have you always lived together?' Nikki asked. She could not imagine a world where she would live with Mum into her senior citizen years and retain her sanity.

'Only since my husband died,' Preetam said. 'How long has it been – *hai*!' she suddenly cried out. 'Three months.' She took the edge of her dupatta and dabbed at the corners of her eyes.

'Oh, enough with the theatrics,' Arvinder said. 'It's been three years.'

'But it's still so fresh,' Preetam moaned. 'Has it really been that long?'

'You know very well it has been,' Arvinder said sternly. 'I don't know where you got this idea that widows have to cry and beat their chests every time their husbands are mentioned but it's unnecessary.'

'She got it from the evening dramas,' Sheena said.

'There. Another reason to cut back on the television,' Arvinder said.

'I think it's very sweet,' Manjeet said. 'I want to be sad like that too. Did you faint at his funeral?'

'Twice,' Preetam said proudly. 'And I begged them not to cremate him.'

'I remember that,' Sheena said. 'You made a huge fuss before passing out and then you woke up and started all over again.' She rolled her eyes at Nikki. 'You have to do these things, see, otherwise people accuse you of being unfeeling.'

'I know,' Nikki said. After Dad died, Auntie Geeta had come over to visit, black rivulets of mascara running down her cheeks. She wanted to mourn with Mum and was surprised that Mum remained dry-eyed, having done her crying in private. When she noticed a bubbling pot of curry on the stove, she became indignant. 'You're eating? I had nothing after my husband died. My sons had to force it into my mouth.' Feeling pressured, Mum refrained from eating the curry and then wolfed it down after Auntie Geeta left.

'You are all lucky to be able to grieve like that,' Manjeet said. 'Women like me don't get a funeral or any sort of ceremony.'

'Now, now, Manjeet, don't go putting it on yourself. There are no women like you. Just men like him,' Arvinder said.

'I don't understand—' Nikki said.

'Are we going to do any work or is this another class of introductions?' Tarampal interrupted. She shot Nikki a disapproving look.

'We have less than an hour now,' Nikki said. She handed the books out to the women. 'There are some alphabet exercises in here. She gave Sheena a letter-writing worksheet she had printed off the internet.

The remainder of the lesson passed slowly and silently, with the women scrunching up their faces in concentration. Some looked tired after a few tries and put their pencils down. Nikki wanted to find out more about the widows but Tarampal's presence kept her nervously on task. As soon as the clock struck 8.30, she told them they were dismissed and they filed out quietly, putting their books back on the desk. Sheena ducked past her and said nothing, clutching her letter in her hand.

The next lesson was on Thursday. All the women were promptly seated when Nikki arrived with an alphabet chart that she had found in another charity shop. 'A is for apple,' she said. They repeated 'Apple' after her. 'B is for boy.' 'C is for cat.' By the time they got to M, the chorus had faded. Nikki sighed and put down the chart.

'I can't teach you to write in any other way,' she said. 'We have to go through the basics.'

'My grandchildren use these books and charts,' sniffed Preetam. 'It's insulting.'

'I don't know what else to do,' Nikki said.

'You're the teacher – don't you know how to teach writing to adults?'

'I thought we'd be writing stories. Not this,' Nikki said. She picked up the chart and went back to the letters, and by the time they got to Z for zebra, the chorus was loud. There was a glimmer of hope – they were trying, at least.

'Right. Now there are a few writing exercises so we can learn about how to form words,' Nikki said. She flipped through the workbook and copied a few words on the board. As she turned, she heard urgent whispers but the women stopped talking when she was facing them again.

'The best way to learn to spell words is to sound them out first. We'll start with the word "cat." Who wants to repeat after me? "Cat".'

Preetam's hand shot up. 'Yes, go ahead Bibi Preetam.'

'What sorts of stories would you have us writing?'

Nikki sighed. 'It's going to be a long time before we can start writing stories, ladies. It's really difficult unless you have a sense of how the words are spelled and how the grammar works.'

'But Sheena can read and write in English.'

'And I'm sure it took her a lot of practice, right Sheena? When did you learn?'

'I learned in school,' Sheena said. 'My family came to Britain when I was fourteen years old.'

'That's not what I mean,' Preetam said. 'I'm saying that if we tell Sheena our stories, she can put them in writing'

Sheena looked pleased. 'I could do that,' she said to Nikki.

'And then we could give each other advice on how to improve the stories.'

'But how will you ever learn to write?' Nikki asked. 'Isn't that why you signed up for these classes?'

The women shared a look. 'We signed up for these classes because we wanted to fill our time,' Manjeet said. 'Whether it's learning to write, or telling stories, it doesn't matter. What matters is that we're keeping busy.' Nikki noticed she looked particularly sad when she said this. When she caught Nikki looking at her, she quickly smiled and dropped her gaze.

'I'd rather be telling stories,' said Arvinder. 'I've survived all this time without reading and writing; what do I need it for now?'

There was resounding agreement. Nikki was torn. If the tedium of learning to write was discouraging these women, she should motivate them to keep going. But storytelling was so much more fun.

In the back, Tarampal called out, 'I don't like this idea. I am here to learn to write.' She crossed her arms over her chest.

'You do your ABC colouring books then,' Arvinder muttered. Only Nikki heard her.

'Here's what we can do,' Nikki said. 'We'll do a bit of writing and reading practice for every lesson, and then if you want to do some storytelling sessions, Sheena and I can transcribe your stories and we can share them with the class. One new story each lesson.'

'Can we start today?' Preetam asked.

Nikki looked at the clock. 'We'll go through vowels first, and then, yes, we can do some stories.'

Some women already knew A E I O U but others like Tarampal struggled with them. Everybody grumbled at her for holding back the rest of the class when Nikki quizzed them. 'The A and the E are pronounced the same,' Tarampal kept insisting. Nikki instructed Sheena to start transcribing in the back of the classroom while she worked with Tarampal.

'English is such a stupid language,' Tarampal said. 'Nothing makes sense.'

'You're getting frustrated because it's new. It will get easier,' Nikki assured.

'New? I've been in London for over twenty years.'

It still came as a mild shock to Nikki that these women knew so little after living here for longer than she had been alive. Tarampal caught her expression and nodded. 'Tell me, why haven't I picked up English? Because of the English.' She said this triumphantly. 'They haven't made their country or their customs friendly to me. Now their language is just as unfriendly with these Ahh-Oooh sounds.'

In the back of the room, there was a rise of giggles and a squeal. Sheena was hunched over her paper, scribbling quickly while Arvinder whispered in her ear. Nikki turned her attention back to Tarampal and carefully said different words with vowels until Tarampal admitted to hearing the slightest difference between them. By the time they were finished, so was the lesson, but the women in the back of the room were still crowded around the desk and whispering urgently. Sheena continued writing, pausing every now and then to think of a correct word, or to rest her wrists. It was nine o'clock.

'Class is dismissed,' Nikki called out to the back. The women didn't appear to have heard her. They continued chatting and Sheena dutifully transcribed. Tarampal crossed the room to pack up her bag. She tossed the women a look of contempt and muttered, 'Bye,' to Nikki.

Nikki felt her spirits lifted by the women and their renewed sense of focus. They wouldn't learn to write this way but they were obviously so much keener on telling stories. As she made their way towards them, the women fell silent. Their faces were flushed. Some were hiding smiles. Sheena turned around.

'It's a surprise, Nikki,' she said. 'You can't see. We're not done yet, anyway.'

'It's time to lock up,' Nikki said. 'You'll miss your bus.'

Reluctantly, the women rose from their seats and picked up their bags. They left the room in a buzz of whispers. In the empty classroom, Nikki put the tables back in their usual place, just as she'd been told to do by Kulwinder.

The light in the classroom in the community centre was still on. Kulwinder could see the window glowing as she walked out of the temple. She slowed down and considered what to do. Nikki had probably left the light on and if Kulwinder didn't go up there to turn it off, Gurtaj Singh might decide that electricity was being wasted on classes for women. But she would not be safe entering that empty building. The phone call from the other night invaded her mind whenever she found herself alone. Before that, there had been two other warnings – one call which came only hours after she returned from her first intentional visit to the station and another one after her last visit. Both times, the police had offered little help, but her caller still felt the need to keep her in line.

She decided not to bother with the light. Walking briskly towards the bus stop she saw the women from the writing class in a huddle. Kulwinder did a silent roll call. There was Arvinder Kaur – so tall that she had to stoop like a giraffe to listen to the others. Her daughter Preetam was perpetually adjusting the lacey white dupatta on her head. So precious and vain compared to her mother. On the edge of the group, Manjeet Kaur spoke in furtive nods and smiles. Sheena Kaur was nowhere to be seen but she had probably sped home in her little red car. Tarampal Kaur had registered as well but she wasn't part of the group. Her absence was a relief.

The women noticed Kulwinder approaching and they acknowledged her with quick smiles. Maybe they could explain why the light was still on. Perhaps Nikki was in there entertaining a lover? It wasn't unheard of for youngsters in the neighbourhood to use these vacant rooms for their filthy interactions. In that case the lights would be off though wouldn't they – but then again, who knew what this new generation found pleasurable?

'*Sat sri akal*,' she said, putting her hands together for all of them. They returned the gesture. '*Sat sri akal*,' they murmured. In the glow of the streetlamp, they looked sheepish, as if caught stealing.

'How are you ladies?'

'Very good, thanks,' said Preetam Kaur.

'Enjoying your writing classes?'

'Yes.' They were a rehearsed chorus. Kulwinder eyed them suspiciously.

'Learning a lot?' she asked.

A sly look passed between the women, just a flash, before Arvinder said, 'Oh yes. We did a lot of learning today.'

The women beamed. Kulwinder considered asking them more. Perhaps they needed a reminder that their learning was the result of her clever initiative. *I do everything for you*, she used to tell Maya, sometimes with pride and at other times, with frustration. The women looked desperate to get back to their conversation. Kulwinder was reminded of Maya and her friends huddled together, their hushed conversation often punctuated with giggles. 'What was so funny?' Kulwinder would ask later, knowing the question was enough to make Maya dissolve into giggles again, and then Kulwinder couldn't help laughing along. The memory was accompanied by a stabbing pain in her gut. What she would give to see her daughter's smile again. She bade the women farewell and continued her journey. She had never been close to these women and she knew they had signed up for her classes for lack of anything else to do. She had loss in common with them, but losing a child was different. Nobody knew the ache of rage, guilt and profound sadness that Kulwinder carried with her everyday.

This main road had some shadowy patches where walls of hedges and parked cars could easily hide a crouching assailant. She reached for her phone, wanting to ask Sarab to come and pick her up but standing still seemed just as risky. She set her sights on the junction of Queen Mary Road and marched onward, aware that her heart had started pounding. After the caller had hung up last night, she had sat up in bed, alert to every creak and shift in the house. She had drifted to sleep eventually but this morning, exhausted and alone, she found herself inexplicably furious, this time at Maya for putting her through all of this.

Laughter broke like fireworks into the air. Kulwinder whipped around. It was the women again. Manjeet waved but she pretended not to see. Kulwinder craned her neck as if she was checking something on the building. From this distance, the glow in the window reminded her of flames. She turned her back on the building and walked so briskly she nearly broke into a run.

Chapter Five

Around the corner from the car park, Nikki had discovered a spot where she could hide and have a cigarette before class. Here the temple was completely cut off from her view. She shook a cigarette from its pack and lit it. Her shift at O'Reilly's last night had felt longer than usual and she found herself looking forward to tonight's lesson.

Nikki finished her cigarette and entered the community centre building, running straight into Kulwinder Kaur on the stairwell.

'Oh hello,' she said.

Kulwinder's nose crinkled. 'You've been smoking. I can smell it on you.'

'I was standing near some smokers, and . . .'

'Maybe these excuses work on your mother, but I know better.'

'I don't think my smoking should be your concern,' Nikki said, straightening her shoulders.

There was heat in Kulwinder's stare. 'The behaviour of an instructor is my concern. The women look to you for guidance. I don't know how they're supposed to respect any instructions that come from the mouth of a smoker.'

'I'm doing everything that's expected of me in the classroom,' Nikki said. She made a mental note to cut short the storytelling session in favour of a grammar lesson in case Kulwinder did a spot check.

'Let's hope so,' Kulwinder said. Nikki wedged past her uncomfortably on the stairs and found that all the women had arrived promptly. Tarampal had chosen a seat a noticeable distance from the others. 'Nikki!' Sheena called. 'I've written a story. It's a combined effort from all of us.'

'Wonderful,' Nikki said.

'Can you read it aloud to the class?' Preetam asked.

'I think Nikki should read it,' Sheena said.

'In a minute,' Nikki said. 'I'll just set some work for Bibi Tarampal here.'

'Don't bother with me,' Tarampal sniffed. 'I'll just be working on my A-B-C book.'

'For what?' Arvinder asked. 'Don't be such a spoilsport.'

'I'll learn to write soon and you'll still be illiterate,' Tarampal shot back.

Nikki pulled up a chair next to Tarampal and searched for the page on linking vowels and consonants. There were pictures representing each simple three-letter word. CAT. DOG. POT. 'I don't know all of these letters,' Tarampal complained. 'You haven't taught them all to me.'

'Do the ones you know,' Nikki said gently. 'We'll work on the others together.'

Nikki was aware that the women were watching her very closely as she began to read their story. Her Punjabi was rustier than she expected and Sheena's rushed handwriting was unlike the careful print in the books she had learned from. 'I'm not sure if I can read this, Sheena,' Nikki said, squinting at the page.

Sheena shot up from her seat. 'I'll do it then.' She took the papers from Nikki. The other women sat up in their seats, their faces wide with anticipation. Watching them, Nikki had the dreadful sense that somebody was out to play a joke on her.

Sheena began to read. 'This is the story about a man and a woman taking a drive in a car. The man was tall and handsome and the woman was his wife. They didn't have any children and had lots of free time.' Sheena paused for effect and glanced at Nikki before continuing.

'One day they were driving along a lonely road and they were running out of petrol. It was dark outside and they were scared. It was also cold, so the man

stopped the car and hugged the woman so she would stop shivering. She was actually pretending to shiver. She wanted to feel the man's body. Although she had felt his body many times before, she wanted to be with him in this dark car.

'He began to feel quite like a hero because he was protecting his wife. He moved his hands down her back to her bottom and gave it a squeeze. She leaned closer to him and gave him a kiss. With her hands, she also moved down—'

'Okay that's enough,' Nikki said. She took the story from Sheena and told her to have a seat. All of the women in the class were giggling except Tarampal, whose face was buried in her book. Nikki scanned the page. A sentence caught her eye: *His throbbing organ was the colour and size of an aubergine, and as she gripped it with her hands and guided it towards her mouth, he became so excited that his knees began to shake.* Nikki gasped and dropped the pages on the desk.

The women were laughing loudly now, and their voices had begun to echo down the corridor. They reached the doorway of Kulwinder Kaur, who turned to listen but the sounds just as quickly settled down.

'What's the matter?' Sheena asked.

'This is not the type of story I had in mind,' Nikki said.

'You can't be too surprised. You read stories like this yourself,' Manjeet said. 'You bought us an entire book of them.'

'I bought the book as a joke for my sister!' That said, *Red Velvet* had graduated from the charity shop bag to Nikki's bedside table, from where she had no intentions of removing it.

'I don't get the joke. Were you supposed to buy her a different book?' Preetam wondered.

'She's a bit reserved,' Nikki said. 'I thought the stories would remind her that she needed to lighten up, that's all.' Were the widows smirking? They appeared to be challenging her. She cleared her throat. 'I think we're done with stories for now.'

The women groaned when Nikki presented the alphabet chart. 'Today we'll review consonants.'

'Oh, not that bloody thing,' Arvinder said. 'A for apple, B for boy? Don't treat me like a child, Nikki.'

'Actually "A" is a vowel. Remember? What are some other vowels?'

Arvinder scowled and said nothing. The other widows stared back blankly as well.

'Come on, ladies. These are important.'

'Last time you said we could do storytelling during these lessons,' Preetam protested.

'Right. I probably shouldn't have said that. The fact is, I was hired to teach you all to write. I need to honour that promise.' She glanced once more at the pages on the desk. If Kulwinder knew about this story, she'd accuse her of deliberately setting the women on the wrong path.

'Why don't you like Sheena's story?' Preetam asked. 'I thought modern girls prided themselves on being open-minded.'

'She doesn't like it because she's just like everybody else,' Arvinder said. 'All those people who say, "Take no notice of those widows. Without their husbands, they're irrelevant."'

'That's not what I think of you,' Nikki protested, although Arvinder's observation was not far off the mark. She had certainly expected these widows to be more impressionable than they turned out to be.

'We'd be invisible in India,' Arvinder said. 'I suppose it makes no difference that we're in England. You must think it's wrong of us to discuss these things because we shouldn't be thinking of them.'

'I'm not saying your story was wrong. It was just unexpected.'

'Why?' Sheena challenged. 'Because our husbands are gone? Let me tell you, Nikki, we have plenty of experience with desire.'

'We talk about it all the time too,' Manjeet said. 'People see us and assume that we're just filling our empty evenings with gossip but how much of that can one do? It's far more fun to discuss the things we miss.'

'Or what we were never given in the first place,' Arvinder said dryly.

Laughter rippled though the classroom. This time the noise pierced Kulwinder's concentration just as she was about to solve a row in her sudoku puzzle.

'Keep your voices down,' Nikki pleaded.

'Come on, Nikki,' Preetam urged. 'This will be fun. I've got a story brewing in my mind. A more satisfying series finale to my favourite television drama.'

'Do Kapil and Anya finally get together?' Manjeet asked.

'Oh, and how,' Preetam said.

'There are stories about men and women that I tell myself when I'm lying awake at night,' Manjeet said. 'It's better than counting sheep or taking Rescue Remedy. It helps me to relax.'

'I'm sure it does,' Sheena said, raising an eyebrow. The women burst out laughing again.

'Even Tarampal has some stories, I'm sure,' said Arvinder.

'You leave me out of this,' Tarampal warned.

Suddenly, the door of the classroom swung open. Kulwinder Kaur stood with her arms crossed over her chest. 'What is going on here?' she demanded. 'I can hear the commotion all the way from my office.'

The women were silent with shock for a moment and then Preetam Kaur said, 'Sorry. We were laughing because I couldn't pronounce a word.'

'Yes,' Arvinder said. 'Nikki said this word in English which means "aubergine" but we couldn't say it.' The women tittered again. Nikki nodded and smiled at Kulwinder as if to say, 'What can you do?' She placed her palm flat on the story on her desk.

It was fortunate that Tarampal was sitting so close to the door. Her workbook was wide open and looked very legitimate. Nikki just hoped she wouldn't say anything. She still looked gravely unhappy with the women.

'I need to talk to you outside for a moment,' Kulwinder said to Nikki.

'Sure,' Nikki said. 'Sheena, can you please write the alphabet on the board? I'll test you all when I come back.' She shot Sheena a stern look and followed Kulwinder outside.

Kulwinder fixed Nikki with a stare. 'I hired you to teach these women, not stand around telling jokes,' she said. 'I don't know what they're doing but it doesn't look like learning.'

Through the window, Nikki could see the women staring at the board and Sheena dutifully writing the letters. Tarampal was hunched over her desk, working her pencil hard into the paper. She looked up to check the roundness of her D against Sheena's on the board. 'Nobody said learning couldn't be fun,' Nikki said.

'This job requires a degree of respect and professionalism. Your respect is clearly questionable because you'll smoke on temple grounds. I have high doubts about your professional standards.'

'I'm handling the job just fine,' Nikki said. 'I'm doing exactly what you asked of me.'

'If you were, then I wouldn't have to remind you to keep the noise down. You realize, don't you, that any small misstep means that these classes could be shut down? As it is, we have very few participants.'

'Look, Kulwinder, I get that you want these classes to go well but I didn't realize I'd be under constant surveillance. The women are learning. You need to back off and let me do my job.'

A storm cloud seemed to take over Kulwinder's expression. Her lips became menacingly thin. 'I think you're forgetting something very important,' she said, her voice suddenly low and steady. 'I am your boss. I hired you. You should thank me for taking you on even though your only skills were pouring drinks. You should thank me for coming here to remind you to remain focused. You should thank me for letting you off with a warning. I didn't come here for a discussion. I came here to *remind* you of your *responsibilities*, something you are clearly lacking. Understand?'

Nikki swallowed, hard. 'I understand.' Kulwinder looked at her expectantly. 'And thank you,' Nikki whispered. Tears of humiliation burned in her eyes.

She waited for a few moments before reentering the classroom. The women's eyes were wide in anticipation. Even Tarampal was looking up from her book.

'We have to get back to work,' Nikki said, blinking furiously.

Thankfully, there were no arguments. Arvinder, Tarampal, Preetam and Manjeet accepted an exercise on consonants. Sheena practised writing a persuasive speech. While the women worked, Nikki couldn't help replaying the humiliating confrontation in her mind. She told herself that Kulwinder probably chastised everybody but her harsh words had hit a raw nerve. *Your only skills were pouring drinks. Lacking responsibility*. Here Nikki had been trying to steer the women back towards literacy to avoid getting into trouble but did Kulwinder recognize her efforts? It didn't matter if Nikki did the right thing. It was still wrong.

The time passed quickly while Nikki was lost in her thoughts. Even her fights with Mum didn't leave her feeling so helpless. If Kulwinder was like this as a boss, imagine what she had been like as a parent to her rebellious daughter. Nikki glanced at the clock.

'Is everybody finished?' she asked.

The women nodded. Nikki took up the consonants worksheets. Arvinder's wobbly handwriting made her H's look like M's but she had persisted until Z, slashed across the lines like a lightning bolt. Preetam's handwriting was more precise but she only reached J before time was up. Manjeet had ignored the consonants entirely, choosing instead to write A E I O U at the top of the page as if revising what she had learned before.

What was there to do besides feeding more worksheets to the women, more rote practices? This reproduced string of alphabets looked as uninspired as any other monotonous task that filled these widows' days. If they continued on this path, the women would stop showing up. Nikki could already sense their restlessness. As she scanned the worksheets, a debate clamoured in her mind. She'd been hired to teach English, yes, but hadn't she only signed up because she thought she'd be empowering women? If the widows wanted to share erotic stories, who was she to censor them?

'You've all worked very hard today,' Nikki said. 'These practices are good.' She handed the worksheets back to the women. Then she smiled. 'But I think your stories would be better.'

The women looked at each other and grinned. Only Tarampal scowled and crossed her arms over her chest. 'I promise to continue to teach you how to read and write,' Nikki said to her. 'But the rest of you are welcome to bring in your stories. We must make sure to be very quiet from now on though.'

'See you on Tuesday,' Sheena said on her way out the door.

'See you all then,' Nikki said. 'Oh, and if you see Kulwinder, remember to say thank you.' *And fuck you*, she thought.

The following Tuesday Nikki made sure to leave time for the quick odour-neutralising routine she had practised to perfection as a teenager. Pre-cigarette, it involved pulling her hair back into a bun and taking off her jacket to avoid clinging smoke smells and then, after, a dose of extra-strong mints and a spray of extra-strong perfume.

Nikki was in the middle of her perfume bath when a face appeared and then flitted out of her view. 'Sorry,' the man belonging to the face said. She only caught a glimpse but she noticed that he was cute. A moment later, she stepped out of the corner and saw him leaning against the wall.

'It's all yours,' she said.

'Thanks,' he said, ducking in. 'I just needed to make a phone call.'

'Sure,' Nikki said. 'Me too.'

'No, you were clearly smoking. It's not very good for you,' he said as he lit his own cigarette. 'You really shouldn't.'

'Neither should you.'

'True,' he said. 'Is it just me or do they taste even better in hiding?'

'Much better,' Nikki agreed. As a teenager, she used to smoke in the park behind her house, her adrenaline surging each time she saw Mum or Dad's silhouette crossing the window. 'Especially when your parents are within sight.'

'Ever got caught?'

'No. You?'

'Oh yeah. It was bad.' Nikki watched as he took a long drag of his cigarette and stared into the distance. His attempt at being mysterious came off as cheesy but surprisingly, she liked it.

'I'm Nikki,' she said.

'Jason.'

She raised an eyebrow. 'Is that an American name for a Punjabi boy?'

'Who says I'm American?'

'Canadian?' Nikki asked. She definitely detected an accent.

'American,' Jason said. 'And Punjabi. And Sikh, obviously.' He gestured at the temple. 'And yourself?'

'British and Punjabi and Sikh,' Nikki said. It had been a long time since she identified herself in all of those terms at once. She wondered if this was what the widows thought of her, and in which proportions.

'So what's your real name?' she asked Jason.

'Jason Singh Bhamra.' Jason squinted at her. 'You look surprised.'

'I was sure it was an anglicized version of something else.'

'My parents gave me a name that Americans could pronounce as well. They were forward-thinkers in that regard. Like yours, I'm assuming.'

'Oh no,' Nikki said. 'I just don't tell people my full name. It's only on my birth certificate. Nobody uses it.'

'Does it start with an N?'

'You're not going to guess it.'

'Navinder.'

'No.' Nikki was already regretting lying about her name. It just seemed more interesting than the truth: "Nikki" meant little and she was a younger sibling so her parents had decided it was apt.

'Najpal.'

'Actually—'

'Naginder, Navdeep, Narinder, Neelam, Naushil, Navjhot.'

'None of the above,' Nikki said. 'I was kidding. My real name is Nikki.'

Jason smiled at her and took another drag of his cigarette. 'That was a missed opportunity. I was going to say "if I guess it, will you give me your number?"'

Oh dear, Nikki thought. More cheesiness. 'Well, I don't think anyone can pull off trying to pick up girls in dodgy alleyways.'

Jason tipped his cigarette packet towards Nikki. 'Another one?'

'No thanks,' she said.

'Your phone number?'

Nikki shook her head. It was instinctive. She didn't know this Jason Bhamra. She snuck another glance at him, noticing the slight cleft in his chin. He was *cute*.

'It's the principle of the thing,' she explained, hoping he would ask again. 'We're at the temple.'

'Damn,' Jason said. 'You have principles.'

'I've got several. I'm thinking of adding "no smoking" to my list but it's hard.'

'It's nearly impossible,' Jason agreed. 'A few years ago I tried quitting smoking, and then I settled for quitting drinking instead. I thought I'd get points for eliminating one vice.'

'You don't drink?'

'I lasted a week.'

This made Nikki laugh. Then she saw her chance.

'Have you ever been to O'Reilly's pub in Shepherd's Bush?'

'Nope. I've been to the pub on the Southall Broadway though. Did you know you can pay in rupees there?'

'That's not very useful if your salary is in pounds.'

'True. This O'Reilly's pub then . . .'

'No rupees required. I'm there most evenings. For work, not because I'm an alcoholic.'

Jason's grin was rewarding. 'So you're there this week?'

'Most evenings,' Nikki said. As she walked away, she felt his gaze on her back.

'Nikki,' he called. She turned around. 'Is it short for Nicole?'

'It really is just Nikki,' she said. She held back her smile until she was out of his view. Their encounter left her skin tingling, as if she was walking through a light mist.

'I've got a story by Manjeet,' Sheena said as soon as Nikki entered the classroom. 'The one she tells herself before going to bed.'

'It's very good,' Preetam said. 'Manjeet told me about it at the market the other day.'

Manjeet waved away the praise bashfully. Sheena handed Nikki three pages of dense scribbles. 'The Viewing,' Nikki read out. '*The flat, dark mole on Sonya's* . . . uh . . . *thing*,' she squinted.

'Sunita,' Manjeet corrected. 'Sunita's chin.'

'Sorry. ' Nikki pointed to the Gurmukhi letters as if her touch could untangle them. '*The flat, dark mole on Sunita's chin looked like shorts. As a cat, she was brittle* . . .' This wasn't right. She looked up at the women helplessly.

'*Hai*,' Preetam said, stricken. 'What are you doing to her story?'

'I'm struggling to read it.'

'Give her a break. We can't expect her to be able to read Gurmukhi well. She's not from India,' said Sheena.

'I can speak better than write,' Nikki admitted.

'Your Punjabi grammar is all wrong,' Preetam sniffed. 'The other day you were saying D for Dog and then you translated Dog to the feminine *kutti* instead of *kutta*. It was insulting. You kept repeating it too – *kutti, kutti*.'

'It was like you were calling all of us bitches,' Sheena said in English.

'I'm sorry,' Nikki said. 'Sheena, can you read your own writing?'

Sheena looked at the pages and shrugged. 'I had to be very quick.'

Manjeet raised her hand timidly. 'I think I have it memorized from repeating it all those nights.'

'Go ahead then,' Nikki said.

Manjeet drew in a breath and straightened her shoulders.

The Viewing

The flat, dark mole on Sunita's chin looked like a stain. As a child, she was brought to a local fortune-teller who predicted that the mole would be a burden. 'A big mole is like an additional eye,' the fortune-teller said. "She will have a wild imagination and she will be too critical of everything."

The fortune-teller was correct. Sunita was often lost in daydreams and she was very quick to judge people. When Sunita came of age, her mother Dalpreet thought she might greaten her chances for marriage if she could choose between two eligible husbands. She arranged for the first family, the Dhaliwals, to see Sunita on Tuesday. The second family, the Randhawas, would see Sunita on Wednesday. However, at the last minute, the Dhaliwals' train was delayed and they could only be there on Wednesday as well. Sunita's mother panicked. She could not refuse them. It would also be impolite to reschedule with the other family.

Sunita was aware of the conflict because she had overheard her mother confiding in a trustworthy neighbour. 'If my daughter were more desirable, perhaps I would have some bargaining power. But Sunita is no catch with that hideous mole. I have to keep these families unaware of each other somehow. I have no choice.'

Although her mother's words stung, Sunita knew she had a point. The mole was very ugly. It made her the target of insults from cruel children at school and it distracted potential suitors from her fine features. Sunita spent all of her pocket money on expensive creams to make the mole fade but they didn't work. Her only hope was to marry a man with enough money to pay for an operation to remove it altogether. For this reason, Sunita was eager to meet multiple suitors. But rather than resigning her fate to the hands of the families, she came up with an idea.

'Mother,' she said. 'Let's host both families at the same time, but keep them separate. The Randhawas can sit in our living room and the Dhaliwals can be in the kitchen. While you're entertaining one family, I'll be pouring tea for the other. Then we'll switch places.'

It was a harebrained scheme, but it might work. They were landowners with a spacious home. The tables in their kitchen and living room were equal in their capacity to host guests. Dalpreet agreed because she could not come up with a better solution. She was becoming increasingly desperate to marry off her daughter. It was said that woman without a husband was like a bow without an arrow. Dalpreet agreed with this saying but she also believed that a man without a wife was even more problematic. Look at their neighbour. He was greying and still single. Some people called him Professor because he spent all his time reading books but Sunita's mother thought he was a madman. One afternoon, while Sunita was clipping the washing to the clothesline, Dalpreet caught him watching her from the window upstairs. Once Sunita became somebody's wife, surely he would consider it indecent to stare like that?

The day arrived. Dalpreet woke Sunita with firm instructions to conceal her mole with an expensive powder that matched her sandy skin tone. 'What difference does it make?' *Sunita briefly wondered.* 'He'll have to see me as I am eventually.' *But she made the mole disappear nonetheless.*

From her bedroom window, Sunita saw the Dhaliwals enter her house. She caught a glimpse of their son. He had broad shoulders and a thin beard but then she heard him speak. His voice was so high-pitched, it could be mistaken for his mother's. As Sunita prepared the tea, she heard the Randhawas entering the front door. She walked out into the living room with a tray of sweets and sneaked a glance at the boy. His eyes were a kind, greyish-brown but his scrawny shoulders jutted painfully through his shirt. He wasn't the manly suitor she had hoped for. Sunita headed back to the kitchen, leaving the Randhawas with polite apologies.

'What do you think?' her mother asked her as they passed each other in the corridor. 'Which one is your choice?'

Sunita felt sorry for her mother. A simple viewing would not reveal what she wanted to know most about these men. She was so busy running between both families that she hadn't had time to think of what it would be like to press her naked flesh against theirs. In Sunita's fantasies, the viewings were entirely different. The men would stand before her, their chests bare and the bulging muscles between their legs exposed. She would give them opportunities to impress her – to put their warm mouths against hers; to titillate her with firm, expert fingers. This was what she imagined doing every night with the neighbour – the Professor. She knew he watched her and this made her want him even more.

'They're both fine,' Sunita said to her mother.

'Fine?' Dalpreet asked. 'What does that mean? Which one do you like better?'

Sunita didn't know how to answer. Her mother interpreted her silence as shyness and let her go. Sunita returned to the Dhaliwals in the kitchen. She sat across from her suitor and looked demurely at the floor. If the family were kind, they would surreptitiously provide opportunities for the couple to study each other more closely. They would deliberately look away or become involved in an animated discussion that allowed the boy and girl to hold each other's gazes. Sunita waited for this moment but it didn't come. Mrs Dhaliwal was not much of a talker and she sat so close to her son, with her thigh so tightly pressed against his that Sunita wondered if she still fed him and washed his bottom too.

Sunita had a few moments before she had to return to the Randhawas. She stared at the tiles and delved into a fantasy about this Dhaliwal boy. 'Kiss me,' she said, drawing him into the lush farmland that bordered her family home. She lay down between tall stalks of grass and could smell the fragrant earth, the soil recently churned. He lay on top of her and slipped his tongue gently into her mouth. His hands roamed from her waist to her breasts, which he cupped and squeezed gently. With a pop, her blouse opened and he was taking her nipples into his mouth. Sweat rolled down the crease between her breasts and he licked it. She sighed and bucked at the movement of his hard, bulging muscle against the velvety cushion between her open legs—

'HEEHEEHEE!'

Sunita's daydream was broken by the Dhaliwal boy's hideous laugh. Somebody had told a joke. Everybody was laughing but this man was the noisiest. His grin revealed a set of big teeth. Sunita could not imagine tender kisses from a mouth like that. 'I won't marry that donkey,' she informed her mother in the corridor.

Her mother looked relieved. 'Good. The Randhawas have a better dowry offer anyway,' she said, ushering Sunita into the living room.

Sunita sat before the Randhawas with renewed interest in their son now that she had eliminated the Dhaliwal boy. The Randhawa boy's boniness was still bothersome but his grey eyes were like the still pools of rain that collected on pavements and glittered with specks of sunlight. She imagined holding her firstborn child and gazing into those eyes. Of course, there was the act that created the baby first. Once again, she fell into her imagination. This time the scene was set in their marital suite. She was wrapped in a bejewelled red gown and he was undressing her slowly. With each glimpse of skin that he revealed, he stopped to marvel at her. Finally, she was naked and standing before him while he knelt at her feet, having removed her shoes. He swept her into the air and laid her down gently on the bed. His fingers made teasing circles on her inner thighs as he kissed her passionately.

The fantasy ended there. It was already too far-fetched. This bony, awkward boy would never have the strength to lift Sunita onto the bed. His fingers would be stiff as sticks and he would jab them into her – she knew this from the feverish, impa-

tient way he dipped his biscuit into his tea. He wouldn't know the last thing about fondling a woman either. He would pinch and twist as if tuning a radio.

'Neither of those men are suitable,' Sunita told her mother after both families left. 'I won't marry them.'

It was just as well. Both families declined Sunita. The Dhaliwals believed she was vain. 'She spent more time looking at her painted toenails than at the in-laws who would take her in. An ungrateful girl,' huffed Mrs Dhaliwal. The Randhawas had overheard Dalpreet's comments about the dowry and they were offended. They mistook the lusty look in Sunita's eyes for greed, not knowing that she was actually attempting to conjure up a fantasy about their son.

Dalpreet cried and fretted. 'What will I do now?' she wept, dabbing the corners of her eyes with her dupatta. 'I have been cursed with a choosy daughter. She'll never get married.'

Helpless to comfort her mother, Sunita climbed onto the roof of her house and stared up into the sky. Somewhere out there was a husband for her. Not a boy. A man. She rested flat on her back. This was a bold thing to do. Anybody looking out of their window could see this single girl lying in the dark, daring the world to join her. A breeze sighed through the fields, lifting and dropping the hem of Sunita's cotton tunic like a winking eye. She spread out her arms and stretched them till the tips of her fingers were touching the furthest points. It still wasn't far enough. On these rooftop visits, Sunita wished to lenghthen her limbs so she could spread across the entire world.

A presence made the hairs on Sunita's neck stand. She sat up and looked around and noticed a bedroom light on in the house next door. A shadow crossed the window. Sunita's heart leapt. She had noticed the Professor when he moved in to the house – rumour had it that he had been married once before but he was now living as a bachelor in his sister's home – but she was never able to maintain her gaze on his face long enough without making her mother suspicious. She sensed from his long, confident strides that he was an experienced man.

Waiting for the Professor to pass the window again, Sunita freed her hair from the chaste braid her mother had made her wear. She combed her fingers through her hair, unweaving it so it fell loosely on her shoulders. She wished she had some kohl for her eyes. She bit her lips and pinched her cheeks to give them colour.

The Professor arrived at the window again and this time he lingered. 'How did you get up there?' he asked. His deep voice stirred something in Sunita.

'It wasn't too difficult,' she said.

'It looks dangerous,' he replied. 'You're not scared?'

She shook her head. Her hair moved back and forth. She could sense that he was watching her. Encouraged by his interest, she smiled. 'Nothing scares me.' Her heart hammered inside her chest.

He returned her smile and climbed out of his window. In a few swift movements, he was on the roof with her. Although his physique was muscular, his steps were quiet. A breeze passed through the village, making Sunita shiver. Without a word, he drew her to his warm and solid body. His smell was intoxicating.

Sunita leaned back onto the roof and closed her eyes. The Professor rolled towards her and slipped his hands under her tunic. His fingers deftly stroked her hard nipples. His was an assured touch. Sunita arched her back and lifted her arms to let him peel off her blouse. His hands didn't return to her breasts; instead, he lowered his head to them and took his time caressing each one with his tongue. The intense prickles of pleasure from this contact made Sunita gasp. All she could feel was his warm, wet mouth on her skin – the rest of her body had melted away. When he began to tug at the strings of her salwaar, she flung her legs apart. He looked up in surprise. He had probably never met such a forward young woman before. Just as Sunita was begin to regret being so eager, the Professor pressed his mouth to the throbbing, private place between her legs. His skilled tongue ran over her warm, wet folds and settled on the pulsing knot that gave her the most pleasure. Something began to build in her – a mounting tension that made her breaths shorter. The weight in her chest made her nervous. She wanted to sit up but at the same time, she wanted this escalation to continue. Never had Sunita experienced two opposing forces within her own body. Her thighs shivered despite the heat in her belly. Her toes curled although her shoulders were slack. She felt as if she was being dipped into a river that was so cold that it burned.

Finally, it happened. A bursting release that spread through Sunita's body and shook her every muscle loose. She moaned, clutching the Professor's hair. He looked up at her and for the first time, she felt shy. She turned her cheek so it was obscured by night shadows. Seconds or hours passed – she could not be sure because time was an illusion in these farmlands after dark.

Eventually, she turned around. The Professor was gone. She sat up, confused. Her salwar was tied tightly around her waist and she was wearing her tunic. Had it all been a fantasy? It couldn't be. Those feelings of pleasure were too vivid. She leaned over the roof and looked into the neighbour's home. The Professor's bedroom window was shut and the curtains drawn.

Sunita didn't want to grieve. Perhaps the powers of her imagination were so strong that she had willed this dream to become a brief reality but that only meant that it could happen again. Climbing off the roof, she thought about the men she had refused that afternoon, sitting with their families and plotting their next bridal viewing. She touched her hands to her mole. Her sweat had worn away the concealing powder. All along, everybody was wrong, Sunita decided. There was nothing unlucky about being able to see the world the way she did.

The women were captivated. They leaned towards Manjeet, sliding to the edges of their chairs to hear more. Manjeet maintained her straight posture throughout, her eyes shut as she drifted into Sunita's world. She opened her eyes and shot Nikki a furtive look. 'Sorry,' she whispered. 'I get carried away.'

'Don't apologize. That was beautiful. Your story has such great details,' Nikki said.

'It all comes from Sunita's imagination, not mine,' Manjeet said.

'Sunita is not you?' Preetam asked. 'You've got a mole as well.'

'Ah, Sunita's mole is a mark of beauty,' Manjeet said. 'Mine is just . . .' She shrugged. Nikki noticed that she kept her hand cupped around her chin to cover her mole.

'It's beautiful, Bibi Manjeet,' Nikki said. 'Just like Sunita's.'

Manjeet grimaced. Her face cheeks flushed with embarrassment. 'Please, there's no need to say such things. My mother was very concerned about my mole. She said it was bad luck and I'd never find anyone.'

'Your mother had a lot to worry about if all you could think about was bedding men,' Tarampal retorted.

'Nobody's saying you have to listen,' Arvinder shot back. 'If you're so focused on your learning, you wouldn't be paying any attention to us.'

Tarampal's face reddened. It was hard to know if she was embarrassed or infuriated.

'Obviously, your mother was wrong,' Nikki said. 'You found your husband.'

'Yes, but I didn't keep him, did I?'

The other widows exchanged looks. 'Now, Manjeet,' Arvinder said firmly. 'I've told you, you mustn't go down that path.'

'Why not?' Manjeet asked. Her eyes streamed with tears.

'Whatever happened, I'm sure you can't be blamed for your husband's death,' Nikki said.

Manjeet let out a short laugh. 'He's not dead. He's still very much alive. He ran away with the nurse who took care of him after his heart attack.'

'Oh,' Nikki said. Poor Manjeet. It made more sense now – the "widow look" that Sheena had mentioned. Manjeet dressed like a widow because it was more acceptable than being separated from her husband. 'I'm very sorry,' she said.

'That's all everyone ever says,' Manjeet said. 'They just apologize. But they didn't do anything wrong. He did.'

'That's right. He did. He and that trampy little nurse,' Arvinder said. 'Not you.'

Manjeet shook her head and wiped her nose. 'If I could live my life again, I'd be more like Sunita,' she said. 'She knows what she wants. That nurse, too. She knew what she wanted and she took it.'

'*Hai*,' Preetam said, dabbing the corners of her eyes with her dupatta. 'It's very tragic.'

'You're not helping,' Sheena hissed. 'Nikki, say something.'

Nikki didn't know what to do. The women stared at her expectantly. She thought back to the details of Manjeet's story and imagined Sunita lying on the roof, anticipating the rest of her life. 'I think what Bibi Manjeet's story has highlighted is that there's a difference between being courageous and being *malicious*,' she said. Sheena quickly gave the women a Punjabi translation of the word. 'I think Sunita's courage is admirable but to take somebody's husband is greedy and hurtful.'

'You have courage too, Manjeet,' Sheena said. 'You wouldn't have told that story if you didn't.'

'I'm too afraid to tell people what he did,' Manjeet said. 'That's cowardly, isn't it? I've been pretending that he died on a trip to India so nobody would ask any questions. I even went to stay with my oldest son in Canada for a while so people would think I was doing my husband's last rites.'

'When did it happen?' Nikki asked.

'Last summer.'

'It's still very new, then,' Nikki said.

'Tell that to them. They've bought a home together,' Manjeet said. 'This nurse came to England from a village in India as well but she's from a different generation, Nikki. Those girls know how to do everything men want before they're married.'

'In my time, you just relied on what your married sisters and cousins told you,' Arvinder said.

Nikki could picture it – a young and blushing Arvinder surrounded by giggly sari-clad relatives, taking turns to offer words of wisdom. There was something enviable about the scene. She couldn't imagine having such a moment before Mindi's wedding. 'That sounds nice,' she said. 'You looked out for each other.'

'It was useful,' Preetam said. 'Like when my cousin Diljeet said "Use ghee to grease things up down there."'

'*I* was the one who told you that,' Arvinder said. 'Oldest trick in the book.'

Sheena burst out laughing. 'Look at Nikki's face!' she cried. So, Nikki was obviously unsuccessful at hiding her mortification then. She had a mental image of Mum in the kitchen spreading a lump of ghee across the surface of a heating *tava* where it melted instantly. Now ghee had an entirely different association.

'That's right,' Preetam recalled. 'It was Diljeet who warned me to be discreet, and to always try to sneak some ghee into a small container during cooking without my mother-in-law noticing. Otherwise it was challenging to get big drums of ghee into the bedroom without the rest of the family seeing.'

'Don't you have those little tubs for the kitchen?' Nikki asked.

'Costco sells them in bulk,' Preetam said. 'Why are you wasting money buying small-small tubs?'

'I was given a useful tip to please my husband if he wanted it during my time of the month,' Manjeet said. 'Let him put it in your armpit, then do this.' Manjeet cranked her arm up and down.

'You didn't!' Sheena exclaimed.

'I did,' Manjeet said. 'He liked it. He said it had the same feeling as my private parts – hairy and warm.'

Nikki had never struggled so hard to keep a straight face. She made eye contact with Sheena, who had her hands cupped over her mouth. Laughter rippled through Sheena's sleeves.

'Many women didn't even know what was expected of them until their wedding night,' Preetam said. 'Not me, thankfully, but can you imagine the surprise?'

'You're very welcome,' Arvinder said. 'I told you everything you had to know.'

'Really?' Nikki asked. 'That's very progressive of you.' Arvinder appeared to be well into her eighties. Nikki couldn't even imagine somebody in Mum's generation discussing the birds and the bees. Once again, she had underestimated Arvinder, and Manjeet as well, with her creative alternative methods of pleasuring her husband.

'*Hanh*, well, I thought it was important,' Arvinder said. 'God knows, I didn't know what real satisfaction felt like until somebody bought me one of those electric shoulder massagers. I tell you what, they're good for releasing tension in many places.'

The women laughed. Nikki wanted to remind them to keep the noise down but a glimpse at Manjeet's face stopped her: the traces of sadness around her eyes were replaced by deep laugh lines. She looked gratefully at the widows, her stark white dupatta slipping off onto her shoulders where she let it rest.

Chapter Six

Kulwinder squinted at the forms, trying to concentrate. A moment ago, the women's voices had risen again, disrupting her thoughts. She had been tempted to storm into the room but they had settled down before she could get up from her chair. Now her inability to focus could be blamed on the silence. Without distraction, she could not hide from these new English words. The visitor visa forms to India for her annual trip had changed recently, with an added layer of perplexing questions and declarations about national security. The reasons an Indian needed a visa to enter India were baffling enough, let alone this complicated vocabulary. She had raised both questions with the Lucky Star Travel Agents who had reminded her patiently that she was a British citizen, and had been for over two decades. 'Officially, you're not Indian,' the agent said. To Kulwinder, this explained nothing.

Her eyes were tired. She had left her trusted pair of bifocals at home and she decided she would need them to finish these forms. She'd already missed the last bus home, so she left the building and cut across the car park. Behind her, there were a few people from the temple but once she went off this main road it would just be herself and the houses with their shuttered windows. She marched quickly, her eyes trained on the distant lights.

As Kulwinder turned on to her road, she became aware of the sound of shuffling feet behind her. Training her eyes on her house in the distance, she picked up her pace. The person following sped up as well. Their close presence made the tiny hairs on her neck stand on end. It was only a matter of seconds before they caught up with her. She spun around, 'When are you going to leave me alone?' she cried.

The follower took a step back. Kulwinder's heart galloped in her chest. It did not slow down when she realized it was Tarampal Kaur.

'I need to speak with you,' Tarampal said.

'About what?' Kulwinder asked.

'A conflict I'm having.' Tarampal lowered her gaze. 'I'm just not sure how you'll react.'

Kulwinder stiffened. She noticed that Tarampal looked shifty. She was clasping and unclasping her hands as if there was something she was meant to be holding. Kulwinder's heart began to race again. She was not prepared to have this conversation with Tarampal in the middle of the street. 'Is this about—' She couldn't continue. She spent so much time trying not to dwell on the connection between Maya and Tarampal that she couldn't even say one's name in front of the other.

'The writing class,' Tarampal said. 'The other women aren't doing very much work.'

'Oh.' The sharp exhalation was involuntary, as if Kulwinder had been punched. Overlapping feelings of relief and disappointment shredded her voice to a whisper. 'The class.' Of course Tarampal wasn't going to talk about Maya. What had she expected? Tears sprang to Kulwinder's eyes. She was suddenly grateful to be standing the shadows.

'I've been keeping up with the writing and reading exercises,' Tarampal said. 'But the other women are just there to . . .' she hesitated. 'Fool around.'

So the women were giggling and being friendly with each other and Tarampal felt excluded. Why was Tarampal coming to her with petty complaints rather than dealing with it herself? 'You need to speak to them. Or to the teacher,' Kulwinder said.

Tarampal crossed her arms over her chest. 'I could complain about the classes, you know. I could tell Gurtaj Singh that they're not very productive. I don't complain because I don't want to create any trouble for you.'

'It's far too late for that.' The words shot out before Kulwinder had time to think.

Tarampal looked hurt. She lowered her gaze. 'I really hope that you and I can be friends again.'

Never, Kulwinder thought but she was careful not to react this time. Tarampal wasn't interested in friendship. She only wanted to keep a closer eye on Kulwinder. Kulwinder wouldn't be surprised if this were why she had signed up for the classes.

The silence only lasted a moment but it seemed to expand, as time always did whenever Kulwinder encountered Tarampal. She knew it would be easier to tell Tarampal the truth: *I've given up. I can't prove anything – the police and the lawyers told me as much. Now I can't even go for walks without receiving a threatening phone call afterwards.* But Kulwinder couldn't allow it. Every now and then she opened her Barclays diary, relived the details, allowing the hope to build that she had simply missed something, some way yet to recover the past.

She still refused to believe what the police had told her. It couldn't be so simple. This was her Maya! Just one week before she died, Maya had been promoted at work. She had bought tickets to a concert. She had probably reserved books at the library, made plans with friends, found a recipe she was keen to try. The last time Kulwinder saw her, Maya had been playing with the neighbour's dog that had wandered over to her driveway. He nearly toppled her when he tried to lick her face and Kulwinder had shouted in fright but Maya thought it was hilarious and buried her face in the dog's fur, telling him what a good boy he was. How could anybody believe she would do such a ghastly thing? And why was Kulwinder getting these threats if Maya's death had been so straightforward? But the police had said no foul play; they had testimonials confirming that Maya *had* been very upset and guilty and *it's understandable to want more answers when you're grieving*, the lawyer had said before warning her it would be take many billable hours to build a case. As the inevitable doubts and frustrations crept into her mind, Kulwinder remembered this: God had witnessed it all. Sarab always said that this was what mattered in the end.

'Thank you, Tarampal, but these days I prefer the company of my husband,' Kulwinder said. 'Have a good night.' *God sees everything*, she thought. It gave her enough strength to walk away from Tarampal. Then, when she got home, she buried her face in a couch cushion and sobbed into it while Sarab watched, the colour draining from his cheeks.

The pipe gurgled so loudly it sounded like a motor. Before leaving for her shift, Nikki added it to a growing list of repair requests, which included a mysterious damp bulge in the ceiling and a wireless internet connection so weak that it only worked if she held her laptop over the sink. The most recent items were squeezed at the bottom of the page in miniscule handwriting. Nikki had promised herself to tell Sam O'Reilly about these problems once she ran out of space, but after their awkward encounter last year, she avoided requesting anything of him.

It had started innocently enough, with Nikki requesting some overtime hours. Sam asked if she was saving up for a holiday. 'Mary Poppins musical tickets,' Nikki had said. Mary Poppins had been her favourite childhood movie, and, aged seven, she had once followed a woman out of the shops because she was carrying a large umbrella and wearing a full skirt. 'I was convinced she would sail into the air and land in one of the chimneys. I wanted to give her directions to our house.'

Sam's eyes had sparkled with amusement. His face, normally lined with weariness, made him look a decade younger when he smiled. Nikki teasingly told him so. Garry, one of the Russian kitchen workers had been passing by. His eyes darted back and forth between Sam and Nikki and, later, there were snickers between him and the other kitchen hand, Viktor. The next day, when Nikki arrived to work, Sam presented her with two tickets to Mary Poppins. 'If you'd like to go with me on Friday,' he said.

Nikki stared at the tickets, blushing furiously. Had he and the other men thought she was flirting? Asking for overtime and mentioning the musical hadn't been intended hints but Sam had obviously taken them as such. 'I can't accept these,' she managed to say. 'I don't think it would be appropriate.'

Sam had understood right away. His lips, pulled to a near grimace from the strain of his gesture, broke into a big grin. 'Oh, of course,' he said, hiding his embarrassment in a sudden flurry of activity. He ran his hands through his hair and began sorting out the glasses behind the counter. Garry and Viktor began making remarks in Russian every time Nikki was around. Sanja, a fellow barmaid confirmed the remarks were about Nikki offering sexual favours in exchange for training and quick promotion. How depressing, Nikki thought – if she was to be accused of sleeping her way up a professional ladder, she would have hoped that bartending at a crumbling Shepherd's Bush pub was not its highest rung.

Nikki folded up her list and put it away. After travelling to Southall twice a week, she was grateful for the thirty-second commute down the stairs from her flat to O'Reilly's. Besides, they always had a good turnout for Trivia Night so she knew it would be a busy and tiring shift. In the pub, Nikki slipped past a group of men crowded near the television and waved at a few regulars. Sanja was vigorously wiping down a table in her usual punishing way. Another barmaid, Grace, often asked after Nikki's mum as if they were old friends. Grace was easily moved by contestants' backstories on Britain's Got Talent and had once arrived to work puffy-faced and sleep-deprived because the little boy magician who had been bullied didn't win.

'Nikki!' Grace called from across the pub. 'How's your mum, luv?'

'She's well,' Nikki said.

'Is she keeping warm?'

Mum's temperature moderation was of utmost importance to Grace for some reason. Grace looked at her expectantly. 'She's got good insulation at home,' Nikki assured Grace.

'Bet it's not as warm as the old village in Bangladesh though,' Steve with the Racist Grandfather called out.

Nikki wished she had a clever comeback but all she said in reply was, 'I was born in England, you fuckwit.' Steve grinned as if she'd just paid him a compliment.

It was a relief to see Olive weaving her way through the tables. Nikki poured Olive a beer and called out, 'I have a present for you.' She drew a folder from her bag.

'Is that what I think it is?' Olive asked.

'Yes,' Nikki said. 'This one's written in English.' It was Sheena Kaur's tale.

The Coco Palm Resort Hotel

The hardest part about planning the wedding was deciding which honeymoon package to buy. Kirpal and Neena spent weeks weighing their options between different locations. Finally they decided on a beach resort called The Coco Palm. Kirpal liked the pictures of the open blue sea and white sand. Neena was drawn by the resort's tagline: Try Everything Once. *This would be her only honeymoon and she was determined to make the best of it. She wanted to try snorkeling and deep-sea diving and all of the other offerings of this resort at least once.*

When they arrived at the hotel, they made sure there was a king-sized bed as promised. The hotel receptionist gave them a list of places where they could dine and told them where the pool was, but Kirpal smiled at his wife, Neena, and said, 'I think we'll be spending most of our time indoors.' Neena's cheeks burned and, down below, a fire was raging. She couldn't wait to be alone with him. For months since booking this honeymoon, she had sneaked glances at the brochure's featured king-sized bed strewn with rose petals. She had imagined them falling onto the bed together in a tangle of sweaty limbs, moaning his name loudly. This wouldn't be possible after the honeymoon. Once they returned to his parents' home, only a thin wall would separate their bedroom from her in-laws'. They would have to muffle the sounds of their sensual pleasures.

Kirpal smiled at Neena. She wondered if he was thinking the same thing. Then, as he reached for their bags, his smile disappeared and flash of pain crossed his face. 'What's wrong?' she asked. 'It's my back,' he said with a grimace. 'I've been having these awful pains since before the wedding but there was no time to see a doctor with all of the preparations. I think the celebrations just made it worse.' Neena tried to hide her disappointment. What this meant, of course, was that they would not be able to make love on their first holiday away together. When would they get the chance then?

A bellhop brought their bags up to the room and received a generous tip. 'Enjoy your stay,' he said. After he left, it was just Neena and Kirpal, alone and together at last but unable to express their love. Kirpal fiddled with the zipper on his suitcase and then sat down on the bed. He slowly leaned back until he was lying flat. Out came a long sigh of relief. 'I'd just like to rest for a while,' Kirpal said. He closed his eyes, his face still faintly contorted in a remaining spasm of pain. Neena realized how much pain he had been hiding. Perhaps something could be done to relieve him.

She lay down on the bed next to him. His body was warm and hard, his breathing soft. His eyes were closed as if he was asleep but when she brushed her lips against his cheek, he stirred. She sucked gently on his earlobe. Although she didn't know if this was what she was meant to do, her husband was enjoying it so much that she couldn't imagine it was wrong. Small groans escaped his lips now and as she lowered her lips to his neck and his chest, she could hear his breath getting deeper and faster. She stopped there, considering her options. She had been warned before getting married that what a couple did together on their first night alone set the tone for the rest of their lives. He had a backache – yes, it was a problem for now, but if they were expected to grow old together, there would be many ailments in the future that could keep one or both of them bedridden for life. What would they do then? As much as she loved her new husband and enjoyed this moment, he needed to know that he had a duty to her as well. She repositioned herself so her head was facing his feet. Confused by suddenly seeing her bottom, her husband began to protest. 'Why did you stop?' he asked. He barely uttered the last word when Neena lowered her lips onto his precious organ. It became rock hard to her touch. She began moving her lips down, feeling every inch of him tense beneath her. She took care not to put too much weight on him because his back was hurting – her weight rested on her knees, which were positioned on either side of his chest. She arched her back slightly, putting her precious parts in his full view. He just had to tip his head upwards slightly so his tongue could tickle the ripe, throbbing bud between her legs . . .

'Whoa!' Olive cried, looking up from the page. 'I was *not* expecting that. I thought these were going to be granny romance stories. These are all-out naughty.'

'Sheena's hardly a granny,' Nikki said. 'I think she's in her mid-thirties. Her husband died from cancer several years ago.' It was a mystery to Nikki that Sheena preferred the company of elderly and conservative women over those her own age.

'There's more.' Nikki scanned the pages and pointed to a middle paragraph.

'Don't bite me there,' he warned her. She obeyed him, but as her lips began to tire of those in-and-out movements, she let her teeth graze his skin and felt the ecstasy shudder through both their bodies like an electric shock. A sound which signalled pain and pleasure rumbled from his lips.

'She's got a flair for writing,' Olive remarked.

Nikki flipped to another page and scanned it. 'Hey,' she said. 'There's a twist. She starts screwing the bellhop.'

Neena got onto her hands and knees and he stood behind her, placing his fingers into her wet lips. Her hips began to rotate in anticipation of his big, hard member. Usually Ramesh was too busy lifting bags and running hotel errands to notice his guests too closely but he had seen her getting out of the airport shuttle earlier that morning. The wind had picked up her skirt and revealed a glimpse of her lacy red panties, which were now crumpled near the bed post. He couldn't believe he was entering her now. She moaned, 'Yes, yes, oh that feels so good.' Ramesh looked up, aware that he was making love to another man's wife.

'Go Neena,' Olive said. 'Try everything once indeed.'

'Her husband's watching though. And enjoying it.'

Ramesh made eye contact with Kirpal, who sat in the chair in the corner of the room. Gripping his own manhood, he watched his wife moan with raw desire as Ramesh glided in and out of her.

'Are the other stories this naughty?' Olive asked.

'Pretty much.'

'Those dirty little minxes,' Olive said. 'Who's reading these, besides you and the widows?'

'Nobody else at the moment,' Nikki said. 'But that could change. I'm thinking that once we have enough stories, we could try to get them published.'

'Hmm,' Olive said. 'I don't know. These are very intimate. The widows might be all right with sharing them with you but it might be another thing to get them out in public.'

'These women are a lot bolder than I thought,' Nikki said. 'I could actually see Arvinder speaking at a Fem Fighters rally. Or Preetam doing a dramatic reading.'

Olive tipped her head and smiled. It was that you're-getting-ahead-of-yourself look that Nikki was familiar with, except she was more used to receiving it from Mindi. 'We could work our way up to it,' Nikki conceded.

Suddenly there was a cry in the kitchen. Nikki pushed open the door and saw Sam hopping about, squeezing his left-hand fingers with his right hand. 'What happened?'

'Got sprayed with hot water. The indicator light on the dishwasher's broken.'

Sanja stepped forward and opened the dishwasher door, turning her face away. An angry cloud of steam rolled into the air. She picked out the dishes gingerly and began stacking them on the counter. Sam muttered something under his breath and walked out of the kitchen with Nikki in tow. At the sound of the kitchen hands' snickers, Nikki paused. She didn't need to see if Sam was okay. Sam was fine. She took her place at the bar. 'Bloody idiots,' she muttered.

'Who?' Olive asked.

'Those guys in the back.'

'Don't let them get to you. They're just resentful,' Olive reminded her.

'Probably,' Nikki said. 'But sometimes I can see where they got the idea from – Sam hired me without any experience. It raises eyebrows doesn't it?'

Olive shrugged. 'He saw potential in you. Maybe he was attracted to you as well, but he tried to ask you out ages after you started working here and you said no. He hasn't treated you any differently since.'

'He has, actually. I used to be able to just chat and laugh with him but since then it's just uncomfortable. It's all Garry and Viktor's fault.' Secretly she blamed herself as well. Why did she have to go and compliment Sam?

'Tell them off then,' Olive said. 'Go on. Put them in their place.'

For all of Nikki's outrage, she squirmed at the thought of confronting those guys face to face. She was afraid of what they might say in response – *you were asking for it*. She was afraid that she wouldn't be able to convince them that they were wrong. 'It's not such a big deal. I can just ignore them,' Nikki said.

Olive raised an eyebrow but she said nothing. The doors swung open and a young man appeared in the doorway. Nikki didn't have time to hide her pleased reaction. Olive followed her gaze to Jason as he made his way to the bar.

'Who's that?'

'This guy I met the other day,' Nikki mumbled, mouth curling into a smile. She busied herself suddenly, wiping down the gleaming countertop. 'Oh hey,' she said casually as Jason approached.

'O'Reilly's pub,' he said. 'There are about seventeen of them. This is my fourth try.'

'I said "Shepherd's Bush", didn't I?' Nikki asked.

Jason considered this. 'Possibly. I missed that.'

'She didn't give you the address?' Olive asked. 'I'm Olive, by the way.

Nikki's lady-in-waiting.'

'Nice to meet you,' Jason said. 'This is really embarrassing, but I have to use the bathroom before I order anything.'

Nikki pointed out the toilets. 'He's cute,' Olive commented once Jason was out of earshot.

'You think so? I don't know,' Nikki said.

'Bollocks. I saw the look on your face when he walked in. How did you meet?

'At the temple, of all places. We were both taking smoke breaks in the same alleyway. I didn't get a chance to ask him what he was doing in the temple in the first place.'

'Praying, perhaps?'

'It's more of a giant social club. People show up to pay their respects for about two minutes and then they join their friends in the dining hall to eat free food and gossip. It's hardly a spiritual place for the majority of young people.'

'So maybe he was there to meet with friends.'

'Ah,' Nikki said. 'That's a problem. I don't date guys who hang out at the temple. I mean, they live in this great big city where the world is at their doorstep and a gurdwara is their social stomping ground?'

Olive gave her a look. 'You're doing it again.'

'Doing what?'

'Being overly critical. Give the boy a chance. He went to every O'Reilly's pub in London to find you. That's keen isn't it?'

'Maybe a bit too keen,' Nikki said.

'Nikki,' Olive sighed.

'All right. I'm resisting him a little. I don't know why.'

'I've got a theory.'

'Don't tell me I've got residual issues with my father,' Nikki warned. 'You've tried that theory before, it only made me feel like shit.'

'Not your dad, your mum. Jason's the kind of boy your mum would want you to date. A nice Punjabi boy.' There was a devious twitch in Olive's smile.

'Oh god, Olive. What if he was at the temple that day to check out marriage profiles?' Nikki asked. 'What if he had checked out Mindi's? That's – that's incest of sorts.'

Olive hushed her as Jason approached the bar. There was an awkward silence between the three of them. The trivia announcer's voice boomed across the pub.

'What is the second most populated city in Mexico? For three points, the second most populated city in Mexico.'

'Guadalajara,' Jason said. He turned to Nikki. 'Can I order a Guinness please?'

'Oh, of course,' Nikki said, springing into action. She noticed Olive studying Jason carefully.

'Jason, can I ask a question to clarify something?' Olive asked.

'Sure.'

'Why were you at the temple the day you met Nikki?'

Nikki froze, her hand wrapped around a glass. '*Olive*!'

'Let's just get it out of the way, shall we? And then I'll get out of your way.'

'You'll have to excuse my friend,' Nikki began but Olive held up her hand to stop her.

'Let the man speak,' Olive said.

Jason cleared his throat. 'I was there to give thanks.'

'Really?' Nikki asked.

Jason nodded. 'My mother was diagnosed with breast cancer a couple of years ago and the doctors just told her that she's in remission. It was a fairly close call, so I wanted to have a little chat with God and let him know that I was grateful.'

Olive shot Nikki a smile and excused herself from the bar, taking her drink with her and disappearing into the crowd of trivia participants. 'I'm sorry to hear about your mum,' Nikki said. 'That must have been hard.'

'It was, but she's better now. I have to admit, I don't turn to religion often, especially not at the temple, but there was a familiar peace to it.'

'My father died a couple of years ago. Heart attack,' Nikki said.

'I'm sorry.'

'Thanks.' Nikki said. 'It was very sudden. Happened in his sleep.' She didn't know why she was telling Jason this. Suddenly her face felt warm and she was glad for the pub's dim lighting. 'So have you got any family in London then?' she asked.

'A distant uncle and aunt. They live near the temple in Southall. When they found out I was moving here for work, they insisted that I live with them. I had to let them down gently. My aunt was most concerned that I would have nobody to cook for me.'

'Parents are like that,' Nikki said. 'My mother recited a whole list of terrible consequences that befell girls living on their own. Starvation was up there after rape and murder.'

'I have to say, it was pretty nice having langar in the temple that day though. I didn't realize how much I missed home-cooked dal and roti.'

'I missed it too,' Nikki admitted. 'Weirdly enough, I never cared for dal when I lived at home. I know if I called my mum to ask her how to cook it, she'd try to use her dal to lure me home. I thought, how hard can it be? I bought some lentils in the supermarket and boiled them and added curry spices to the mix. I think I put in too much turmeric – that was one of the problems with my recipe anyway – and it came out fluoro-yellow and completely inedible. By the end, I just wanted it to *look* like dal at least, so I tossed in some instant coffee mix to make it browner.'

'Please tell me you didn't eat it?'

'I tossed it into the alleyway. The next morning my boss Sam came in, grumbling about how somebody had vomited next to the pub and I thought, no that's just Nikki's Venti Dal Latte.'

Nikki was so comfortable chatting to him that the remaining hours of her shift passed quickly. When Jason asked her what she had been doing at the temple that day, Nikki shifted her attention to a new group of customers at the bar and busied herself with their orders. The distraction bought her some time to return with an answer. 'I teach a writing class there – adult literacy.' She decided that this would be her standard answer to anyone besides Olive; it was safer.

Olive returned to the bar after the final round of trivia was completed. 'Jason, your answer to the Mexico question was correct. Guadalajara.' Her voice was pitched slightly higher than usual.

'Uh-oh. Tipsy Olive,' Nikki teased. 'Teaching those nasty Year Nines with a hangover must be horrid.'

Olive ignored her. 'Nikki, did you hear what I just said? Jason is very clever. You guys are cute together. You and Mindi should have a double Punjabi wedding.'

'Mindi's my sister,' Nikki explained to Jason. 'And Olive, shut up.'

'Mindi's looking for a husband,' Olive continued. 'Do you have anyone in mind, Jason? Friends? Brothers?'

'I've got a brother but he's only twenty-one. He's famous though, if that counts for anything.'

'What is he famous for?' Nikki asked.

'Have you heard of the interactive website *Hipster or Harvinder*?'

'Yes,' Nikki said at the same time Olive said, 'No.' Nikki launched into an explanation for Olive. 'It's a website where people can submit photos of themselves sporting trendy beards and visitors rate them according to how closely they resemble pictures of this Sikh man named Harvinder. He's got an insanely bushy beard.'

'My brother did a study abroad year in India and befriended the famed Harvinder during a trek in a tiny village. They got to talking about how beards represent identity in Sikh culture and how they've become very hip in the Western world lately and the idea for the website was born,' Jason said.

'Your brother created *Hipster or Harvinder*? That's so cool.'

'Yeah. He returned from India with a big beard as well. It was self-expression thing. He tried getting me to grow one but I looked like a hobbit,' Jason said.

'You're too tall to be a hobbit,' Olive said kindly.

'Thank you,' Jason said.

'Have you got any friends we can set Nikki's sister up with then?' Olive asked. 'Tall ones?'

'I don't really believe in the whole Indian set-up thing.'

'Why not?' Olive asked.

'Too much pressure. Everyone gets so involved – friends, parents. They start putting deadlines on everything, as if every relationship between a woman and a man must lead to marriage. It's stressful.'

'Exactly!' Nikki said. 'Imagine going out with someone your mum picked for you. That's an immediate turn-off.'

'Then if it doesn't work out, you have all of this explaining to do.'

'And people to avoid.'

'Too much drama,' Jason agreed.

Nikki noticed Olive's attention switching between them as if she was watching a tennis match. She slipped back to the trivia tables, giving Nikki a wink over her shoulder as she left.

A wild wind battered the bus windows with rain. Passengers hurried off the bus and ran, huddled, towards the temple. Nikki gripped the edges of her rain jacket hood but the wind bit at her cheeks. Last night, after she closed the pub and had her last cigarette outside with Jason, they had discussed quitting smoking. 'I'll quit with you,' he said. 'We can help each other out. Of course, this means I'll have to have your number. You know, for tracking my progress and inspirational pep talks.'

Now after braving the rain and managing to arrive at the temple's wide awning, Nikki contemplated having her last cigarette. She made her way along the edge of the building and cut across the car park, ducking into the alleyway. The cigarette was well worth it. She took a long draw and wondered how she was going to quit, but the idea of having an excuse to talk to Jason made it worthwhile.

Deep in thought, Nikki finished her cigarette and stepped out of the alleyway. Behind her, a gruff voice called out. 'Excuse me,' he said.

She turned around to see a stout young man wearing a checked shirt with the top buttons undone to expose the curly hairs on his chest.

'Is this the temple?' he asked. Something in his voice gave Nikki the impression that he wasn't asking, but telling.

'Yes,' she said. 'Are you lost?' She matched his stare. His lips curled back in disgust as he stepped towards her.

'Your head should be covered,' he said.

'I'm not in the temple yet,' Nikki replied.

The man stepped towards her. There was a hard look in his eyes. Nikki's stomach fluttered with nerves. She glanced around and, with relief, noticed a family milling in the temple's entrance.

His eyes followed her gaze. 'Cover your head in the presence of God,' he said eventually through his teeth. He stalked off, leaving Nikki bewildered.

All of the women were already in the classroom when Nikki arrived. They were busy in their conversations and Nikki did nothing at first to interrupt them. She was distracted by her encounter with the man. She had never seen somebody so aggravated by an uncovered head on temple grounds. Who was he to order her around?

Tarampal Kaur trailed in after her and took her seat at the furthest end of the room. She laid out her pencils in a row and then looked up expectantly at Nikki. 'I'll be with you in a moment,' Nikki told her. The other women looked up as if noticing Nikki for the first time.

'We talked about our stories on the bus all the way here,' Manjeet said.

'On the bus? Couldn't other people hear you?' Tarampal asked.

'Nobody eavesdrops on old lady chatter. To them it's all one buzzing noise. They think we're discussing our knee pain and funeral plans,' Arvinder said.

'You could at least try to be discreet,' said Tarampal.

'Ah, being discreet gets us nowhere,' Preetam said. 'Remember playing coy and pretending not to want it?'

'And not talking about it afterwards. I always wanted to know – was it good for him? Could he try to last longer next time?' Manjeet said.

'Or possibly add a few more tricks to his repertoire,' Arvinder added. 'There was so much of this.' She reached out and squeezed two imaginary breasts, then pantomimed a man rocking rapidly back and forth. 'Then it was over.' The women screeched with laughter and applauded the reenactment.

'You'll be caught for talking about these things,' Tarampal said. 'And then what?'

The women fell silent and exchanged looks. 'We'll deal with it if it happens,' Sheena said finally. 'Like Arvinder said, nobody listens to us.'

'Come on, Tarampal,' Manjeet said with a nervous smile. 'It's just a bit of fun.'

'You're taking a big risk,' Tarampal said. She began gathering her things. 'If you're found out, it's not my problem.'

The look of dismay on Manjeet's face was clear. Arvinder reached out and squeezed her arm comfortingly. 'The only way we'll be discovered is if somebody tells,' Arvinder said. 'Are you planning on reporting us? Because if you dare do it, Tarampal, then we're all witnesses to the fact that you were in this class as well.'

'So what?' Tarampal asked.

Preetam stood up and walked slowly to Tarampal. Suddenly she had the gait of a fierce matriarch from one of her dramas – tall and powerful, with her chin tipped upwards at an angle so she could stare down Tarampal.

'We'll say that you started all of it and then became resentful when we didn't like one of your stories. That's the word of four women against one. And Nikki, who can convince people because she has a law di-gi-ree,' Preetam said.

'Um, I don't have a law degree, and also, surely there's a better way. . .' Nikki started.

'You're shameless, all of you,' Tarampal spat. She stormed out of the classroom.

'Wait, Tarampal, please,' Nikki called, following her. In the hallway, Tarampal paused, clutching her bag to her chest. Her knuckles had gone white. 'Tarampal, before you rush to tell Kulwinder about our classes, just please—'

'I don't plan on going to Kulwinder again. I tried. She didn't want to hear it,' Tarampal said.

'Oh,' Nikki said. She didn't know whether to be angry at Tarampal or pleased with Kulwinder. 'Then who are you so afraid of?'

Tarampal didn't answer Nikki's question. She glanced at the small window in the classroom door. 'Did you see how the women ganged up on me in there?' she asked. 'I've known them for years and they've just turned their backs on me. What makes you think you can trust them?'

'They were just trying to protect themselves,' Nikki said.

'You're sure about that?' Tarampal asked.

'Yes,' Nikki said. But when she peered at the widows, an uneasy feeling came over her. They were chatting amongst themselves, their voices tinny and barely audible in the hallway. She knew nothing of their world.

'Why don't you come back inside, Tarampal? We can work something out.'

Tarampal shook her head. 'I'm not going to risk being associated with these classes. Those women have no integrity. They don't care about their late husbands' reputations. I have Kemal Singh's good name to uphold. Do me a favour and throw out my registration sheet. I want nothing to do with these stories.' She stalked off.

'We should ask her to come back,' Manjeet was saying when Nikki returned to the classroom. 'You know what she's capable of.'

'Listen, Manjeet. Didn't we stand by you when Tarampal found out about your husband leaving you? She left you alone once she knew she was outnumbered,' said Preetam.

'What do you mean?' Nikki asked. 'What was Tarampal going to do?'

'Nothing now,' Arvinder declared. It didn't answer Nikki's question. Arvinder's chest was puffed out with pride. 'Don't worry, Manjeet.'

'*Hai*, but her bus just left. She's going to have to wait twenty minutes now for the next one,' Manjeet said.

Nikki watched the temple's car park from the window. Tarampal emerged from the building and walked briskly towards the street. A silver BMW slowed down next to her and a window rolled down. Tarampal stooped to chat with the driver and then got inside.

'She just got into someone's car,' Nikki said. 'Is that safe?'

The women looked at each other and shrugged. 'What would a dangerous man want with old ladies like us?' Arvinder asked.

'Tarampal's only a couple of years older than me,' Sheena said defensively. 'She's in her forties.'

This shouldn't have been surprising to Nikki. The smoothness of Tarampal's face bore such contrast to the dreary widow's clothing she draped herself in. That stooping walk, that sigh as she sat at her desk, were just affectations to play the withered and weary character expected of widows. 'It's okay to just hop into someone's car and be driven home here?' Nikki asked.

'It's probably not a complete stranger. People offer me lifts home from the market all the time. They usually identify whose son or daughter they are first,' Arvinder said.

'Was it a silver BMW?' Sheena asked. Nikki nodded. 'It was probably Sandeep then, Resham Kaur's grandson.'

Preetam let out a *humpf* at the sound of Sandeep's name. 'That boy who thinks he's too good for any girl in this community. He even rejected Puran Kaur's great-niece from America. Remember her? She visited for a wedding. Skin like milk and her eyes were green.'

'Resham told me they were contact lenses,' Manjeet said.

'*Hai*, Manjeet, you believe everything you hear. Of course Resham would go around spreading rumours about the girl and claiming she wasn't good enough for her precious boy,' Sheena said. 'She's one of those old-fashioned Indian mothers, completely infatuated with her sons. When her eldest got married, she slept in the bed between him and his wife for a month to prevent them from having relations.'

'It took him a month to ask his mother to leave his bed? What a wimp,' Preetam declared. 'If that were me, I would have pretended to cry loudly in my sleep every night like a terrified new bride until she got sick of it and left us alone. I would say, "Make a choice! Your mother or me?" And he'd choose me.'

'My mother-in-law did the same thing,' Arvinder said. 'Not on the wedding night, she left us alone that night. But many nights I'd fall asleep and wake up to see her snoring peacefully between us. I asked my husband,

"Doesn't that noise bother you?" He said, "Noise? What noise? She's my mother."'

Nikki's mind was still on Tarampal. 'Why does Tarampal have to maintain her husband's reputation if he's dead?'

The women exchanged looks. 'Kemal Singh was a religious pundit,' Manjeet said, 'good at telling fortunes and doing special prayers for people. Some people still pay respects to him. She's being a devoted wife by making sure that his reputation stays clean.'

Arvinder snorted. 'Devoted wife? She's got better things to do with her time.'

'She still has an image to keep, doesn't she? She depends on it. I wouldn't be surprised if she came knocking on all our doors tonight with a special prayer,' Manjeet said.

'I'd show her these and she'd leave in an instant,' Arvinder replied. She held out her palms. The women snickered at what was clearly another one of their inside jokes – something about Arvinder's fortune lines, Nikki guessed.

Sheena looked up. 'Nikki, don't concern yourself too much with Tarampal,' she said. 'As long as the men don't find out about these stories, we're fine.'

Nikki thought about the temple's dining hall, and the strict divide that ran like an invisible force field between the men's and women's designated sides. 'I trust that won't be a problem,' she said. 'None of you really chat with the men, do you?'

'Of course not. We're widows. We don't have any more contact with men. We aren't allowed,' Preetam said.

'Not such a bad thing,' Arvinder said.

'Speak for yourself,' Sheena retorted. 'I didn't have as many good years with my husband as you all did with yours.'

'Good years? Between the cleaning, cooking and fighting, where was the time for good years?' Arvinder looked up at Nikki. 'The girls in your generation are luckier. At least you get to know the person before marrying him. You can separate the idiots from the bloody idiots.'

Manjeet giggled in appreciation. Sheena remained pensive, her eyes downcast. Nikki could sense that it was time to change the subject. 'Who has a story to share?' Nikki asked.

Arvinder's hand shot confidently into the air.

The Shopkeeper and His Customer

The shopkeeper was busy stocking his shelves when the door of the shop opened and a woman walked in. She was slim but her hips were wide and she was wearing modern English clothes but she was Punjabi. He asked her, 'Can I help you?' She ignored him and went to the back of the shop. He thought she might be a shoplifter but then he wondered how she would smuggle the stolen goods out of the shop in such tight-fitting clothes. He followed her to the back of the shop and saw her looking at the rows of spices.

'Which one do I use for making tea?' she asked.

The correct answer was cardamom and fennel seeds but the shopkeeper did not want to say. He wanted her to keep asking questions in her very sweet voice.

'I don't know,' he said. 'I don't make tea.'

'If you tell me, we can make tea together,' the woman said. She smiled at him. He smiled back and leaned close to help her with her choices. 'Maybe it's this one,' he said, picking out a packet of mustard seeds. He held it to the woman's nose to give her a whiff. She shut her eyes and inhaled. 'No,' she said. She laughed. 'You don't know anything.'

'I may not know anything about brewing tea, my dear,' the shopkeeper said, 'but I do know how to keep that smile on your face.'

He put the packet of seeds back on the shelf and tucked her hair behind her ear. She leaned towards him and gave him a kiss on the lips. He was surprised. He was not used to this sort of behavior in his shop, even though he had started flirting with her first. The woman took his hand and led him to the back room of the shop and turned around to face him.

'Why is she leading him to the back room? Shouldn't he take her? How does she know where it is?' Preetam asked.

'Don't interrupt me,' Arvinder snapped. 'Do I butt in when you are narrating a story?'

Sheena put down her pen and gave her wrist a stretch. 'This is hard work,' she commented in English to Nikki.

'It's not making any sense,' Preetam argued, 'unless she has actually been there before. Maybe she is a girl that he wanted to marry but his parents wouldn't allow it so she has come back in a disguise.'

Arvinder looked irate but Nikki could see that she was considering the suggestion. 'Okay, Sheena, put in that detail as well.'

'Where?' Sheena asked.

'Just anywhere. So anyway, we're getting to the best part. *The woman started taking off her clothes. She twirled around until her sari had completely unwound from her body*.'

'I thought she was wearing modern clothes,' Sheena said. 'Why is she dressed in a sari now?'

'Saris are a better image.'

'So change that as well? No modern clothes?'

'No woman wearing a sari would be as forward as that.'

'Rubbish. All over London women are carrying on like this, no matter what they wear.'

'London, maybe. The *goris* do this, but not in Southall,' Manjeet said.

'In Southall too. You know that hill behind Herbert Park? Young boys and girls are always meeting there. We had relatives visiting one summer and we took them there in the evening to see the sunset. We saw a Muslim woman wearing a full hijab dashing from one parked car to another – from one man to another. All kinds of things happen,' Preetam said.

'Is that where Maya got caught then?' Manjeet asked. The room became a vacuum. The women shifted in their seats, reminding Nikki of the uncomfortable looks on the faces of those women in the langar hall when the Green Dupatta had been holding court. Something about Kulwinder's daughter made people react in this way. 'What?' Manjeet asked, looking around. 'Tarampal isn't here any more and I never got the full story because I was in Canada.'

'He found text messages on her phone,' Preetam said. 'That's what I heard anyway.'

'You heard, but what do you know?' Arvinder asked, turning to her. 'I didn't raise you to speak ill of the dead.'

'*Hai*, but everybody knows now, nah?' Preetam said. 'It's been nearly a year.'

'Not everybody,' Sheena said, nodding at Nikki. 'And she doesn't need to know. I'm sorry Nikki, but this is a private matter. It's not something Kulwinder would like us discussing.'

It was another reminder that the women did not fully trust her. *Why can't I know?* she wanted to ask as the women exchanged looks and glares. Sheena looked particularly annoyed. It all made Nikki more intrigued by Maya and her salacious past. It was more for curiosity's sake that Nikki wanted to find out about Maya, but perhaps she'd also have a better chance of building her relationship with Kulwinder if she knew. She considered bringing this up with the widows – after all, it was in their best interests that Kulwinder thought the English classes were going well – but Sheena suddenly took over directing the class.

'Go on with your story then, Arvinder,' Sheena said. She pointed to the clock. 'We don't want to be here all night.'

There was a noticeable pause. The women looked at Nikki. 'Yes, let's move on,' Nikki said. 'We were right in the middle of it.' She gave Sheena an appreciative smile, which was returned. The others began to relax.

Arvinder shrugged. 'I don't know where to go next.'

'Describe his organ,' Sheena offered. 'Big or small?'

'Big of course,' Arvinder scoffed. 'What's the point of a skinny carrot entering you?'

'There are ones that are too big. You wouldn't want a sweet potato. *Hai*, that was my problem,' Sheena said, shaking her head. 'No amount of ghee could make that first entrance a pleasant one.'

'A banana is ideal,' Preetam said. 'Nice size and shape.'

'How ripe?' Arvinder asked. 'Too ripe and it would be like my first experience – a pile of mush.'

'Why are you using vegetable and fruit names?' Nikki interrupted. These conversations were starting to put her off going to the supermarket.

'We don't always,' Manjeet said. 'Sometimes we say *danda*.' The Punjabi word for stick. 'Nobody talks about these things. All of our knowledge and language was passed down from our parents. They certainly didn't discuss what men and women did together.'

'You're right,' Nikki said, failing to come up with the Punjabi word for penis herself. She would have to get used to these replacement words even though they sounded bizarre to her. In a previous lesson, none of the widows had batted an eye when Sheena read out, 'She gasped and whispered, "Oh my darling, that feels so good" as he thrust his cucumber into the depths of her lady pocket.'

'But we do know the English words,' Preetam said. 'That we learned quickly from television and our children. Like swearing – we heard the way they said it and knew it was wrong.'

'Cock,' said Arvinder.

'Balls,' Preetam chirped. 'Tits.'

'Pussy?' whispered Manjeet. Nikki nodded. Manjeet beamed.

'Tits, fucking, pussy, arses,' Arvinder declared in a sudden fit.

'All right, then,' Nikki said. 'We can stick to the produce names if that's what you're comfortable using.'

'Vegetables are the best,' declared Preetam. 'Tell me, is there anything that gives you a better idea of how it would feel and taste than a description of it as a juicy-juicy aubergine?'

Before class the following week, Nikki sprinted from the bus through icy rain to get to the temple. Still shivering in the langar hall, she spotted Sheena sitting alone. She lined up to fill her plate with chickpea curry, dal and roti and then asked Sheena if she could join her. 'Of course,' Sheena said, moving her bag.

Nikki tore a piece of roti and used it to scoop up the dal. With a teaspoon, she dabbed on a bit of yoghurt. 'Mmm,' she said, chewing the roti. 'Why is temple dal always so delicious?'

'Do you want the religious answer or the real answer?' Sheena asked.

'Both.'

'The dal is made with God's love. And it's full of ghee.'

'Noted,' Nikki said, taking a less generous scoop with her next piece of roti.

'Don't let it stop you from enjoying your meal,' Sheena said. 'But whenever I try on a pair of trousers and they feel too tight, I know what's to blame.'

'You don't always eat here before class, then?' Nikki said. Sheena was a slim woman who did not look like she had ever suffered an overdose of fatty dal.

'I usually go home after work and cook dinner for my mother-in-law and myself before coming here. The traffic was so bad today because of the storm that I decided to just come here straight from work.'

So Sheena still lived with her mother-in-law even though her husband had passed away. Nikki wondered if she did so out of a sense of duty. As she often found herself doing, she sneaked a glance at Sheena, seeking clues from her modern dress and demeanor as to how traditional she really was.

'She's got dementia, the poor thing,' Sheena continued, interpreting the unspoken question. 'Sometimes she asks after her son. I can't imagine leaving her to live on her own, confused and disoriented all the time.'

This reason made more sense. 'She was a good mother-in-law then?' Nikki asked. 'All I seem to hear are the horror stories. I worry about my sister who wants a traditional marriage. Your mother-in-law obviously treats you well though.'

'Oh yes. She was like a friend,' Sheena said. 'We kept each other entertained at home. She didn't have any daughters, so she really enjoyed having me around. There was no question that I'd remain in the family after Arjun died. Living with them took some getting used to at first, but everything's about adjusting. Tell your sister that. Is she having an arranged marriage?'

'Sort of,' Nikki said. 'I posted an ad for her on the marriage board.'

'Oh, some of those profiles are hopeless, aren't they?'

'I like the one that mentioned the guy's blood type,' Nikki said. 'Wifely duties probably involve donating a kidney in that family.'

Sheena laughed. 'When my parents were arranging my marriage, I was mortified that they kept touting my "wheatish" complexion like it was my most important asset.'

'Yes!' Nikki said. 'As if it attracts any more candidates if you compare your skin to barley.'

'Unfortunately, it works,' Sheena said. 'The whole Fair and Lovely thing. Arjun's whole family was darker than mine and when we couldn't have children, someone had the nerve to say, "Well, now you don't have to worry about them taking after his side."'

'That's messed up,' Nikki said, yet she remembered having a go at Mindi for buying face lightening cream in India, and Mindi replying, 'It's easy for you to judge, you're at least three shades lighter than me.'

'Are you next then?' Sheena asked. 'After your sister?'

'Oh goodness, no,' Nikki said. 'I can't imagine having my marriage arranged.'

Sheena shrugged. 'It's not that bad. Takes the effort out of it on your part. I don't think I would've been very good at dating.'

'But doesn't it all feel very . . . set-up?'

'Not if you play your cards right,' Sheena said. 'See, when my parents were looking for a boy for me, I did a bit of looking myself. I'd seen Arjun at a wedding, and when my parents asked about my preferences, I basically described him without mentioning his name. They went out and fetched him within the week. Luckily he'd noticed me at the wedding as well. Everyone was very pleased with themselves.'

'That's actually quite romantic,' Nikki admitted. She could only hope for Mindi to have such luck in her search.

'If you want something, always make your parents or in-laws think it's their idea,' Sheena said, pointing her finger at Nikki. 'Take this old lady's advice.'

Nikki laughed. 'All right, Bibi Sheena. How old are you anyway?'

'I've been turning twenty-nine for the past six years,' Sheena said. 'You?'

'If you ask my mum, I'm still an infant and I will never earn the right to think independently. But seriously, I'm twenty-two.'

'Do you live on your own?'

Nikki nodded. 'In a flat above a pub. Don't think I could spin that one to make it seem like it was my parents' idea.'

Suddenly, Sheena's face lit up. With a discreet flutter of her fingers, she waved at somebody. 'No, Nikki, don't turn around,' she said quickly when Nikki swivelled in her seat.

'Who's over there?'

'Nobody,' Sheena said.

'What's Nobody's name?'

'You're very nosey.'

'Nobody Singh?'

'Will you stop looking, Nikki? Ok, his name is Rahul. Rahul Sharma. He does *sewa* at the temple three days a week because when he was laid off from his previous job, he ate all his meals here. It saved him. Now he volunteers in the kitchen to pay it back.'

'You sure know a lot about him. Do you guys talk, or just make lovey-dovey faces in the langar hall?'

'There's nothing going on between us,' Sheena said. 'Nothing official. We work at the Bank of Baroda together. I was in charge of showing him the ropes when he started a few weeks ago.'

'You're blushing.'

'So?'

'You're in love.'

Sheena leaned towards Nikki. 'Sometimes he stays back after work to chat with me. We make sure to have our conversations in the car park behind the bank so nobody on the main road can see us. But that's it.'

'Have you gone out on a date? Get into your little red car and drive out of Southall so nobody will see you if that's what you're worried about. Or pick a meeting point somewhere.'

'It's not that easy,' Sheena said. 'One date leads to another and next thing you know, we're in a relationship.'

'So?'

'I'm still very much a part of my late husband's family. It could get complicated. Plus, Rahul's Hindu. People will talk.'

People will talk. How Nikki hated that cautionary adage. Mum had used it on several occasions to try to talk her out of working at O'Reilly's.

'Who would talk about you and Rahul? The widows?'

'I don't know what the widows would think. I think there may be a limit to what they can tolerate, especially if we carried on in public. Widows aren't supposed to remarry, remember, let alone go on *dates*.'

'I've often wondered why you're friends with them,' Nikki blurted out.

Sheena raised an eyebrow. 'Excuse me?'

Immediately, Nikki felt embarrassed at what she had said. 'Sorry, that came out wrong.' A moment passed. She avoided Sheena's eyes, scanning the hall instead for a distraction. Then she noticed a clique of women sitting in the centre. Their shimmering outfits and impeccable make-up gave them the same air of glamour as the women in Preetam's favourite Indian dramas.

'I just see you as being more suited to be friends with those women over there. In terms of age and values.'

'I can't keep up with that lot,' Sheena said. Nikki observed that Sheena didn't even turn to look at them. 'I tried. I went to school with some of them. But Arjun was diagnosed with cancer shortly after we got married – that was strike one. People are sympathetic at first but when the illness drags on, they start avoiding you, like your bad luck is contagious. Then, because of the chemotherapy, having children was out of the question. That was strike two. They were all having babies and forming mothers' groups and they couldn't relate to me. Then after being in remission for seven years, Arjun relapsed and died. I became a widow.'

'Strike three,' Nikki said. 'I see.'

'It's no huge loss to me. The widows are more down-to-earth. They understand loss. Those women over there married wealthy men who own family businesses. They don't work and they've got standing appointments at Chandani's.'

'Who's Chandani?'

'Priciest beauty salon in Southall,' Sheena said. 'It's one of those places where you take yourself for a rare treat but otherwise you make do with a cheaper manicure from one of those smaller salons off the Broadway.' Sheena flashed her glittery fingernails at Nikki and grinned. 'I've been doing them myself for years. Hot pink base with gold glitter – that's my standard one.'

'It looks great,' Nikki said. She inspected her own nails. 'I don't think I've ever had a manicure.'

'I couldn't live without them,' Sheena said. 'Shame I didn't marry a rich man. I'd be spending my whole days at Chandani's, talking about everyone. It's a cesspool of gossip. Worse than the langar hall. Those women can't be trusted.'

Tarampal's warning about the widows flashed into Nikki's mind. But Sheena seemed trustworthy. Nikki felt at ease speaking with her. 'Hey, can I ask you something?'

Sheena nodded.

'Tarampal was really concerned that we'd be found out. Is she that scared of Kulwinder?'

'She was talking about the Brothers,' Sheena said.

'Whose brothers?'

'No, *the* Brothers. A group of young, unemployed men who consider themselves Southall's morality police. A lot of them were working at the scrap metal factory before it closed down. Now they patrol the temple grounds and remind people to cover their heads.' As Sheena said this, her hand travelled to her neck. She played with a thin gold chain that rested on her collarbone.

'That happened to me,' Nikki said, astonished. The memory of the man's sneer brought back a prickling sensation of anger. 'I just thought he was very religious.'

'There's nothing religious in their thinking. They're bored and frustrated. The more zealous ones station themselves on the Broadway, doing spot checks in children's bags for cigarettes, questioning girls about their whereabouts and activities to make sure they're keeping the community's honour intact. I've heard they offer services to families as well.'

'What kind of services?'

'Bounty hunting, mostly. A girl runs away from home with her Muslim boyfriend and the Brothers send the word out through their network of taxi drivers and shop owners to spot her and bring her home.'

'And people haven't said anything? Nobody's complained about being terrorized like this?'

'Sure, there's some grumbling but nobody would dare to speak up against them. Plus, people are afraid of them but also find them useful for keeping their daughters in line. You don't want to complain too loudly because you don't know who feels obligated to them.'

'Is that guy one of them?' Nikki asked. A young, muscular man had just strode into the langar hall. He looked formidable enough to scare a schoolgirl into obeying her parents.

Sheena nodded. 'They're not hard to spot. They walk around like cowboys so everyone knows they're here.' Bitterness laced her voice. Nikki noticed once again that she was playing with her necklace but now she had tugged it out from under her collar. A locket in the shape of a letter G was visible. When Sheena noticed her looking, she tucked the locket away. 'Just a gift from my husband,' Sheena explained. 'For a pet name he used to have for me.'

The locket looked similar to something Nikki's grandmother had sent from India when she and Mindi were born, cartoonish initials molded from gold. It was a child's necklace – the chain was delicate and short. Sheena's hurried explanation struck Nikki as strange but she was distracted by a bigger question: What would the Brothers do if they found out what went on in her writing class? Goose bumps prickled her skin as she realized she already knew the answer.

Chapter Seven

The wheel on the screen had been spinning for nearly a minute. Nikki pressed the CONFIRM button again and received a stern warning: *Pressing CONFIRM again will re-submit your order. Do you want to re-submit?* 'No,' she muttered. 'I wanted it to work the first bloody time.' Her arms ached from holding the laptop in its usually prime wifi connectivity position over the sink and she felt woeful for failing at her simple mission to make an Amazon purchase. During the last class, Sheena had asked if she could take a break from transcribing because of the strain on her wrist and Nikki had agreed to buy a recording device. She peered out the window – some clouds, but not a terrible day for a walk. There were some electronics shops in the area that she could try.

It began spitting with rain halfway through Nikki's journey to King Street. She broke into a jog and took refuge in the Oxfam shop. When she entered, she was breathless, stray hairs plastered to her forehead. The cashier smiled sympathetically at her.

'Took a ghastly turn out there, didn't it?' she said.

'Just terrible,' Nikki said.

On the electronics shelf, next to a box of second-hand hairdryers and adapter plugs, Nikki spotted a tape recorder with a glossy red finish. This could work. It would probably be easier than teaching the widows to use a digital recorder with all its bells and whistles anyhow. She took it to the cashier. 'Have you got any blank cassette tapes by any chance?'

'I've got a boxful somewhere,' the cashier replied. 'I'm also dying to get rid of our story cassettes. The library donated a whole Enid Blyton *Famous Five* series years ago but I haven't had the heart to throw them out. We have to clear out some storage room in the back now and if I don't find them a home . . .'

'I could take some,' Nikki said. She couldn't bear the thought of those tapes being thrown out either. Mum used to borrow them from the library when she was too little to read so she could follow along with Mindi.

The cashier disappeared into the back room. While she was away, Nikki browsed the shelves. She came across the Beatrix Potter book again and flipped through it. 'You don't happen to have more books about Beatrix Potter, do you?' Nikki called.

'Everything we've got is on the shelves,' the cashier said, emerging into view again. 'Which book are you looking for?'

'It's not one of her stories, exactly. It's a collection of her early sketches and journal entries. It's very hard to find because it's a collection of glossy pictures of the actual extracts rather than pages of typed up. I saw it a few years ago in a bookshop but didn't buy it.'

'I hate it when that happens. Book regret. You come across something and think, I don't want that, and later, you're obsessed with getting it and it's no longer available.'

Nikki's regret was bigger than that. '*Beti*, what is this? A picture book?' Dad had asked when he noticed her browsing it in a bookshop in Delhi. 'It's your exam year. These are cartoons.' With no rupees of her own, Nikki was unable to purchase it herself. 'It's not a picture book,' she'd said in frustration. 'They're Beatrix Potter's journals.' This meant little to Dad. Nikki had been sullen and resentful for the rest of the trip.

The cashier looked up curiously at Nikki. 'Any particular reason you're buying a tape recorder in the twenty-first century?'

'I'm teaching English to some older women,' Nikki replied. 'I don't have much of a budget for learning aids and we're recording conversations and improving accents.' This was the line she had practised in case Kulwinder asked about it. She planned on staging a few recorded conversations with the students as a decoy.

The cashier handed her a box filled with *Famous Five* story tapes. 'Pick whichever you want.' She smiled. 'This one's my favourite.'

It was the story of a secret passageway. Only a few sentences, but Nikki was instantly transported to her childhood when Mum would play these tapes at night, rarely saying anything as Mindi followed the words on the page with her finger and Nikki sat captivated by the ebb and flow of the narrator's voice. Despite her elite education in India, Mum must have lost confidence in her pronunciation once she arrived in England. Nikki thought of Tarampal Kaur with a rush of guilt. The woman just wanted to learn English and Nikki had all but ignored her yesterday when she stormed out in a rage.

'How much are they?'

'They're only ten pence each.'

Nikki glanced at the box. It was hard to resist. 'I'll take them all then.' She paid for the tape recorder as well and walked out into the downpour hugging her purchases close to her chest.

After zipping up her suitcase, Kulwinder stacked her papers and passport neatly together and put them in a pouch. She shut her eyes, pulled her dupatta over her head, and asked Guru Nanak to bless her with a safe journey.

A creaking noise downstairs made her eyes fly open. Kulwinder had to fight the panic that rose into her throat. It was just Sarab, she assured herself. He was home early from his shift. Her heartbeat resumed its normal pace as she named each sound of his arrival – there he was, padding about the kitchen, the back door hinges squeaking as he stepped out to the second freezer in their garage where she had stored meals for each night of her absence. She opened her eyes and called out his name. There were some fresh rotis and a pot of tea on the table for lunch but he hadn't seen it. Making her way to the top of stairs to call his name again, she realized that he thought she was already gone.

Kulwinder deliberately stepped on a loose board. The stair groaned loudly in protest. 'I'm here,' she said when she reached the foyer. Sarab was in the living room watching television.

'Oh,' he said. 'What time is your flight?'

'Four thirty,' she said. 'I need to be there two hours before. Three hours is preferred but I think two hours is just fine.' The less time running into Punjabis at Heathrow, the better.

'We'll leave at two,' Sarab said. Kulwinder wasn't sure if she imagined the resentment in his voice. They'd quarrelled again yesterday about her trip. He'd demanded to know why she was still going. 'We go every year,' she'd reminded him. There were relatives to visit, weddings to attend. Of course they'd understand if she missed a year, but her life in London had changed enough lately. India would be the same, as if she had never left it and, more than ever, she craved the noise and chaos of her less complicated past. She wanted to breathe in the gritty air and elbow her way through bustling markets. Sarab's refusal to go to India was deeply disappointing; it widened the chasm between them that grief had created. Kulwinder didn't understand why he preferred to cope with loss in stillness. She would travel the entire world if it would help her escape.

'What are you watching?' Kulwinder asked.

Sarab was never unkind, just detached. An expression of mild irritation rippled across his features. 'Just a television show,' he replied.

Kulwinder retreated to her bedroom and drew a chair to the windowsill, watching the pavement below. Out of habit, she turned her head at an angle to keep Tarampal's house in the furthest corner of her vision so it was just a pesky blur. A pair of grandmothers wearing woolly cardigans over their salwar kameezes dragged overflowing trolleys back from the market. Crossing their paths, a couple and their three small children formed a single file line to let them pass. There were polite thanking nods between both parties. One of the old women reached out to stroke a child's face and when the child turned her face up and smiled, an acute pain punctured Kulwinder's heart. Did Sarab experience Maya's loss in these same little ways? She couldn't ask.

Across the road, a young woman came into Kulwinder's view. She squinted and pressed her nose against the window. That hurried walk was unmistakably Nikki's. What was she doing here? Nikki's satchel bounced against her hip as she traipsed across the road. She was carrying a carton. Kulwinder craned her neck and saw Nikki ring the doorbell at Number 18. The door opened and Mrs Shah appeared. What did Nikki want from Mrs Shah? They spoke for a few moments and then Mrs Shah pointed to the house next door before retreating back into her home.

Number 16. Nikki had come to visit Tarampal. Kulwinder took in a breath and let her gaze follow Nikki to Tarampal's doorstep. Her heartbeat accelerated; it was always like this when she came face to face with that walkway, that door. For weeks after Maya died, Kulwinder was haunted by visions of her walking in and never coming out.

Nikki rang the doorbell and waited. A few moments later, she placed the carton on the ground and knocked on the door. Kulwinder continued to watch as Nikki drew a notebook and pen from her bag and scrawled a note that she tucked into the carton. Reluctantly, she stepped off the porch, turning back a few times to see if Tarampal had materialized.

Kulwinder waited until Nikki was completely out of view, and then she hurried down the stairs. 'Just going next door to say goodbye to the neighbours,' she called over her shoulder.

Just as she was about to cross the road, Kulwinder stopped. What was she doing? She was curious to see what Nikki had left on the doorstep but was it worth the visit? Tarampal's house drew and repelled her in equal measure, keeping her on the pavement switching her feet in a reluctant dance. *It's for your classes*, she convinced herself. There was something shifty about Nikki and she needed to find out what it was before her classes were affected. She scrambled across the road, looking to her left and right for cars and nosy neighbours. The last thing she needed was somebody spotting her rooting through Tarampal's belongings on her doorstep.

Nikki's carton was not properly sealed because there were cassette tapes bulging out of the top, pushing through the flaps. Enid Blyton and *Famous Five* tapes. Kulwinder plucked the note from the carton. It was written hastily and the Gurmukhi spelling was all wrong, but Kulwinder got the gist of it.

> *(To Tarampal's daughter: Please read this note to her. It is from Nikki) I'm very sorry about last lesson. Here are some story tapes so you can return to learning English.*

Return to learning English? What exactly was going on in that class? Kulwinder replaced the note and returned to her house. Her heartbeat thrashed in her ears. She took out her phone and searched for Nikki's number. It was a good thing she had thought to save it that night so she could call Nikki to reprimand her if she left the community building lights on again.

Kulwinder waited for her hands to stop shaking and then she typed a message.

> *Hello, Nikki. Letting you know that I will be in India longer than expected. Returning 30 March. Any issues please contact Sikh Community Association offices.*

She pressed Send. Her return was actually scheduled for 27 March. That gave her three days to make a surprise drop-in on the classes to find out what Nikki and the women were up to.

Moments later, she received a reply from Nikki.

> *Okay! Have a good trip!*

'Let's play a game,' Manjeet suggested when Nikki entered the classroom. Nikki wasn't listening – she was distracted by the sight of four elderly, white-clad women wandering the halls.

'Does anyone know who those ladies are?' Nikki asked. The women floated past the window. One pressed her wrinkly face against the panel and then pulled away.

'They're some friends of mine. They want to join in as well,' Arvinder said.

'So why don't they come in?' Nikki asked.

'They will.'

'They're staring at us,' Nikki said. A pair of eyes at the window met hers and then disappeared.

'Let them make their own way,' Arvinder said. 'They've never been in a classroom before. The thought of telling these stories is very daunting.'

'We told them there's nothing to worry about,' Preetam said. 'They're just a bit afraid of you.'

'You're too modern for them,' Arvinder explained.

'Too modern?'

'You're wearing jeans. You always wear jeans,' said Preetam. 'And everybody can see your bright pink bra because of the wide neck of that sweater.'

'It's off-shoulder,' Sheena said in Nikki's defense. 'That's the fashion.'

'Fashion-fashion is fine for you young girls, and we don't have a problem with it, but to these ultra conservative ladies, you're an alien,' Arvinder said.

'You might as well be English,' Preetam said.

'This is ridiculous,' Nikki said. 'It's like we're in a zoo enclosure.' The women outside were taking turns to peer at her now. One scanned her from head to toe and then whispered to her friend.

'Excuse me, Nikki. What is enclosure?' Manjeet asked.

'Like a cage,' Nikki said.

'Sometimes you mix the English words with the Punjabi words,' Manjeet said.

'That's also a problem for you all?' Nikki asked.

Manjeet nodded very apologetically.

'And you're not married,' Preetam blurted out. 'How are these women supposed to talk to someone about these intimate things when she's not supposed to have experienced them?'

'Are you getting married, Nikki?' asked Manjeet. 'Are you looking? You shouldn't wait too long.'

'When I decide to get married, Bibi Manjeet, you'll be the first to know,' Nikki replied.

'Don't do that,' Arvinder said with a frown. 'Tell your family first.'

'That's it,' Nikki said. She marched to the door and opened it against the class's rising protests. She gave the women her brightest smile and brought her palms together. 'Good evening,' she said. '*Sat sri akal*.'

The women drew together and stared at Nikki. 'Welcome to the class,' she continued. 'Come on in.' The air between them was still. Nikki's smile began to hurt. 'Please,' she said.

As the ladies began to retreat, Arvinder came rushing out the door. She apologized to the women as they disappeared down the stairs in a slow, hunchbacked procession. Arvinder gripped Nikki by the shoulders and steered her back into the class. 'Where are they going?' Nikki asked.

'You've scared them. They weren't ready for this.'

'Well, when they come back, I'll apologize and start over. It's just—'

'They won't come back,' Arvinder snapped. Her stare was like a hot white light. 'We are not all the same, Nikki,' she said. 'There are some very reserved people in this community.'

'I know that, but I just— '

'You *don't* know,' Arvinder said. 'Our little group were the only widows to sign up for writing classes. That may seem like nothing to you but for some, it's a very brave and frightening thing. Those women are shy and scared. They got no attention from their husbands – not the kind they wanted anyway—'

'Oh Mother, please,' Preetam said.

Arvinder turned to face her. 'Please what?'

'Nikki, those women came from a very traditional village. That's all. And you,' Preetam said, nodding to Arvinder. 'You always make it sound like you had a terrible husband. I don't remember Papa being half as bad as you make him sound.'

'You wouldn't know anything about my private life with your father.'

'But that night before my wedding, when you gave me all of that advice? Your cheeks were shimmering. You were like a new bride yourself. Don't tell me it all came from your imagination. You knew what passion was. He had to have shown it to you at some point.'

Arvinder's lower lip quivered. Nikki noticed her biting it, either to stop from laughing or saying something. Either way, she knew that she had to put an end to the conversation. She pulled the tape recorder out of her bag and laid it on the table. 'I bought us a tape recorder so Sheena doesn't have to transcribe and you all can tell your stories without having to pause.' She busied herself with plugging it in and feeding it a new tape. 'Shall we test it?' she asked brightly, pressing the record button. 'Somebody say something.'

'Helloooo,' Manjeet said, giving the tape recorder a wave.

Nikki turned it off, rewound it and played their recording. Their voices came through clearly. The silence from the other women was captured as well.

'Could you give me the tapes at the end of each lesson?' Sheena asked. 'I'll play them at home and transcribe the stories.'

'You still want written versions of the stories?' Nikki asked.

'If it's not too much trouble for Sheena,' Manjeet spoke up. 'I like that what I imagine gets put onto paper.'

'Me too,' Arvinder agreed, shrugging off her huff. 'I can't read the words but I can see them. It will be my only chance to see my words in print, even if I can't read it myself.'

The class registration forms were still in Nikki's bag from her visit to Tarampal's house earlier. Somebody – one of Tarampal's children, she assumed – had printed her name, address and telephone number in block letters, and hers was not the only form that looked rushed by another's hand. Did these ladies look at those words and feel a sense of pride that they represented them as a person? Or was there shame at being unable to decipher the alphabet?

'What's your game, Manjeet?' Nikki asked, recalling Manjeet's exclamation as she had entered the classroom.

Manjeet looked very pleased. 'Let's each come up with a story for these pictures.' She produced a magazine from her bag. On the front cover, a naked woman lay on her back, her full breasts glowing in the natural light that poured through an open window.

'Is that an old *Playboy*?' Nikki asked, feeling her eyes bug out slightly.

'Confiscated from my son thirty years ago. I buried the magazine in a trunk because I was afraid that the neighbours might see it in the rubbish. I came across it this morning while sorting through all of our old things.'

Playboy from the eighties. The women had big hair and the photographs were tinted in sepia, giving the images an instantly nostalgic look. Some of the men had trim moustaches. The women passed the magazine around and flipped through the pages. Arvinder held up a centrefold of a model sitting naked on the bonnet of a sports car. Her bronze skin glowed against the car's red finish. 'This woman is waiting in the garage to surprise her lover. He's a mechanic.'

'He spends the whole day tuning people's cars and when he returns, he's ready to be tuned up himself,' Sheena offered.

'Only problem is, she's getting sick of waiting. Plus, when he comes back, he has to shower to get all the grime and sweat off him so he can smell nice for her,' Manjeet said.

'So she decides to put her clothes back on and go for a drive around the neighbourhood. The first handsome man she sees, she'll find and take him back to her house,' Preetam said.

The magazine was still in Arvinder's hands. She flipped to another page. 'This man,' she said, pointing to a picture of a muscular, tanned man. The women murmured their approval.

Nikki said nothing else as the story was passed from woman to woman, taking shape. Eventually, there was a pause between lines. 'I think we're done,' Sheena said.

'But they've only been using their hands,' Manjeet protested.

'What of it?' Arvinder asked. 'They're both very satisfied. Besides, let her save the real thing for her lover. She's still going to go to bed with him tonight.'

'True. By the time she's finished with this man, it's evening and her lover is returning.'

'Won't he be able to tell that she's been with another man?'

'She can take a shower,' Sheena said.

'Then she'll be too clean. It's suspicious,' Arvinder said.

'Too clean?' Preetam asked. 'What man would be bothered by that? I always showered right before my husband came home.'

'She can spray on some perfume then,' Sheena suggested.

Arvinder shook her head. Her voice rose with certainty. 'Here's what she does. She takes a shower and then walks out the door. She passes the old village well and mingles with other housewives at the small market. She finds some extra errands to do – paying the chaiwallah in advance for a week's worth of afternoon tea, bringing water to the farmhands. That's about as much activity as she'd have done throughout the day. Her skin glows with a light sweat but she's not dirty. That's how she covers it up.'

When she was finished, she was out of breath, exhilarated, triumphant. She had revealed much more than she had said and the force of the confession seemed to knock her windless. The women stared at her. Preetam in particular looked horrified.

'Those were all places near our home in Punjab,' Preetam finally said.

'Replace them with shops in this *gori*'s life then,' Arvinder said. 'Nikki, tell us, what's within walking distance of your place?'

'A pub,' Nikki said.

'There,' Arvinder said. 'Add that, Sheena.'

'Who was it?' Preetam asked quietly. 'When?'

Arvinder sucked in her breath and said nothing.

'Who was it?' Preetam cried.

'There's no need to raise your voice at me, Preetam,' Arvinder said. 'I am still your elder.'

'You've just admitted to doing the most dishonourable thing,' Preetam said. 'Who were you cheating on my father with? Did you wreck another family?' Preetam looked around wildly. This was the role of a lifetime for her, Nikki realized. All of her angst and theatrics finally had an outlet. 'Who was it?'

The other women shrank back into their seats, their eyes intently darting back and forth between mother and daughter. Nikki was reminded of her first impression of these two women. Their resemblance had been so obvious that she had mistaken them for sisters. But this conflict illuminated their differences. The sleeves of Arvinder's white tunic hung loosely at her bony wrists and the hems had greyed slightly while Preetam's widow attire was a classier affair – lacey trim on a cream dupatta. While Preetam's eyes were bright with rage, Arvinder's stare was distant and watery, her whole body heaving in the aftermath of her revelation.

Preetam fanned her face with her hands. '*Hai*, Nikki. I might faint.'

'That's not necessary, Preetam,' Sheena said.

'Sheena, don't get involved,' Manjeet said quietly.

'Did you think about our family?' Preetam asked. 'About what you would have had to do if Papa found out? It's still happening, you know. Look at how Maya ended up.'

'*That's enough*,' Arvinder snapped. Preetam burst into tears and bolted from the room.

'I think it's time for a break. Ten minutes and then we'll meet back here,' Nikki announced. The women filed out silently. Nikki sat back in her chair. Her head throbbed from this whirlwind of revelations, the most confusing of which was the mention of Maya. How did she end up? The hints about her death, about being caught with texts on her phone. There was nobody to ask, no appropriate moment to do so. From the window, she could see them emerging from the building and walking towards the temple. Sheena and Manjeet walked together, giving space to Arvinder who lingered behind them. She stood under the temple's awning and stared off at the distance, at the cars lined on the concrete lot. Nikki contemplated approaching Arvinder but she was wary of prying after her misstep with the old women earlier. Arvinder stepped into a puddle of warm light, which gave her white garments a soft, yellowish appearance. She wasn't a widow any more, but a lithe young woman hungering for affection.

A navy sweater stretched across Jason's shoulders to show off his physique. As they waited in line outside the art-house cinema, Nikki couldn't help stealing glimpses at him. A shaving cut on his jawbone looked recent. She wondered if he had taken as long as she had to get ready. She had bought mascara, lipstick, eye shadow and new foundation from Boots after an eager salesgirl convinced her to let her do a mini-makeover. She chided herself all the way home for acquiring these things that she usually railed against. Make-up was oppressive. It created an ideal of women . . . didn't it? But when she caught her reflection in a shop window, she discovered a version of herself with fuller lips and bolder eyes – and she liked it.

By the time they got to the front of the line, tickets for every film were sold out except for a French movie. 'This one got good reviews,' Nikki said. 'It starts in an hour and a half though. Shall we take a walk and find a place to eat?' Jason nodded.

'Ever been to Paris?' he asked Nikki as they strolled down the street.

'Once,' she said. 'With a lover.' She had meant to sound mysterious but it came out like a title for an erotic story. *Once, With A Lover*. She giggled.

'That good, huh?' Jason asked.

'No, awful, actually. I met this French film student at a party last year. I got some cheap Eurostar tickets and went away to Paris for four days. It was meant to be romantic.'

'But it wasn't?'

'We were both broke. He was out most of the day working – not on his art, mind you. He was working in McDonalds. I spent most of the day sitting in his flat watching television.'

'You didn't go out? Take in the City of Lights?'

'He kept promising that we'd do that together when he came home. The flat was in a very unsafe area and my French is hopeless, so I was happy to wait. But each night he came back, brooding and tired. It went downhill quite quickly.'

'That's too bad,' Jason said.

'And you?' Nikki asked. 'Been to Paris?'

Jason shook his head. 'Went to Greece and Spain with my ex. It was all the travel she was interested in doing. I never got to Paris.' A shift in his voice caught Nikki's attention. When he noticed her peering at him, he changed the subject. 'There's a place which does delicious gourmet pizzas up that way.'

As they headed in the direction of the restaurant, they passed a bookshop called Sally's and something stirred in the back of Nikki's mind. 'Do you mind if we duck in? I want to check if they have something,' Nikki said.

'No problem,' Jason said. As soon as they entered, he made a beeline for a section at the back. Nikki approached the counter and inquired about *The Journals and Sketches of Beatrix Potter*. The clerk looked it up on her system and said, 'It's out of print. Have you looked for used copies online?'

'I have,' Nikki said. And she had found two, but they were in very poor condition, the spines threadbare and the pages dog-eared. One copy appeared water damaged, with wrinkly, bloated pages as if somebody had dropped it into the bath. She thanked the clerk and searched for Jason. He was in a section marked Eastern Philosophy. She gave him a wave and headed to the Anthologies section. Scanning the titles, Nikki could not help hearing the voices of her Southall storytellers, urgent and rhythmic as they wove their sensual tales.

She went to join Jason. 'What were you looking for?' he asked.

Nikki told him about the Beatrix Potter book. 'It was in this little bookshop in Delhi which was crammed from floor to ceiling in textbooks and novels. You could spend a whole day there,' she said.

'You don't remember the name of the shop?'

'No. Just that it was on Connaught Place, sort of wedged behind a boutique in one of those restored colonial buildings.'

'Amongst at least ten other bookshops of the same description,' Jason said with a smile. 'I know people go to Connaught Place to escape the mayhem of Delhi but I'm drawn to the pushcarts and makeshift stalls that find their way in somehow.'

'Exactly. The more I think of it, the more I want that very copy, not something new. I still remember it had a tea stain on the cover in the shape of a leaf. My dad had looked at it and said, "This book isn't even new." That just made me angrier. Here I was, so excited about the contents of the book and all he could see was a superficial mark on the cover.'

They went to the cashier together where Jason purchased a book called *Japanese Philosophy*. 'This completes my set,' he explained to Nikki as the cashier rang up his purchase. 'I've got all the books in this series – Chinese, Indian, Western and Islamic. Oh, and Sikh of course. But I've got another entire shelf for Sikh philosophy books.'

Nerd, Nikki thought with a twinge of delight. 'Are your parents religious?' Nikki asked.

'Not really. Traditional, but not religious. That's what prompted me to study Sikhism in the first place. It seemed like there were so many rules they kept imposing that had no basis in religion. I started reading the scripture to be able to argue with them.'

'I'm sure they loved that,' Nikki said.

'They sure did,' Jason grinned. 'My parents grudgingly admit to learning a few new things now and then but it's hard work. Yours? Traditional?'

'My mum has always been a bit more traditional than Dad. Dad was quite supportive of me. Mum seemed to think that she had to rein me in all the time. It was hard when Dad died.'

'You guys were close?' Jason asked. Then he hastily added. 'Sorry. That's a stupid question. I hated people asking me that when my mother was sick. As if our closeness mattered – she's family, whether we're close or not isn't really the point.'

'It's okay,' Nikki said. 'And yes, we were. He was very encouraging of me, but before he died, we'd had this massive argument. I dropped out of Law school. He was furious. I'd never seen him so upset before. We didn't speak, and then he went to India with Mum to get away from it all and he died there.' Nikki said it all so matter-of-factly but when she was finished, she felt the tears boiling in her chest. She panicked. Was she really going to cry over Dad for the first time *now*, while on a first date? 'Sorry,' she choked.

'Hey,' Jason said. Up ahead, there was a small park with an iron bench facing the road. He gestured to it and Nikki nodded. She was grateful that her face was obscured by shadows as they sat down. The pressure of tears subsided.

'It's hard because it was so sudden that I'll never know if he came to terms with what I did or not. My mum gets really antsy when I try to ask her what his last conscious moments were like, so I imagine he was still upset with me. I don't know which feeling is worse – guilt or grief. Or which one I'm supposed to feel. '

'Grief, I suppose,' Jason said. 'There's little use in feeling guilty.'

'But if I hadn't dropped out . . .'

'You can't do that to yourself,' Jason said. 'I get it. My parents would have freaked out if I'd switched out of Engineering. Luckily for them, I actually like it. But you can't sentence yourself to all of this torment over what might have happened if you'd decided to stay in law school. It's likely that you'd be miserable.'

Nikki took in a breath and felt it come easily. Jason's assurances were not new; Olive had given her a similar talk after Dad's death. But Jason was the first Punjabi person to attempt to convince Nikki that she had made the right decision. Only now did it occur to her that she was expecting him to repeat Mindi's concerns. *What about duty?* Instead all she saw on his face was understanding.

'Thanks,' she said.

'No problem. We've all had to come to terms with letting our parents down.'

'You can't have been too troublesome being a first-born male and an engineer,' Nikki teased. It might have been a trick of passing headlights, but she noticed a stricken look crossing Jason's face. He laughed, but it was a beat too late. Nikki was curious but she felt it was too soon to pry. 'I was kidding,' she added.

'I know,' Jason said. 'There's a lot of pressure to succeed though. I had to tick all of the success boxes right from the very start. It makes me think of banana chips.'

Nikki stared at him. 'You've lost me.'

'See, when I was in pre-school my parents discovered I was left-handed. They had a meltdown. My dad sat me down every night to train me to write with my right hand. I hated these sessions, but there was one way to motivate me – Dad bribed me with a dried banana chip for each line of the alphabet I traced out with my right hand. I loved those things. It was a couple of years before I discovered real junk food, of course.'

'What was so bad about being left-handed?'

Jason pulled a serious face. 'I was starting out life with a devastating disadvantage, Nikki. I would never be able to use scissors properly. Tying shoelaces would be complicated. And worst of all, my work would be untidy. Dad had a left-handed cousin in India who was always punished by teachers for leaving pen smudges on his assignments.'

'A couple of banana chips and you were converted. You wouldn't hold up well as a spy.'

'I stuck to my guns and remained left-handed. I got told off every time I came home from grade school with smudged ink on my left hand. My mother had this complex about being an immigrant – she thought people would think we weren't clean. She used to scrub my hands each day with grainy blue laundry soap but she couldn't change who I naturally was.'

'What a rebel,' Nikki teased.

Jason grinned. 'All I'm saying is that I've always been aware of the pressure to follow the rules and meet expectations. The eldest child is meant to pave the way. If I fail at anything, my siblings are doomed, according to my parents.'

'Sometimes I think that's why my sister is making such a project out of finding a husband,' Nikki said. 'She wants to set things right, hoping that I'll take her lead.'

'You'll be posting your particulars on the marriage board then?'

'Never.'

'Good. It's bad enough that you picked me up at the temple.'

'I did not pick you up,' Nikki retorted, giving Jason a thump on the arm. He laughed and stood up. 'Come on, let's get some dinner,' he said. He reached out his hands, palms up, inviting Nikki to place her hands in them and then he pulled her up. She teetered forwards and nearly fell right back onto the bench if not for his arms, suddenly bracing her waist. They kissed then. The street around them dissolved into a peaceful silence, which lingered even after they gently drew away from each other and began walking, wordlessly, towards the restaurant.

At dinner, Jason asked Nikki how her job at the temple was going. 'Good,' Nikki said, sawing a knife through her margherita pizza. She took a bite and looked up to see Jason staring expectantly at her. 'There's not much to say about it, really,' she shrugged. 'I'm just teaching old ladies to read and write.'

'It sounds very rewarding.'

'It is,' Nikki said. She could hear, above the restaurant's din of voices and cutlery clashing, the women's audible sighs after a particularly steamy story had been read out.

'Is it something you've always wanted to do?'

'Sure,' Nikki said, and now she could not help breaking out into a smile. 'I've always wanted to do some sort of community service, and this involves writing, so it combines my two passions.' The word *passion* made her giggle.

'Look at you, so excited about what you do. It's great,' Jason said. 'Your mum and sister must be proud at the very least that you're helping women in the community.'

An image flashed into Nikki's mind: Mum and Mindi sitting in the back of Nikki's classroom, pencils poised primly over their notebooks and confusion descending over their faces when the women started describing sex scenes with vegetables. She burst out laughing. It was the sort of uncontrollable, gasping laughter that made her belly ache. She shook her head and shut her eyes, shaking with laughter and when she opened them, Jason was peering curiously at her.

'Oh my goodness,' Nikki said. 'I'm sorry.' Tears streamed down her face. 'I have to tell you, don't I?'

'Tell me what?'

'I'm not a teacher.'

'What do you do then?'

'I'm running an erotic storytelling workshop for Punjabi widows.'

Jason blinked. 'What do you mean?'

'Exactly that. Twice a week, we meet in the temple community centre on the pretence of learning English but the women come up with these sexual stories instead.'

'You're kidding,' Jason said. 'You have to be.'

Nikki took a sip of her wine with flourish, pleased at the widening smile on Jason's face. 'No kidding,' she said. 'We all pitch in with feedback and suggestions to make the story more convincing. Sometimes one story takes up a whole lesson.'

The frown on Jason's face worried Nikki a little. Maybe she shouldn't have said anything. 'What's wrong with my amazing job?' she asked lightly.

'Nothing's *wrong*. I'm just struggling to believe this,' Jason said.

'"*She felt her pulse throbbing in the sweet, secret spot between her thighs*,"' Nikki said. 'A widow wrote that.'

Jason shook his head slowly, a curious smile appearing. 'So how did this come about?'

Nikki found herself at the very beginning, telling Jason about how she had been fooled into thinking she'd be teaching a literacy class. His growing smile made her slightly lightheaded. 'Are these proper widows? Like my grandmother?'

'I don't know. Does your grandmother harbour any fantasies of kneading dough for your grandfather's roti with her bare bottom? Because that's a story we did recently.' It had been Arvinder's idea. Both members of the couple had been aroused by this act – the half-naked woman grinding her bum over the gooey raw dough and the man eating the roti later which he claimed was velvety soft because of this secret method.

'I can't imagine her being savvy enough to come up with a scene like that.'

'Not to you maybe. But I'll bet she talks about these things with her friends.'

'You'll bet my sweet, innocent Nani-ji talks dirty with her prayer group?'

Nikki smiled. 'A month ago, I would've thought that was crazy as well but there's such a range of creative stories coming from just four widows. There must be so many more.' She couldn't help looking at all elderly women differently now, not just the Punjabi ones.

'My grandmother can't even write her own name. She saw me playing computer games when I was a kid once and she thought there were actual men inside the computer, with miniature guns in this tiny little city gone amok. There's no way someone with that little exposure to the world could come up with such detailed sex stories.'

'But sex and pleasure are instinctive, right? Good, satisfying sex makes perfect sense to even the most illiterate person. You and me, we're just used to seeing it as an advanced invention because we learned about it after we learned the other basics – reading, writing, learning how to use a computer, all of that. To the widows, sex comes before all of that knowledge.'

'I didn't hear a word of that because I'm thinking about my grandmother making sex-roti,' Jason said with a grimace.

'Bum bread,' Nikki said.

'Tushy toast,' Jason laughed. He shook his head. 'I'm still in shock. What made these women feel comfortable telling you everything? Besides your obvious charm, of course.'

'I guess they didn't think I'd judge them because I'm a modern girl. They don't tell me everything though.' She thought about Preetam's outburst about Arvinder's affair and the way Maya's name had rankled everyone once again. No explanations had been provided after the women returned from their break and Nikki sensed it would be a long time before she could ask about it. 'Enough about my job. Tell me about engineering.'

'You sounded bored just asking about engineering.'

'Tell me! About! Engineering!' Nikki said, pumping her fists into the air. Jason's laughter boomed across the restaurant. A waiter gave them a dirty look.

They did not make it to the film in the end. They stayed on at the restaurant, ordering more wine, glancing only once at their watches and quickly agreeing that they preferred conversation. Jason only wanted to hear about the stories. Nikki studied his face as she spoke; there was not a hint of outrage or disgust. He didn't bat an eye when she casually mentioned that she felt like she was making a feminist foray into these women's lives. The word didn't seem to chafe. Olive was right, Nikki realized. Most men would be turned off by a woman making it her mission to help other women talk about their sexuality.

Afterwards, they walked outside together. It was a cool night and the London lights glowed on the streets. Nikki drew close to Jason and he slipped his arms around her waist. They kissed again. 'It's those raunchy stories' fault,' Jason said. Nikki laughed. *No, it's you,* she thought.

Chapter Eight

Nikki laid out the three Indian blouses and took a picture. She sent it to Mindi with a text: *Which one for me?* The stall owner, a small man with a snowy beard and a large pink turban, rapidly listed their merits: 'One hundred per cent cotton! Very breathable! Colours don't bleed in the wash – even the red dye doesn't come off!' His overenthusiasm gave Nikki the impression that these were likely polyester blouses that would smell like armpits after ten minutes of wear and make a crime scene of her other laundry if she so much as put them in the same basket.

Mindi rang her back. 'Since when did you start wearing kurti tops?' she asked.

'Since I discovered a Southall clothing bazaar that sells them much cheaper than vintage shops anywhere else in London,' Nikki said.

'The bluish-green on the far left is the best.'

'Not the maroon?'

'It's not my favourite,' Mindi said. 'The black one is nice too, because of the silver embroidery on the collar. Could you buy me one as well?'

'Are we going to dress the same like Mum forced us to in primary school?'

Mindi groaned. 'That was the worst, wasn't it? Everybody asking if we were twins?'

'Then when we begged her to stop, she told us we were being ungrateful.

Some children don't have clothes at all!' The idea of naked children had sent Nikki and Mindi into hysterics.

The tarp above the stall began to sag from the weight of rainfall. Nikki rubbed her hands together. At the hot chai stall next door, a queue was forming. 'What else have they got in this bazaar? Anything good?' Mindi asked.

'Some produce, a couple of masala stalls, Indian sweets,' Nikki said, looking around. 'There's a woman who can dye your costume jewellery stones to match the exact shade of your outfit. There's an entire row for those jingly-dangly wedding decorations and I also spotted a guy with a parrot who picks your fortune out from a hat.' Women roamed from stall to stall, their handbags clutched tightly under their arms. Earlier, Nikki had sidled up to a group of older ladies comparing aubergines. To her disappointment, they were only sharing a recipe.

There was a lot of clattering in the background. 'Are you at work?' Nikki asked.

'I'm just leaving. I'm sorting through these make-up samples that Kirti gave me for tonight. Can't decide between two eyeliners.'

'It's more for you than the guy, isn't it? He probably won't notice the difference.'

'I'm actually only meeting women this week,' Mindi said.

'In that case you'll need to check if the gurdwara does lesbian weddings.'

The clattering stopped. 'I thought I told you about this.'

'I think I'd remember.'

'So, I wasn't having much luck with the temple profile. I decided to get a trial membership with Sikhmate.com. It's more discreet than I expected and you can set up these really specific filters.'

'And you've determined that your husband must have a vagina?' Nikki asked, forgetting for a moment where she was. The turbaned vendor staggered as if he'd been shot. 'Sorry,' Nikki mouthed. Out of guilt, she pointed at all three blouses and gave him a thumbs-up. He nodded and put them into a thin crinkly blue plastic bag.

'On Sikhmate, there's an option to meet the women of the families first before meeting the guys. You get a coffee with them, and if you hit it off, they introduce you to their brothers, nephews or sons.'

That sounded like a total nightmare. 'That's so much more pressure though,' Nikki said. 'They'd be screening you.' Not to mention the creepiness of marrying into a family where the sisters and mothers selected mates for their men.

'It's meant to be less pressure,' Mindi said. 'If I got married, I'd be spending a lot of time with the women of the family anyway, so I guess they want to see if we're compatible.'

'Do I get to screen guys for you then?' Nikki asked. 'Do I get to veto the ones I don't like? Or does it only work one way? Honestly, Mindi, this sounds like a terrible plan. I'd almost welcome the idea of you meeting some of the less desirable temple profile guys over meeting these Sikhmate aunties first.'

There was renewed clattering in the background. 'I think I'll go with the plum eyeliner,' Mindi said. 'It's more subtle. Leaves a better impression.' It was a clear signal that Nikki's advice was not needed. 'I'll let you know how it goes.'

'Good luck,' Nikki muttered. They said their goodbyes and hung up. Nikki paid the vendor. She joined the chai queue, watching people scatter under cover as the downpour got heavier. She held the bag of blouses close to her chest. Mindi probably didn't know this, but Nikki had enjoyed dressing alike. She had been secretly sad when they won the war against Mum to let them be individuals.

Arvinder and Preetam were not speaking. They arrived at the class ten minutes apart and sat at opposite ends of the room. Between them, Sheena's bag, mobile phone and notebook sat on a desk but Sheena was nowhere to be seen. Manjeet was also missing.

'We'll just wait for the others,' Nikki said. She gave Arvinder a smile. Arvinder's gaze darted away. Preetam fiddled with the lace edge of her dupatta, folding it into tight corners. The silence reminded Nikki of her first moments with these widows. She glanced at the seat where Tarampal had sat, dutifully tracing dotted letters in her workbook.

'I'm here, I'm here,' Sheena said breathlessly, entering the room with three women. 'This is Tanveer Kaur, Gaganjeet Kaur and the late Jasjeet Singh's wife. We just call her Bibi. They'd like to join our class.'

Nikki surveyed the women. Tanveer and Gaganjeet appeared to be in their late sixties but Bibi was closer to Arvinder's age. They were all dressed in white. 'You are all friends of Sheena's?' Nikki asked. The women nodded. 'Oh good,' she said. 'So you know what we discuss in these classes.' The last thing she needed was another earnest English-learner like Tarampal.

'I still tell most people I come to these classes to improve my English,' Sheena said. 'Unless I really trust them.' She smiled at the new widows.

From her corner, Arvinder spoke up. 'You can't rely on everyone's friends to be trustworthy though. The people you tell might spread the word to others who can't keep a secret.'

Bibi was indignant. 'I can keep a secret.'

'She's just saying we should be cautious,' Sheena assured Bibi.

'You all are very welcome here. We just have to make sure we're not found out by the wrong people,' Nikki said. While crossing the Southall Broadway after her market trip, she had caught sight of three young Punjabi men patrolling the bus stop and bullishly reminding schoolgirls to go straight home.

Preetam's scanned the bead-lined hem of Nikki's new blouse, prepared to engage now that it wasn't just her and Arvinder. 'I like what you're wearing,' she said.

'Thanks,' Nikki replied. 'No bra straps visible.'

'Yes. Very nice,' Gaganjeet said. Suddenly her face distorted – eyes bulging, lips drawn back to reveal her dentures. She let out a deafening shriek. In its aftermath, Nikki looked around to see that only she was rattled.

'*Waheguru*,' Arvinder said to bless her.

'That was a sneeze?' Nikki asked.

'*Hanh*, I'm recovering from a cold. All weekend I've been sneezing and coughing,' Gaganjeet said.

'It's going around,' Preetam said. 'I saw Manjeet at the temple early this morning and she said she wouldn't be attending class tonight. I suppose she's unwell too. She looked a bit pale. You should take something for that cold, Gaganjeet.'

'I had some chai,' Gaganjeet said. 'I put extra fennel it in.'

'I mean take some medicine. Isn't Boobie Singh's pharmacy near your place?'

'It's Bobby,' Sheena corrected.

'He charges too much, that Boobie,' Gaganjeet complained.

'Do any of our other new members have a story to share?' Nikki asked, lest the discussion digress any further. This was the other risk of adding more members. In the warm-up to telling stories, the women often traded gossip: what colour lengha a friend's granddaughter wore to her wedding reception; what time the bus to the market arrived on Sunday when there were disruptions; who had recently misplaced her sandals at the temple and allegedly taken another pair, starting a chain of thefts by people who had to replace their footwear.

'Nikki, wait a while, *nah*? We are just getting to know our new friends,' Arvinder said. 'I heard that Kulwinder is away in India. This means we can stay in the building longer.'

'And make more noise,' Sheena said.

'I don't think we should take Kulwinder's absence as a reason to relax,' Nikki said, although she felt much less tense knowing that the office down the hall was empty for the next four weeks. 'I'd rather not stay till late. I have to catch the train home.'

'You take the train home at night by yourself? Where do you live?' Bibi asked.

'Shepherd's Bush,' Nikki said.

'Where's your house? Near the market or far from it?'

'It's not in Southall. I live in West London,' Nikki said.

'It's safe to walk around here at night,' Bibi said. 'I do it all the time.'

'You can do it because you're an old lady,' Tanveer said. 'What would a man hiding in the bushes want from you?'

'I happen to have a lot of pension money,' said Bibi with a huff.

'Tanveer means that you wouldn't be assaulted,' Sheena said. 'Younger women have to worry about that.'

'Is that what happened to Karina Kaur?' Tanveer asked. 'I saw the advertisement for the new television program about the anniversary of her murder. It happened a few years before we moved here from India. Honestly, if I'd known that this could happen to one of our girls in London, we might not have come here at all.'

At the mention of Karina's name, a noticeable hush fell over the room. A moment passed in which everybody seemed to be thinking and Nikki sensed her outsider status more acutely than usual. She cast her gaze over the group and noticed a visible tension on Sheena's face.

'I remember that. People said she was walking around alone in the park. Meeting her boyfriend,' Arvinder said.

'And that's punishable by murder is it?' Sheena snapped.

Arvinder looked taken aback. 'Sheena, you know I didn't mean it like that.'

'I know,' Sheena said quietly. She blinked and then gave Arvinder a small nod. 'Sorry.'

Nikki had never thought Sheena could become so unnerved. She did a quick calculation. From what she could remember of the case (not that her mother would let her forget it), Karina and Sheena would probably have been around the same age when it happened. She wondered if they had known each other.

'Don't be scared by these stories, Nikki. Southall is very safe,' Gaganjeet said brightly. 'Why don't you live here? It's full of our people.'

'Nikki's a proper modern girl,' Arvinder informed the others. 'You just can't tell because she's dressed like a good Punjabi girl today. Nikki, you should wear some bangles.'

Nikki kept an eye on Sheena, who appeared lost in thought. Her fingers fluttered at her collarbone where she touched her necklace as if making sure it was still there. Nikki took a step toward her and was about to ask if she was okay when Gaganjeet called her name.

'Nikki, are you looking for a husband? I might have someone for you.'

'Nope,' Nikki said.

'Why not? I haven't even told you about him yet.' Gaganjeet looked hurt. She blew her nose into a crumpled tissue. 'He has property,' she added.

'Does anyone have a story?' Nikki asked, stepping back to the front of the room. 'We're running out of time.'

'Okay, okay, no need to be impatient,' Arvinder said. 'She's still very bossy,' she muttered to the others.

'I've come with a story,' Tanveer said. She hesitated. 'It's a bit unusual though.'

'Believe me, every story told in this class is unusual,' Preetam said.

'I mean, this story has an element of something quite different,' Tanveer said. 'Quite shocking.'

'Well, I could not possibly be more shocked that I was last lesson,' Preetam said. She threw a dirty look at Arvinder.

'Tell us your story, Tanveer,' Nikki said before there was a quarrel.

'All right,' Tanveer said.

Meera and Rita

Everything had a designated place in Meera's home because she liked order. She and her husband even had a schedule for their nighttime intimacies. They did it on Tuesdays and Fridays, right before going to bed. The routine never changed. She would take off her clothes and lie down on the bed, staring up and counting the tiny pockmarks on the ceiling while her husband thrust into her, one hand gripping her right breast. There were no surprises, although Meera always made sure to say, 'Oh! Oh!' as if opening a present she didn't really like. After his final grunt, her husband would roll off her and instantly fall asleep. It was this part of their ritual that filled Meera with mixed emotions – relief that it was over and disgust that he did not clean himself afterwards. Wednesdays and Saturdays were for washing the sheets.

The detergent Meera used for this specific task was a special floral-scented powder. She kept it on the top shelf, above the regular detergent that was used for washing the clothes of her husband, their sons and her husband's younger brother, who also lived in this house. When the younger brother announced that he had fallen in love with a girl named Rita, and that he was going to marry her, Meera's first thought was, 'Where will Rita's place be?' Everything would have to be rearranged to fit this new bride into their lives. She shared this concern with her husband, who reminded her that she was the elder. 'You're allowed to give orders to her.' He said this generously, as if, after years of bossing her around, he was finally giving her the privilege of doing the same to somebody else.

It occurred to Meera to be kind to the new girl – to share with her rather than intimidate her. Meera had always wanted a daughter instead of the two noisy sons who trailed dirt all over her freshly vacuumed carpet and wrestled like baboons over everything. But at the wedding, jealousy overtook Meera. Rita was young and vibrant. The cropped blouse of her wedding lengha showed off the tight, honey-smooth skin of her midriff. In Meera's day, such outfits were considered scandalous. Meera felt a twinge of jealousy observing the way Rita's husband watched her during the wedding reception. His eyes roamed over her body, hungrily taking her in. 'Wait till they've been married a few years,' Meera told herself. 'His wonderment will wear off.' These thoughts were satisfying, yet Meera was aware that her husband had never looked at her like that, even in the early days.

After the newlyweds returned from their honeymoon, Meera gave Rita a tour of the house, making sure to point out where everything was – from the spare sofa covers to the winter jackets. Rita appeared to be paying attention but that night, after washing the dishes, she stacked the plates haphazardly and wedged the cutlery into every available space. Fuming, Meera plucked all of the dishes from the drainer and started over. It took her some time to finish the chores for the evening because Rita ignored her system of wiping down the tables and thoroughly sweeping beneath the counters to get rid of stray rice grains. When she finally finished, Meera was glad that it wasn't a Tuesday or a Friday – she was too tired and irate to put up with her husband's routine thrusts.

As she settled into bed, her husband already snoring soundly, Meera heard noises from the adjacent room. A giggle followed by a 'Shhh!' Then the unmistakable laughter of her brother-in-law. Meera pressed her ear against the wall. Rita's voice was commanding. 'Good,' she was saying. 'Keep going. Do it harder.' Meera recoiled from the wall. No wonder Rita didn't take instructions from her. She was too busy being the boss in her marriage. This won't do, *Meera thought. There could be only one ruler of this household and it was going to be her. She decided to be extra stern with Rita the next day. She would insist on taking Rita through another tour of the house and she would quiz her afterwards.* 'Where does the Windex go? What about the spare plastic bags from the grocery store?'

Through the walls, she could hear Rita's moans escalating now and the bed creaking to a frantic rhythmn. Didn't the girl realize that there were other people living in this house? Meera purposefully opened her room door and shut it loudly to remind the newlyweds of the way sound travelled in this home. The noise ceased for a few moments, but eventually it resumed, with Rita's moans swelling through the house like notes in an opera song. Meera burned with envy. She tiptoed out of the room and noticed with disappointment that Rita's bedroom door was shut. If it were just slightly ajar, she would be able to see what was going on. For some reason, she could not picture it. All she could see when she shut her eyes was Rita's smooth, flat tummy. Her mind's eye roved higher and she could picture the girl's firm, round breasts, her nipples flushed pink and alert. She pictured a pair of lips closing around those nipples and she was horrified to realize that those lips belonged to her. She chased the image out of her mind and blamed her tiredness for making her imagination run wild.

Meera sprang out of bed the next morning, ready to start and finish her chores. She passed Rita's room and noticed that the door was still shut. While Meera made tea, the sound of giggling drifted into the kitchen. Meera's sons tipped their heads up towards the ceiling and then they exchanged curious glances. 'Finish your breakfasts,' Meera ordered. Above her, Rita could be heard making demands again. 'Use your tongue,' she was saying. 'Yes, just like that.' Meera reddened. Again, she felt a strong tingling, a sensation that she was experiencing what Rita was asking for.

Rita finally came downstairs after her husband had left for work and the boys for school. The house was still. Meera threw herself into her chores. 'Can I help with anything?' Rita asked. Meera coldly replied that she didn't need any help. 'All right,' Rita said with a shrug. Meera could feel the younger woman watching her. She felt self-conscious.

'You must think I'm very uptight,' Meera said finally.

'I didn't say that.'

'But you're thinking it.'

'Are you?'

'No,' Meera said. She picked up the laundry basket and marched to the washing machine. 'I'm practical. I'm considerate of others. I'm not interested in hearing your nighttime activities.'

'We'll keep it down next time.' Rita's casualness infuriated Meera further. She searched the house for an impossible task for Rita to complete – perhaps washing the windows. The water spots always dried and left milky circles on the glass, making it look unclean. She was about to give her orders to Rita when she noticed that the laundry detergent was missing.

'Where is it?' she demanded. 'Didn't I tell you to keep the detergent on the shelf?' Rita calmly pointed out that the detergent was better placed in the storage closet with the other cleaning supplies.

'Rubbish,' said Meera. 'Is this how you expect to run a home?' She marched over to the storage closet and found the laundry detergent. In the closet her hand also brushed across a box that she had not seen before. She reached into the box and found it full of clay sticks. They were rounded at the ends, with a particular thickness. They resembled a part of a man's body that Meera had long forgotten about. She was about to return to Rita to confront her when she felt a breath on the back of her neck.

'I didn't think anyone would find those,' Rita whispered.

'I didn't think you would need these,' Meera replied, turning around. Her throat was dry but she managed to get the words out. It was rumoured that older women molded these sticks out of clay and baked them to keep aside for when they were feeling an urge that their husbands could no longer satisfy. 'You're too young,' Meera said.

Rita's laughter was like birdsong. 'Too young? Oh, Meera. There's so much I can teach you.'

'You? Teach me?' Meera retorted. 'I'm your elder.' But as she spoke, Rita had leaned forward and kissed her on the neck. Lightly, with her tongue, she traced Meera's collarbone. Meera gasped and shrank back into the closet as Rita brushed her lips against Meera's cheek and then finally, a full, deep kiss on the mouth. 'I can show you lots of things,' said Rita.

Here, Tanveer stopped. The colour in her cheeks was high. She pressed her lips together and waited. The room was so silent that Nikki could hear the air stirring through the heating vents.

'What happens next?' Nikki asked.

'They help each other out,' Tanveer said. She couldn't seem to meet the stares of the other women. Nikki nodded encouragingly at her. 'I haven't imagined that part yet.'

'It's definitely unusual,' Sheena said, clicking off the tape recorder. The story seemed to have roused her spirits. She sat upright and regarded Tanveer with curiosity. Tanveer bowed her head as if expecting to be chastised. 'Not in a bad way though,' Sheena assured her. 'Just different. Right, Nikki?'

'Right,' Nikki said, but she was aware of the thickening tension in the room. Arvinder was lost in thought. Gaganjeet had held a tissue to her nose to catch a sneeze that seemed frozen in place from the time Rita and Meera made intimate contact. Bibi nodded slowly and sagely, still processing the story's details. Then she spoke.

'This kind of thing is more common than you think,' she said. 'Two girls in my village were rumoured to serve each other as well, but I believe they just used their hands.'

These words unfroze Gaganjeet. There was a sudden flurry of activity in her seat – sneezing, coughing, zipping up a purse and picking up a walking stick. 'I really shouldn't be in class when I am unwell. My apologies,' she told Nikki. Her knees made a pistol-snap sound as she stood up and hurried out of the classroom.

'You've scared her,' Preetam accused Tanveer. 'Why would you write such a story? This isn't a class for women who do perverted things.' Tanveer dropped her head once again. Nikki felt a flash of irritation with Preetam. 'Tanveer has told a story about pleasure,' she said. 'I don't think it matters who Rita and Meera find that pleasure with.'

'It's unnatural. It may as well be science fiction,' Preetam said. 'And these two women have husbands. They're cheating.' She shot a pointed look at her mother.

'Maybe they consider it practice. Or something which enhances their bedroom lives,' Sheena said. 'In the next scene, their husbands return home and our Rita and Meera put on a little performance for their husbands. That's a good night for everyone.'

'Why do their husbands have to come home?' Arvinder asked. 'Maybe these women are content like this. We don't have to have men in all the stories.'

'Intimate relations are to be shared between men and women,' Preetam said. 'You're encouraging these sorts of stories as if all of us were dissatisfied with our husbands.'

'You're lucky your husband treated you well. Not everybody had that luxury,' Arvinder shot back.

'Oh, Mother, please. He provided for you didn't he? He gave you a roof over your head? He worked; he fathered your children. What more could you want?'

'I would have liked some of what the women in these stories are getting.'

'It sounds like you did get it,' Preetam muttered. 'Just not with the man you were married to.'

'Don't judge me, Preetam. Don't you dare,' Arvinder said.

Preetam's eyes widened. 'I don't have any secrets. If you accuse me of anything, you're just lying.'

'That's right. You don't have any secrets. You have no reason for any secrets. Your marriage was happy. Have you ever stopped to think about why that was? Because *I* let you have choices. I said no to the men who emerged from every corner as soon as you came of age. I didn't care if they said my daughter was pretty and could fetch a high dowry – I wanted you to have your pick.'

'Maybe we should stop for a while,' Nikki suggested, but Arvinder shushed her. 'Nikki, don't try to play the peacemaker. Some things need to be said and they're going to be said now.'

Arvinder returned her firm stare to Preetam. 'The adjustment period for some women was horrific. You weren't still a little girl like Tarampal. She was ten. You weren't like me – hastily mismatched with a man a foot shorter than you because both families were trying desperately to consolidate some drought-stricken land before it lost its value. Your father felt so small around me that his stick was limp all the time, and when I dared to complain once that we never had sex, he threatened to throw me out of the house.'

The outburst stunned everybody into silence. Nikki's mind raced. Of all the revelations hammering around in her mind, she could only focus on the most horrific. 'Tarampal was ten?' she whispered. The room was so silent her words seemed to echo across the walls.

Arvinder nodded. 'Her parents brought her to a pundit when she was ten and according to his palm reading, she was destined for nobody else but him. He told them that she would have five sons with him, and that they would all be wealthy landowners who would not only take care of her but also ensure the prosperity of their grandparents. They were so excited by these prospects that they disregarded his age – thirty years her senior – and got her married to him. They came to England about ten years later.'

'What happened to his predictions then? Tarampal only had daughters,' Sheena said.

'I imagine he blamed her for it. They always do.' Bitterness laced Arvinder's voice.

'Most of us were about that young but we weren't sent to sleep with our husbands until we were older,' Bibi said.

'How much older?' Nikki asked.

Bibi shrugged. 'Sixteen, seventeen? Who can remember? The next generation got away with marrying a bit later. Surely your mother was about eighteen or nineteen.'

'My mother went to university first,' Nikki said. 'She was twenty-two.' Even that seemed an impossibly young age to make such permanent choices.

'University.' Arvinder looked impressed. 'No wonder your parents raised you in proper London. They're modern.'

'I've never considered my parents modern,' Nikki commented. She considered all the arguments about short skirts, talking to boys, drinking, being *too British*. Pleasing them had been an endless battle that she was still fighting.

'But they were. They knew how to speak English before they came here. We built Southall because we didn't know how to be British.'

'Better to keep to our own kind, or that's the idea at least,' Sheena said. 'My mother was so nervous coming to England. She'd heard stories of Indian kids being beaten up at school. My father arrived here first and convinced her that Southall was a place with our kind of people and we would fit right in.'

'If you had any problems in this new country, your neighbours would rush to your side and bring you money, food, whatever you need. That's the beauty of being surrounded by your community,' Arvinder said. 'But if you had a problem with your husband, who would help you to leave him? Nobody wanted to be involved in other families' personal affairs. "You should be grateful," they said if you complained. "This country is spoiling you."' She directed a stern look at Preetam. 'I gave you all the happiness I couldn't have. You loved your husband, your marriage. Good for you. I *survived* mine.'

Once the last woman had trailed out of class, Nikki hurried from the building, a clear plan in her head. The high street was bright and warm with the lights from shop windows. The Sweet Shop owner beckoned to Nikki from the doorway. 'Gulab jamun and barfi all fifty per cent off,' he offered. At the newsagents next door, a large poster announced the arrival of three Bollywood actors whose faces and names Nikki vaguely recognized from Mindi's film collection. Her cheeks burned from the winter chill. Droplets of misty rain clung to her hair.

Number 16 Ansell Road was a compact brick structure with a paved driveway, identical to most other houses on this street. A strong wind current carried the scent of cumin through the streets. Nikki knocked on the door. She heard the rapid thumping of steps and then the door cracked open. Through the chain loop, Tarampal's eyes peered out into the world. Nikki saw the recognition, then the flare of anger in her eyes.

'Please,' Nikki said. She braced her hands against the door to keep Tarampal from slamming it shut. 'I just want to talk to you for a moment.'

'I have nothing to say to you,' Tarampal said.

'You don't have to say anything. I just want to apologize.'

Tarampal remained still. 'You already said sorry in your note.'

'So you received the tapes?'

The door clicked shut. The hairs on Nikki's arms stood straight against the chilly breeze. It began to drizzle. She took cover under the awning and knocked rapidly on the door. 'Can I just talk to you for a moment?' From the corner of her eye, she noticed Tarampal's figure in the living room window. She went to the window and started knocking on it. 'Tarampal, please.'

Tarampal flitted out of Nikki's view. Nikki carried on rapping her knuckles against the glass, aware that she was causing a commotion. It worked. The main door flung open and Tarampal stormed out onto the front steps. 'What do you think you're doing? The neighbours can see you,' Tarampal hissed. She ushered Nikki into the house and shut the door behind them. 'Sarab Singh will tell his wife I've got lunatics visiting my house.'

Nikki didn't know who Sarab Singh was, or why his wife mattered. She cast a glance down the hallway. This was an immaculate home, with the strong smell of varnish suggesting a recent renovation. She recalled the langar hall ladies mentioning damages to Tarampal's property – clearly she had fixed up the place since. 'Are your children here? Your grandchildren?'

'I have daughters, all married. They live with their husbands.'

'I didn't realize you were all alone,' Nikki said.

'Jagdev found a place near his new job but he still visits at weekends. He was the one who read your note to me.'

Who was Jagdev? Nikki had trouble keeping up. 'I'm not familiar with a lot of people in this community—' she began.

'Oh yes, you're a proper London girl,' Tarampal said. A look of scorn crossed her face when she said the city's name. In her own home, she had a haughty confidence. She was still wearing a widow's outfit but an updated version of the white tunic – the neckline bare and the waist cinched to show her figure.

The rain was spitting against the windows now. 'Could I trouble you for a cup of tea?' Nikki asked. 'It's very cold out there and I've come all this way.'

It was a small victory when Tarampal grudgingly said, 'Yes.' It would be easier to convince Tarampal to return to the class over tea. Nikki followed Tarampal into the kitchen, where granite counters ran the length of the room beneath a sleek row of cupboards. The electric stove was the state-of-the-art model that Mum coveted, with a white coil seemingly drawn onto the surface, the heat filling it instantly in a digital glow. Tarampal had switched it on and was rummaging through her cupboard. She produced a dented stainless steel pot and an old cookie tin that rattled with the sound of seeds and spices. Nikki had to suppress a smile. If Mum had an ultramodern kitchen, she would probably still store dal in old ice-cream containers and use her simple pot for boiling tea leaves as well.

'You want sugar?' Tarampal asked.

'No, thank you.'

The kitchen became briefly awash in headlights. 'That's probably Sarab Singh leaving for his night shift,' Tarampal said as she added the milk. 'I don't think he likes being home alone. A few years ago when Kulwinder and Maya went to India for a holiday, he worked double shifts every evening. God knows he needs even more distraction now.'

'Kulwinder lives there?' Nikki asked. She went to the living room and looked through the window. The driveway of the opposite home matched

Tarampal's.

'Yes. You came to Maya's wedding *sangeet* didn't you? It was there. I thought they should have rented a hall because there were so many guests but . . .' Tarampal threw her hands up as if to say it wasn't up to her. Nikki had no time to correct the assumption that she had been a wedding guest. Tarampal had returned to the kitchen and was bringing out two cups of steaming tea. Nikki followed her.

'Thank you for this,' Nikki said, taking her cup. 'I don't have homemade chai everyday.' The chai from the market stall earlier had been too thick and sugary.

'You British girls prefer Earl Grey,' Tarampal said. She wrinkled her nose.

'Oh no,' Nikki said. 'I enjoy a cup of chai. I just don't live at home.' The aroma of cloves made her surprisingly nostalgic for the afternoons spent visiting relatives in India. An idea came to her. 'Would you be able to write down the recipe for me?'

'How would I do that? I can't write,' Tarampal said.

'Maybe we could work on that together. If you came back to the classes.'

Tarampal set down her teacup. 'I don't have anything to learn from you or those widows. It was a mistake signing up in the first place.'

'Let's talk about it.'

'No need.'

'If you're concerned about people finding out about the stories—'

At the mention of the stories, Tarampal nostrils flared. 'You think those stories aren't a big deal, but you have no idea what they can do to people's minds.'

'Stories aren't responsible for corrupting people,' Nikki argued. 'They give people a chance to experience new things.'

'Experience new things?' Tarampal snorted. 'Don't give me that. Maya was a big reader as well. I saw her reading a book one day – the cover had a picture of a man kissing a woman's neck outside a castle. On the cover!'

'I don't think books are a bad influence.'

'Well, you're wrong. Thank goodness *my* daughters weren't like that. We pulled them out of school before they could get any funny ideas.'

Tarampal's sternness was frightening. 'How old were your daughters when they got married?' Nikki asked.

'Sixteen,' Tarampal said. 'All were sent to India when they were twelve, to learn to cook and sew. The matches were made there and then they returned here for a few more years of school.'

'What if they hadn't agreed to the matches? They were so young.'

Tarampal gave a dismissive wave. 'There's no such thing as disagreeing. Only accepting and adjusting. I had to do that when my marriage was arranged. And when my daughters' time came, they knew their duties.'

This interpretation of marriage sounded like an endless list of chores. 'It's rather unexciting,' Nikki said. 'I would think that girls who grew up in England would want romance and passion.'

'*Hai*, Nikki. That just isn't how we did things. *We* didn't have these choices.' Tarampal almost sounded wistful.

'So when it came time for your daughters to get married, you wanted them to have no choice as well?' Nikki asked, knowing she was on dangerous ground but not knowing how to tread lightly on this subject. The softness in Tarampal's gaze vanished.

'Nowadays, girls run around with three or four men at the same time, deciding when *they* want it to happen. You think that's right?'

'What do you mean?' Nikki asked, leaning toward Tarampal.

Tarampal looked away. 'I didn't say you were like that.'

'No – what you said: deciding when they want it to happen. When they want *what* to happen?'

'Oh, don't make me spell it out, Nikki. Girls here are spoiled by their choices. A man can't just storm into a room and take off a young girl's clothes and tell her to spread her legs. Somebody at the temple told me that there's a law in England against a husband doing it to his wife if she doesn't want to. His own wife! Why does a man get punished for doing this? Because the English don't value marriage like we do.'

'It's punishable because it's wrong, even if they're married. It's rape,'

Nikki said. It was another one of those words surrounded by such taboo that she had never learned its Punjabi equivalent, so she said it in English. No wonder Tarampal resented the other widows. Although they appeared reserved like her, their storytelling went against everything she had been trained to believe about marriage.

'That's what husbands did back then. We didn't complain. Being married is about growing up.'

At the corners of Tarampal's eyes, fine lines were just beginning to emerge. Her hair was still dark and thick, unlike the white buns worn by the other widows. She was young, yet she'd been a wife for three-quarters of her life. This detail struck Nikki hard. 'How old were you?' she asked.

'Ten,' Tarampal said. Her face shone with a pride that made Nikki's stomach roil.

'Weren't you afraid? Weren't your parents afraid?'

'Nothing to be afraid of. It was such good fortune, being destined for Kemal Singh, the Pundit himself,' Tarampal said. 'Our horoscopes matched, you see, so there was no denying our match even though there was a huge age difference.'

'Was there time for you to get to know each other?' Nikki asked. 'Before the wedding night, I mean.'

Tarampal took a longer pause to sip her tea and in that time, Nikki thought she noticed a cloud cross her face. 'I'm sorry. I shouldn't press,' Nikki said. 'It's obviously personal.'

'It doesn't happen like that,' Tarampal said. 'It is much simpler and you will want it to be over as soon as it starts. The romance, the consideration for each other's needs – that comes later.'

'So it came, then?' Nikki said. She wasn't sure why she felt so relieved but her sentiments were mirrored in Tarampal's features. An unexpected smile twitched on her lips. 'Yes,' she said, her cheeks high with colour. 'All of the good things came later.' She cleared her throat and turned her head away, clearly embarrassed that Nikki had seen her reminiscing.

'What's wrong with writing about them then? Sharing them?' Nikki asked gently.

'*Hai*, Nikki. Those stories are vulgar. Why must these private things be written for everybody to see? You're defending these stories because you're unmarried; you don't know anything yet. You must be picturing it with somebody – you have a boy in mind, do you?'

'Uh, me? No.' Tarampal would probably chase Nikki out and bleach the seats if she knew that Nikki had been with several men already, none of whom she had ever considered marrying. Then there was Jason. Last night, he had come to the pub and she had invited him back to her flat after her shift. The floorboards had creaked dangerously with their shifting steps as they tumbled onto her bed. Afterwards, Nikki had suggested that they spend their next evening in Jason's flat. 'My place isn't an option,' he'd said. 'I've got a flatmate who's always there and the thinnest walls in the world.' A catch in his voice suggested this was an excuse. She wasn't dwelling on it. She couldn't. She liked him too much.

A moment passed. Nikki turned towards the window, looking at Kulwinder's home. The curtains were drawn shut and the porch light was off, giving it the shadowy appearance of a house in mourning. Turning back to face Tarampal, Nikki's gaze landed on an item on the fridge: a Fem Fighters magnet clip.

'Is that yours?' Nikki asked, surprised, pointing to it.

'No, of course not. It was Maya's,' Tarampal said. 'She left it here. Kulwinder and Sarab came through and took everything, of course – all of her clothes, her books, her photos. All that was left after they came through were the little things – a paperclip here, a sock there. This magnet as well.'

'She lived here?'

Tarampal stared at her strangely. 'Yes, she was married to Jagdev. How can you not know this? Weren't you friends with Maya?'

'No.'

'How do you know Kulwinder then?'

'I responded to an advertisement for the job.'

'I thought you were one of Maya's friends. I thought Kulwinder offered you the job as a favour.'

Nikki looked at the magnet again. No wonder Tarampal thought they were friends; they clearly had a few things in common. There was such contempt in Tarampal's voice every time she mentioned Maya, yet they had been practically related. 'So Jagdev is your nephew?'

'He's a family friend from Birmingham. No relation. He came to London to look for work after he got laid off from his job. Kulwinder insisted on introducing him to Maya because she thought they'd be suitable for each other.' Tarampal sighed. 'But she was wrong. Maya was a very unstable girl.'

Jagdev: the son Tarampal always wanted. Nikki could see her relishing the role of possessive mother-in-law. She wished there were some way to teleport Mindi into this conversation, to show her what she was getting herself into. Tarampal wasn't even related to Jagdev and she could hardly hide her disdain. What were Mindi's chances of winning approval with a real mother-in-law? 'So it was set up then? How long did they have to date?'

'Three months,' Tarampal said.

'Three *months?*' Even Mindi and Mum would balk at that time frame. 'I thought Maya was a modern girl. Why the hurry?'

'The widows didn't tell you all about this?'

'No,' Nikki said.

Tarampal sat back and eyed her. 'I find that surprising. All they do is gossip.'

'They're not gossips,' Nikki said, rushing to the widows' defense. For all her frustration at being excluded from conversations about Maya, Nikki admired Sheena's protectiveness. 'Sheena's especially loyal to her. I suppose these stories get distorted and she wants to prevent that from happening.'

'There's only one story,' Tarampal said. 'Sheena's like Kulwinder – she doesn't want to believe the truth. *That's* the truth.' She pointed at the back door. A small window in the door provided a view of the garden but it was dark. Again, Tarampal was assuming Nikki knew this truth. She looked at the Fem Fighters magnet clip; if Maya were alive, maybe she'd be teaching the women's classes and finding some way to sneak in erotic stories under Kulwinder's nose. What was this terrible fate that nobody wanted to discuss? If Nikki wanted to know more, she had to play along. 'Well, I did hear some rumours that Maya was not very honourable,' she said.

'Maya was seeing an English boy, did Sheena tell you that? *Hanh*, she wanted to marry him. Came home with a ring on her finger and everything. Kulwinder put her foot down and told Maya she had a choice – marry the boy and leave her family forever or leave the boy and have her family.'

Leave the family, Nikki thought immediately. *Good riddance to old-fashioned parents*. Then she was struck by a sobering memory of her first few weeks alone in her flat. It had been lonely enough without giving up her family forever. 'And a forced marriage was part of the deal?' Nikki asked.

'An *arranged* marriage by the people who had her best interests at heart,' Tarampal replied flatly. 'We all cared for her, you know. I was a close friend of Kulwinder's and I had seen Maya grow up. We knew what she needed.'

'Were they compatible, then?' Nikki asked. *A good blood-type match?* she refrained from asking.

'Sometimes Maya and Jaggi got along but they fought a lot too. Most of their arguments were in English but this body language, everybody can understand.' Tarampal puffed up her chest and tilted her head upwards to challenge an invisible adversary. 'One day she purposely said in Punjabi, "We should get our own place." She wanted me to hear it.'

Nikki sensed a bit of excitement in Tarampal's reenactment. Auntie Geeta got similarly carried away whenever she arrived at Mum's place with fresh gossip. 'She just wants to connect to people, the poor thing,' Mum always said in her defence, though Nikki knew Mum found it unsettling, this eagerness to vilify people for entertainment's sake. Yet Nikki found it just as difficult to suppress her curiosity. 'Did they move then?'

'She was very unstable, you know.' It was the second time Tarampal had mentioned this. 'The question is, why did she want so much privacy? In our community, girls move in with their in-laws once they're married – since I was offering very reasonable rent, Jaggi decided to stay here and this became their marital home. See, Maya didn't want to accept her life.

She was trying to live as if she had married that *gora*.'

She thought she could make it work, Nikki thought sadly. 'So they stayed here?' she asked, looking around. Even a contemporary home like this one would feel confining to a woman trapped in an unhappy marriage. 'I'm guessing Maya wasn't happy about it.'

'Not at all. Then Jaggi began confiding in me. He suspected that she was having an affair. Maya put on perfume in the morning before going to work in the city. She stayed late at the office and was driven home by a man from her office. Who would drive all the way to Southall just to drop off a girl unless they were getting something in exchange?'

'A friend. A kind colleague,' Nikki said.

Tarampal shook her head. 'Nonsense.' Her pronouncement was absolute. 'Maya and Jaggi had a big quarrel about it. She packed her bags and went home to Kulwinder's place.'

Here Tarampal paused and stared out the window. Nikki followed her gaze. The plain curtains in Kulwinder's bay windows were drawn tightly together. What happened when Maya decided to leave? Nikki imagined Kulwinder's lips set in that stern line as she shook her head and ordered Maya to do her duty.

'And then what?' Nikki asked.

'Maya was home for about a week, and then she was sent back. Things were peaceful at first but it didn't take long for the fighting to resume once she returned.' Tarampal sighed. 'You can't expect the world from your husband. The sooner you girls understand that, the fewer disappointments you'll face.'

Mindi's dating profile picture flashed into Nikki's mind, that shimmer of hope in her eyes. Nikki felt a sudden relief on Mindi's behalf. She had far more control over her situation than Maya had. Although Nikki still had her doubts about Mindi meeting the women of the families first, at least she had choices. She could say no, and she certainly wasn't going to be bullied into a three-month courtship. Mum would never allow it. 'My sister is looking for a husband but she's being selective,' Nikki informed Tarampal. 'She wants to avoid being let down.'

'Good luck to your sister, then,' Tarampal said. 'Let's hope she does not end up losing her mind like Maya.'

A silence stretched between them, during which Nikki's eyes scanned every available space in the house to avoid Tarampal's intense stare. The kitchen opened out onto a living room with a plush suede sofa facing a modern stone fireplace. A row of three framed wedding portraits lined the wall space above the mantel. Each bejewelled bride wore a large gold hoop on her nostril and a pattern of sequined bindis that studded the arch of her eyebrows. The overwhelming jewellery partially obscured their facial expressions.

'How did Maya die?' Nikki asked softly.

'She took her own life,' Tarampal said.

'How?' It was a morbid question but Nikki had to know.

'The way women in our culture do it when they are filled with shame,' Tarampal said. She blinked and turned away. 'With fire.'

Nikki stared at Tarampal in horror. 'Fire?'

Tarampal nodded at the back door. 'There is still a patch of burnt grass in the garden. I don't go out there any more.'

So that was what Tarampal had pointed to earlier. It was too much to take in. The revelation left Nikki slightly short of breath. From the corner of her vision, the back garden was shrouded in shadows but she adjusted her seat so she could cut it out completely. How could Tarampal stand it? No wonder the house had been so lavishly remodelled – an attempt to move on from the memory of Maya's ghastly suicide. Nikki felt a lump in her throat as she thought of Kulwinder and Sarab living across the street from the site of their daughter's death. 'Was anybody else home at the time?' she asked. *Surely somebody could have stopped her*, she thought, with a fierce and desperate longing to save Maya from herself.

'I was at the temple. Jaggi was halfway up the road. He had found some messages on Maya's phone from the man she had been sleeping with. He told her he wanted to divorce her. This sent Maya into a panic. She didn't want to be divorced. She was afraid of never being able to face the community or her parents again. Maya was in hysterics and begged him to stay.

Jaggi stormed out of the house, saying "this is over." That was when she ran out into the back garden, doused herself in petrol and lit the match.'

'Oh my goodness,' Nikki said. She shut her eyes but the violent scene played out in her mind. Tarampal kept on speaking but her voice sounded far away. 'That's the problem with having too much imagination, Nikki. Girls begin to desire too much.'

This flawed and rigid logic was maddening. Nikki didn't have any idea what Maya looked like but she pictured a younger, slimmer version of Kulwinder, wearing jeans and her hair in a loose ponytail. A modern girl. The callous words of those langar hall ladies returned to her. *A girl with no honour*. If people in the community were ready to brand her as such, she probably saw no reason to keep living.

'Poor Kulwinder and Sarab,' Nikki said.

'Poor Jaggi,' Tarampal said. 'You should have seen him at the funeral – clutching his hair, falling to the ground, pleading for her to come back, despite everything she did to him. He suffered much more.'

Surely grief wasn't a competition. 'I'm sure it was difficult for everyone, including yourself,' Nikki said.

'It was *more* difficult for Jaggi,' Tarampal insisted. 'Think of what Kulwinder and Sarab have been saying about him: that he drove Maya to it, that he never took care of her. Why should his reputation suffer?'

Discomfort swelled in Nikki's stomach. Where exactly had the conversation taken this turn? Less than an hour ago, she had rushed across the Broadway thinking that she might convince Tarampal to return to the classes but she was more wilful than Nikki had expected.

'You have a lovely home,' she said quickly before Tarampal's rant could spiral any further into this dark territory of honour.

'Thank you,' Tarampal said.

'My mum wants to do some remodelling,' Nikki said. 'Do you have the contact information of your guy?' Mum would like that – a Punjabi contractor, someone who would understand her need to make the house look luxurious for Mindi's future wedding.

Tarampal nodded and left the kitchen. It was a relief to be left alone.

Nikki took in a deep breath and finished her tea, gulping down even the gritty remnants of seeds and leaves that had escaped through the sieve. The house was silent except for the chorus of rain outside. She plucked the Fem Fighters magnet from the fridge and rolled it in her palm. To think that she had handed out hundreds of these at a Hyde Park rally and that somewhere in that pulsing summer crowd, Maya might have been present.

Tarampal returned with a brochure for a contractor. Attached at the top was a name card with the contractor's name in gilded raised lettering: RICK PETTON HOME RENOVATIONS

'He's English,' Nikki said with surprise.

'I had Jaggi help me with communicating,' Tarampal said. 'He's back in Birmingham but he visits every so often.'

'Like a good son,' Nikki said.

Tarampal flinched. 'He's *not* my son,' she said.

'Of course,' Nikki said. What a punishing existence it must have been for Tarampal with her failure to produce a son for the community's spiritual leader. She was sorry that she mentioned it. A look of unease lingered on Tarampal's face as Nikki picked up her satchel.

Passing the living room on her way out, Nikki could feel the stares of Tarampal's daughters from their portraits on the wall. Their eyes glistened with youth. It was difficult to discern their emotions beneath the heavy coat of make-up and wedding jewellery. Was it excitement? Nikki wondered. Or fear?

Chapter Nine

Nikki stretched her leg and pinched the edge of the curtains between her toes to drag them across the window. Jason stirred at her side. 'Leave them open,' he mumbled.

'Such an exhibitionist,' Nikki teased. 'I'm just trying to keep the sunlight out.' It was late morning. Last night, all night, they had been up reading stories to each other with pauses in between to reenact the best scenes.

Jason gave her a light smack on the bum. 'Naughty,' he said. He reached over her and drew the curtains shut. Dropping his head back to the pillow, he landed a wet, delicious kiss on Nikki's ear. She sank back into his chest and pulled the covers over both their heads.

Jason shifted and rolled to his side. There was a rustling sound. He returned with a slightly crumpled sheet of paper. 'There was once a village tailor . . .' Jason narrated.

'We already did the tailor one.'

'I'm writing the sequel,' Jason said. He slipped his hands under the sheets and ran them down the length of her back. Nikki shivered. Jason brushed his lips against her neck, travelling up and down its length with light, dusty kisses. He reached between her legs and began tracing his fingers in circles along her inner thighs, inching upwards and then drawing away. Nikki sank back into the softness of her bed.

Charred flesh.

The image flashed into her mind so suddenly that Nikki sat up. Startled, Jason jolted away. 'What happened?' he asked. His face was so full of concern that Nikki felt foolish.

'Nothing,' she said. 'I must have had a bad dream last night and it came back to me.' Fragments of this dream remained in her consciousness. She could catch a faint whiff of burning and the wide-open mouth of an anguished scream. She shook her head. Three times since her visit to Tarampal she had dreamt of Maya.

Jason placed a light kiss on her collarbone and rolled back to his side, keeping an arm wrapped around her waist. 'Do you want to talk about it?'

Nikki shook her head. It had been a week since her visit with Tarampal and she had tried to forget it. She succeeded only partially – snatches of conversation no longer drifted in her mind, but certain images shot into her view without warning.

'Was it a nightmare, or a bad dream,' Jason asked.

'What's the difference?'

'A nightmare is scary. A bad dream can be a little . . . bad' Nikki turned to see a smile playing on Jason's lips. 'Like the story of a woman who, despite her best efforts to keep her house under control, can't seem to find time to enjoy her husband.'

Nikki recognized the beginnings of a widow's story. Jason continued. 'She decides to go ahead and hire a maid without her husband knowing. The maid enters the house after her husband goes to work and leaves before he comes home. Now the woman is free to do whatever she wants during the day because she has no more obligations – no school pick-ups, no grocery shopping. She spends her whole day at the spa and exploring all those sights of London she's never had a chance to see.'

'The plan is working out well,' Nikki said. 'Until the husband returns to the house one day because he's forgotten some papers. He sees the maid dusting the tops of cabinets. "Who are you?" he asks.'

'She spins around and sees a tall man advancing towards her,' Jason said. '"Please, don't be angry," the maid says. She explains the wife's plan. "She just wants some time to herself. I'm helping her."'

'The man doesn't know how to react. He stares at the maid, wondering how long this has been going on. The maid can't help but notice that he's very attractive. "I can do everything your wife can do," she says softly, walking towards him. "I've ironed all of these shirts.' She touches his collar. "I've bought a new set of shaving razors." She strokes his cheek and feels a light prickle of stubble. "What else does she do?"'

'The maid doesn't wait for him to answer. She unzips his pants and out springs his man hammer,' Jason said.

Nikki burst out laughing. 'Is that what you call it?'

'It's quite the tool.'

'*You're* quite the tool,' Nikki said, giving Jason a shove.

'I walked into that one. All right, his instrument?'

'That implies something clinical,' Nikki said. 'Like a surgical instrument.'

'Or something that makes sweet, sweet music,' Jason offered.

'Try a vegetable.'

'Out springs his parsnip.'

'Think of a more consistent shape.'

'You're very bossy about this vocabulary.'

'I want to get it right.'

'All right, his zucchini.'

'They're called courgettes here.'

'Oh, I like that. It sounds sophisticated now, like a corvette.' Jason said.

'His courgette feels silky to her touch,' Nikki continued.

Jason frowned. 'The last time I cooked using courgettes, they were rough and bumpy before being peeled.'

'Surely you've encountered a smooth courgette.'

'Nope.'

'Where do you shop?'

'You've lost me.'

'How about now?' Nikki asked. She threw leg over Jason's side and straddled him.

'Now I've completely forgotten everything I ever knew,' Jason said, staring at Nikki's bare breasts.

'They have sex in every room of the house. The man feels terrible afterwards and confides to his wife. To his surprise, she looks pleased. "I thought that might happen," she says. Turns out she had hidden the husband's papers so he'd have to come home to look for them. She planned for the maid and her husband to meet. Now she wants to watch them while they have sex. It turns her on.'

'Where can I find a girl like that?' Jason joked.

'Close your eyes,' Nikki ordered. She lowered her face towards his and kissed him, breathing in the musty smell of his hair. 'She's watching us now,' she murmured into his ear. 'Are we turning her on?'

Jason looked up. 'Yeah.' A ring trilled through the flat, sending a jolt through both of them. Jason's smile suddenly vanished as he reached past Nikki for his phone, which was in his jeans pocket under the bed. 'Sorry,' he mumbled, looking at the screen. 'I have to answer this.' He stepped into his pants and pulled them up.

It could be work, Nikki thought, but it was Sunday, and Jason's face looked grimmer than somebody being chased by a demanding boss. This had happened twice already. A sudden phone call and then Jason was out so quickly that she could practically see the dust he kicked up as he exited the room. 'Who is that?' she asked last time. She didn't want to seem nosy, but the call had interrupted a movie, when he insisted on leaving his phone on vibrate. He had left the theatre for twenty minutes. 'Just some work stuff I have to take care of,' Jason had said.

Nikki strained to listen now but Jason's voice was muffled and hushed. He was in the bathroom. She tiptoed into the corridor to listen but a floorboard creaked, betraying her presence. She hurried into the kitchen and busied herself making breakfast for the two of them.

'I'm out of coffee,' Nikki said when Jason emerged from his hiding place. He looked tired. She tried not to notice. He sat down at the table and put his head in his hands. Nikki pulled out a chair next to him and squeezed his shoulder. 'Who was it?'

'Just work,' he said. Nikki watched him hastily putting his clothes on, his face cloudy and lost in thought.

'I was going to make us omelettes,' Nikki said, opening the fridge. 'Do you want two eggs again or just one?'

'That's fine,' Jason said.

'Two eggs it is,' Nikki said.

Jason looked up. 'Oh hey, sorry.' He smiled. 'Just one egg would be great. Thank you.'

Nikki nodded and turned to the stove. 'So, I was thinking we should try to catch that French film. I'd still like to see it.'

'Good idea,' Jason said. 'Is it still playing?'

'That cinema runs the same films for ages,' Nikki said. 'I think that weekend was its first showing. They screened a documentary about slums in Calcutta there a couple of years ago. My parents went to see it three times over six months.'

'Thank goodness for people who like re-watching movies then. They're keeping that cinema going.'

'My parents had very different tastes, though. Dad liked his historical or current affairs shows and Mum only watched Indian dramas or Hollywood rom-coms. They found something that they could both enjoy in this film.' She smiled at the memory of Mum and Dad coming home from another matinee of the same film, their cheeks shining like new lovers.

'It sounds like they made the whole arranged marriage thing really work,' Jason commented.

'They did,' Nikki said and she was surprised at this realization. Her eyes became hot with tears. 'Now, do you want cheese in your omelette?'

'Sure,' Jason said. His phone rang again. Nikki turned around to see him frowning at the screen. 'I need to take this again, Nikki. Sorry.' He hurried out of the flat. Nikki fought the urge to tiptoe to the doorway to eavesdrop on his conversation. She could hear him pacing the cramped corridor outside. When he returned, he attempted another reassuring smile but it fell flat.

'What's going on?' Nikki asked.

'It's just a work thing,' Jason said. 'Kind of hard to explain. Things are going to be busy for a while.'

Nikki served the eggs and they both ate in silence. Something had descended heavily on the flat. Had Jason sensed her attempt to keep him around for breakfast so she could ask – casually of course – where their relationship was going? Perhaps it was too soon, but they had been seeing each other nearly every night since that first date. Intense beginnings were exciting but they fizzled out quickly and Nikki wanted more than a fling.

Jason finished his breakfast and then left with another round of apologies and promises to call Nikki later. *He has a demanding job. He had to leave for an important work thing*, Nikki told herself, testing out the line for veracity. It wasn't convincing.

Nikki descended into O'Reilly's that evening to find a young woman she had never seen before standing at the bar. Her brown hair was pulled back in a ponytail and her make-up was so heavy that her eyes looked drawn on. She gave Nikki a quick smile and then returned to twisting the end of her ponytail in her finger. 'Hello,' Nikki said.

'I'm Jo,' the girl said with no other explanation.

Sam emerged from the back room. 'Oh good – Nikki you've met Jo, Jo this is Nikki. I'm training Jo to work at the bar so I'll need you in the kitchen this evening.'

'All right,' Nikki said. If she had known of this arrangement in advance, she would have prepared herself to spend the evening with those two buffoons in the kitchen, but it seemed that nothing was working out her way today. Heading for the kitchen, she tossed a glance at Jo. She was an attractive young woman, and the snickering Russians were sure to comment again on Sam's dodgy hiring judgment. Jo looked disinterested in anything Sam was saying as he leaned close to her. *Come on, Sam*, Nikki thought. She wished Olive were here but it was half-term holidays and she was in Greece with her teacher friends. She pulled out her phone and sent her a quick text:

London sucks at the moment. When do you come back??

The reply was a photo of a pristine and sunny beach landscape. Nikki wrote back:

Stop rubbing it my face

I'd like to rub this in MY face hahahaha

A moment later, a picture appeared on Nikki's phone. It was a shirtless, tanned man on the beach with such defined stomach muscles, they looked hand drawn. His arm was around Olive's bare waist and her cheek was pressed against his chest. One of her eyes was squeezed shut in a wink. Bring me one, Nikki wrote back.

The kitchen was a flurry of activity and foreign language when Nikki entered it. The Russians called out to each other and Sanja flitted between them. The moment they noticed Nikki, their voices dropped. They shared a smirk. Nikki could tell from a slight tension of recognition in Sanja's face that she had heard and understood their joke. Outside the kitchen, the pub rocked with applause and laughter. It was another trivia event and the quizmaster was warming up the crowd with a bit of stand-up comedy.

Garry appeared at Nikki's side. 'You didn't hear me?' he asked. 'I said take these to Table Five.'

'Sorry,' Nikki said.

'You have to listen,' he said. 'This is kitchen, not Sam's office.' He made a wiggling motion with his hips.

'Look, Garry. I think it's really inappropriate of you to imply—'

Garry walked off before Nikki could complete her sentence. She took the order out, her cheeks burning with indignation. She passed Jo, who was busy checking her phone. 'I think you've got customers,' Nikki said. Jo scowled back.

On her return back, she saw Sanja at the door. 'Don't bother with them,' she said. 'They're arseholes. They want to work at the bar because they think they'll impress girls that way.'

'I don't think working at the bar will help them in that department.'

'Me, I prefer the kitchen work. But maybe I'm better than the new girl.'

'Anyone's better than that,' Nikki said. 'I don't know what Sam's thinking.' Noticing the line of cleavage that Jo exposed as she leaned towards a customer, Nikki thought, *or maybe I do*.

Nikki returned to the kitchen and focused on the orders, wishing for the night to pass quickly. She wanted to return to her flat and just curl up on her bed. The kitchen clattered with noise and each time the door swung open, she could hear the quizmaster's booming questions.

'Native to Australia, this amphibian mammal lays eggs.'

'Which actress played Marta in The Sound of Music?'

'What did Jesus send his disciples out with? A) Sticks and stones B) Bread and Money C) Scrip D) Staves.'

What's a scrip? Nikki wondered as she pulled open the dishwasher door. A burst of scalding steam rushed to her face. She yelped and shoved the door close. Sanja rushed to her side. 'Here, open your eyes and let me see.'

Nikki blinked a few times to clear her blurry view of Sanja's face. 'You be careful with that thing,' Sanja said, tossing a look of contempt at the dishwasher. 'The alarm beeps before the dishes are dried. I should have warned you.'

Garry called out to Sanja. She snapped back at him in rapid Russian. 'Thanks,' Nikki said. She opened her eyes. 'And thanks for standing up for me.'

'You don't know what I said.'

'It sounded like the Russian equivalent of "fuck off."'

'Correct,' Sanja said.

Sanja's kindness helped the remaining hours of Nikki's shift pass a little more quickly. The trivia crowd was good-natured tonight, even after Steve with the Racist Grandfather answered a question about North Korea with, 'Me love you long time!' Yet by the time Nikki's shift was over, her anger at Sam still had not subsided. She marched to Sam's office and rapped on his door. 'Come in,' he called.

Nikki entered. 'The dishwasher's got issues,' she said.

'Yeah I know,' Sam said, not looking up from a spread of papers on his desk. 'I'll get it fixed soon.'

'You need to get it fixed sooner than that,' Nikki said. Her voice wavered.

Now Sam looked up. 'I'll fix it when I've got the money, Nikki. If you haven't noticed, things are tight round here.'

'It's a hazard,' she replied. 'Besides, if you haven't got the money, why are you hiring new staff? What's the deal with this Jo, Sam?'

It was satisfying to see Sam look so taken aback. 'Am I supposed to check all my hiring decisions with you?'

'I think I'd have a more professional opinion than you.'

'Is that right?' Sam asked wryly.

'Do you know what those idiots in the kitchen have been saying about me? That you hired me because I seduced you. Is that right, Sam? Because I sure don't remember it that way. Here I was thinking I got this job because I was a hard worker but—'

'Nikki, I'm going to stop you right there.' Sam's tone was infuriatingly calm now but distinct worry lines scored his forehead. 'I haven't hired Jo. She's my niece – my sister's kid. Remember my weekend in Leeds? It was to bring Jo back down here. I'm training her as a favour. She just turned eighteen and has no idea what she wants to do with her life. She and my sister haven't been getting along very well, so I thought I'd step in.'

That sounded like something Sam would do. 'That still doesn't excuse—' Nikki began.

Sam waved away Nikki's words. 'I should have talked to you about that whole asking you out thing. I was too embarrassed. I had no idea those guys were giving you a hard time about it. I'll have a word with them.'

'You don't have to do that.'

'Won't it make things easier if I tell them to stop?'

'I'd rather they hear it from me,' Nikki said. 'If you rush out there to defend me, it'll just confirm what they think.'

'Fine then,' Sam said. 'As long as you know that I hired you because you're reliable. You're a good worker. I could see that in you right away.'

'That's the opposite of what my law tutor said. He pretty much said I didn't even bother trying.'

'You knew what you didn't want to waste your time with. That's a skill in itself. Honestly, I wish I'd listened to myself more before taking on this pub. It's a crumbling mess at the moment and I wish I loved it as much as I'm going to have to pay to keep it from falling apart.'

Nikki still could not help feeling self-conscious about her outburst. She returned to her bag to get the business card for Tarampal's contractor.

'Sam, if you're interested, these guys are supposed to be quite good and I'm guessing they're affordable because they've done some renovation work for this lady I know in Southall.'

Sam took the card and then whistled. 'You're joking. Affordable? I know this company. I called them for a quote when I wanted to remodel the restrooms. They charge through the roof.'

'Really?' Nikki asked, taking the card back and examining it. How did Tarampal, living on her own without an income, manage? 'Hey Sam, these cutbacks aren't going to affect my job are they?'

Sam shook his head. 'As far as I'm concerned you could work here forever.'

Nikki smiled with relief. Sam continued. 'But that doesn't mean you should. Try something else, Nikki, with that brain of yours and that way you have with people.'

'I still don't know what that is.'

'You'll figure it out,' Sam said. He sighed, looking around. 'I'd do things differently if I were in my early twenties. I inherited this pub from my dad because it was something to do, but if I hadn't, I'd have opened a bicycle rental shop on a beachside resort somewhere. I'm tied to this place now. It was charming at first and for a while I loved stepping into my dad's shoes but once the novelty wore off, it became just a workplace. I don't think it would be like that with bicycles, but as long as the pub is standing, I've got to stand here with it.' He shrugged. 'Obligations, you know?'

Dancing in the Rain

He liked to take long showers to wash off the stresses of his long day at work. His wife complained that she never saw him; he was out the door first thing in the morning and then in the evenings he was washing off a day's worth of grime and sweat from his construction job. The water bills were very high and by the time he was finished, all the hot water was finished as well. 'I can't do anything about it,' he insisted. 'This is my only chance to relax.' The woman was hurt. 'There are other ways to relax that we can both enjoy,' she reminded him. The man looked at her in confusion as his wife walked away. He shrugged and went into the bathroom and started taking off his clothes. He could feel the soreness in every muscle and the tightness in his shoulders.

A moment later, the bathroom door opened. His wife appeared, wearing just a towel. The man began to understand now but he still just wanted to be alone. He held up his hands and waved his wife away, chiding her for interrupting his private time. The wife paid no attention to his protests. She raised her arms, letting go of the towel. As it fell onto the floor, the man could not help noticing his wife's body and he tried to remember when he last saw her standing in front of him completely naked like this. He turned around to turn on the shower and felt her drawing close to him, her nipples hard against his bare back. The water splashed on their faces as if they were dancing in the rain but they were actually moving very slowly. Her delicate hands ran smoothly across his body, wiping away the grit and soil from his work in the depths of the earth, so removed from small luxuries like the first drizzle of clean water after a punishing hot day. He shuddered as she moved down to his large shaft and began stroking it. She kissed his face, his lips, his neck. Her strokes increased in speed to match his short, sharp breathes. He pumped his organ into her palm. With the other hand, she scraped her nails lightly against his back. Her fingertips spelled out words of adoration in the sheen of water on his skin. He jerked suddenly into her hand with a throaty moan. 'We've never done it like that,' he gasped. She smiled and buried her face in his hair. There were many things they had never done together.

When it was his turn to return the favour, he was very attentive. She stood with her back pressed against the wall and parted her legs. He flicked his tongue against the tight bud at her centre. The water continued to fall on them. Her legs shook with the intensity of pleasure and she clutched his hair, feeling waves of warmth radiate within her as she came closer and closer to bursting. It was almost painful – her skin tingled with the sensation of the water on her skin; every part of her was suddenly aware and sensitive. She cried out loudly. 'Don't stop,' she called. 'Don't stop.' He didn't.

The class applauded. Preetam blushed. It was an unusual story for her, Nikki thought, and then she noticed a detail missing.

'What are the names of the people in your story?'

'They don't have names.'

'Oh, give them names,' Arvinder said pityingly, as if compelling her to give sweets to a child.

'John and Mary,' Preetam said.

The room broke out in a mix of giggles and protests. 'Give them Punjabi names. Or Indian ones at least,' Bibi urged.

'I just can't see Indians doing this kind of thing,' Preetam said.

'How exactly do you think babies are made?' Arvinder asked.

'Not that,' Preetam said. 'This couple isn't making babies. They're just pleasuring each other.'

'Where did you get the idea for this story from, Preetam?' Tanveer asked, squinting slightly at Preetam.

'From my imagination,' Preetam said.

Tanveer turned to Nikki. 'Nikki, what is it called when you present work that isn't originally yours? You can get expelled from university for it – Satpreet Singh's son got caught doing it. There's an English word.'

'Plagiarism,' Nikki said.

'Yes,' Tanveer said. 'I remember that word because nobody knew what it meant; even Satpreet Singh was confused. He didn't think the punishment would be so severe for copying a few paragraphs from a book he found in the British Library – "my son was using his wits," he kept saying. But the English are very fussy about the truth. Preetam, you have done plagiarism.' The word was mangled by her accent.

'You're mad,' Preetam said but she did look a bit worried. 'I can't read English books. Where would I get this story from?'

'Channel Fifty-Six at 1 a.m.'

Surreptitious glances shot about the room. Nikki didn't have to ask what was on Channel Fifty-Six at 1 a.m. because their knowing smiles told her everything. 'There was a movie on the other night about a couple. The man came home wearing one of those fluorescent vests – he was a miner or something, and then he said something in English and his wife led him into the bathroom. They did exactly what you described.'

'It wasn't in English,' Arvinder said. 'It didn't sound like English; it was French or Spanish I think.'

'The German ones are the best,' piped up Bibi. 'Their men are so sturdy looking.'

'Your secret's out, Preetam,' Tanveer said with a grin.

Preetam squirmed. 'There's nothing to watch on the Indian channel late at night,' she protested.

'Maybe we should move on,' Nikki said.

'I've got the rest of my story now,' Tanveer offered.

'The one about Rita and Meera?' Arvinder asked. Tanveer nodded.

'Yes, please, tell us what happens,' Bibi said.

Rita led Meera to her bed. The sheets were lightly tousled from the night before but Meera refrained from telling off the young girl for not making the bed. She felt a strong and urgent pulsing in her loins as she lay down on the bed and

closed her eyes on Rita's instructions. Rita's breath was hot on Meera's skin. They kissed passionately, playfully flicking their tongues. After unbuttoning Meera's top, Rita gave her nipples gentle bites through the fabric of her bra. Meera gritted her teeth. The sensation of this young woman teasing her flesh made her want to scream with ecstasy but she knew there was even more pleasure to come. Rita stroked the peach between Meera's legs. There was such heat radiating from Meera that Rita knew she was ready. She peeled off Meera's clothes and put her fingers into her wet, swollen centre. Meera whimpered with delight. Her whimpers became deep moans in rhythm with Rita's steady movements. Rita's fingers rotated gently in a circle, preparing Meera for what would come soon. The clay stick lay on the bedside table. Meera glanced at it occasionally. Rita shook her head. 'Not yet,' she said firmly. She knew it was cruel to withhold pleasure from this woman who so badly wanted it but Rita wanted to prolong this experience. She had great power over Meena now. She could get her to do anything she wanted. How Rita managed this moment could determine the course of the rest of her life in this home.

Rita pulled away from Meera and took out a bottle of coconut oil from her dresser drawer. She and her husband had used coconut oil together on their first night, and sometimes, to surprise him, she rubbed it all over her body and then waited in bed for him, naked and glistening. She made a show of it now, stripping for Meera, who watched her every move. Then she tipped the bottle of oil into her hands and rubbed them slowly over her breasts and stomach and thighs. She was aware of how sexy she looked – a goddess with glowing bronze flesh. She returned to bed and reached for the clay stick, which she rolled over her body, from her neck to her stomach, till it was slick with oil. Meera enjoyed the show. She turned on her side and watched Rita, mesmerized. 'Show me what you do with it,' Meera said.

Rita lay down and spread her legs and slipped the stick into her silken folds. She guided it in and out of herself, bucking and sighing the way she did with her husband. With one hand, she clutched at her naked breast, twisting her hard nipples between her fingers. She met Meera's gaze. 'You get it now?' she asked.

She drew the stick out and sat up. 'It's your turn,' she said. 'Lie down.'

Meera shook her head. 'You keep going,' she said.

'Oh don't tell me you want to stop now.'

'I don't want to stop.'

'Then what is it?'

Meera cast a shy gaze over Rita's naked body. 'All this time I spent envying you, I was actually lusting after you. I want to keep admiring your body.'

It was Rita's turn to go shy. 'I had no idea,' she said. 'I thought you resented me.'

Meera pressed her lips to Rita's. They shared a long and passionate kiss during which Meera reached down and wrapped her hands around the stick. She slipped it into Rita and began to pump it slowly. 'What do you want me to do?' Meera asked.

Rita's eyes flew open in surprise. She never thought she would be in the position to ask anything of Meera, yet here the older woman was, ready to serve her. 'Go faster,' Rita commanded. Meera obeyed. 'Faster,' Rita said. She groaned and tipped her head back. Meera's feverish movements were making her thighs quiver. She raised them so that the stick could be driven in deeper. 'Ah! Ah!' she cried. Beneath her, the sheet was soaked in her sweat and her juices. She pulled Meera's face to hers. 'I'm very close,' she whispered.

Meera pulled out the stick. She lay on top of Rita and rubbed against her. The feeling of Meera's hot flesh against Rita's made her excitement mount quickly. She wrapped her legs around Meera's waist. Each grinding movement made her gasp and moan. Both women clutched each other, trying to prolong these sensations. Their climax arrived quickly. Meera shuddered and dropped her head to Rita's collarbone. Rita stroked her hair. In this short moment, both women were closer than they had ever been but they were also lost in their own thoughts. Meera was wondering if she would ever be able to go to bed with her husband after experiencing Rita. Rita was thinking about the order of Meera's life that she had just disassembled. From now on, I will decide where everything belongs, *Rita thought.*

'My, my,' Arvinder said. 'A chilling twist.'

'Very good,' Bibi remarked.

'Thank you,' Tanveer said.

'Don't you think it's a good story, Preetam?' Arvinder asked. 'It's very original.'

Preetam, who was feigning a sudden preoccupation with her nails, muttered a quiet 'Yes.'

After the women were dismissed, Sheena hung back at Nikki's desk. 'I have some news about Manjeet.'

Nikki had noticed that Manjeet was absent for the second class in a row. 'Is she all right?'

'She's left Southall.'

'What? Why?'

'Her husband had another stroke last week and that nurse girlfriend of his decided she wasn't cut out to take care of him any more. She left him. When Manjeet heard that he was sick and alone, she packed up everything and went up north to take care of him.'

'She's gone permanently?' Nikki asked.

Sheena shrugged. 'This is only what I heard from one of her daughters who came to the bank the other day to transfer some money over to them. She said Manjeet was talking like everything was back to normal, like he'd never left.' She shook her head. 'After everything he put her through! And she's staying in that house that he bought with his girlfriend in Blackburn. I don't know whether to consider her a loyal wife or a huge pushover.'

Both titles sounded like the same thing to Nikki. She surveyed the empty classroom. 'I wish I'd had a chance to talk her out of it, or at least say goodbye. It's a good thing we've added Tanveer and Bibi to the class. With Tarampal and Manjeet both gone, it will start to look like we have too few students to continue running the classes.'

'Yeah,' Sheena said. 'There's something else I need to tell you.' She hesitated. 'You have to promise not to be angry.'

'Whatever you did, I'm sure it's nothing which can't be fixed.'

'You won't be angry?' Sheena prompted.

'I won't be angry.'

Sheena drew in a breath and released her confession in one rapid stream. 'I made copies of the stories to show to a few more friends.'

'Oh.'

'Are you angry?'

Nikki shook her head. 'I suppose that's to be expected. The stories would probably have got around by word of mouth, so a friend reading them isn't so bad.'

'The thing is, my friends were really into the stories, especially the one about the tailor. They made some photocopies for their friends. Their friends might like to come to class as well.'

'How many friends are we talking about here?'

'I don't know.'

'Three?'

'More.'

'Five? Ten? We need to make sure that we don't raise any suspicions.'

'More. Women outside Southall want to come to the class as well.'

'How did this happen?'

'Emails. Somebody scanned a story and all of a sudden they were being sent to mailing lists everywhere. One woman who approached me at the temple today lives all the way in Essex.'

Nikki stared at Sheena. 'You promised not to get angry,' Sheena reminded her.

'I'm not angry,' Nikki said. 'I'm shocked. I'm . . .' She looked around the classroom, at the empty seats, and remembered the anticipation with which she had arranged the tables on that first day. 'I'm sort of impressed,' she said. 'I thought about compiling them into a book, but it never occurred to me to just make copies and send them around like that.'

'I must admit, I didn't intend for the stories to get around either. I just made that first copy for my friend who dropped in for a visit from Surrey because she was grumbling that she didn't have anything good to read. She called me up right away and said, "Send more!" I scanned a few more but

I made a mistake. I left the originals on the copier at work. Guess who returned it to me?'

'Rahul?'

Sheena blushed. 'He pretended he hadn't noticed the words on the page but they must have caught his attention. At lunch the next day, he said, "You seem to have quite a colourful imagination."'

'Ooh,' Nikki said. 'What was your response?'

'I just smiled mysteriously and said, "There's a blurry line between imagination and reality."' -

'Very smooth.'

'Rahul won't tell anyone,' Sheena said.

'I'm not worried about him,' Nikki said. 'My concern is that we won't be able to keep these stories a secret from the Brothers.'

'Mine too,' Sheena said. 'But if we hide, we're letting them have all the power, no?' The question was tentative but a new and noticeable strength edged Sheena's voice.

'That's right,' Nikki said. She opened the cassette player and pulled out the tape rather too enthusiastically, leaving a trail of brown tape caught in the machine.

'Here, spool it back,' Sheena said, handing Nikki a pen. Nikki took a closer look at the tape. 'I've ripped it,' she said. 'Bloody hell. Tonight's stories are gone.'

'It's all right. I can remember most of the details. I'll write down what I can and I'll read it aloud to the group next time,' Sheena offered.

'Thanks, Sheena,' Nikki said. She gathered the unspooled tape and wrapped it neatly around the plastic casing. 'That was my last cassette too.'

'You don't have any spares?'

'I must have left them in the box I took to Tarampal,' Nikki said. She was met with a questioning look from Sheena. 'I took some story tapes to Tarampal's house last week because I felt bad about not teaching her English. It was an apology of sorts.'

'How did Tarampal react?' Sheena asked.

'She's still keen to learn English but she refuses to come back to our class. I tried to persuade her but—'

'Don't let her come back,' Sheena said. 'It's better without her.'

'You dislike her that much? I know she's a little more traditional, but I thought you all were friends.'

'Tarampal isn't *anybody's* friend,' Sheena said.

'I don't understand.'

The seconds ticked by almost audibly as Sheena studied Nikki, deciding. When she finally spoke, her voice was firm. 'Whatever I tell you stays in this room, all right?'

'I promise.'

'First let me ask you something. Did you go inside Tarampal's house?'

'Yes.'

'What was it like? Your first impression.'

'It was really nice,' Nikki said. 'Everything looked recently renovated.'

'Did you ask her how she paid for all those renovations?'

'No, I thought that would be rude. I was curious about it, though. I got her contractor's card and when I recommended those services to my boss, he said they were very expensive.'

'I'll bet they are. You'd only use top-notch contractors if other people were footing the bill,' Sheena said.

'Who?'

'The community,' Sheena said, gesturing at the window. The curve of the temple's dome was visible in the window. People milled in the car park, their chatter rising to fill the pause. 'Anyone with money is paying Tarampal to keep quiet about their secrets.'

'Tarampal *blackmails* people?'

'She doesn't call it that,' Sheena said. 'She considers it a form of help. It's the same thing her husband used to do.'

'Has she ever asked you for money?' Nikki asked. 'Would she try to blackmail us over the classes?'

Sheena shook her head. 'Very unlikely. She only targets the wealthy.'

Nikki remembered Arvinder holding out her palms and saying Tarampal wouldn't be interested in them. Now she understood what Arvinder meant.

They were empty; there was nothing to take from a widow. 'She knows it's not worth it,' Nikki mused. 'How do you know all of this, Sheena?'

'For my birthday last year, I decided to pamper myself with a manicure from Chandani's. The girl doing my nails told me about it. She said that Tarampal's main victims are also the salon's regular clients – those rich women we saw in the langar hall the other night. Tarampal's husband left behind a list of people in the community who had consulted him about their indiscretions. He had records of what people told him and the prayers he prescribed to them. Tarampal uses the list against people. Maintaining an honourable reputation in this community is worth a lot of money to those families, especially those who can afford it. Like the parents of Sandeep Singh – that boy who picked her up in the white car after she stormed out of class that night. He's gay. His mother had approached Tarampal's husband to get him to adjust his behaviour somehow. Sandeep often drives Tarampal around to pay off his debts.'

'How much do people have to pay her?' Nikki asked.

'Whatever she demands. Of course, she doesn't put it that way. She tells them that she's continuing her husband's work, that she puts in requests for special prayers in India to put them on a righteous path again. She claims that the money goes towards fees to cover long-distance calls and travel expenses for her prayer agents. It's all done with lots of sympathy and smiles but everyone knows she's running a thriving enterprise on shame and secrets.'

'Wow,' Nikki said. She recalled the hardened look that crossed Tarampal's face when she talked about honour and shame. No wonder she took it so seriously; it was her livelihood. 'It's hard to imagine Tarampal running any sort of enterprise.'

'She's very skilled. She truly believes she's making things right, offering some sort of service to restore people's pride. The people who pay her end up believing it too, otherwise they wouldn't part with their money.'

When discussing Maya's suicide, Tarampal had struck Nikki as rather unsympathetic, her concern largely focused on Jaggi's reputation. Nikki had thought Tarampal was simply being overprotective but now it made more sense. 'It's sort of ingenious,' Nikki admitted. Sheena narrowed her eyes and started to say something. 'Not that I condone it. I won't be inviting her to return to our classes,' Nikki added.

'Good,' Sheena said. She looked relieved. 'I don't need her poking around in my business.'

'That's fair enough. The only one permitted to poke around in your business is Rahul,' Nikki said with a grin.

'Nikki.'

'I couldn't help it.'

'There's nothing going on between Rahul and me.'

'Still?' Nikki asked. 'Come on.'

Sheena dropped her voice and gave an exaggerated flutter of her eyelids. 'We met up for dinner last weekend.'

'And . . .?'

'It was very nice. He took me to a restaurant in Richmond. We drank wine on a restaurant that overlooked the Thames. After dinner we walked along the river. He wrapped his jacket around my shoulders when the breeze became too chilly.'

'How lovely,' Nikki said. Sheena's eyes glistened with the excitement of new love. 'Are you going to keep seeing each other?'

'Maybe,' Sheena said. 'If we can keep meeting up outside Southall for a while, then yeah. I didn't run into a single Punjabi person in Richmond. At first I was afraid of being seen – it's not that far away and my in-laws have loads of relatives nearby in Twickenham. But I forgot about all of that. You don't notice who's watching when you're enjoying yourself. You don't care either.'

'Would Tarampal try to blackmail Rahul as well if she found out?' Nikki asked. The tension returned to Sheena's face.

'He wouldn't have enough to offer her,' Sheena said. 'She's more interested in wealthy people, remember?'

Nikki shook her head. 'Here I was feeling sorry for her, being caught in the middle of that awful tragedy.'

Sheena looked at Nikki sharply. 'She spoke to you about Maya?'

Yes, Nikki began to say, but then she considered what Sheena had revealed about Tarampal. A seed of discomfort lodged itself in her chest. Once again, she felt like a complete outsider. For every question she asked, there were hundreds more that went unanswered. 'I only know what she told me,' Nikki finally said.

'And I'm sure she told you a very good story,' Sheena said. She clutched her handbag and made her way towards the door so quickly that Nikki had no chance of asking her to stop.

Chapter Ten

Kulwinder's bones told her she was back in London. Before the pilot announced the landing, she felt the rheumatism seep wetly into her body. In India, she had been able to climb flights of stairs and to push her way through the throngs of people. Her sandals had clapped against the soil of her ancestral land, announcing her arrival. Now she was in Heathrow, wearing trainers with an old salwaar kameez and being ushered by a grim-faced attendant into the customs queue.

Her last trip to India had been with Maya. They had spent hours in bazaar stalls, feeling the fabric of exquisite saris crinkle beneath their touch. Kulwinder had bought Maya a pair of small gold hooped earrings. 'Oh Mum,' Maya had said, a smile spreading across her face as she picked them out of the box. 'You didn't have to.' But Kulwinder had been overcome by a sense of generosity towards her daughter during that trip, and she kept on buying her things – as if knowing that their remaining days together were numbered, she had been tempted to give her the whole world.

'Passports – Internationals over here, British citizens here,' the attendant called, forcing her back to the present. The line began to break as people moved into their designated rows. The attendant made her announcement again when Kulwinder was approaching the front of the queue. She held Kulwinder's gaze.

'Can I see your passport, ma'am?' she asked. She wasn't unkind about it exactly, but expectant, as if she already knew Kulwinder's story. Kulwinder handed over her passport. 'British,' she informed the attendant, who returned her passport and walked away, pretending not to hear her. This had happened before. She had grumbled to Maya about it, who didn't understand. *What do you expect them to think, Mum?* Maya would ask, staring pointedly at Kulwinder's clothes in a way that made her wonder how it was possible to love your daughter and dislike her so much at the same time.

Sarab was waiting on the other side when she got out. He gave her a chaste squeeze of the hand and asked, 'How was it?'

'Good,' she said. 'It was home.' As she said this, her heart filled with sorrow. Maya had occupied more space in her trip than she'd hoped. She had visited temples and lit candles for Maya, and for the truth of Maya's death to emerge. In the middle of a distant relative's wedding ceremony, she had left, clutching her side so people thought she was ill but it was actually the unbearable pain of watching the bride and groom take their solemn steps around the Holy Book together.

London had not changed. The wind whipped her face, spraying her hair with mist. She pulled her shawl over her head and followed her husband to their car. The city's flat outskirts greeted Kulwinder with the usual dismal views: walls covered in swirls of graffiti, scaly rooftops and the wide glowing lots of petrol stations.

'Are you hungry?' Sarab asked as they neared Southall.

'I had something on the plane.'

'We can stop for something if you'd like.'

This was his way of saying he had not eaten dinner. Kulwinder calculated the number of meals she had left behind for him. There would have been enough for every night she had been away, including tonight. 'Maybe McDonald's,' he said. Kulwinder said nothing and Sarab pulled in swiftly to the drive-through. She pictured him sitting there every evening, ordering his regular meal – Filet-O-Fish and Chicken McNuggets – and chewing slowly to pass the time. The prepared dinners would still be in the freezer when she got home, and she would defrost them for dinner for the next few weeks. This happened every time she went away without him. In a strange way, it was comforting. If Sarab couldn't eat home-cooked meals without her, it meant he had missed her, a sentiment he would never express in words. It also reminded Kulwinder that he would survive without her.

'Let's sit inside,' Kulwinder said. 'I don't like to eat while the car is moving.'

He agreed. They parked and entered the restaurant, finding a booth in the corner next to a window. The restaurant was noisy with the sounds of teenagers; it was Friday night. Out of the corner of her eye, Kulwinder noticed a few Punjabi girls but she was too jet-lagged to try to figure out whose daughters they were.

'Your writing classes have certainly been very popular,' remarked Sarab. 'I was at the temple the other day and saw some women heading into the building.'

'Which women?' Kulwinder asked. While in India, her problems with Nikki had become as distant as London itself.

'I don't know who exactly,' Sarab said. 'I did run into Gurtaj Singh at the langar hall the other day. He asked me what was being taught in those classes. I told him Nikki was teaching the women to read and write. He said, "That's all?"'

'Was he suspicious?' Kulwinder asked. She recalled the note Nikki had left on Tarampal's doorstep. It still didn't make sense – why had Nikki apologized? But if class sizes were increasing, it meant that Kulwinder's initiative looked successful to Gurtaj Singh.

'He seemed impressed,' Sarab said.

They ate their meals and returned home. The house smelled familiar and foreign at the same time. Kulwinder breathed it in and felt a hard hit in her gut. *Our daughter is dead.* She turned to Sarab, hoping to make eye contact but his face was clouded over. He brushed past her to the front room and moments later the broadcast of the Punjabi news blared into the living room and drowned the silence.

Kulwinder propped her suitcase against the bottom stair and left it there. Sarab would bring it up for her and then he would go back downstairs to the sitting room and fall asleep in front of the television. She drifted up the stairs to her room and unzipped her kameez. It made her shoulder ache to reach back but she felt skittish asking for Sarab's help. What if he thought it was an invitation to touch her intimately? Or worse, what if he didn't? Kulwinder shook away these thoughts. She managed to tug at the zip and drag it down eventually. Making her way to the bathroom, she passed Maya's room and paused. The door was open. Once a shrine to all things Kulwinder detested about Maya's Western lifestyle, the room had been hollowed out during the move to her marital home – the piles of magazines thrown into recycling, the door hook which held a dozen handbags tossed into the garbage, the high heels, the lipstick, the ticket stubs from concerts, the novels all chucked into boxes. Kulwinder did not remember opening the door. Sarab must have gone in there in her absence.

Would he ever forgive her? There were times when she wanted to break the silence by shouting: *it was my fault, wasn't it?* She had given Maya that impossible choice. She had set up the marriage, considering it such good fortune to find a willing and available groom across the road where she could keep an eye on Maya. 'Don't embarrass me again,' Kulwinder had said when Maya came home and declared her marriage over. In her lowest moments, Kulwinder believed that everyone was right: there was no mystery to Maya's death. She had ended her life because Kulwinder had sent her back.

Kulwinder took a furtive glance at the window and saw the ghostly outlines of curtains in Tarampal's living room window. She turned away. Regret struck her one bolt at a time. At the wedding, a clutching worry when Tarampal gave Jaggi a tight embrace that lasted longer than necessary. The flash of fear that crossed Maya's face. The questioning look Sarab shot Kulwinder. The way Kulwinder, on the drive home, dismissed Sarab's concerns and said, "She's married now. She'll be happy."

If a man calls, always answer the phone with 'Oh hey. I was just in the shower.'

It projects an instant image into their minds. This was the only tip Nikki remembered from a dating advice column she'd read in one of Mindi's women's magazines. It would finally prove useful; she was in the shower and the phone was trilling outside with the ring tone she had programmed for Jason's calls. She was annoyed with herself for being excited. She reminded herself to be aloof. *Aloof*, she thought as she rang him back. *Cool. Casual. I wasn't waiting by the phone.*

'Hi Nikki,' Jason said.

'Oh, hey man, whashappening? I had a shower,' she blurted.

'Cool,' Jason said.

'I mean, I was in the shower when you called.'

'Oh. All right. Sorry to interrupt.'

'No it's okay. I was pretty much finished – you know what, it's not important. How are you?'

'I'm all right. Things have been a little crazy.'

'Work stuff?' Nikki offered.

There was a split second pause. 'Yeah,' Jason said. 'And other stuff. I need to talk to you about something. Could we meet up?'

'I've got a double shift at O'Reilly's tonight,' Nikki said.

'Can I meet you there?'

'Okay. It gets a bit busy after eight on Wednesdays, so some time before?'

'All right.'

'Hey, Jason . . .'

'Yeah?'

'This is weird.'

'What is?'

'This – you. You calling me out of the blue like this and then wanting to meet.'

'Do you not want to meet tonight?'

'I do. It's just that – that I haven't heard from you in a while and all of a sudden you call and you say let's meet and . . .' She was struggling. 'Do you know what I'm getting at?' Jason's silence sparked her anger. 'Look, I'm a bit tired of feeling like I have to be available whenever you are,' she said. 'The way you left my place the other morning was very rude.'

'I'm really sorry about that.'

'I like you,' Nikki said. 'I can be honest about it. It's not that complicated for me.'

'It's complicated for me. I need a chance to explain myself. There are circumstances which are quite out of my control.'

'It's always circumstances, isn't it? Some foggy power that guys can't control.'

'That's not fair.'

Nikki went quiet. Jason continued. 'I like you too, Nikki. A lot. But I need to talk to you in person about where I am at the moment. Can I see you tonight?'

Nikki didn't want to give in so easily but she also wanted to see him. She let the silence linger. 'Nikki?' Jason asked. His voice was soft and uncertain.

'Yeah, all right,' Nikki said. *Last chance*, she thought, though she couldn't bring herself to say it.

Steve with the Racist Grandfather had a girl with him. Her long strawberry-blonde hair swayed across her back as she tipped her head to laugh at whatever he was whispering into her ear. This was worthy of announcement. Nikki texted Olive:

Steve has a girlfriend!

Olive's immediate reply:

Is she inflatable?

A live one! Can't believe someone would go out with him

I know! All the good men are taken and all the shit men aren't even learning how shit they are.

Any luck overseas?

Nope. Greek Boy doesn't speak much English. My intellect needs as much stimulation as my other places.

Nikki replied with a winking face and returned her attention to the customers. Grace was taking orders from a group of men in suits on the end of the bar. She gave Nikki a wave. 'How's yer mum, darl?' she asked.

'She's good.'

'Not too cold any more. Tell 'er summer's coming.'

Grace was right. The chill in the air seemed duller by the day and there were moments of lingering warmth in the afternoons. Soon, summer would arrive. The café next door would open its outdoor courtyard and the occasional American tourist would pop in for an authentic English pub experience and find O'Reilly's distinct lack of charm disappointing. Nikki would still be working here. This bothered her more than usual. She had a quick vision of herself growing into Grace, her raspy voice chatting up customers she had served for decades.

Steve's loud laugh broke Nikki's thoughts. 'Nikki, check out this guy on TV. Nola's saying he should drop the musical act and focus on being Osama Bin Laden's body double.' A skinny turbaned man wearing a traditional kurta sat on the vast stage and expertly slapped the heels of his palms against a tabla.

The girl shifted uncomfortably. 'That's what you said,' she protested.

The camera closed in on the panel of judges watching the drummer with intensity. It was *Britain's Got Talent*. Nikki returned to the bar to search for the remote control. Although Grace was busy with customers, they couldn't afford to have her crying over some contestant's heartrending backstory. Where the hell was the remote control? She rushed to Sam's office and knocked on the door. No answer, but the door wasn't locked. His desk was a mess of paperwork and coffee stains. Nikki found the remote control on his chair, where he must have absent-mindedly left it. She returned to the bar and switched the channel.

'We were watching that,' Steve said.

'Now you're watching *Top Gear*,' Nikki said.

Customers trickled through the door. None were Jason. Nikki took note of the time – it was past nine now. She checked her phone for missed calls. Nothing. She sent him a text. 'You still planning on coming tonight?' Her thumb hovered over the Send button. It sounded whiny. Desperate. She deleted the message.

The kitchen door opened. Garry emerged, balancing two large plates on his arm. 'You seen Sam?' Garry asked when he returned from serving.

'He's not in his office,' Nikki said.

'Tell him I'm going,' Garry said. 'I quit.'

'What? Right now?'

'Now,' Garry said.

'What happened?'

'Wages here is shit,' Garry said. 'I ask for raise – he say, maybe, maybe. Then nothing. Viktor also quit.'

Through the glass panel on the door, Nikki could see Viktor packing up his belongings. 'Garry, it's really busy.'

Garry shrugged.

'Can't you finish up your shift and then talk to him?'

Viktor came out of the kitchen. 'Talking don't work for us,' he declared. 'Maybe Sam give special raise to you when you go in his office.'

The comment gripped Nikki in the throat. She saw that somebody had changed the channel on the television again. A close-up shot of the tabla man showed him thanking the judges with his palms humbly pressed together in front of his chest. Steve pointed at the screen and chuckled. Outrage rippled through Nikki like a tidal wave.

'Listen, you little fuckwits,' she seethed. 'I have never slept with Sam. But if I did, it would be none of your damn business. You two can quit if you like – that would make my life much easier. But if you change your minds and decide to stay, I'd suggest you focus on doing your damn jobs properly. Maybe then Sam might consider you competent enough to pay you the wages you feel entitled to.'

A hush fell over the pub. Thin applause crackled on the television screen as the tabla player left the stage. From the corner, Steve let out a low whistle. 'You tell it like it is, Nikki,' he said.

Nikki whipped around to face Steve. 'Oh, don't you pretend to be any better. I've put up with your racist rubbish for too long. I don't care that you're a customer. You can pack up your ignorant comments and get out as well.'

Nikki strode to the middle of the room. 'For everybody's information, the entertainment in this establishment is decided upon by the management.' She pointed a thumb to her chest. 'Me. I decide what's playing on that screen. Whoever's got the remote, you have ten seconds to return it to me or at least change the channel *because we're not watching* Britain's Got *Bloody* Talent.'

Grace stepped forward and produced the remote control with a guilty duck of her head. Somebody in the back of the room started an ill-advised slow clap, which quickly died. Nikki changed the channel and went back behind the bar, where Garry and Viktor shared a nervous glance and retreated to the kitchen.

'Why don't you take the rest of the shift off, luv? I've got this,' Grace said.

'I'm fine. It was just . . . they say such insulting things and I've started getting angry at myself for not saying anything and—'

Grace's face was wide with understanding. 'You said what you had to say, darling. No need to explain.'

'I didn't mean to be so harsh about the remote control,' Nikki said.

'That's quite all right,' Grace said. 'I don't know what that show does to me but the tears start coming and I just can't stop crying. You've seen it.'

'I have,' Nikki said.

'My husband says "It's women. It's in your chemical make-up. You can't control being overwhelmed by emotion." But I don't get that way about sad movies or even those news items. Little girl diagnosed with rare cancer on the news the other day – I frowned and said, "What a shame" and moved on. But that man working two jobs to be able to pay for his sister's contortionist classes so she can one day perform in the *Royal Variety Show* . . .' Grace choked on her words.

At this point, anything was better for this pub than *Britain's Got Talent*. Nikki gave Grace a sympathetic squeeze of her shoulder and flipped to the next channel. They landed on a grim scene: police combing through dense foliage and then a sergeant talking to the camera. *Perfect*, she thought. Customers politely avoided Nikki, leaving her idle at the bar. She checked the time on her phone once again and surveyed the pub. No Jason. That was it. She searched for his contact details, took in a breath and deleted his number. She didn't want to be tempted to call him.

In the corner, Steve leaned over to whisper something to Nola and Nola sprang from her seat and left the pub in a huff. Steve's grin disappeared. He scrambled after Nola. Grace raced over to the entrance, blocking his way. 'You've got a tab to pay,' she reminded him. Then she said something that Nikki couldn't hear. Sulking, Steve pulled out his wallet and threw some bills at Grace and left. Grace picked up the money and brought it over to Nikki. 'He's an accidental tipper,' she said. 'Here's your share.'

'Oh Grace, no. You've been serving him tonight.'

'You've been putting up with him for years,' Grace said. 'You deserve a reward. I told him Sam would have him removed if he tried to come back. He's no longer welcome here because he makes our staff and patrons uncomfortable.' She pressed the bills into Nikki's hand.

Grace's gesture stirred something in Nikki. She couldn't believe how much she missed Mum all of a sudden – Mum who had pushed money into her hand the same insistent way the first time she returned home for dinner after moving out.

Nikki's phone was still in her hand. She searched for Mum's number and began composing a message but the words didn't come to her. She called her instead. After several rings, Nikki was tempted to hang up but then Mum picked up. 'Nikki?'

'Hi, Mum. How are you?'

'I was just thinking about you.'

Those simple words warmed Nikki's heart. 'I was thinking about you too, Mum.'

'I need you to do me a favour.' There was an edge of slight panic in Mum's voice. 'Aunty Geeta is coming over tomorrow and I have no Indian snacks to serve. The shop I usually go to in Enfield is closed temporarily – death in the family, I heard – and the other shops don't have enough variety. Can you go to Southall and buy some gulab jamun, ladoo, barfi, jalebi – whatever they have – and bring them here? I also need some cardamom for tea. The cardamom at Waitrose is too expensive.'

Here Nikki was thinking they were about to have a bonding moment. Her schedule for tomorrow was wide open. 'Sure, Mum,' Nikki said. She knew better than to ask Mum why she still bothered socialising with Aunty Geeta, for whom an unsatisfactory afternoon tea was probably symbolic of a woman's failings.

'Why is it so noisy?'

'Um, I'm at a movie.'

'The new job is going well?'

'Uh huh.'

'You're liking teaching? Maybe this is a new career path for you?'

'I don't know, Mum,' Nikki said, eager to cut the conversation short. 'I have to go. I'll see you tomorrow afternoon.' Mum said goodbye and Nikki slipped her phone back in her pocket. She didn't know if she was disappointed, relieved or amused at how the call turned out. If only Jason were around; they'd laugh over it together.

A customer approached Nikki tentatively and asked if happy hour was still on. 'Sure,' Nikki said, although it had ended fifteen minutes ago, and she poured him a lager. Despite her best efforts to stop thinking about Jason, she couldn't help looking at the door again and wishing that he'd just show up and apologize for being late.

Nikki's phone buzzed in her pocket. She checked it to find a message from Mum:

Another thing. Pls be careful in Southall. They are showing what happened to Karina Kaur on Channel Four now – don't walk around there at nite!!!

Nikki looked up at the television screen. The Channel Four logo glowed in the bottom corner. The narrator's voice was barely audible in the buzz of pub conversation so Nikki switched on the close captioning.

[ON APRIL 8th 2003, A GIRL WAS REPORTED MISSING AFTER SHE DID NOT RETURN HOME FROM SCHOOL.]

[KARINA KAUR, A YEAR TWELVE STUDENT AT SOUTHALL SECONDARY COLLEGE, WAS ONLY WEEKS AWAY FROM SITTING HER FINAL EXAMS.]

[AFTER A 48-HOUR PERIOD, A SEARCH BEGAN FOR THE MISSING STUDENT.]

Two young women waved at Nikki from their table. 'Is it still happy hour?' one of them asked.

Nikki shook her head. The woman glanced at the customer nursing his lager. 'You sure?' she asked.

Nikki took their orders, keeping an eye on the screen. The next set of captions accompanied footage of small flickering flames. Then the camera zoomed out to show a crowd of high school students in uniform holding candles.

[AFTER THE DISCOVERY OF KARINA'S BODY, A VIGIL WAS SET UP OUTSIDE HER SCHOOL.]

'Thought I told you to take the evening off. Go on. Get some rest,' Grace said, setting down a tray.

Nikki nodded vaguely at Grace but she couldn't tear her attention away from the screen. Filling the television screen, a young Punjabi woman stood at the tall iron gates of a school. She gripped a lit candle with two manicured hands – the nails hot pink with glittery gold tips. The flame illuminated the streaks of tears down her face and the gold pendant which rested on her collarbone, in the shape of the letter G.

The man behind the counter at Sweetie Sweets probably thought he was paying Nikki a compliment. 'These gulab jamun are worth the calories,' he had said, looking her up and down. 'Not that you need to worry, hmm? Not yet anyway.' He chuckled. 'Before marriage, my wife was also skinny—'

'If you could just pack these in a box for me, that would be great,' Nikki said quickly, cutting him off.

'No problem, dear. You having a little party? Am I invited?' he grinned, leaning closer.

Nikki was very close to smashing a gulab jamun on the guy's forehead when his wife emerged from a back room. Suddenly, he became busy finding a box for the sweets. The wife glared at Nikki as she paid and left.

She checked the time on her phone. It was too early to go to Mum's without having to sit through countless questions that she wouldn't be able to answer about her teaching job. She strolled along the Broadway, where the pavement was crowded with discount clothing racks and vegetable crates. A crooked line of men had formed outside a mobile phone shop selling overseas calling cards. Stacked atop these stores were more businesses, overlapping signs popping out from the buildings like cartoon speech bubbles: Pankaj Madhur Accounting, Himalaya Guest House, RHP Surveillance Pte Ltd. What Nikki used to consider chaos now felt very much like home as she wove through the throng of people, the box of sweets tucked under her arm. Eventually, she came to an intersection and crossed it to find herself standing at the entrance of the Bank of Baroda.

Sheena was sitting at a counter and assisting a customer when Nikki walked in. 'Next,' called the woman in the window next to hers.

'No thank you,' Nikki said. 'I'm here to see Sheena.'

Sheena looked up. She returned to the customer and then walked out to greet Nikki with an air of professionalism that belied the confusion on her face. 'Kelly, I'm going on my lunch break,' she called.

Once they were outside, Sheena's smile vanished. 'What are you doing here?' she asked.

'Can we talk?'

'Oh, Nikki, I knew I should have asked you before passing those stories around. You're upset, aren't you? Listen, the women coming to the next class are trustworthy. We'll talk tonight about what to say to the Brothers if they question us.'

'It's not about the stories,' Nikki said. 'It's Karina Kaur I'm curious about.'

The concern on Sheena's face faded. 'You're interrupting my lunch hour,' she replied.

'I can't talk to you about it at the temple because there are too many eavesdroppers. I had to come here.'

'What makes you think I know anything?'

Nikki described the footage of the school candlelight vigil. 'I'm pretty sure that was you.'

'That's impossible,' Sheena said. 'I wasn't at school then. I was a newlywed when Karina died.'

'It was someone who looked a lot like you then. She had that glittery pink manicure.'

'Lots of women in Southall have those,' Sheena said.

'It was you. We both know it. You were wearing that necklace with the letter G pendant.'

Sheena winced as though Nikki had jabbed her. She only recovered after adjusting the collar of her blouse to conceal the fine gold chain. 'What for, Nikki? Why do you want to know? Because if you're just plain curious, I'm not here to indulge you. This community's problems are real.'

'This isn't for entertainment.'

'What's it to you then?' Sheena pressed.

'It's my community too,' Nikki said. 'I don't live here, but I'm part of it now. In my entire life, I have never felt so frustrated, amused, loved and bewildered as I have been in these past two months. But there seem to be layers of things going on that I'm not allowed to know about.' She sighed and looked away. 'I'm not so naïve to think that I can help, but I'd like to be aware of what's happening.'

Sheena's face softened. A speck of afternoon sunlight peeped through the clouds and deepened the orange of her hennaed hair. Nikki was unwilling to drop her gaze, even when Sheena looked past her, deep in thought.

'Let's go for a drive,' she finally said. Nikki followed her round to the car park and Sheena's little red Fiat. Sheena put her key in the ignition. A bhangra tune poured from the speakers. They said nothing to each other on the drive, which took them past rows of bone-white houses. The road curved out and the houses disappeared behind them, replaced by parkland. Sheena slowed down on a gravelly road that opened out onto a small lake. The sun glinted on the water.

'The girl you saw in the documentary was Gulshan Kaur. She was one of my best friends,' Sheena said. 'She died in a hit-and-run accident not far from here. The driver never came forward.'

'I'm so sorry,' Nikki said.

'Her mother gave me her birth necklace after she died. I didn't want to accept it at first, but she insisted. There's a superstition about keeping a deceased woman's gold in her own home. It brings bad luck. Most people decide to sell or reshape their gold but Gulshan's mother insisted that I have it. I've worn it every day since her death.'

'You touch it sometimes,' Nikki said. 'Like you're remembering her.'

'If Gulshan were alive today, we'd see each other every day,' Sheena said. 'She'd still be my friend even though those other women distanced themselves from me and thought I was bad luck after Arjun's cancer. She cared about the truth. That's what killed her.'

'What do you mean?'

Sheena took in a quivering breath. 'Karina was Gulshan's cousin. Gulshan and I were a few years older than her, so whenever she mentioned her cousin Karina, I just knew her as the lively girl that Gulshan played older sister to. Karina was rebellious. She got suspended from school for selling cigarettes to younger kids once, and she sneaked out to meet boys. Gulshan used to counsel her. Karina's father was highly respected in the community and each time Karina did something bad, people muttered, "What's wrong with that girl? She comes from such a good family. There's no excuse." Gulshan knew the truth though. Karina's father drank heavily. He did it behind closed doors. A few times, Karina showed Gulshan the bruises she had from her father's beatings.'

'What was Karina's mother like?' Nikki asked.

'Not around. This was part of the reason Karina's father was so strict – he had no idea how to control a daughter. She was punished for every little thing and the beatings became more frequent. He pressured her to leave school and marry an older man in India. One day Gulshan got a call from Karina from a payphone. She said she was running away with her boyfriend and that she would call again once she was safe. Gulshan tried to talk Karina out of it but Karina said, "It's too late. If I go home now, my father will murder me." Gulshan didn't tell anybody that Karina had called her, but a few days later, somebody managed to track her down.'

'A bounty hunter, I'm guessing,' Nikki said.

'Yes. A taxi driver who was after the reward money. He found her miles away, in Derby. Imagine that, Nikki. She got that far away and the community still managed to find her.' Sheena choked on these last words.

'She was sent home?' Nikki asked softly. Sheena nodded. She took a tissue out from her purse and dabbed the corners of her eyes.

'After Karina returned, Gulshan didn't hear from her. Gulshan's parents warned her to stay out of it but one day, she broke down and said, "Sheena, something terrible is going to happen to my little cousin. She is going to die." Even I struggled to believe it at first. Karina's father had started a charity drive for newcomers to the country. He had come to my family's assistance when we first arrived in England. He had helped to fill out all the paperwork, tax forms, employment, everything. I reminded Gulshan that young girls have a tendency to exaggerate. I was sure this man wouldn't kill his daughter. Karina was probably on her way to India to get married to save the family's honour.

'Then I turned on the news one night and Karina had been reported missing to the police. It was her father who had reported her missing. That's when it hit me.' Sheena paused. In the quiet, the sound of another car could be heard making its way down the gravel path. It pulled up near them and a family with two children emerged and made their way across the field. Sheena stared past them and continued.

'If her father was telling the police that she had disappeared, then he knew that she wasn't coming back. A few days later, her body was found in the wooded area near Herbert Park. That was a frightening time for the community. Everybody shut their daughters away at home, convinced that a killer was on the loose.'

'But Gulshan suspected the father of murdering her,' Nikki said. A sense of dread crept into her body.

'Yes,' Sheena said. 'She didn't know for sure. But after the fuss was over and the media went away, she started asking her own questions. Wasn't it strange that Karina's father had reported her missing to the police, but had kept things quiet the first time she ran away? Why hadn't he hired another bounty hunter? He must have known that she was dead. Then one day, Gulshan called me up. She was very excited. She said, "Sheena, there's proof now." She had gone with her parents to Karina's house to pay their respects at a prayer session. She had managed to sneak away to Karina's room, which she searched until she found a diary. There were entries detailing Karina's worst fears – that her father would murder her to save his reputation. Gulshan couldn't take the diary out of Karina's house without being noticed so she put it back where she found it. She thought it would be safer to call the police and tell them to search the room. But then . . .' Sheena bit her lip.

'The accident,' Nikki said. 'Gulshan died before she could contact the police.' She closed her eyes as if momentarily shutting off the world would ease the injustices of Karina's and Gulshan's story.

'Somebody must have told Karina's father about the questions Gulshan was asking, about her seeing the diary,' Sheena said. 'The – the diary was never found.'

'Who else did Gulshan tell about the diary?'

'She told me,' Sheena said softly. 'And I told my mother-in-law. It was the early days of my marriage and we were bonding. I didn't think anything of it. Likewise, she didn't see the harm in telling a friend, who told another friend . . .' Sheena shook her head, her words catching again. 'Out of a sense of duty, somebody felt it necessary to stop Gulshan. Stop her before she embarrassed the community. Before she made us look a group of barbarians who killed their own daughters.'

'Oh, Sheena,' Nikki said. 'I'm so sorry.'

'Me too,' Sheena whispered.

Sheena's secret hung heavy in the air. They both stared straight ahead, watching the lake shimmer and ripple like a jewel. A breeze ran through the surrounding parkland, turning up blades of grass revealing their dark underside. London's buildings were mere outlines in the distance.

'Do you come to this spot often?' Nikki asked.

Sheena stared out the window. 'All the time. Gulshan didn't live far away and she went jogging here three times a week. She had to put up with comments, you know – Punjabi girl running around bare-legged.'

'The driver of the car would have known where to find her then,' Nikki said.

'Exactly. After Gulshan died I visited the scene of the accident and saw how the road curved. There's a blind spot. The council petitioned to have a sign put up to warn pedestrians after the accident. Perhaps she had her earphones in and wasn't paying attention. You try to tell yourself it could just be an accident, that the simplest explanation is the most likely.'

'Maybe that's all it was,' Nikki offered. 'An accident.' The coincidence nagged her immediately. She could only imagine the struggle this created within Sheena.

'I won't ever know for sure,' Sheena said. 'But in this community I'm suspicious of accidents. A few years later, Karina's father was hospitalized with liver cirrhosis. I heard from people in the community that he was in great pain and I thought, *serves him right*. He had stopped hiding his drinking. People blamed Karina's death. They called him a broken man, a mourning father. I didn't have an ounce of sympathy for him. At his funeral, I wore Gulshan's necklace for the first time. People stared but they said nothing. They all knew.'

Nikki could practically feel the burn of those stares. 'You're very brave for doing that,' she said.

With one hand, Sheena rolled her pendant between her thumb and forefinger. She shrugged. 'It was just a small gesture. I'm sure nobody even remembered afterwards.'

'They probably did.'

'Or they didn't,' Sheena said. The force in her tone surprised Nikki. Perhaps Sheena felt responsible for Gulshan's death in the first place. Nikki said nothing else, waiting for the tension to leak away.

'Let's head back,' Sheena said. She twisted the key into the ignition and backed out of the park. The radio came on and an old Hindi love ballad filled the car. As they gained distance from that lonely park, Sheena seemed to relax. She hummed along with the song.

'You know this song?' Sheena asked as the singer reached his chorus.

'My mum would know it,' Nikki said.

'Oh, definitely. It's a classic.' Sheena turned up the radio. 'You can actually hear the sorrow in his voice.' They listened to the singer crooning about his heavy heart and his longing. Nikki had to admit that the tune touched a nerve. The streets of Southall came into view, the ballad providing a soundtrack to the passing rows of jewelry shops and samosa stands. Despite the sinister story that Sheena had just told, Nikki could understand how this place could be home, and why leaving would be unimaginable to some.

They were pulling into the bank's parking lot when Sheena muttered, 'Shit.' Her eyes were trained on a figure in the distance. 'Is that Rahul?' Nikki asked, squinting. Sheena nodded. She parked in the farthest spot from the entrance and turned off the engine but made no move to leave the car. 'I'll wait till he goes back inside,' she said.

'When are you going to stop avoiding each other in public?' Nikki asked.

'At the moment we're avoiding each other in private as well,' Sheena said.

'Why? Why happened?'

Sheena twisted the keys in the ignition. The engine purred and a tune floated from the radio. 'We started becoming quite physical with each other.'

'And?'

'It's all happening too quickly. My husband courted me for months before we even held hands. With Rahul, I went from kissing on the cheek to the most intimate level within two dates.'

'I'm sure things are fast-paced now because you're passionate about each other and it's new. Besides, you're not inexperienced any more. You can't compare a romance at this stage in your life to your first marriage fourteen years ago.'

'I know that,' Sheena said. 'But I miss the thrill, the build-up.'

'You should try discussing it with Rahul.'

'Discussions won't work. I can tell *you* these things but I can't talk to him about it.'

'Try it.'

Sheena sighed. 'I told him last night that we need some distance. He's managed to stay out of my way all morning. I don't want to cross paths with him now or he'll think it's some silly game, like I'm playing hard to get.'

Sheena suddenly gasped and ducked. Her movement startled Nikki. 'He's coming this way,' Sheena hissed. Rahul was indeed advancing on the car. All of a sudden, Sheena became very busy. She fiddled with the radio tuner and leaned over Nikki to open the glove box and search through a mess of old parking tickets. Rahul knocked on the window.

Sheena rolled down the window. 'Oh, hello,' she said breezily.

'Hi,' Rahul said. 'Is everything okay?'

'Hmm? Oh yes,' Sheena said. 'We're in the middle of a conversation, so if you don't mind excusing us . . .'

'Sure. I noticed your car parked here but the lights were on, so I was checking to see if there was anyone inside. I was afraid your battery would die.'

'Thank you,' Sheena said. 'We're fine here.' The high colour in Sheena's cheeks indicated that she was anything but fine.

'Okay,' Rahul said. They watched him walk away and when he entered the bank, Sheena let out a huff of air. 'Do you think I did a good job playing cool? I don't know. He's thrown me off now.' She flapped her hands at her cheeks. 'Now I'm going to be late returning to work because I can't walk in there, all flushed like this.'

'I shouldn't have taken up so much of your time,' Nikki said, glancing at the clock on Sheena's dashboard. 'I'm not sure what I was expecting, marching into the bank and thinking we'd just chat over the counter about it.'

Sheena continued fanning herself. It looked as if she were waving away Nikki's apology. 'You weren't expecting a complicated story. Nobody does. If a girl is killed, it's unimaginable that her loved ones would have a hand in it. People don't consider it unless they know what goes on in this community.'

'I thought I was well aware,' Nikki mused. 'When Tarampal told me about Maya's suicide, I was shocked but then I remembered that honour was a big deal in this community. I didn't think there was more to it . . .'

Here Nikki's voice trailed off. *Maya's suicide.* Out loud in this small space, the words were jarring. A dreadful question began to form in her mind. Clearly, Sheena noticed. She abruptly stopped fussing over her face and dropped her hands to her lap. In the heavy silence that followed, Nikki summoned the courage to ask her question.

'Did Maya really commit suicide?'

Sheena's reply was unexpectedly swift. 'Do you think she'd do something like that?'

'I didn't know her,' Nikki said.

The impatience in Sheena's sigh was noticeable. 'Come on, Nikki. A modern girl leaving a note confessing to her "sins" and "ruining the family's honour?" Maya was too Westernized to have such concerns.'

Tarampal had not mentioned a note. Her version of events had made the incident sound more spontaneous – Jaggi's threats of divorce sending Maya into an immediate panic. 'Who wrote the suicide note then?' Nikki asked.

'Probably the person who killed her.'

'You're not suggesting . . .' Nikki felt her legs growing cold from the shock. 'Jaggi? Because of the affair?'

'If there *was* an affair, but who knows?' Sheena said. 'Jaggi was the jealous sort. Tarampal didn't help things by spying on Maya and assuming that every smile she gave a man meant that she was sleeping with him. She meddled in their marriage.'

'There was no police investigation? How is that possible?'

Sheena shrugged. 'I know that Kulwinder tried talking to the police once, but they didn't believe there was any evidence of foul play.'

'So they just closed the case?' Nikki asked.

'There were testimonies – some of Jaggi's friends' wives reported that Maya had been considering suicide for a while. They made it sound like they were really tight – a social club of wives – but I can tell you that Maya hardly spoke to them. She had friends of her own.'

'And where were they?' Nikki demanded. 'Why didn't they come forward?'

'Fear, I guess,' Sheena said. 'Everybody's too afraid to fight for Maya. The risks are too high and nobody knows for sure if anything suspicious really happened. Even Kulwinder avoids the police now. I see her taking the long route from the market sometimes so she won't have to pass the station. Somebody probably warned her not to rock the boat.'

A chill passed through Nikki. She had brazenly entered the home where a murder may have taken place – a *planned* one. 'Tarampal wasn't there when it happened, was she?'

'No. I remember seeing her at a temple program that night. But Kulwinder has never forgiven her. Tarampal told the police that Maya had threatened to burn down the whole house the night before her death.' Sheena rolled her eyes. 'If Maya ever said such a thing, I'm sure it was taken out of context. Tarampal's testimony made Maya sound like an agonized wife from a Hindi movie.'

Unstable, Tarampal had repeated. 'And it made the suicide seem more plausible.'

'Yes,' Sheena said. 'Tarampal's loyalties are with that boy one hundred per cent.'

The son Tarampal always wanted. Nikki shook her head. 'This is so . . .'

'Twisted? Messed up?' Sheena offered. 'Now you see why I warned you about prying? It's dangerous.'

Nikki understood but she still didn't want to back away. 'What about the note? Was it in Maya's handwriting?'

'It must have been close enough. The police were convinced it was a suicide note. They told Kulwinder the words were smudged, like Maya had been crying.'

'A good detail,' Nikki said drily. 'Sounds like they were eager to latch onto any scrap of evidence that suggested suicide. No messy investigations, no can of worms to open.' Poor Kulwinder.

'I suppose so. Kulwinder didn't have a chance of getting into Tarampal's home, let alone searching it for a sample of Maya's handwriting.'

Nikki dropped her head to her hands. 'It's sickening, Sheena,' she said. 'We're sitting here, almost certain that an innocent woman was murdered.'

'But there's no way to prove it,' Sheena said. 'Remember that, Nikki. Don't try to be a hero here. It doesn't work.' Before stepping out of the car, Sheena adjusted her collar in such a way that it swallowed her pendant and made it disappear.

Chapter Eleven

Geeta was gesticulating wildly. Her henna-dyed beehive quivered from the force of her movements. 'Then they told him his shoes were too muddy to enter their country. Can you believe these people? Luckily Nikki and Mindi don't have to travel anywhere for work. These Customs officials can be so fussy.'

'I thought Customs in Australia was strict about muddy shoes from overseas because of foreign soil particles mixing with theirs,' Harpreet said, ignoring Geeta's subtle jibe at her daughters whose unimportant jobs didn't take them overseas.

'*Leh*. Foreign soil. What's so foreign about Britain's soil? No, I'm telling you, these people were giving him a hard time because they thought he was Muslim.'

Having already invited herself to Harpreet's home for tea, Geeta was pleased to have an audience for her grievances. Her intentions of boasting were never subtle. In the past ten minutes, she had mentioned her son's trip to Sydney no less than four times. Harpreet wished she had gone to the temple yesterday. She had avoided it because she knew Geeta was an avid attendee of all Enfield gurudwara's weekday programs; then she ran into her in the Sainsbury's car park. She checked the clock. Still at least an hour before Mindi would finish her hospital shift and return home.

'Suresh said Sydney is very much like London,' Geeta tried again.

'What was he doing there?' Harpreet asked.

'His company sent him there for a conference. All expenses paid. They even flew him on business class. He said, "Mummy-ji, only the bosses fly on business class. There must be some mistake. Nowadays there are so many budget cuts that even the CEOs are flying in economy. But they said, no, no, there's been no mistake. All part of the company perks.'

'That's very nice,' Harpreet said. She had no news of her children to boast of. Mindi remained unmarried and Nikki – well Nikki had not said anything about her Southall job since starting. Earlier this afternoon Nikki had brought the box of sweets and then hurried off, claiming to have some appointment just as Harpreet was about to ask again how her job was going and what exactly she was planning to *do* with it. Harpreet got the vague sense that the job was not a subject Nikki wanted to discuss, which likely meant that she had quit, just like she quit university.

Geeta responded to Harpreet's silence with a look of pity. 'Children will do as they please,' she said generously.

Not your children, Harpreet thought. But then who wanted sons like Geeta's – grown men who still called her Mummy? 'How is your yoga class going?' Harpreet asked to change the subject.

'Good, good,' Geeta said. 'Improving my blood flow. We need this kind of exercise. The teacher is a very lean woman but she's in her fifties. She says she's been practicing for only a few years but she's gained a lot of flexibility.'

'*Hanh*, yoga gives you a lot of strength.'

'You should join us on Tuesday evenings.'

Harpreet could think of nothing worse than attending a yoga class with Geeta and her gaggle of friends who spent more time backwards boasting than downward dogging. 'Personally, I prefer the gym.'

'You joined a gym?'

'A few weeks ago,' Harpreet said. 'I just brisk walk on the treadmill and ride the stationary bike sometimes. I like going in the mornings. It gives me more energy.'

'Energy for what?' Geeta asked. 'At our age, we should be slowing down.' Disapproval clung to her words.

'Everybody is different,' Harpreet said.

Leaning forward to pick up a piece of ladoo, Geeta's kameez blouse dipped forward, revealing a deep line of cleavage. 'What I like about yoga is that it's all women. Is your gym unisex?'

Harpreet's face burned. She was trapped into answering Geeta's question. So what if there were men at her gym? 'Yes,' she said.

'Come to yoga,' Geeta said. It was a reprimand. 'There are other women like us there,' she added.

'*Hanh*, women like us,' Harpreet said vaguely. If a uniform and a code of conduct could be issued to Punjabi women over the age of fifty, Geeta would have designed it.

'How is Mindi doing?' Geeta asked.

'She's well. Working today.'

'Found anybody yet?'

'I'm not sure,' Harpreet said. This would be the default answer until Mindi was ready to get engaged. The truth was, Mindi had been seeing someone but she hadn't mentioned him lately. Harpreet was afraid to ask. On one hand, she wanted Mindi to find someone and settle down. But it meant returning each evening to an empty home and Harpreet wasn't ready for that.

'She'd better find somebody quickly, nah? If she spends all this time looking and comes up empty, it looks bad.'

'She'll find someone,' Harpreet said. 'There's no use pressuring the girl. She can think for herself.'

'Of course she will,' Geeta murmured.

Harpreet poured the last of her pot of chai into Geeta's cup. Black specks of Lipton leaves dotted the surface. 'Come, I'll filter them out,' she said, taking the cup from Geeta's hand. In the kitchen, she searched for her sieve and remembered having to throw away the one her mother had given her to take to England after Nikki and Mindi used it to scoop their goldfish out of its tank. She felt a pang of sadness. What was home without her family?

Geeta was brushing crumbs off her lips when Harpreet returned. 'No sugar, please,' she said with the nobility of a dieter. But no combination of yoga poses would eliminate those ladoo calories, Harpreet thought with smug satisfaction.

'Now tell me,' Geeta said after taking a sip of tea, 'have you heard about these stories?'

'What stories?'

'The *stories*,' Geeta said.

Harpreet found it difficult to mask her irritation. Why did people prefer repeating rather than explaining themselves? 'I don't know what you're talking about.'

Geeta set her cup on its saucer. 'The stories that have been passed around the entire Punjabi community of London. When Mittoo Kaur told me about them I laughed and didn't believe her. Then she brought one of the stories to my house. She said that she had read it aloud to her husband and after that . . .' She shook her head. 'Well, people get affected by these things.' She stared at Harpreet as if this would help her absorb her point. 'They had sex on her sofa,' Geeta whispered.

'*What?* She *told* you this?'

'I was surprised as you are but the story was very involving.'

'What's the book called?' Harpreet asked.

'It's not a book,' Geeta said. 'They're just typed-up stories. Nobody knows exactly where they're coming from.'

'What do you mean? The author's anonymous?'

'Supposedly there's no single author. These stories haven't been published anywhere. They're just being copied, scanned, emailed and faxed all over London and they're reaching an intended audience. Mittoo Kaur has read three already, and all three have completely transformed her relations with her husband. During yoga class the other day, when the teacher asked us to lie on our backs and pull our knees to our chests, Mittoo winked at me and said, "Just like last night." At our age! Can you imagine?'

'No,' Harpreet said quickly. 'I can't.' She *was* imagining though. She was picturing herself with Mohan. 'Did Mittoo tell you where she got the stories from?'

'Her cousin passed them to her. Her cousin got them from a friend at the Enfield temple, who first heard about them from a Punjabi colleague who lives in East London. She lost the trail there because her cousin never asked the colleague where the stories came from but Mittoo Kaur isn't the only person I know who has come across these stories. Kareem Singh's wife told me she's come across them as well. The one she told me about was very graphic. A Punjabi woman brings her car to a mechanic and they end up having sex on the bonnet. She ties his wrists to the wing mirror with her dupatta.'

'They're that detailed?' Harpreet asked. 'I've never come across stories like that with our people in them.'

'Rumour has it the stories are coming from Southall.'

'That's ridiculous,' Harpreet said with a laugh. 'I'd believe it if you said they were from Bombay, but if they're from England, they're not from there.'

'No, it's true. Her aunt has a friend who attended a class there on how to write dirty stories.'

That made no sense. 'There would be riots in the community if such a thing existed,' Harpreet said.

'That's why it's advertised as an English class.'

'That's imposs—' Harpreet froze. Southall. English class. Harpreet swallowed and kept quiet. She reminded herself that Geeta was a gossip. Geeta exaggerated. There was no reason to think—

'You know what else she told me? The stories are being written by older women whose husbands have died. Can you imagine? Women like us.'

'*Hanh*,' Harpreet croaked. She took a gulp of tea. 'Women like us.'

* * *

By the time Nikki got to Southall station the next day, she was grumbling under her breath. The train had been delayed and she was running so late that there wasn't even time for that cigarette that she badly craved. Bloody Jason and his plan for them to quit together. The bus dutifully climbed the hill and descended slowly onto the Broadway. Vegetable peels littered the ground outside the market and sequins twinkled like constellations in the sari shop windows. A couple emerged from the steps of Fast Track Visa Service clutching papers against their chests. As the bus pulled up to the temple, Nikki checked the time on her phone: class had started half an hour ago.

A humming noise was coming from the community centre building. Nikki climbed the stairs. The noise grew. Distinct voices – Arvinder's and Sheena's – could be heard over an ocean of excited chatter. Nikki walked into the room and gasped. There were women everywhere – sitting cross-legged on tables, nestled comfortably in chairs, leaning against the walls, perched on the teacher's desk at the front of the room.

Nikki was speechless. She stepped back and stared at the women, unable at first to take in what she was seeing. There were many widows, distinct in their white attire, but clusters of women from other age groups had joined the classes as well. The presence of younger women was chaotic – the clink of bangles, the clouds of perfume. The voices of the middle-aged women rang out with an enviable certainty.

It was the widows who noticed her first. One by one, they pulled away from their conversation and focused on Nikki. The noise bled from the room gradually until Nikki was facing a completely quiet group of women. She felt the sudden need for air and wondered if she had been holding her breath this whole time.

'Is that the teacher?' one woman asked.

'No, the classes are being run by a *gori*.'

'What *gori* can speak Punjabi?' another woman asked. 'No, it must be her.'

The chatter commenced again, voices bouncing across the walls. Nikki stepped through the crowds and found Sheena.

'When did they all show up?' Nikki asked.

'The first ones were standing outside the building about an hour ago. I noticed them from the langar hall and hurried over to tell them that the classes hadn't started yet. They said, "That's all right, we're waiting for the others." Then another crowd arrived,' Sheena said.

'When you said that the stories had spread all over London . . .' Nikki said, looking around.

'I didn't think there would be this many women either,' Sheena said. 'But we couldn't turn them away.'

'But what will we do when Kulwinder returns?'

'We can make up a roster,' Sheena said. 'The women can sign up for sessions.'

'Or we can start our own classes in our areas,' a woman sitting nearby called out. 'Anyone else here live in the Wembley area?'

A few hands shot up. *Oh shit*, Nikki thought. If the stories were spreading, they had probably reached Enfield as well. She did a quick scan for Mum's friends and saw nobody that she recognized.

'Everybody listen,' Nikki shouted. The women were momentarily stunned into silence. Nikki rushed to maintain the pause. 'Welcome to all of you. I want to thank you for coming tonight. I wasn't expecting such a large turnout, and we'll need to put a limit on class sizes in the future.' She looked around the room. 'I also want to emphasize the need to be discreet, although I'm not sure if it's realistic.' Her heartbeat quickened at the thought of the Brothers discovering them. 'We could be in a lot of trouble if the wrong people find out about these classes.'

Quick glances darted about the room. Nikki's heart sank. 'They already know, don't they?' she asked.

From a back corner, Preetam raised her hand. 'Dharminder here says she found out about the classes because one of the Brothers came knocking on her door asking if she knew anything about the stories.'

Dharminder, a stout widow whose low dupatta hung over her eyes, nodded. 'Yes. If anything, they're the ones spreading the word.'

It wouldn't be long before they went knocking on Kulwinder's door then. Panic tightened Nikki's chest. They had to stop the classes – they had to, otherwise the women were in danger. *She* was in danger. 'I'm not sure if this is a good idea then,' Nikki said.

'We can't shut down the classes now, Nikki,' Sheena said. 'These women have come from all over. Let's go on with the session tonight and then we'll think about what to do later.'

The room was silent now. All eyes were fixed on Nikki. Sheena was right – these women had turned up to support the class. She couldn't stand the thought of turning them away and losing all of these new voices.

'Who has a story to share?'

Hands shot into the air and voices began to overlap. Nikki gestured for quiet. She searched the room. A bony middle-aged woman wearing a long maroon kurti stretched over black tights was waving a piece of paper.

'My story is incomplete,' she confessed when Nikki called on her. 'I need some help with it. Oh, I'm Amarjhot, by the way.' She giggled shyly. Her mannerisms reminded Nikki of her first encounters with Manjeet. 'Why don't you start us off, Amarjhot,' Nikki said.

As Amarjhot approached the front of the room, the other women clapped. Amarjhot cleared her throat and began.

There was a young, beautiful woman by the name of Rani. She looked like a princess but she was not treated like this by her parents. Being the youngest daughter of a poor family, Rani had to do all the housework and she was rarely let out of the house. Many people in her village did not even know she existed.

There was an audible yawn in the back of the room. Amarjhot's reading was very slow. She continued describing Rani – her hazel brown eyes, her fair skin with cheeks you could mistake for apples, her slender waist. Then one day, a man came to ask Rani for her hand in marriage. She stopped here. She stared at her page and then turned to Nikki. 'After this, I couldn't find the words. They wouldn't come. I remember what I wanted to say though.'

'Say it then. Skip to the wedding night,' Preetam called out. 'What did Rani and this man do together?' Anticipatory giggles floated through the room.

Amarjhot closed her eyes briefly and a smile flashed across her face. She began to laugh.

The more vocal women in the room were more than happy to bring the story forward. 'He unwound her wedding outfit and laid her on the bed.'

'He took off his clothes. Or she took off his clothes for him and touched his body.'

'He had a big one.'

'Massive. Like a python.'

'He used it gently though, because she knew so little. He let her hold it first and move her hands along it.'

'And then he kissed her,' continued Amarjhot. 'She eased at the touch of his lips on hers. As they kissed, he traced his fingers over her body as if he was drawing her. He circled a flat palm over her nipples. They hardened at his touch. He then put his lips to one nipple and began sucking while rolling the other gently between his fingers. Rani was in ecstasy.'

'But she began moaning a name which wasn't his,' Bibi called out.

Gasps and murmurs of appreciation. 'Whose name was she calling out?'

'No, don't – this Rani was a virtuous girl who was feeling love for the first time – why ruin it?'

'Nobody's ruining anything. We're just adding masala,' Tanveer said.

Their heckling faded into the background for Nikki. She carefully stepped past the women to the desk, where the enrolments list was kept. It would be a good idea to record names and details. Looking through the paperwork, she came across Tarampal's registration form. Nikki couldn't help another wave of panic – where was 16 Ansell Road on the Brothers' canvassing trail?

'Maybe they try it at first but they discover that he's too large,' Preetam suggested.

'So they do it from behind,' another woman said.

'Eww,' a few women squealed. There was then a small and precise lesson in what 'behind' meant. 'Not in her bum,' Tanveer said helpfully, to their relief.

'Oh, why not though? That's not so bad. It's different.'

'Have you not heard how big this guy's garden pipe is? It's more like a fire hose. Would you really want something that size entering your exit-zone?'

'Where the hell is their ghee?' somebody asked desperately.

The discussion continued. It was finally decided that Rani and her husband would turn their crisis into an exciting adventure. They would try a variety of positions.

Spot fires of conversation broke out across the classroom. Casual confessions drifted into earshot. 'My husband and I tried that one,' Hardayal Kaur sniffed. 'It only works if you're very flexible. My knees were too stiff from farm work, even at age twenty.'

'Mine tried to put his banana between my breasts once. I don't recommend it. It was like seeing a canoe trying to edge its way through two hillsides.'

Amarjhot glanced helplessly at the page in her hands. 'I think I have to consider this story a bit further,' she said. She returned to her seat.

'*My tongue will stoke your burning fire; a hot, licking flame of pure desire,*' boomed a voice from the far left corner of the room. All heads turned to Gurlal Kaur. She was a vision of peaceful meditation with her legs crossed and her eyes closed. Her words commanded silence. She continued.

'*You are the suppleness of soil, the strength of stalks. Let me lay atop you, my manhood growing like a root into your velvety soft embrace. When it rains, I feel your slick wetness against my body and I breathe in your musky scent. We will rock together in a joint rhythm, our fiery passions evoking the strongest thunder and lightning to crack onto this earth.*'

All that could be heard was the breathing of women. Nikki was the first to speak. 'Did you just make that up?' she asked.

Gurlal shook her head. She opened her eyes. 'There was a terrible drought in my village the year I was supposed to marry. My parents couldn't afford a dowry but they knew I wouldn't settle for anyone less than my dear Mukesh Singh, whom I had met once during a bridal viewing and fallen madly in love with. My parents knew I wouldn't be happier with anybody else; they had seen the way our eyes lit up when we first saw each other. *You're the one*, we both said silently.'

'That's beautiful,' Preetam said. 'The land was barren but their love grew.' The other women shushed her.

'Each morning and night, special prayers were said for the rain. They were being said in Mukesh's village as well, where the situation was no better. It was from those daily prayers that he became inspired to write poetry. He sent the poems to my home. I had to be careful to collect them from the mailman before my parents got to them, although they wouldn't have been able to read the poems anyway. They were both illiterate. That year, my father often grumbled that my schooling had given me too many choices because I was stubbornly insisting on marrying Mukesh. I took out one of the letters and pretended that it was a note from Mukesh's relatives, praising my father for raising such an educated daughter. That appeased him. That poem is my favourite.'

'Do you still remember it?' asked Sheena.

'Of course.' She drew a breath and closed her eyes again. '*My beloved. Your body is an entire galaxy; your moles and dimples a sprinkling of stars. I am just a weary desert traveller, my lips parched and searching for refreshment. Each time I am ready to give up, I look up, and there you lay in the stretch of midnight skies. Your hair billows around you and your hands fall away from your chest, revealing your pale, round breasts. At their tips, your nipples point to greet my puckered lips. I kiss them tenderly and feel the shudder of sensation rock through your body, your world. Between your legs, a flower is moistening itself, its lips plump with anticipation. Your body is an entire galaxy of its own accord. I explore you with my lips, grateful for my thirst to be quenched and when I reach your forbidden garden, my thirst becomes your hunger. Your long legs are draped around my neck, your hips thrusting against my mouth. My lips become wet with your dew. I press them inside you and feel the throb of your blood pulsing into your most intimate places. How grateful I am to have my lips against yours in this way, to connect these blushing parts of ourselves together.'*

A serene smile gave Gurlal's face an ethereal quality. She dipped her body forward into a modest bow.

'Tell us what it was like when you two finally got together. Just as good?' Preetam asked.

'Oh, I bet it was. If his hands could spell out such beautiful poetry, imagine what they could do in the bedroom,' said Sheena.

'It was very good,' Gurlal said. 'He wrote a poem for every single night that we were together. I can recite every single one.'

The impossibility of this claim bothered none of the ladies. The room was filled with a hallowed silence.

'Go on then. Tell us another one,' Arvinder urged. Gurlal opened her eyes and was about to respond when suddenly a visible jolt shot through her. The room filled with a quick rustling. Nikki looked up and felt a stab in her gut from the sight.

Kulwinder Kaur was standing in the doorway, her mouth agape.

Nikki crossed to the front of the room with a smile plastered on her face. She could not know how much Kulwinder had heard but excuses were already forming in her mind. Maybe she could convince Kulwinder that the women had been discussing alternate endings to an Indian drama.

'I want to see you outside now,' Kulwinder hissed. Nikki followed her into the corridor.

'You've just dropped in at an unfortunate time,' Nikki began. Kulwinder held up her hand to silence Nikki.

'How long has this been going on?' Kulwinder asked.

Nikki looked at her feet. She was about to mumble a reply when Kulwinder spoke again. 'To think that I trusted you to lead these women into literacy. All this time you were filling their heads with filth.'

Nikki's head jerked up and she stared Kulwinder straight in the eyes. 'The women wanted this.'

'Rubbish,' Kulwinder retorted. 'You've been corrupting this community right under my nose this whole time.'

'I haven't! Look – many of these women's husbands don't know they're here. Please don't tell them.'

'I have better things to do with my time than go around poking my nose into other people's lives,' Kulwinder said. She looked past Nikki into the room full of women. 'How did you get all of these new women to sign up? What did you tell them?'

'I didn't have to tell them anything,' Nikki replied. 'Word spreads quickly in this community, as you well know. The women wanted a place to express themselves.'

'*Express* themselves?' Kulwinder retorted, showing Nikki just what she thought of her response. She pushed her way into the room, her palms open in a silent but clear instruction: *give them to me*. The few women who had written stories reluctantly handed them over. The majority could give her nothing. The eldest women reacted admirably. They stared at Kulwinder, their lips tightly pressed together as if to protect their stories from being stolen right from their minds. As Kulwinder's raid continued, women scooted out of the way to create a path for her. She reached the desk.

'Where are the rest?' she asked.

'In my bag,' Nikki croaked. Her satchel was closed. She could not imagine any other circumstance where she would allow somebody to open her bag and search it as Kulwinder was doing now, her thick fingers extracting the binder like it was a diseased organ. Kulwinder strode out the door and down the hallway, the binder held tightly against her chest. Nikki went after her.

'Kulwinder, please. Just let us explain.'

Kulwinder stopped walking. 'There's nothing to explain,' she said.

'So much work has gone into those stories,' Nikki said. 'You have no idea. Please give them back to us.' She had thought of scanning the pages into a back-up copy but she hadn't got around to it. 'You weren't even supposed to be back yet,' she accused.

'And you thought that as long as I was away, you'd make a mockery of my English classes? Thank goodness I had the sense to check up on you.

You've never taken this job seriously.'

'You advertised for an instructor for a storytelling class. That's what I wanted to do, and that's what the women wanted out of these sessions as well.'

'Don't you dare blame me for this,' Kulwinder said, pointing her finger inches away from Nikki's face. 'I should have known you were going around recruiting women to sabotage my classes and turn them into something corrupt.'

'The women came on their own,' Nikki said.

'You were knocking on doors on my street just before I left for India. I saw you.'

'I only visited Tarampal because I wanted to—'

'You went to Mrs Shah's house before that. I saw you from my window.'

'I got the address wrong,' Nikki said. 'Honestly. I wasn't going around—'

'That's enough. You are lying to my face now.'

'Well, it's true. You can ask Mrs Shah if you want. The form said 18 Ansell Road but Tarampal lived on 16 Ansell Road. She had written 16 but the ink was smudged and it looked like 18 . . .' Nikki paused. It didn't sound like the truth. Tarampal did not know how to write her own address.

'I don't want to hear any more excuses. You've gambled with my reputation. Do you know what people will say once this gets out? Do you realize how hard it was to ask the men of the Board to fund these classes?' Kulwinder asked.

Nikki nodded absent-mindedly. Her mind was still on the form. She recalled Jason's story about his mother scrubbing the ink stains from his left hand.

'And with so many women joining the classes, did you really think you could hide this from me? How long were you going to—?'

'Kulwinder,' Nikki said.

'Don't interrupt me.'

'Kulwinder, this is important,' Nikki said. The urgency in her voice must have struck Kulwinder. For a moment, she looked concerned.

'What is it?' she asked irritably.

'Your son-in-law, Jaggi. Was he left-handed?'

'What are you talking about?'

'More importantly, was Maya right-handed? Because . . . because . . .'

'What on earth are you—?'

'Just, please, I know this sounds crazy.' Nikki rushed back into the classroom and returned with Tarampal's registration form. 'This is Jaggi's handwriting. You could show this to the police and they could compare it to the note. The note was smudged too, wasn't it? Those weren't tears – his hand just brushed against the ink and—'

Kulwinder snatched the form from Nikki's hands. She didn't even look at it. Her anger made her chest heave up and down. 'Who the hell are you to bring my daughter into this?' she asked, her voice suddenly low and frightening.

'I know that you're afraid to investigate it but there might be something here,' Nikki said. She pointed at the registration form. 'Just consider it, please. I could go to the police with you. There's evidence.'

'What happened to Maya has nothing to do with you,' Kulwinder said. 'You have no right—'

'I have every right if I think an innocent woman was killed and the culprit could be caught.'

'You're trying to change the subject to distract me,' Kulwinder said. 'I won't have you using my classes or the women of this community to carry out your agenda – whatever it may be.'

'I don't have an—' Nikki attempted to argue, but Kulwinder's silencing palm had shot up again like a wall. She stared her down. 'I want you to go back into that room and clear them out. These classes are suspended. You are fired.'

Chapter Twelve

Kulwinder marched home against the brisk winds, clutching the folder against her chest. Her rage was in danger of spilling out onto the streets. She wanted to scream and for a strange moment, she invited thoughts of running into Jaggi now. One fiery look would send him scuttling away.

She arrived home with wild hair and flushed cheeks. Sarab was in the living room as always, the television lights flickering against the windows. She marched in and commanded his attention with a wave of the folder. 'Did you know about this?'

He looked up, the remote control poised as if to pause her. 'Know about what?'

'The English classes. The other day, you said the classes have become very popular. Did you know what was going on?'

He shrugged and looked down. A movie heroine raced across the screen, her faithful dupatta trailing behind her like a red banner. 'There has been some talk, sure. The English classes are not what they seem.'

'What are people saying exactly? What are the men saying?'

'You know I don't listen much to idle conversation. There were just a few comments that some wives were becoming more outspoken. They had an entirely new vocabulary to describe . . .' He shrugged and watched the heroine, who was inexplicably wearing a completely different outfit now. Kulwinder took the remote from him and turned off the television.

'Describe what?' she demanded.

'Their desires.' His face flushed. 'In the bedroom.'

'Why didn't you tell me this?' she asked.

'Kulwinder,' he said calmly. Her heart missed a beat. It had been very long since he said her name. 'When have I been able to tell you anything you don't want to hear?'

She stared at him in disbelief. 'Those women's conversations aren't just about their bedroom lives. They told Nikki about Maya. For all I know, they've been discussing it openly for weeks and putting our lives at risk.' She hadn't recognized half the women in that room – what versions of the story had they spun and how would she control it?

'Do they know something?' Sarab asked. The hope in his voice broke Kulwinder's heart.

'Nikki thinks she has some proof but it's nothing, Sarab. We shouldn't get our hopes up.'

As Kulwinder relayed Nikki's discovery about Jaggi's handwriting, she remembered the police telling her about the note and its contents. The constable had to brace her fall as she staggered onto a chair. What had the note said? Something about being sorry, something about being ashamed. 'They're not my daughter's words,' Kulwinder had managed to say. 'My daughter was not concerned about *izzat*.' When had Maya ever used Punjabi words when an English one would suffice? The writer of the note had been careless and hasty in this imitation of her daughter.

Sarab stared and stared. He looked at Kulwinder as if she had materialized suddenly out of thin air. 'Jaggi's left handed.'

'So what?' Kulwinder asked. 'It doesn't mean—'

'There's something we can do.'

'Will they accept it?' Kulwinder asked. 'Or will they just repeat what they've always said: that Maya was distressed, that it's natural to look for somebody to blame? Then what if the police won't help us and Jaggi finds out we've gone to them again?' The first time Jaggi called in the middle of the night, there were no threats. He simply told her that he and his friends knew what time Sarab left work on his late shifts. 'The important thing is to stay safe now,' she reminded Sarab.

'Is it?' Sarab asked angrily. 'Are we meant to live our whole lives in fear?' He crossed the room and pulled open the living room curtains, exposing the view of Tarampal's house across the road.

'Please,' Kulwinder said, turning her back on the window. 'Close the curtains.' Sarab did as she told. They sat in the shadows, listening to the low hum of the house lights. 'Sarab, if something happened to you—' She couldn't complete her sentence. She was aware of Sarab's heaving breaths from across the room. 'I lost Maya. I can't lose you as well.'

Sarab's lip trembled. *Say it to me now*, Kulwinder urged silently but he looked past her. She wondered if he had been lonely when she was away or relieved not to avoid speaking to her. She could see them drifting further apart, sleeping in separate rooms, politely waiting for each other to vacate the living room before settling in front of the television. Just the thought made her feel terribly lonely, as if it was already happening.

'How about Nikki?' Sarab asked.

Kulwinder narrowed her eyes. The last thing she wanted to do was talk about Nikki. 'What about her?' she asked impatiently.

'Where does she live?'

'Somewhere in West London.'

'Tell her she needs to be careful.'

Kulwinder thought back to her heated confrontation with Nikki. Not once had she mentioned to Nikki that she might be in danger. Did Jaggi know about Nikki's questions? And what if the Brothers found out that she was the ringleader of these classes? Kulwinder shook her head to dismiss the thought. Nikki lived outside Southall. There was no need to panic about her safety. 'I don't know where she might be now,' Kulwinder said.

'Go to the next class and—'

'I've suspended the classes,' Kulwinder said. 'I fired Nikki.'

Sarab looked up sharply. 'Kulwinder, think about the girl,' he said. He drew himself away from her. She felt the emptiness of the room as he vacated it but her indignation remained. It was Nikki who had put them in this situation. If she had just done her job, none of this would have happened. Kulwinder opened the folder. Weeks and weeks of deception were written in these pages. Picking through the folder, she saw that one of the illiterate widows had put her artistic talents to use and filled a page with illustrations. A man hovering over a woman's breast, his mouth slightly open to capture her nipple. A woman straddling a man, the crease down her spine to her buttock defined to show the slight arching of her back. Filth.

Kulwinder tossed the papers back into the folder and went to the kitchen to make some tea. She poured the water into the pot. While waiting for it to heat up, she could not help thinking about the angles of the man's body as he crouched over the woman. She shook her head and focused on the pot. Tiny bubbles were beginning to surface on the water. She crossed to the spice cabinet and took out the fennel and cardamom seeds and there, again, she paused and shut her eyes. Spots of light danced around as her vision adjusted to the darkness. Then, instead of disappearing, the spots took shape. A man. A woman. Fingers skilfully gliding across bare skin. Red lips pressing into glistening flesh. Her eyes flew open. She went to the stove and took the pot off. She glanced at the folder. She supposed there was no harm in reading one story, just to review the information. After all, if she were to be questioned by the council over this, she needed to have all the details.

Kulwinder picked out the first story.

The Tailor

Centuries ago, on the fringes of a palace city, there was a talented but modest tailor named Ram. Ram's customers were women who wanted to look like the royals who lived behind the palace walls. These women travelled for miles to see Ram, carrying with them a list of seemingly impossible demands. It was said that Ram had a gift for putting together the most regal and fashionable creations out of nothing. He could spin a simple yellow thread into gold and turn an ordinary pale green into the rich emerald shade of a rare jewel.

Many of Ram's customers were enamoured with him. They noticed the way he handled his modest sewing machine, his fingers deftly moving between layers of cloth and they drew conclusions about what a talented man he must be between the sheets. During fittings, some women purposely loosened their top garments and leaned forward to give him a sneak peek at their cleavage. Some left a gap in the curtain of the changing space to give Ram a chance to peek. Ram paid no attention. While working, he preferred not to be distracted by temptations. One day he would have time for a lover but for now there were too many orders. Word had spread all over India that Ram was the best tailor. The popular rhyme went:

The tailor Ram is the best in town
You'll feel like a royal in a fancy gown
His prices are good, his prices are fair
You'll be a queen with a crown in her hair

But for every piece of praise Ram received, there was also a curse. Jealous tailors all over India were furious with him for luring their clients away with his magical skills. Ordinary men cursed him for catering to the demands of their wives, who, when wearing such fine saris, expected royal treatment.

One afternoon a woman came to Ram asking for his help. Her hazel eyes made Ram's heart skip. 'For once, I would like to look like a rich woman,' she told him in a voice that he wanted to hear whispering in his ear. She handed him an old shawl. 'I can't afford to buy something new but can you stitch a border onto to this?'

'Of course,' Ram said. For you, I would do anything, *he thought. 'Your husband must have bought this for you.'*

The woman smiled and tucked a stray hair behind her ear. 'I have no husband,' she said to Ram's delight.

This beautiful woman was fit to look like a queen. Ram decided that he would not accept any payment from her when the shawl was completed – all he wanted was a chance at another conversation so he could find out her name. Ram's passion for the woman ignited his creativity. He blended dyes to create threads of the most brilliant colours to impress her. The border of the shawl would be lined with a parade of turquoise and magenta peacocks. In the centre of the border, Ram would embroider a replica of the palace with a miniscule image of the woman standing in one of its windows. He would point it out to her, this secret, so she would know that she was his queen.

A scene with this level of detail required Ram's fullest concentration. He was so focused that he dismissed the voices of the children playing outside. It was only when he heard his name that he stopped working and paid attention.

The tailor Ram is the best in town
You'll look like a princess in a fancy gown
His prices are good, his prices are fair
But he'll never be a part of a loving pair

This was the worst curse in existence because it banished its victim to a lifetime of loneliness. Ram ran outside. 'Where did you hear that?' Ram asked. The children scattered. Ram chased them up the street before he realized that he was still holding the shawl. It was ripped and covered in mud from being dragged along the ground. 'Oh no!' Ram cried out. He returned to his shop and tried his best to repair the shawl but it was ruined. That evening, when the woman returned to check on the shawl's progress, Ram hung his head in shame and said that he had lost the shawl. The woman was outraged. Gone was the warmth from her hazel eyes. 'How could you do this?' she screamed. 'You're the worst tailor in the world!'

Ram closed his shop the next day. He wept at his workstation, seeing the curse darkening his future like a storm cloud. He had never wished for anything before but now he wished for a chance at intimacy. Why didn't I bed a woman when I had the chance? he asked himself. He went to sleep dreaming of the milky thighs of the customers who had bared their bodies to him. In his dreams, he was bold enough to bury his face in their bosoms and breathe in their sweet scent. In another dream, Ram saw himself bent over a woman, kissing her plump lips as she stroked his manhood with one hand and tickled her own private parts with the other . . .

Suddenly, Ram woke to a rustling noise. A burglar! Ram leapt out of bed and *rushed to his storage room first. Nobody was there. The rustling noise started again. Ram shone his lamp in the direction of the noise and noticed that his fabric was moving. He picked it up and noticed that it was heavier than usual, almost solid. He brought it to his workstation to see it in a better light. The fabric twisted away from his grip and fell to the floor. Its shape shifted in waves until a woman fully emerged. Ram staggered back against the wall, staring at this ghostly thing in his home.*

'W-what are you?' he stammered.

She had the sorts of eyelids that swept as dramatically as butterfly wings each time she blinked. Her skin had a golden hue and her shimmering hair let off the sweet scent of jasmine. The curves of her body were very arousing. She followed his gaze across her chest and reached for him. Her touch was soft. Her fingers, now fully formed, ran along her body to show him that she was real. She drew attention to parts of the body that Ram had never had to consider as a tailor – the bone jutting from her collar, the sharp edge of her elbow. Her toenails were curved and white like half-moons. Her belly button was a dark crater in the golden desert of her body. Ram reached out to clutch a handful of flesh above her hip. It was as real as his own.

'Call me Laila,' she said.

She put her lips to his earlobe and sucked it gently. Shivers of delight ran through Ram like an electric current. He ran his hands down her back and grabbed her buttocks, drawing their hips together as they fell back against the bed of fabric. She unwound the loose cloth that covered the top of her body and exposed her breasts to Ram. Ram flicked his tongue against a dark nipple. Laila gasped with pleasure, grinding herself against him. Ram switched to the other breast. She tasted salty and musky, the way he could never have imagined. Daringly, he brought his fingers to her mouth. She licked and sucked on them. Ram's manhood throbbed with anticipation of what Laila's sweet, silky mouth might do for him. His fingers were slick with saliva when he pulled them away from Laila's lips and into the silky crevice between her legs.

'You're so real,' Ram uttered.

Laila spread her legs wider and allowed Ram to stroke her. The fabric beneath her darkened with shadows of sweat. With both thumbs, Ram gently parted the folds of her womanhood and used the tip of his tongue to tickle her protruding button. Laila's giggle turned him on even more. She rolled over him, pulling off his pants fiercely. His manhood was stiff. Laila teased him. She brushed her wetness against the tip of his manhood and watched his face contort with pleasure. 'How does that feel,' she breathed into his ear. Her breasts dangled over his lips. He replied with a groan. 'That's not a proper answer,' Laila said sternly. With a scowl, she lowered herself onto him and began riding vigorously on his hard, thick stick.

The angry look on Laila's face was the only remnant of the punishing nature of the curse. Ram gave Laila's bottom a hard squeeze. Her scowl deepened. 'How dare you?' she asked. He gritted his teeth, the tension building inside him. He felt Laila's muscles clenching at the same time as his. She cried out his name and let out a long, shuddering moan. Witnessing Laila's ultimate pleasure triggered Ram's quick, hot release. He grabbed her hips and moaned loudly. Laila's body was slick with sweat. She continued to rock slowly on his stick as tiny aftershocks sent quivers through his body.

As they lay together, Laila explained that she had been created from Ram's wishes to be with a woman. The curse had not been as strong enough as his desires. Aware that wishes, just like curses, have a lifespan, Ram asked Laila how long they would be together. 'As long as these rolls of fabric,' Laila said. They looked around. The fabric had unspooled and spilled across Ram's modest studio. Rich, deep hues of orange and dazzling silver threads stretched as far as they could see.

Kulwinder's tea was cold. She barely noticed it as she brought the cup to her lips and gulped it down. Her face, her hands and feet felt very warm, almost hot. She could feel the pulsing of her heart and another pulsing in very private place. There was a faint recollection of this feeling, from many years ago when she first discovered what it was that men and women did, and why they did it. Her earlier appalled façade forgotten, she was enthralled. She even dared to think that it was worth living the rest of her life for, this closeness with another human being.

She put the story back into the folder and pulled out another one. This was by Jasbir Kaur, a widow who lived in South London. Kulwinder had attended the engagement party of her grandson a few years back. She began reading Jasbir's story and felt the blood surging through her body with such urgency that she had to put it down. She stood up and left the cup of tea on the table. A wave of energy swept over her and carried her up the stairs. Lying on the bed, Sarab was staring at the ceiling. Kulwinder took his hand and laid it gently on her breast. He stared at her in confusion at first, and then he understood.

Nikki knew without ever having had the experience that she would be pretty hopeless in a fight. A wrestling scenario played in her mind and immediately she saw herself being pinned to the ground by one of Kulwinder's meaty arms. She winced; even in a fantasy, she was losing. She would have to use her wits. The stories, she would explain, had never been intended to make a mockery of the classes, or of Kulwinder. The stories were inspired by the women, and yes, they were raunchy, but weren't they learning language all the same?

If these tactics didn't work, Nikki would just grab the folder and leave. For this scenario to work, the folder would have to be within reach of course. It occurred to her with a pang that Kulwinder might have already tossed the stories out in the rubbish.

The night breeze picked up and rustled through the trees. On the main road, the headlights of cars shone intensely like eyes. Nikki turned to a side street and walked briskly to warm herself. At night, the houses seemed to crouch together behind dim patches of porch lights. Nikki's phone buzzed in her pocket. A text from Sheena.

All the women still want to meet regularly. Can you think of a place?

One problem at a time, Nikki thought, shoving the phone back into her pocket. In Kulwinder's living room, the television flashed like a siren against the windows, which had curtains only partly drawn. Nikki rang the doorbell and waited but nobody came. She tried again and then peered into the window. She could see into the whole bottom story from here. She squinted at the kitchen – lights on, a steel teapot and matching cup on the table, but nobody. Nikki shivered from the cold. The rain was getting heavier now. She tugged the hood of her jacket around her head. Opposite Kulwinder's lit house, Tarampal's home was completely dark.

Nikki crossed the road and hesitated on the edge of Tarampal's driveway. She was hoping for a better view of Kulwinder's house but she would have to go closer to Tarampal's porch. It was clear that nobody was home but this was only a small comfort. The house still loomed menacingly, its gaping windows like blackened eyes. She forced herself forward. At least the awning on the porch provided some shelter from the rain. On the second level of Kulwinder's house Nikki could see that the dim bedroom lights were on. She squinted, searching for more. At one point, she thought she saw a shadow crossing the window but it could easily have been a sheet of rain being carried by a strong gust.

What am I doing here? The question struck Nikki as the awning rattled with the thrum of rainfall. Even if she knocked on the door and Kulwinder answered it, what were her chances that Kulwinder would calmly return the stories? The pages didn't really matter. The women could retell them. There were recordings. What Nikki wanted to do was talk to Kulwinder. Explain how the stories came about. Compel her to see that these women who had started one quiet rebellion could come together to fight a bigger injustice. Her heart and mind were still racing from her discovery about Jaggi's handwriting. She just needed to convince Kulwinder that the case was worth pursuing.

Nikki ducked out from under the awning and made her way back to the main road. She would not confront Kulwinder today. It was too soon. Let her cool off; this was probably what she was doing now. On the main road, Nikki made a left towards the station. Her satchel swung against her hip without the usual weight of the stories. The windows of houses shone with a warm and familiar light. Nikki felt an ache for home. As the rain pelted down, she recalled the long walks through the city after quitting university, her face wet with rain and tears. She had entered O'Reilly's on a particularly wet afternoon, so grateful to belong somewhere, to be hidden.

Nikki stopped in her tracks. The pub! The widows could continue their meetings in the back room. She strode quickly through the rain and pulled out her phone.

'Sheena, I've found us a place to move the story classes. O'Reilly's, where I work. It's quite empty on weekday evenings.'

'You want those old Punjabi widows to meet in a pub?'

'I know it's a bit unorthodox, but—'

'I'm picturing it now.'

'I am as well,' Nikki said. Her vision switched between a scandalized Preetam refusing to enter and a drunk Arvinder swinging from the chandeliers. 'But listen, Sheena, once we get the stories started, they won't notice where they are. The important thing is to keep meeting. It can be a temporary place until we find a better solution.'

'I could drive a few of the older women,' Sheena said. 'I could find a friend to take some others and give them directions. You tell me where it is and I'll sort it out.'

'You're sure you don't mind?'

'No problem,' Sheena said.

'Another thing,' Nikki said. She paused. Sheena was not going to like this. 'There might be way to incriminate Jaggi.'

'*Hai*, Nikki!'

'Just listen.' Nikki rushed to explain the smudged registration form before Sheena could protest.

'What did Kulwinder say?' Sheena asked when Nikki was finished.

'She didn't want to hear it,' Nikki said. 'I think she was too caught up in her shock and anger about the classes. I'm still in Southall at the moment. I thought of going to her house but I've decided to give her some distance.'

'If you're near Kulwinder's house, you're not far from mine. Do you want to come over? It's really pouring out there.'

'That would be nice,' Nikki said. 'I'm on Queen Mary Road. There's a bus stop here and a little park across the road.'

'Okaaay . . . oh! I can see you now.'

'Where are you?' Nikki squinted. Through the rain, she could see the outlines of people in their homes but no specific view of Sheena.

'I'm across the road. I live near the park – but Nikki, don't stop. Keep walking quickly.'

'What's going on?'

'Just go straight and make a left at the next junction.'

Nikki felt a dreadful prickling sensation, and from the corner of her eye, she noticed a shadow. 'I'm being followed?' she whispered.

'Yes,' Sheena confirmed.

'Who is it? Can you tell?'

'It might be one of the Brothers,' Sheena said.

'I'm going to turn around and say something.'

'Don't be stupid,' Sheena hissed. Her tone startled Nikki. 'Keep walking. Stay calm. There's a 24-hour supermarket. Go to the car park and wait for me. I'll come get you.'

'No, Sheena. I'll be fine.'

'Nikki—'

Nikki hung up. Her stalker would recognize Sheena's little red car. Being on foot was an advantage. She picked up her pace. Her breath caught in her throat. She could hear the person behind her, not slowing down, not turning. He was waiting to see where she would go. She dropped back to a casual pace, her eyes darting left and right to keep track of the shadow. She crossed the road to the supermarket and took refuge in the white, open expanse of the car park. Only then did she dare to glance over her shoulder. A young Punjabi man was staring intently at her. Nikki matched his stare with all the calmness she could muster while her heartbeat thrashed in her ears. Eventually, he walked away, but not without casting a menacing look at Nikki over his shoulder.

Chapter Thirteen

Kulwinder woke. She sat upright. The duvet fell away from her, revealing her naked body. She gasped and pulled the sheet up, tightening it across her chest and tucking it beneath her armpits. Sinking back into bed she noticed the coolness of it against her bottom, her calves. She recalled the events of last night as she spotted her clothes tossed around the room carelessly. Her salwaar hanging from the corner of the ironing board, her top crumpled in the corner, her pants – her pants! – scrunched into a ball on the dresser and slowly unfurling.

She closed her eyes in embarrassment. *Oh what have we done?* she thought. Behaving like *goreh*, getting carried away in their excitement. They had wrapped themselves around each other last night like giddy lovers, moving up and down, left and right, *twisting* even. Where had it come from? The stories had provided no instructions, but they had known anyway how to bring each other to such heat. The thought of it sent shocks through Kulwinder's body and then she was overcome by a wave of shame.

But why?

She was startled by the question, uttered so clearly that it broke the silence in the room. Why was she ashamed? Because she was supposed to be; because women, especially at her age, did not ask for these sorts of pleasures. She blushed, thinking of the uninhibited moans that escaped her mouth – from every part of her body it seemed – as she drew Sarab in closer and closer. What if the neighbours heard? It had not even occurred to her last night.

Sarab's side of the bed was empty as usual. He was always awake before her. His morning routine involved showering and then sitting in the living room with his newspaper. What was he thinking of her now? He was probably wondering what happened; what had inspired her to reach out for him like that? Worse, he would think that there was something wrong with her, he would think that she *liked* it, couldn't get enough of it. That would be humiliating. Disgraceful.

Why?

Well, Kulwinder thought, *he* had liked it too hadn't he? She recalled his grunts, his gasps of surprise. If he enjoyed it, then who was he to complain or ask her why it happened?

'Sarab,' Kulwinder called out. It was best to settle this now. To explain to him that last night's behaviour was a response to those stories, nothing else. A moment of weakness. They did not have to discuss it any further.

There was no answer. She called out for him again. Nothing. Swinging her legs over the edge of the bed, Kulwinder held the sheet taut against her breasts, leaned out the door and bellowed her husband's name. He called back. 'I'm in the kitchen,' he said.

Curious, Kulwinder scurried around the room finding her clothes. As she descended the stairs, she could make out faint sweet spices in the air. She sniffed her way to the kitchen and found Sarab standing at the stove, a pot bubbling in front of him. Black leaves and spices bubbled to the surface in a soupy mixture – too thick, Kulwinder immediately noticed, but she was too surprised to say anything. 'Since when did you start making tea around here?' she asked.

'You have made it every morning for the last twenty-seven years,' Sarab replied. He stirred a spoon through the mixture. 'I have seen you do it countless times. I'd like to think I know how to make a cup of chai.'

Kulwinder stepped up to the stove and turned it off. 'You're burning it,' she said. 'Sit down and I'll make you a new pot.'

Sarab lingered on the spot and watched her pour the leaves out to start again. She looked up to see him smiling at her. 'What?' she asked irritably, her glance darting away. He reached out and gently tipped her face towards his. Their eyes met and her lips twitched. The laughter that they shared filled the room, a shot of intoxicating warmth like the first hint of summer. When they stopped laughing, they started again, and they noticed that they were both crying as well. They wiped each other's tears away.

'Those stories,' Sarab gasped. 'Those stories.' He was delighted.

Chapter Fourteen

A ghostly mist floated between the parked cars and trees as Nikki walked briskly to the supermarket for her weekly shopping, hiding her face in the fleece-lined collar of her jacket. As she was about to leave the store, her phone buzzed in her pocket.

'Hey, Min. What's going on?'

'Listen, I was just having lunch with the girls, and Kirti's fiancé is here – did I tell you she's already engaged to a guy she met at speed dating?'

'Nope,' Nikki said. 'Congratulations to her.' She began walking briskly back to her flat, scrunching her face against a spray of rain.

'But I called to ask you something. Kirti's fiancé Siraj was saying there's a class being offered in the temple in Southall for old bibis. Some sort of sex ed course.'

Nikki nearly dropped the phone. 'Sex ed?'

'I told him, my sister teaches English classes there and if there was such a thing I'd know all about it. Can you imagine? A sex ed class! For old Punjabi ladies! Hang on, I'll put you on the phone to him.'

'Wait,' Nikki said. 'I don't want to talk to him. Where did he hear that?'

'He said he heard it from some friends. Men can be worse gossips than women.'

'What sorts of friends?' Nikki asked.

'I don't know. Don't worry, Nikki, nobody believes it. It's not going to affect the reputation of your English classes, if you're worried about that. Who would believe that a bunch of old bibis would be sitting around talking about sex?'

Nikki couldn't help feeling protective over the widows. A fierce and sudden wind ripped through the air and sent Nikki's hair flying in all directions. 'You can tell Siraj that he's wrong,' Nikki said.

'You're wrong, Siraj,' Mindi called. 'My source is confirming it.' In the background, Nikki could hear the irritating cooing of Kirti's voice. 'Aw, darling, it was a good story though, innit?'

'Tell Siraj that my students *write* erotic stories. They don't need sex education; they're very well versed in what goes on the bedroom. They have wisdom which comes with age and experience,' Nikki continued.

There was a long silence from Mindi. Nikki could hear the background noise of the restaurant fading away.

'Say that all again. I couldn't hear very well in there so I've gone outside.'

'You heard me fine,' Nikki said.

'Nikki, are you serious? *You're* running those classes?'

'I wouldn't call them classes. They're more like sharing sessions.'

'For old women to share what? Sex tips?'

'Fantasies,' Nikki said.

There was a sound that Nikki would have mistaken for a shriek of glee if she didn't know her sister better. Nikki stopped mid-pace, letting her shopping bags slip from her wrists to the pavement. 'Mindi?' she asked uncertainly. Laughter, raw and wild, poured down the phone line.

'I can't believe it. The old bibis of Southall are writing erotic stories.'

'You're finding this funny?' Nikki asked. 'Mindi, are you drunk?'

Mindi giggled and her voice dropped to a whisper. 'Oh Niks, I wouldn't normally, but we had a little bit of champagne at lunch to celebrate the engagement. I felt like I had to drink just to mute the sound of Siraj's voice. He's a nice guy but he's very loud. When he was telling us about the classes, I felt the whole restaurant turning to look at us.'

'Where did he hear the rumour from?'

'I told you, some friends.'

'Do you have any names specifically? Could you find out?'

'I did ask before but Siraj was very vague, *oh, just people I know*. That's why I thought it was all completely made-up. I could ask him again.'

'No, don't,' Nikki said, changing her mind. She didn't know this Siraj and she didn't want it getting back to his friends – however remotely connected they might be to the Brothers – that she was searching for them.

'Mindi, I should go,' Nikki said. 'I'm just walking home from the shops. I'll call you back later.'

'Noooo,' Mindi moaned. 'I have so many questions for you about these classes. Plus, I have something to tell you. I'm seeing someone. I want to talk to you about him. I think he's the one.'

'That's great, Mindi. Does Mum know?'

'She's acting funny about it.'

'Funny how? Has she met him?'

'Not yet. It's still really new. She's just been in a mood lately. She doesn't want me to get married because then she'll be all alone in the house with nobody to talk to.'

'I'm sure she doesn't feel that way.'

'She does. She said so. She went, "Nikki left, now you're in a haste to leave as well. What am I supposed to do?"'

'She'll have her freedom,' Nikki said. But then she thought about it. Mum would be completely alone, with nobody to talk with, nobody to fill the long evening silences.

Mindi hiccupped.

'Maybe we should chat when you're sober,' Nikki said.

'That's the kind of thing I would say to you.'

'Not any more, you drunkard.'

Mindi giggled and hung up.

In the early evening, Nikki left her flat for the pub, her satchel slung around her waist, noticeably lighter without the women's stories. She was still smiling from her conversation with Mindi in the afternoon. When Nikki turned the corner, her smile vanished. Jason was standing in the pub's entrance.

'Nikki,' Jason said. 'I am so sorry.'

Without a word, Nikki breezed past him. He followed her to the door. 'Please, Nikki.'

'Go away, Jason. I'm busy.'

'I want to talk to you.'

'That's nice. Do I get any say in when we get to talk?'

'I couldn't come in that day. I should have called, but . . . look, my mind is completely muddled and—'

'And you've forgotten basic manners?' Nikki snapped. 'You could have texted. It takes ten seconds.'

'I wanted to speak to you in person. I'm so sorry, Nikki. I came here to talk to you, to apologize.'

Nikki entered the pub but sneaked a glance at Jason's face. He looked more tired than sorry. Nikki felt herself relenting but she didn't want to. 'What did you want to talk about?' she asked crossly.

'It's really a sit-down sort of conversation,' Jason began.

'I'm busy right now. Sheena told my class to be here at seven.'

'The writing-class women? They're meeting here?'

Nikki nodded. She had arranged for Sheena to drive one group and a friend of hers would bring the others.

'What happened to the community centre?' Jason asked.

'Kulwinder discovered what was really going on and she cancelled the classes. I was effectively fired.'

'How did she find out?'

'She walked into class and heard everything. We had lots of new members and we weren't being careful enough. Anyway it's a long story, and I don't want to get into it right now. Sheena's driving them over, and they're due any minute.'

'Can we meet after your class is finished? I'll come over.'

'I've got a lot on my mind at the moment and clearly, you do as well.'

'I'd like a chance to explain myself to you,' Jason said. 'If you'll just hear me out. Just tell me when and where to meet you and I'll be there.'

'Just one chance,' Nikki said. 'Nine thirty, my place.'

'I'll be there.'

Nikki raised an eyebrow.

'I'll be there,' Jason repeated firmly.

The first few women appeared nearly forty-five minutes after the start time. They stood tentatively in the doorway and peered in, their faces scrunched up with distaste. Sheena pushed through.

'That was hard bloody work,' she muttered to Nikki. 'Once they figured out I was taking them out of Southall, they started asking all these questions. Where exactly are we going? Which part of London? I don't recognize that sign – where are we? I finally pulled over and said, "We're going to Nikki's pub, all right? If you don't want to go, you can get out here and take the bus home."'

'And?'

'They all stayed,' Sheena said. 'They were too scared. Preetam started praying loudly.'

Nikki approached the doorway. 'It's me, ladies.' She smiled. 'It's so lovely that you made it.'

Arvinder, Preetam, Bibi and Tanveer huddled together and stared. 'Is this everyone?' Nikki whispered to Sheena.

'There was another car of women following me but they may have got lost,' Sheena said, checking her phone. 'Or maybe they decided to turn around.'

'Come in,' Nikki said. 'The weather's taken another turn for the worst, hasn't it? It's warm and cosy inside.' The widows' silence rattled Nikki's confidence. This was going to be harder than she thought. 'We serve soft drinks and juice,' she said. The women did not budge. 'And chai,' she said. This was an exaggeration – they had Earl Grey but she could throw in some milk and cinnamon. Bibi's expression brightened slightly. Nikki noticed that she was rubbing her hands together. 'It's cold out here,' Nikki said. She gave an exaggerated shudder. 'Why don't you come in and have a warm drink?'

'No,' Preetam said just as Bibi took a tentative step forward. 'This is not a place for Punjabi women. We don't belong here.'

'I live here,' Nikki said. 'In the flat upstairs.' She felt a fierce and sudden pride in this decrepit pub. 'I've worked here for nearly three years.'

'If we go inside, people will stare at us,' Tanveer said. 'That's what Preetam means. It'll be like when we first arrived in London. They'll see us in our salwaar kameez and they'll be thinking, "go back to where you came from."'

'They used to say it,' Bibi said. 'Now it's not so common but we can still see it in their eyes.'

Arvinder shifted uncomfortably from one foot to the other. Nikki took her pinched expression as agreement. 'You're all afraid, I know,' Nikki said. 'I'm very sorry that people have been unkind to you. But I chose this pub especially because it's the kind of place where everybody is welcome.'

Bibi continued rubbing her hands. 'What if they make us drink beer?'

'Nobody can force you to drink beer,' Nikki said.

'What if they pour the alcohol into our tea while we're not looking? Hmm?' Bibi asked.

'I'll watch very closely to make sure it does not happen,' Nikki assured her.

Suddenly, Arvinder pushed past the women and entered the pub. Nikki was just about to feel proud of her persuasive skills when she heard Arvinder's loud broken English: 'Excuse me please toilet where?'

'I told her not to drink all of that water before we left,' Preetam grumbled. 'She kept complaining about how dry her throat was.'

Tanveer coughed. 'I think she's catching my bug,' she said. 'Nikki, did you say there was tea?'

'Yes.'

'I would like some, please,' Tanveer said. She wrapped her arms around Bibi's frail shoulders and rubbed them vigorously. 'Come, Bibi. You can warm up inside.' Both women shot apologetic glances at Preetam as they ducked into the pub.

It was just Preetam left. '*Hai hai*,' she whispered. 'I've been betrayed.' It wasn't clear if Preetam was addressing Nikki or some invisible audience.

'There's a television inside,' Nikki said.

'So?'

'There are some good English soap operas on.'

Preetam turned up her nose at this idea. 'I won't understand them.'

'You're very good at making up stories based on what's happening on the screen though,' Nikki reminded her. 'Why don't you come in and do that? The other women love your tales.'

It probably signified nothing, but Preetam hesitated for a moment before she said 'no.' Nikki sighed. 'You're all right with waiting for us out here then? We might be a while.'

Preetam adjusted her dupatta. 'That's fine,' she said stiffly.

'Suit yourself,' Nikki said. Inside the pub, the widows had gathered by the table closest to the entrance. They were right about being stared at. The few customers and bar staff looked at them with mixed expressions of amusement and curiosity.

'Why don't we find a quiet corner,' Nikki suggested, leading the way to the back room, which was actually just a less popular part of the main area. Arvinder, Bibi and Tanveer shuffled along silently, clutching their bags tightly.

They settled around a long table far from the other customers. Above them, there was a window facing the pavement. Preetam's feet shifted into view and then disappeared. Nikki noticed Arvinder watching her. 'Shall I try to get her inside?' Nikki asked.

'Nah,' Arvinder said. 'Let her get to know your neighbourhood.'

Bibi looked around. 'Does it have to be so dark? Why do these *goreh* all like to come into these dark caves to do their drinking?'

'It's not just white people who come in to this place,' Nikki said. 'I've served drinks to Indians here as well.'

'I had a bit of whisky once. Just the bottom of my husband's class. I was having a very bad cold and he said it would soothe my sinuses but it was terrible. It burned my throat,' Tanveer said.

'I used to drink wine with my husband,' said Sheena. 'The doctor told my husband it was a healthy alternative to drinking beer all the time, and that he could have one or two glasses a night. I started drinking it with him.'

'The *doctor* recommended this?' Bibi asked. 'An English doctor, I'm sure.'

Sheena shrugged. 'Yeah. It wasn't my first time drinking alcohol. I used to go to after work drinks with my colleagues when I worked in Central London.'

Nikki's phone pinged in her pocket. She opened a message from an unknown number.

> *Hey Nikki. Once again I'm so sorry. I'll explain everything tonight xx Jason.*

Nikki looked up. The women were now bickering over whether Sheena's doctor should be jailed for recommending wine instead of medicine. Nikki glanced out the window. Who was that talking to Preetam? A man in a familiar pair of slacks whose face was blocked by the bus stop sign. Preetam shooed him away with a wave of her dupatta. 'Get away from me, you idiot!' she shrieked suddenly. Nikki shot up from her seat and ran outside. It was Steve with the Racist Grandfather.

'Namaste,' he said with a grin and a wave. 'I was just trying to direct this lady back to the Tandoor Express.'

'Go home, Steve. You're banned from the pub.'

'I can still hang around outside,' Steve said. He turned to Preetam and dipped forward in a deep bow. 'Chicken tikka masala,' he said solemnly.

Preetam turned on her heels and marched right into the pub. When Nikki caught up with her, she said, '*Hai*, anything is better than standing outside in the cold with that lunatic.' Nikki laughed and gave her a hug. 'I'm so glad you've decided to join us,' she said, steering Preetam towards the group. The widows cheered when they saw her and she blushed and waved.

'Who has a story to share?' Nikki asked.

A moment passed, and then one tentative hand appeared. Bibi. 'I thought of mine on the walk to the bus stop,' she said.

'Go on,' Nikki said. She relaxed into her chair.

'The Woman Who Loved To Ride Horses,' Bibi said. The women broke into giggles.

'Did she also like to ride rickshaws on particularly bumpy roads?'

'And lean against the washing machine while it was on the vigorous spin cycle?'

'Quiet,' Bibi commanded. 'I'm trying to tell my story.' She cleared her throat and started again. '*The Woman Who Loved To Ride Horses. Once upon a time, there was a woman who lived on a large plot of land. Her late father had passed it down to her and had given her instructions: don't marry anybody who is money-minded, because he will try to transfer ownership of the land . . .*'

All of the women were attentive except Sheena, who slumped in her seat next to Nikki. 'Do you want to help me with the tea?' Nikki asked quietly. Sheena nodded. They excused themselves and headed to the bar. Nikki prepared a tray of cups and put the kettle on. 'Would you like something to drink?' Nikki asked.

'Some wine would be nice,' Sheena said. She threw a look over her shoulder. The widows were too engrossed in Bibi's story to notice their absence, much less the wine that Nikki poured for Sheena.

'You look tired. Is everything okay?'

'Just a hectic day at work without enough sleep last night. I was up till late talking to Rahul,' Sheena said. 'I told him that things were moving too quickly.'

'How did he take it?' Nikki asked.

'Eventually, he was all right. We had a long conversation. But his initial reaction surprised me. He became defensive. He said, "But you're enjoying it!"'

'So he thought you were accusing him of disrespecting you?'

'Yeah. I said, "Just because I like it, doesn't mean I can't change my mind and decide to take things slow, all right?" And this look crossed his face – it was like he was taken aback but also impressed.'

'You gave him something to think about.'

'The funny thing is, I was surprised as well. I didn't realize what I wanted to say until I said it. That's why I avoided talking to him in the first place.' Sheena took a few sips of her wine and sneaked another quick look at the widows. 'These storytelling sessions are good fun but I think I've also learned to speak up for what I want. *Exactly* what I want.'

Nikki remembered the unexpected rush of confidence she felt when she stood up to Garry and Viktor. 'Me too,' she said. 'And I didn't think I needed any help in that department.' They exchanged a smile. At that moment, Nikki felt an overwhelming sense of gratitude for Sheena's friendship.

They returned to the widows after Sheena finished her drink and Nikki handed out cups of tea. Bibi's gaze had gone dreamy as she built her story. '*Straddled on the back of this magnificent stallion, she commanded his every move. His muscles moved steadily beneath her, grinding against her most intimate places—*'

Bibi's narration was interrupted by the arrival of another pair of Punjabi women. They looked out of breath and were so relieved to have a seat that they didn't seem to mind being inside the pub.

'I'm Rupinder,' one woman said.

'I'm Jhoti,' said the other. 'Manjinder is coming too. She's just finding a place to park.'

'We were right behind the rest of you,' Rupinder Kaur said. 'But Jhoti here spotted someone she recognized and we had to pull over a little side street and duck down while she tried to figure out if it was him.'

'Ooh, who was? A secret lover?' Tanveer teased.

'Rubbish,' Jhoti said. 'It was Ajmal Kaur's son.'

Of course the women had a radar for detecting members of the community, even when they were outside Southall. Arvinder caught Nikki's smile. 'You know him?' she asked.

'No,' Nikki said.

'Better that you don't. He was smoking a cigarette,' Jhoti said.

The women tsk-tsked. 'Oh, here we go again,' Sheena said in English, rolling her eyes at Nikki.

'Smoking?' Arvinder Kaur said. 'He doesn't strike me as the type. I've seen him at the temple a few times.'

'He's got respectable parents as well. Remember his wedding? There wasn't anything like it.'

'A very lavish wedding,' Tanveer said. 'Both bride and groom were firstborns. The celebrations were a week long.'

'I've heard there are problems in that marriage, by the way. My daughter works closely with the wife's family's neighbours. They say she's moved back in with her parents. That's why I was surprised to see him. I thought he would have gone home as well, but I guess he's stayed to work things out.' Jhoti said.

'Where is he from, again?' Arvinder said. 'His family is from Canada, no?'

'California,' Tanveer said. 'There was a misunderstanding, remember? The girl's father said, "My daughter is marrying an American" and everybody thought he was a *gorah*.'

'They thought so because his name didn't sound Punjabi,' Preetam said. 'It was Jason.'

Something seized Nikki. 'Jason?' she repeated. The women nodded.

'Such a pretty bride, no? And the mehendi was so dark on her light skin. Everybody was teasing her, saying, "This means your husband will be wealthy, this means that your mother-in-law will be kind."' Preetam said.

Nikki excused herself to the ladies and pulled out her phone once she was out of the widows' view. She felt as if her insides had been scooped out. *Jason is married. He was married all along.* Two forces of temptation pulled her in opposing directions: to call him and tell him what a bastard he was; to block his number and let him spend the rest of his life wondering how she figured it out. A silent reel of recent memories played on a loop in Nikki's mind. She saw herself kissing him, in bed with him while his wife wrung her hands in another corner of London. She had never felt so foolish before.

Finally she sent a response to his message.

Don't bother coming over. We're done.

Without hesitating, she pressed Send.

Chapter Fifteen

Kulwinder's phone was buzzing on the countertop where she had left it. When she noticed the unfamiliar number, she felt a flash of anxiety. She picked up just before it rang out, but did not say anything.

'Hello?' It was Gurtaj Singh.

'*Sat sri akal*,' she said with relief. He greeted her back hastily and then said, 'I take it that your writing classes went over time today.'

She glanced at the clock. It was quarter past nine, not that the women would be in the classroom anyway. She had locked the door. 'The classes aren't running.' She stopped herself from saying 'any more.' 'Today,' she said instead.

'Are you telling me that the lights have been on since the last lesson?' Gurtaj asked.

'The lights?'

'I was driving past the temple after dinner out tonight and I noticed the light on in the windows. You do realize, don't you, that money will have to come out of the budget to pay those electricity bills?'

Kulwinder pulled the phone away from her ear so Gurtaj's complaints became distant. She recalled shutting the room doors and locking them, and before that, as always, turning off the lights. Or had she forgotten? It was possible that she had been so enraged that she had left the lights on. Doubt rollicked in her stomach like a wave; something was not right. 'I'll go back in and turn off the lights,' she said.

'No need to leave your house in the middle of the night,' Gurtaj said.

Did he just call to have a go at her then? 'I never said I was at home,' Kulwinder replied. She left a question as to where she was and what she was doing, and pictured the surprise on Gurtaj's face.

Kulwinder marched briskly to the temple, her handbag tucked under her arm and her legs taking lengthy strides. It occurred to her that she might be followed again, but she felt a brazenness from earlier flowing through her blood. Sikhs are warriors, she remembered telling a very young Maya, whose eyes glowed with this knowledge, frightening Kulwinder. 'But girls must act like girls,' she had added. Since Maya's death, Kulwinder had only allowed herself to feel the absence as short, shocking sparks. Now they had ignited something and Kulwinder felt she could breathe fire on anybody who crossed her.

All of the windows were black with night except the classroom and Kulwinder's office. She felt a twist of fear but pushed on until she reached the third floor corridor. 'Hello?' she called out, taking measured steps towards the door. There was no response. The light glared through the small window in the door. With a gasp, Kulwinder saw the damage first. The room seemed upside down. The tables and chairs lay toppled and helpless, their legs sticking up in the air. Papers were strewn in every direction, and streaks of red spray paint crudely marked the blackboard and the floor. Kulwinder clutched the fabric of her blouse because this was the closest she could get to her heart. She hurried to her office.

The vandals had done the same work here – turning over every surface, ruining the order of her work. The file folders had been tossed to the floor and one window bashed through.

There was the sudden slap of approaching footsteps. Kulwinder scurried through the door into her office and searched wildly for a place to hide. The footsteps became louder. Kulwinder picked up the heaviest thing she could find – an office stapler – and clutched it with both hands. The footsteps stopped and a woman appeared in the doorway. Wearing a midnight blue tunic with a silver chain-stitched border, this woman looked both familiar and strange.

'What happened here?' the woman asked, staring at the mess. Then Kulwinder recognized Manjeet Kaur. Kulwinder hadn't seen her out of widow's clothes in the last year.

'Somebody . . .' Kulwinder gestured helplessly at the mess. She had no more words.

'Where are the other women?' Manjeet asked. 'I've been away but I returned to Southall today. I could see the classroom light on from my house and I walked over to give them a surprise.'

'They're not meeting here any more. I cancelled the classes.'

'Oh. You found out, then?'

Still numb with shock, Kulwinder continued to survey the mess. The tidy desk at which she always sat with such pride had been gutted. One drawer hung open lewdly like a tongue.

'I guess we should start cleaning up the place,' Kulwinder said.

'Absolutely not,' Manjeet replied. 'I started my day with leaving my husband. I'm not going to end it with cleaning up after another man.'

Kulwinder looked up in surprise. 'Your husband? I thought he was'

Manjeet shook her head. 'He left me. Then he wanted me back. I went to him thinking it was my duty but all he wanted was somebody to cook and clean after his new wife ran off. Once I realized it, I packed my bags and came home. The whole journey on the train, every time I felt anxious about what I had done, I just remembered that the other widows and Nikki would be cheering me on.'

Kulwinder felt a pang of regret. 'This wouldn't have happened if the women had been in this building. I shouldn't have sent them away.'

Manjeet stepped over the papers and put her arm around Kulwinder. 'Don't blame yourself. Nobody can stop these fools.' She took a moment to look around the room. 'I thought the Brothers had more respect than to break in and destroy things like this, especially in the gurudwara.'

Kulwinder crouched to the floor to pick up a folder and, noticing its contents were soggy, she recoiled. The acrid smell of urine wafted to her nostrils. She stepped back to the doorway and felt a surprising sting of tears in her eyes. She wiped them away furiously. Manjeet had a point. The Brothers were capable of vandalising the cars and homes of women gone astray but temple grounds were sacred. From this distance, Kulwinder could see that everything had been tossed around a bit too deliberately, as if to give the impression of senseless vandalism.

'Did they even find the stories?' Manjeet asked.

Kulwinder shook her head slowly. 'You're right – I can't imagine the Brothers doing this.'

'Then who?

Kulwinder was about to reply when the open desk drawer caught her attention again. It was completely empty, unlike the others. It was the right-hand second drawer, the only contents of which had been Nikki's résumé and job application. She recalled clearing that drawer of its dusty old files after Nikki applied for the job, pleased to have her own official paperwork to store away.

Kulwinder searched the floor. The résumé, the application, Nikki's personal particulars . . . Panic began to rise in her throat.

'I think I know,' Kulwinder said.

Chapter Sixteen

A fierce wind stung Nikki's face as she paced the pavement outside O'Reilly's, smoking her third cigarette. She had certainly earned this one after struggling through that session with the women, the revelation about Jason turning in her mind. A group of men passed by and one looked back. 'Give us a smile, luv,' he called out. In the window of a passing bus, Nikki could see her reflection, her face knotted with rage. She glared at the man, who gave his friend a nudge and strolled off, chuckling.

Making her way up the stairs to her flat, Nikki's phone buzzed in her pocket. She stopped on the stairwell and answered.

'Go to hell, Jason.'

'Nikki, please, let's just talk.'

Nikki hung up and had an urge to hurl her phone out the window just so she could break something. She carried on up the stairs and reached for her keys. Now the tears began to pour, splashing onto her hands as she fumbled through her pockets. She didn't notice Tarampal standing there until she reached the top step.

'What . . .?' Nikki started. With the back of her hand, she wiped the tears from her eyes.

'Are you all right, Nikki?' Tarampal asked. 'What happened to you?'

'It's a long story,' Nikki muttered. *What are you doing here?*

Tarampal reached out and gave her a squeeze on the shoulder. 'You poor thing,' she said. Her pity felt genuine and gave Nikki a bit of comfort but she still could not hide her bafflement. Had Tarampal heard about the classes in the pub and decided to join? It was unlikely. She nearly laughed at the absurdity of this situation: here was Tarampal at her doorstep, comforting her over her apparently married boyfriend.

'I was wondering if we could have a chat,' Tarampal said. She looked expectantly at the door.

'Oh. Uh . . . sure,' Nikki said. She opened the door to the flat and showed Tarampal in. 'You don't have to take your shoes off,' she said, but of course, Tarampal did before hesitating in the doorway. 'Please, make yourself at home,' Nikki said, suddenly conscious of the inadequacy of her hosting skills. She gestured at the small table in the kitchen. Tarampal stepped daintily through the flat in her bare feet, startled by the noisy floorboards. 'Have a seat,' Nikki said. Tarampal remained standing. A bra had been slung over one of the kitchen chairs; Tarampal stared at it until Nikki removed it and tossed it into her bedroom. A lighter and a pack of cigarettes were also displayed in full view. Nikki decided that removing them would draw more attention.

'Nikki, I think you have the wrong idea about me,' Tarampal said when they were both seated.

'Is that what brought you here?' Nikki asked. She wondered how Tarampal had got her address. Tarampal looked so woeful that Nikki refrained from asking. 'I don't have any ideas about you,' Nikki added.

'I think you do,' Tarampal replied. 'I think the widows told you that I'm not a good person. It's just not true.'

'Is it true that you take money from people in exchange for prayers?' Nikki asked.

'Yes, but they come to me. They want help.'

'That's not quite what I heard.'

Tarampal lowered her eyelids and shuffled her feet like a schoolgirl being reprimanded. Gone was the embittered mother-in-law of the dishonourable Maya. She had been replaced by this lonely, helpless creature, the same person whose illiteracy had compelled Nikki to bring storybook tapes to her home. 'How would *you* survive, Nikki?' Tarampal asked, 'if you were a widow with no skills? Didn't I try to learn English to become employable? You and the women turned me away.'

It just didn't make sense, Tarampal coming all the way here just to clear up some misconceptions. 'What is it that you want, Bibi Tarampal?' Nikki asked.

'I'd like us to be friends,' Tarampal said. 'I really would. All those things I said about Maya, they must have scared you off. You must think I wanted her to die. What kind of person would that make me? I just wanted peace in my home. I wanted Jaggi to be happy. I never expected Maya to take her own life. This is something Kulwinder will never accept.'

'Can you blame her?' Nikki retorted. 'Her daughter died under your roof.'

'At her own hands,' Tarampal said. 'She was unwell, Nikki. Her mind was not right.' She tapped her temple with her fingers and nodded knowingly. Nikki realized that this was not a practised gesture; Tarampal was telling the truth she knew. Whatever story Jaggi had spun, she had bought it.

'You don't think something else might have happened that night?' Nikki asked.

Tarampal shook her head. 'Jaggi would never do anything to hurt anybody. He's not that kind of man.' Her eyes shone and a small smile played on her lips. 'He's such a good man.'

Yuck, Nikki thought. She couldn't help thinking of the widows' conversations about mothers-in-law sleeping between their sons and their wives. She wondered what Maya's fate would have been if Tarampal had had sons instead of daughters. Perhaps she would have been less zealous about Jaggi. Or perhaps Maya would have been forced to marry one of her sons.

'Look, I know that you care for Jaggi very much but it's possible that you don't have all the details,' Nikki said.

Tarampal shook her head. 'Kulwinder's just out to get him because she's feeling guilty.'

'Are you sure about that?' Nikki asked gently. 'I think you've been misled.'

'You're the one being misled, Nikki,' Tarampal insisted. 'I know you think you've got some supposed evidence against Jaggi but I can tell you, it's not real.'

'How do you know about that?'

'I spoke to Kulwinder earlier this evening. She came around to my house and told me she was going to the police. I tried to talk her out of it; I finally convinced her to give me your address so I could talk to you myself.'

'Kulwinder gave you my address?' What was Kulwinder playing at, sending Tarampal here? And why go to Tarampal's house to gloat about finding evidence? Something did not make sense. 'I don't have the registration form, if that's what you're here for.'

Tarampal's face fell. 'Who has it then?'

'Kulwinder does. She didn't show it to you?'

Tarampal's eyes darted away from Nikki's. 'No, she said you have it and she told me if I wanted it, I needed to talk to you.' Her voice wavered. She was clearly lying.

In her mind, Nikki could see the registration form neatly folded in her satchel, which she had kicked under her bed after taking out her phone and going downstairs for the pub session with the widows earlier. 'I don't have it,' Nikki said. She noticed Tarampal looking around the flat, searching desperately. Nikki stood up. 'I think you should leave, Tarampal.'

'I've come all this way,' Tarampal said. 'At least make me a cup of tea? I offered you that courtesy when you came to my home.'

'I'm sorry, I haven't got tea. I wasn't expecting guests,' Nikki replied. She knew she was being uncivil but this visit was making her uneasy. Tarampal cleared her throat loudly and nodded. She stood up and walked ahead of Nikki towards the door, no longer careful to avoid the creaky floorboards. While putting on her shoes, she cleared her throat once more and began to cough.

'Oh,' Tarampal cried. 'Oh, I've got this terrible cough from being out in the rain.' With a thud, she leaned her weight against the door and continued to cough. 'Could you please just put the kettle on and warm some water for me before I go back out there?'

Tarampal's theatrics rivalled Preetam's. 'Fine,' Nikki said. She returned to the kitchen and filled the kettle with water, sneaking glances at Tarampal. She coughed again. Nikki wished she didn't feel a little bit sorry for her. She opened her cupboard. If Tarampal didn't mind an Earl Grey, maybe Nikki should just make her a cup before sending her on her way.

'Tarampal, would you like—' Nikki looked up and stopped. The door was open and Tarampal was leaning outside, whispering urgently to someone. 'Who's there?' Nikki demanded. The door flung open and a man barged into the flat, ushering Tarampal back inside, kicking the door shut behind him. A scream rose and died in Nikki's throat. It was the man who had followed her the other night.

'What the hell is going on?' she gasped.

'Block the door,' he said to Tarampal. She scrambled to the door and pressed her back against it. He pointed a finger at Nikki. 'If you scream, you'll pay for it,' he said in a low voice. 'Do you understand?' She nodded quickly. Over the man's shoulder, she could see that Tarampal's eyes were wide with attention, not surprise. She had helped him enter her flat. This had to be Jaggi.

'I saw you the other night,' Nikki said. 'You . . . you were following me.' He must have overheard her talking about the form.

Jaggi glared at her. 'You've been stirring up trouble since the day you got to Southall. You wanted to teach dirty stories to widows, fine. Why poke around in our lives as well?' He looked around the flat. 'I'm going to make this simple: all I want is the form. Give it to me and we'll leave you alone.'

'You think you can just break into my home—'

'You let me in,' Jaggi said, pointing at the door. 'No signs of forced entry.'

'I haven't got the form,' Nikki said. She noticed Tarampal shifting her weight from one foot to the other, her arms almost comically splayed across the door like she was guarding a goal post. She felt her courage building. 'You can search the place if you want.' She prayed he would not look under the bed first so she could buy some time.

'I'm not searching the place. I want you to bring it to me,' Jaggi said.

'I don't have it,' Nikki said. From the corner of her eye, she could see the kettle filled with boiling hot water. If she inched her way closer to the counter without Jaggi noticing, she could grab it.

Jaggi took her by the arm and pushed her onto a chair. 'Tarampal, come here and keep an eye on her,' he said.

Tarampal obeyed, moving to stand over her. She crossed her arms over her chest but there was the beginning of fear in her eyes. Behind her, Jaggi could be heard tearing through the bedroom. 'Just give him the form and he'll go,' Tarampal whispered. 'You're making things more difficult for yourself.'

'Do you still believe he's innocent?' Nikki asked. 'He got you to help him break into my flat. Now he's searching for evidence to destroy.'

'You don't know him,' Tarampal said. Nikki could hear Jaggi cursing now. For a supposedly "good son-in-law," Jaggi certainly had no qualms about swearing in Tarampal's presence. He had called her by her first name as well, a sign of familiarity that Nikki found jarring.

'He's not very respectful towards you, is he?' Nikki asked. She could guess from the nervous way Tarampal kept casting glances towards the bedroom that she had never seen him like this. 'I mean, as a son— '

'I've told you, he's not my son,' Tarampal interjected.

'I mean you're his elder.'

Tarampal balked. 'I'm only twelve years older than him.'

Could they be . . .? A fresh suspicion began to take root within Nikki. Then a crashing sound chased the thought away. A lamp had fallen. It was enough to distract Tarampal for a moment. Nikki shot out of the chair and pushed past Tarampal, who chased after her into the bedroom. 'Get out of my flat!' she shouted, hoping that somebody would hear her.

Jaggi lunged for her and clamped his fingers around her neck. 'Give me the form,' he said through gritted teeth.

Nikki gasped for breath. 'Jaggi, don't!' Tarampal cried, trying to pry his hands off. He released Nikki and with one powerful swing, he threw

Tarampal off, knocking her off her feet. Nikki took in a big gulp of air and held up her arms in surrender. 'Okay,' she said. 'Okay. I'll get it.' She had to think quickly. 'I hid it in the kitchen cupboard.'

Jaggi crouched next to Tarampal. 'Bring it to me,' he ordered Nikki. She took in another shaky breath and hurried back to the kitchen. The kettle was right there but she hesitated to reach for it. Jaggi was strong; if her escape didn't work, he'd kill her. She knew that much from the way his fingers had dug into her throat.

'Why did you do that to me?' Tarampal whimpered. Jaggi murmured back a reply that Nikki couldn't hear. Her heart pounded in her chest – there was only so much stalling she could do. She grabbed the kettle and spun around just in time to see Jaggi tucking Tarampal's hair behind her ear. It was a gesture too intimate to mean anything else.

They were lovers.

The realization clanged in Nikki's head like a bell. She put the kettle back on the counter. The sound alerted Tarampal, who looked up and withdrew quickly from Jaggi. She avoided Nikki's gaze.

'How long has this been going on?' Nikki asked her.

Tarampal shook her head. 'Nothing's going on,' she said. She tugged her dupatta to hide her face. *All the good things come later*, Tarampal had told Nikki, her cheeks turning red like this.

'Is that why you did it?' Nikki asked Jaggi in English. 'Because Maya found out about you two?'

Jaggi could not conceal his surprise. He held Nikki's stare but she knew she had caught him. 'She didn't know how to keep her mouth shut,' he said. Tarampal looked back and forth between the two of them, trying to decipher their conversation.

'Both your reputations were worth a woman's life? That was a reason to kill Maya?' Nikki asked.

At the mention of Maya's name, Tarampal tensed. Nikki switched back to Punjabi. 'He just admitted it, Tarampal. He killed her.'

'I didn't say that,' Jaggi said through gritted teeth. He turned to Tarampal. 'It happened so quickly. It was an accident.'

'It was an accident,' Tarampal repeated but she looked confused. 'What do you mean?'

'She knew about you two,' Nikki said.

'You need to keep your mouth shut,' Jaggi warned, but Nikki noticed the panic registering on his face.

'*She knew?*' Tarampal asked. She drew her dupatta over her chest. 'I don't sleep with people's husbands. I don't do that,' she added quickly to Nikki.

Just like she didn't blackmail people. Wording was the key to Tarampal's denial. As long as she announced her innocence aloud, it was true. 'He's a murderer,' Nikki said, pointing at Jaggi. He stood up and began to advance towards her. Nikki backed herself against the counter, her body flooding with with cold, hard fear.

'Jaggi,' Tarampal said. He stopped and turned around.

'Did Kulwinder know about us?' Tarampal asked.

'No.'

'Are you sure?'

'I'm sure.'

'Because Maya was going to tell her about us?' Tarampal asked softly. Jaggi turned back to look at Nikki. 'Please answer me,' Tarampal said.

'We don't have time for this,' Jaggi said.

'Oh Jaggi,' Tarampal murmured. 'Why?'

'She got upset and said she was going to tell everybody. I started thinking about you and your reputation in the community, and I couldn't let that happen to you. It was all so quick. I threw the petrol on her to frighten her and she said, "You wouldn't dare do it." I took the box of matches and pushed her outside. I was still just trying to scare her.'

Tarampal stared at Jaggi in horror. 'You told the police you weren't at home.'

'Tarampal—'

'You lied to me.'

'Don't let Nikki influence you,' Jaggi said. 'What would you have done? What would you have wanted me to do?'

Tarampal's hands were pressed against her lips and her eyes were bright with tears.

'You're a better person than that, Tarampal, you know you are. You wouldn't have wanted Maya to die, would you?' Nikki asked. 'That's what you told me earlier.'

'You wanted her out of our lives so we could be together,' Jaggi said, stepping between them to force Tarampal to look at him. 'What other way was there?'

Tarampal hesitated. *Death over dishonour*, Nikki thought. Did it matter if it was Maya's death over Tarampal's dishonour?

'I don't know,' Tarampal said. She directed her response to Nikki. It was the first honest thing she had said in a while. All of the colour had drained from her face. 'I. Don't. Know,' she repeated, her voice catching on a sob. She looked like she was ten years old.

'Tarampal,' Jaggi said. He crouched down again and put his hand on her waist. 'There's no need to make a scene. We can talk about this later.'

Tarampal bit her lip and shook her head, her tears splashing on the floor. Jaggi reached out with his other hand to touch her cheek. Something seemed to snap in Tarampal then and, pulling away from Jaggi, she gave him a sharp slap on the face. The sound was like a clap of thunder.

It stunned both Jaggi and Nikki and he stood frozen for a second and then he grabbed her by the throat and began to shake her.

'*No!*' Nikki shouted. She picked up the kettle and flung it as hard as she could – it missed him by a whisker but the hot water splashed across his back. He yelled out and dropped Tarampal, flapping his shirt away from his skin to try to cool the burning.

'Let's go,' Nikki cried, pushing him away from her and leaning down to grab Tarampal's hand. Tarampal gasped for breath as she was hauled up from the floor but before she could take a step, Jaggi caught her wrist and pulled hard, throwing her back on the floor behind him. Nikki straightened up to face him and tried to take a step back but tripped over the leg of a chair. As she lurched forward, she saw his fist coming fast the other way. All she heard was the crack of her head against the kitchen counter and then everything went dark.

Sheena's car was still moving when Kulwinder and Manjeet opened the door and hopped in. '*Hai*, wait! You're going to hurt yourselves,' Sheena cried. But there was no time to stop.

'Do you remember where the pub is?' Kulwinder asked.

'Of course. I was just there,' Sheena said.

'Hurry up then. There's no time.' Sheena pushed down on the accelerator. Kulwinder clutched her seat instinctively as the car shot out of the temple lot.

When Manjeet called her, Sheena had been on her way home after dropping off the other widows. 'Manjeet!' Sheena's voice had burst over speakerphone. 'You're well?'

'I'm back in Southall. I'll update you later but first we need to go to Nikki's place,' Manjeet replied.

'She's in trouble,' Kulwinder added. Sheena did not ask any questions.

'Give me five minutes.'

Kulwinder was relieved they would not have to call Sarab. He might say, 'Kulwinder, are you sure? Try calling her again – you know how young people never answer their phones.' And he would stop at all the yellow lights that Sheena was speeding through.

They arrived in front of the pub and Sheena let them out. 'Go, go,' she said. 'I'll park and come inside.' Kulwinder and Manjeet burst into the pub, hollering at each other to find the stairs. They were so involved in their mission that they didn't notice the other customers, who had all stopped to stare.

Kulwinder made a beeline for the bar. 'You know where is the flat of Nikki?'

'Just upstairs,' the girl replied. She looked amused. 'Are you her mum?'

'How do we get inside?' Kulwinder asked.

'You need a key to access that door outside on the left. Only residents have the key. You'll have to call her and she can let you in.'

'I try calling her, she don't answer. Please. There could be a bad man upstairs.'

The girl bit her lip to keep from laughing. Kulwinder saw what she saw then – a pair of frantic Indian aunties trying to stop something immoral from happening to one of their daughters. 'He is a killer,' she said desperately.

'I'm sure he is. Look, I can't let anybody in, so—'

Kulwinder sniffed the air. 'Manjeet, do you smell that?' she asked.

Manjeet's eyes widened. 'It's smoke.'

Sheena came running into the pub. 'Fire! Get out! Everybody out!' Sheena commanded. The bartender blinked at them in confusion as customers ran out the door.

'They haven't paid,' she cried.

Kulwinder pointed to the window. 'Look. Smoke! Give us the keys.'

The girl's eyes widened. She dived under the counter to rummage for the keys and finally held them aloft triumphantly. Kulwinder snatched them from her hands. 'Let's go!'

They raced out of the building, dupattas flying, fumbled with the door key, and then burst through the door, sandals slipping off and tumbling down the stairs behind them as they raced upwards, shouting. 'Nikki! Nikki!' The smoke thickened as they got closer to her flat door. Kulwinder searched through the smog for the doorknob and flinched at its warmth. To her surprise, the door was unlocked. That bastard must have started the fire and then run off.

As the door opened, smoke began to pour into the stairwell and the three women began to cough. Kulwinder pushed on, ducking to see under the billowing black clouds.

'Stay here! Let me see if I can find her!' she shouted.

She could see the flames and through the smoke, she could see a figure on the floor. It was Nikki. Trying to stay as low as possible, Kulwinder grabbed Nikki's ankles and pulled. She inhaled some smoke and coughed violently, her shoulders shaking. She pulled again and felt Nikki start to move across the floor. It was a long way back to the door. She pulled again with all her weight. Another wave of coughing made her body convulse. Her eyes itched madly and tears ran down her face. She wanted to yell but she couldn't. She dropped to her knees. The impact sent jolts through her body, bringing her back to the moment she found out that Maya was dead. *No, no, no*, she had cried. *Please, please, please.* Frantically wishing for time to reverse itself was as desperate as suffocation. Kulwinder gave the girl a last futile tug.

Suddenly a hand gripped Kulwinder's ankle; another wrapped around her waist.

'Wait! Stop!' She couldn't leave Nikki here. Thinking quickly, hearing her own laboured breathing and nothing at all from Nikki, she pulled off her dupatta and tied it around Nikki's ankle, and then with Sheena and Manjeet's help, the strength of three women allowed them to start dragging Nikki towards the door.

'We've got her!' she heard Sheena shouting.

Chapter Seventeen

Nikki could only see shadows through her narrow, squinting vision. There were snatches of conversation but they amounted to nothing. Somebody was holding her hand. As her eyelids fluttered open, she heard the hushed excitement of Mindi's voice. 'She's waking up.'

The hospital room was glaringly bright and Nikki groaned. The light gave her a headache. Mindi squeezed her hand. Next to her, Mum was leaning anxiously towards Nikki, tugging the edges of her blanket so they covered her legs. 'Mum.' It was all Nikki could manage before she went back under.

When she next woke, it was evening. Two police officers stood beside Mum and Mindi at the foot of her bed. Nikki blinked at them in confusion. She remembered a powerful knock that sent her tumbling backwards. After that, there was only the sharp pain in her head.

'Hello, Nikki,' one of them said gently. 'I'm Police Constable Ables and this is PC Sullivan. We've got a few questions for you when you're ready to answer them.'

'Maybe just give me a little bit of time,' Nikki said. There was a growing pain on her leg and her mind was not clear.

'Sure,' said PC Ables. 'Right now, I just want to inform you that the man who entered your home has been found and charged. We've got him in custody. Are you willing to make a statement about what happened?'

Nikki nodded. The constables thanked her and left. She slumped back against the pillow and stared at the ceiling. 'Why does my leg hurt?' she asked. From the corner of her vision, she saw a look passing between Mindi and Mum.

'You got burned,' Mindi said. 'Not seriously, but it's going to be sore for a while.'

'Burned? How long am I going to be here?'

'The doctor said you'll be all right to come home tomorrow,' Mindi said. She glanced at Mum. 'We'll set up your old bedroom . . .'

Mum abruptly turned on her heels and left the room. *What's her problem*, Nikki wanted to ask.

Mindi watched Mum as she headed out the door. She looked back at Nikki and seemed to read her expression. 'Don't worry about her. So you don't remember anything?'

'I remember he hit me. After that I blacked out,' Nikki mumbled. Patches of events appeared and dissipated in her memory. 'There were two people,' she said.

'They set fire to the flat,' Mindi said.

'Fire?' Nikki struggled to sit up.

'Shh,' Mindi said, gently pushing her back to the bed. 'Don't try to get up so quickly. It's all right – there was a kitchen fire. They lit it and then ran off but it didn't catch onto much else.'

'Luckily,' Nikki said. She pictured the flat engulfed in flames and she shuddered.

'Very lucky. It could have been a lot worse. You're lucky those women were around. They saved you, or at least that's what I understand from the police.'

'What women?'

'Your students.'

'They were there?'

'You didn't know that?' Now Mindi looked confused. 'What were they doing in your neighbourhood?'

Nikki struggled to remember that day but she had a vague recollection of having the class there. Then finding out about Jason. But hadn't some time passed between then and the man attacking her? Jaggi. Tarampal. It came back to her in fragments. When did the widows arrive? Why? Maybe they had been warned somehow.

'They came to save me,' Nikki said, tears burning in her eyes.

Kulwinder's doctor told her she had suffered from smoke inhalation. 'We'll keep you here for a night to monitor your symptoms and then you can go home,' he said.

When he left the room, Sarab took her hand. His eyes were red and weary. 'What were you thinking, running towards a fire?' he asked. Kulwinder opened her mouth to speak but her throat was dry. She pointed at the water pitcher on the side table. Sarab filled a glass for her and waited while she sipped.

'I was thinking about Maya,' Kulwinder said.

'You could have died,' Sarab said. A sob escaped his throat and he buried his face in her hands. As he cried for his wife, for his fear, for his daughter, his tears spilled down her arms, soaking through her sleeves. Kulwinder was still stunned. She wanted to comfort Sarab but all she could manage was a squeeze of her hand.

'And Nikki?' she asked.

Sarab looked up and wiped his eyes. 'She's fine,' he said. 'I spoke to her sister in the hallway just now. She's injured but she'll recover.'

Kulwinder slumped back against the pillow, closing her eyes. 'Thank God.'

She was afraid to ask the next question. She looked at Sarab and he seemed to understand. 'They've arrested him,' he said. 'I spoke to her mother in the hall. The police want to question Nikki before charging him, but he's in custody now for breaking into her home and assaulting her.'

'And for Maya?'

'It looks like they'll open up the case,' Sarab said. 'He could go to jail for a long time.'

Now she began to cry. Sarab mistook these as tears of relief, but

Kulwinder had been transported to the past, when she had given this boy her blessings. He had turned out to be a monster, but at one point, she had called him her son.

Chapter Eighteen

Traces of Nikki's teenage years still existed in her childhood bedroom. The walls were marked with traces of sticker residue from the posters she had put up and a few old photographs remained in picture frames on the dresser.

She used to tape her cigarette packets to the back of the bed leg, but when the packet fell one day, she upgraded to a Velcro adhesive tape. Now she wondered if there was a packet left there. She could use a smoke. Crouching next to the bed and reaching into the narrow space between the leg and the wall, Nikki heard footsteps coming up the stairs. She withdrew but her elbow got caught. Mum appeared in the doorway to find Nikki wriggling on the floor like an insect.

'Uh . . . I just dropped an earring,' Nikki said. Mum's stony face indicated that she knew the truth. She dragged the bed out to free Nikki's arm and left the room. Nikki followed her down the stairs and into the kitchen. 'Mum,' she began.

'I don't want to hear it.'

'Mum, please.' How long was this going to go on? Since she'd been discharged from the hospital this morning, Mum hadn't looked her in the eye.

Mum continued to bustle about, attending to her morning routine of putting last night's dishes away. The plates clattered loudly and the cupboard doors slammed. Over the noise, Nikki wanted to scream *I'm a bloody adult!*

'Mum, I'm sorry about the cigarettes,' Nikki began.

'You think this is about the cigarettes?'

'It's about everything. The moving out, the pub, the . . . just everything. I'm sorry that it wasn't what you wanted for me.'

'The lying,' Mum said, staring squarely at her. 'Those classes you were teaching. Here you had us thinking you were teaching women to read and write but instead they were . . .' She shook her head at a loss for words.

'Mum, some of these women spent their married lives wondering what it would be like to enjoy their husbands. Others missed the intimacy they used to have with their husbands and just wanted to relive those experiences.'

'So you come in and think you can save the world by making them share these tales.'

'I didn't get them to do anything,' Nikki corrected. 'They're strong women; you couldn't *force* them to do anything.'

'You had no business getting involved with other women's private lives like that,' Mum said. 'Look at the trouble you got yourself into.'

'I didn't get myself into trouble,' Nikki said.

'That man attacked you because you were meddling.'

'That had nothing to do with the classes, that was about Maya, the girl he killed.'

'If you hadn't got involved in the first place—'

'So I was asking for it?'

'I didn't say that.'

'What are you so angry about then?' Nikki asked.

Mum picked up a dishrag as if she was going to begin cleaning and then she dropped it. 'You have a double life. I'm the last person to know anything. You're always hiding things from me.'

'Mum, I don't know how to be honest with you,' Nikki said.

'You spent all this time talking about such personal things with complete strangers. You were honest with them.'

'The last time I told the truth in this house, there was an epic argument and I moved out. I was called selfish for not wanting what everybody else wanted for me.' Nikki said.

'We know what's best for you.'

'I don't think you do.'

'If you had told me what you were doing, I could have warned you about the dangers of it, and if you'd listened, that man wouldn't have come after you. Tell me: was it worth it? This thing you've started in Southall – was it worth nearly dying for?'

'But those women came to save me,' she said. 'Even Kulwinder came. I had to be doing something worthwhile if they risked their lives for me. Mum, I didn't just start a little bit of mischief in Southall and I don't intend on leaving it at that either. Those meetings gave those women a strong sense of acceptance and support. For the first time in their lives they could openly share their most private thoughts and know that they weren't alone. I helped them to discover that, and I became willing to learn from them as well. Those women were used to turning the other cheek when injustices were committed because it's inappropriate to get involved, or to go to the police and betray your own. But they didn't hesitate to help me and put themselves at risk when I was in danger. They know that they're capable of fighting.'

Nikki was breathless. She had spoken rapidly, expecting an interruption from Mum but there was none. Mum's steady gaze had softened. 'This is why your father thought you'd be a good lawyer,' she finally said. '"*That girl can find the logic in anything*," he always said.'

'I couldn't convince him to accept that I didn't want to be lawyer though.'

'He would have been convinced eventually,' Mum said. 'He wouldn't have cut you off forever.'

'It feels that way,' Nikki confessed. 'All the time, it feels like I created this eternal wall of silence between us. He died angry at me.'

'He didn't die angry,' Mum said.

'You don't know that,' Nikki said.

'He was very happy when he died. I promise.' At first Nikki mistook the shine in Mum's eyes for tears but then she noticed the tiniest twitch in Mum's lips as well.

'What do you mean?'

Mum's lips contorted further into a smile. A flush spread across her cheeks. 'When I told you that your father died in bed, I didn't mean that he died in his sleep. I let you believe that because . . .' She cleared her throat. 'Because he died from strenuous activity. In bed.'

Nikki suddenly understood. 'His heart attack was brought on by . . . by you two?' Nikki flapped her hands helplessly in a vague pantomime of her parents having sex.

'Strenuous activity,' Mum said.

'I didn't have to know that.'

'*Beti,* I can't let you keep blaming yourself. Dad was having heart problems before you dropped out of university. He didn't die from misery or disappointment. It appeared that way because he was so sullen when you last saw him, but in India he started to put things in perspective. We went to visit relatives one afternoon and your uncle was going on about how advanced the Indian education system was compared to ours. You know what they're like – any chance they get they turn a family reunion into a competition. Your uncle was talking about all of the complex school projects his daughter Raveen was expected to complete and she was only in primary school. He said, "Raveen's school is ensuring that all of its students are successful. What more can I want?" Dad replied, "My daughters were taught to make their own choices about success."'

'Dad said that?' Nikki asked.

Mum nodded. 'I think he surprised himself. Your dad has never been the type to return to the motherland to brag about his successes abroad. But something changed that day. Out of all the opportunities Britain offered us, choice was the most important thing. He just didn't fully realize it until he had to say it aloud to your uncle.'

Nikki blinked back tears as her mum reached for her. The touch of her hand on Nikki's face released the sort of giant hiccupping sob she had not experienced since she was a little girl. She pressed her cheek to Mum's palm, which caught her warm tears.

In the evening, Olive came around. Slung across her shoulder, a large canvas bag overflowed with essays to mark and she carried a box of Nikki's possessions. Nikki's face was still puffy from crying. 'It's been an emotional day,' she explained.

'I'd say it's been a hell of a week,' Olive said. 'How are you coping?'

'I've still got headaches but other than that, I try to avoid being reminded of it all.' But she could not escape the vivid dreams that descended on her every night. The inescapable grip on her throat, flames licking her feet. She shuddered. In the dreams, she was not always rescued. In one version, she managed to break free on her own but with no way to escape, she resorted to jumping from the flat's open window. She plunged to her death and jolted awake, shaking with fear and fury.

'I dropped by the pub last night to see if Sam needed anything. There wasn't much damage to the pub itself, just the ceiling, but for health and safety reasons, he had to shut down for a while.'

'Is Sam all right?'

'Yeah, he's managing. The insurance will cover the damages, and his profit losses.'

'It looked like the only way he was going to fix all of the pub's problems was by burning it to the ground and starting over. Or just cutting his losses and leaving.'

'Well, there you go. It's not exactly burnt to the ground but the pub is the last thing on anyone's mind. He's most concerned about you. Keeps asking. I told him I was dropping in to see you today. He sends his love.' Olive surveyed the house. 'This place brings back memories.'

'Yeah,' Nikki said with a sigh.

'Growing up here can't have been that bad.'

From where they stood, Nikki could see Dad's old armchair. 'Nah, it wasn't,' she said.

Olive reached into her bag and drew an envelope. 'Now, I've got something for you, and I'm under strict instructions to make sure you receive it.' She handed Nikki the envelope.

Nikki thought it was a final paycheck from Sam but when she opened it, she found a letter instead. *Dear Nikki*, it started and it was signed, *Love, Jason*.

'I can't,' she said, thrusting the letter back to Olive.

'Nikki, just read it.'

'Do you even know what happened?'

'I do. He's been coming round to the pub everyday like a lost puppy, hoping to see you. Both Sam and I refused to give him your home address but I said I'd deliver the letter.'

'He's married.'

'He's divorced,' Olive said. 'He filed for divorce before he met you. The poor bugger was so desperate to prove himself that he brought the paperwork to the pub to show us. I can vouch for the fact that it's genuine.'

'Why did he hide it then?'

Olive shrugged.

'It still doesn't make sense. If he wasn't involved in his other relationship, who was calling him all the time? Why did he disappear all of a sudden?'

'I'm sure he explains it all there,' Olive said, pointing to the letter. 'At least read it.'

'Whose side are you on, anyway?'

'I'm always on the side of truth,' Olive said. 'Just like you. And the truth is he was scared and he acted like a fool. He's definitely got some explaining to do but you should give him a chance, Nik. The two of you looked genuinely happy together. He seems like a decent guy who did a really stupid thing.'

Nikki held the letter. 'I might need to read this on my own,' she said.

'No problem. I have these horrid essays to mark.' Olive picked up her bag then leaned forward and planted a firm kiss on Nikki's forehead. 'You're the bravest person I know,' she said.

Nikki returned to bed right after dinner. In the box that Olive had brought over, she found her Beatrix Potter biography. She opened it and began reading, wishing again that she could locate that tea-stained copy of *The Journal and Sketches of Beatrix Potter*. Outside, the skies had darkened and streetlights glowed dully like embers. Nikki's satchel was packed flat at the bottom of the box beneath her worn out trainers and a few more books. Nikki put the box aside and pulled the blanket up to her chin. She didn't have the emotional strength to unpack the rest of the box just yet. It was depressing thinking that one box contained everything she owned.

Then there was Jason's letter, which remained on her dresser. She could see the corner of the envelope but each time she thought of opening it, she felt a churning in her gut and sank further into bed. The letter could contain all the apologies in the world but she wasn't ready to hear them.

Chapter Nineteen

On Kulwinder's walk home from a morning service at the temple, the sky was so dense with clouds that it appeared to be made of stone. How she had hated this weather when she first arrived in England. *Where's the sun?* she and Sarab had asked each other. Then Maya was born. 'Here's the sun,' Sarab had been fond of saying. Cradling her tiny body in the crook of his elbow, the smile on his face had seemed eternal.

Sarab was in the front garden chatting with another man when Kulwinder got home. Kulwinder recognized the man: Dinesh Sharma from Dinesh Repairs. 'Hello,' she said.

Despite not being Sikh, he held his palms together and greeted her with '*Sat sri akal*.' She liked that. She offered him a cup of tea.

'No, no, don't trouble yourself,' he said. 'I'm just here to give a quick quote.'

'I've asked him to fix the letterbox and help out with a few more things around the house,' Sarab said. 'The screen door is coming off its hinges and my eyesight isn't so good, so I don't want to use the drill.'

'All right. Carry on,' Kulwinder said. From the corner of her eye, she noticed a shape moving in the window of the house opposite. Her heart caught in her throat. Tarampal. Was she there? No, she couldn't be. It was a trick of the light. She had fled back to this house after that night, taking refuge in the only place in London that she knew. The next morning, she was gone. A neighbour had seen her piling suitcases into a taxi and rumour had it she was in India now, far from all the whispers and speculation. It was said that she wanted to avoid testifying against Jaggi, but the courts could make her return if they thought it necessary. There was constant talk of Tarampal now – people claimed she had had multiple affairs, that her daughters were not even Kemal Singh's offspring. These were most likely untrue, the tendency of temple gossips to exaggerate compounded by everybody's relief that she was gone. When offers of such information came Kulwinder's way, she declined politely but firmly. After all, she never wanted Tarampal's unravelling to be fodder for community gossip. What Tarampal refused to believe about Maya's death was worth a lifetime of shame.

With the folder tucked under her arm, Kulwinder stepped out of her home once again and walked up Ansell Road. She passed rows of houses and wondered about their inhabitants. Who had read the stories? Whose lives had changed? A misty rain hung almost motionless in the air and speckled her hair like jewels. She tightened her grip on the folder.

There were two boys working in the photocopying shop. Kulwinder went straight for Munna Kaur's son. If it was possible, he seemed to have grown since she last visited this shop a few months ago to get those flyers copied. His shoulders appeared broader and his movements were more assured than before. A man was ahead of her in the queue. He offered to let her go first, but she politely declined, taking time to observe the boy.

'Hello,' she said brightly when it was her turn.

'Good afternoon,' he muttered back, his eyes downcast as he tore an order form off a pad. 'Photocopy?'

'Yes, please,' Kulwinder said. 'It's a rather large order so I can come back.' She pushed the folder to him. 'A hundred copies, spiral-bound.'

The boy looked up and his eyes met hers. Kulwinder gave him a warm smile but she felt the pace of her heart quickening. 'I can't do that,' he said.

'I can come back,' Kulwinder said.

The boy pushed the folder back to Kulwinder. 'I'm not making copies of these stories,' he said.

'Let me speak to your manager then,' she said.

'I'm the manager here. And I'm saying, take your business elsewhere.'

Rising to the tips of her toes, Kulwinder tried to see past the boy. The other worker was a Somali teenager who looked too young to have any authority over this boy. 'Son, what's your name?'

He stared at her. 'Akash,' he said finally.

'Akash, I know your mother,' she said. 'What would she say if she knew you were being so rude to me?'

Kulwinder knew her words were futile the moment she said them. Some other moral obligation was overriding all customs of politeness here. Akash drew back and for a moment, Kulwinder thought he might spit at her.

'Are you aware of what these stories are doing to our community? Destroying it,' Akash hissed. 'If I make copies, you're going to spread them to even more homes.'

'I'm not destroying anything,' Kulwinder said, as the truth dawned. 'It's you and your narrow-minded gang of thugs who want to destroy things.' This was how the Brothers recruited such passionate members, she realized. A few months ago, this boy had been so timid. Kulwinder recalled Munna Kaur saying that she pushed her boy to get a part-time job so he could practice interacting with people more. 'No girl will want to marry a boy who doesn't have confidence,' she had said. Now his confidence was a hot liquid spilling over.

Another customer entered the shop. Kulwinder briefly considered creating a fuss so dramatic that the boy would comply just to placate her. But there was no point. Turning to leave, Kulwinder caught his reflection in the glass doors. His stare was hateful. She uttered a quick prayer for him. *Let him find balance and moderation in all things; let him listen to himself and not the noise of others.* Noise. That was all the Brothers had created. They hollered and stomped around Southall, but after what she and widows went through rescuing Nikki, the Brothers didn't frighten her. Kulwinder noticed there were fewer of them patrolling the Broadway now, and earlier at the temple, she had seen one of them actually serving langar like a proper Sikh instead of keeping watch on the women in the kitchen. 'They're a little afraid of us now,' Manjeet had said. But hadn't the Brothers always been afraid? Now they knew the full force of the women's strength. 'They have more respect for us now,' Kulwinder corrected Manjeet, who nodded and squeezed her hand across the table.

Outside, Kulwinder pulled out her mobile phone and scrolled through the list of names, landing on Nikki's.

'Hello,' Nikki said.

'This is Kulwinder speaking.'

There was a pause. '*Sat sri akal*, Kulwinder,' Nikki said.

'*Sat sri akal*,' Kulwinder replied. 'How are you feeling?'

'I'm . . . well, I'm all right.' There was a nervous laugh. 'And you?'

'I'm well. Are you back at home?'

'Yes. I've been back for a few days now.'

'You'll be staying there for a while?'

'I think so. I can't go back to my old flat.'

'Did you lose many things in the fire?'

'Nothing of much value,' Nikki said. 'Most importantly, I got out alive because of you. I owe you my life, Kulwinder. I actually wanted to call you sooner but I didn't quite know whether to say thank you or sorry.'

'There's no need to say sorry,' Kulwinder said.

'There is. I deceived you into thinking I was teaching those women to read and write. I'm very sorry.'

Kulwinder hesitated. Although she hadn't called Nikki looking for an apology, it was nice to hear. '*Hanh*, yes, yes, but it's all water under the tables now,' she said, pleased to have remembered an English idiom.

'That's very generous of you,' Nikki said.

'It's true. If you had stuck to teaching the women to write, they wouldn't have made up those stories.' *What a loss it would be*, Kulwinder thought, wishing she had some way of conveying this to the photocopier boy. 'I've read a few,' she added.

'And what did you think?' Kulwinder could hear the anxiety in Nikki's voice.

'I rescued you from a burning building,' Kulwinder said. 'I liked them that much.'

Nikki had Maya's unfettered laugh. *Don't show your teeth*, Kulwinder would snap at her teenaged daughter. *Men will think you're inviting them to have fun*. She had inherited the warning from her own mother. Now she laughed along with Nikki and hearing their notes of joy ringing out in unison brought on a wonderful relief.

'I want the stories to be shared with the community,' Kulwinder said. 'Not just the widows who know about the classes.'

'I do too.'

'I tried getting copies made here in Southall but the boy at the counter refused to fill the order for me. Is there a photocopying place near you? I will pay for it. We can get them bound as well. Perhaps we could find someone to design a cover.'

'You're sure you want to do this? It could lead to more trouble.' Nikki said. Kulwinder was both surprised and touched by the caution in her voice.

'I'm sure,' she said.

Kulwinder returned home, still hugging the folder to her chest. Dinesh was no longer in the garden and the mailbox had been uprooted and gently laid on its side on the lawn. 'Where will the postman put our letters?' she asked Sarab.

'It's only for a day. Dinesh is coming back tomorrow.' Sarab eyed the folder. 'And what were you doing with those?'

'You'll see,' Kulwinder said. From the corner of her eye, she saw a flicker from Tarampal's house again.

'Is somebody there?' she asked Sarab, nodding toward the house. 'I keep seeing something.'

'There were detectives investigating earlier. That's probably who you saw.'

But the person in the window had moved about surreptitiously, as if knowing it was a fleeting vision. Kulwinder did not believe in ghosts but she briefly wondered if there was a spirit floating about in that home, wanting to be freed.

'Things are changing,' she had said last night at dinner. Sarab nodded. He thought she was referring to the seasons. Kulwinder didn't clarify. It was becoming warmer. Daylight would soon stretch to nine o'clock and in the early evenings children could already be heard running down the street. When their mothers called them in, she heard herself pleading with them for more time. Outside, the whole world beckoned with intoxicating thrills. In five more minutes, they could reach the end of the street and see the buses heading towards Hammersmith, the trains departing for Paddington Station. They could return to their homes but in their minds, plot the routes that might one day take them through this vast, magnificent city. She put the folder on the coffee table and headed out the door.

'Where are you going now?' Sarab called but Kulwinder didn't answer. She crossed the road and walked up Tarampal's driveway. The sun had come out and washed the white houses in a brief but generous light. Kulwinder peered into the window. She was aware of the neighbours' gazes; she could practically hear them whispering, asking each other what she was looking at.

Through the narrow slit between the curtains, Kulwinder could only see the entryway and the staircase. The vision in the window had been a trick – the sun emerging and disappearing with uncertainty, not quite knowing its rightful position in this time between seasons. A sensation of relief fanned across Kulwinder's body like a fever was breaking. She kissed her fingertips and then pressed them to the window.

It was finally time to let Maya go.

Chapter Twenty

In the evening, a bubbly after-work crowd filled the tube and tumbled out with Nikki. Mindi was waiting at the station wearing a black dress with a glittering neckline that formed a suggestive V-shape above her bust. 'Nice outfit,' Nikki said.

'Thanks. I think it's going to happen soon,' Mindi said.

'What's going to happen?'

Mindi leaned towards her and whispered. 'Sex.'

'You guys haven't slept together yet?'

'I was waiting till everybody approved of him.'

'So if I say yes, you'll do it in the ladies while I order the entrees?'

'Don't be so crude,' Mindi scolded.

'Do you not find him attractive, Mindi?'

'I do, but I don't want to sleep with someone I'm not going to marry. And if you see a red flag that I've missed, well, I might think twice about getting engaged to him.'

'You don't need me to say yes. I thought I already told you that,' Nikki said. 'You don't need *anyone's* approval.'

'But I want it,' Mindi argued. 'You still don't get it, Nikki. This whole arranged marriage thing is about choices. I know you see it as the opposite of that but you're wrong. I am making my own decision but I want to include my family in that decision as well.'

Mindi waved at a man in the distance. Nikki could only see a crowd of German backpackers, and then amongst them emerged a scrawny man that she recognized. 'Oh my god, I remember him,' Nikki said. She turned to Mindi. 'He found your profile on the marriage board, didn't he?'

'How do you know?'

'I met him when I was putting up your profile. He was – oh hello!' Nikki said.

'Hi,' Ranjit said, with a surprised, nervous laugh. 'You're Mindi's sister.'

'Nikki. We've met.'

Mindi looked back and forth between them. 'If you two met while Nikki was putting up my profile, does that mean you were the first man to see my profile?' Her eyes brimmed with adoration.

'You guys go ahead,' Nikki said when they reached the restaurant. 'I'll be there in a minute.' She waited for Mindi and Ranjit to disappear inside and then she lit a cigarette. The pavement glistened with rain and people trotted past, their conversation and laughter mingling with the sounds of traffic. Nikki felt for her phone and then she drew her hand away. *Don't even think about calling him*, she scolded herself. She only finished half the cigarette before stubbing it out and going into the restaurant.

At the table, the waiter asked for their drink orders. 'Shall we share a bottle of wine?' Nikki asked.

Mindi shot a glance at Ranjit. 'I won't have any wine, thanks,' she said.

'Ranjit?' Nikki asked.

'I don't drink,' he said.

'Oh. Right. I guess I'll have the whole bottle to myself then.' The waiter was the only one who broke into a smile. 'It's a joke, guys,' Nikki said. 'Just some sparkling water for me, thanks.'

'You can order a glass for yourself if you want,' Mindi said.

'That's all right,' Nikki said. She thought she saw Mindi's shoulders drop slightly with relief.

* * *

They did not talk about Ranjit on the tube ride home. Nikki waited patiently for Mindi to ask for her opinion. Finally, as they stepped into their house and went up the stairs to their respective bedrooms, Nikki tossed her bag on the bed and followed Mindi into the bathroom.

'A little privacy please,' Mindi said, wiping off her eye make-up.

'You haven't asked me what I think of him,' Nikki said.

'I don't need to know,' Mindi said. Both her eyes were closed now as she rubbed the wipe across her lids.

'What happened to wanting my approval?'

'Honestly, I'm reluctant to ask.'

'Why?'

'You hardly said anything once our meals arrived. Ranjit tried to get to know you and you gave him one-syllable answers.'

'I don't have much to say to a guy like that.'

'Like what?'

'You know.'

'Enlighten me, please,' Mindi said.

'He seems quite conservative.'

'What's wrong with that?'

Nikki gave Mindi a long look. 'Is he going to be uncomfortable every time I have a drink? If I smell like cigarettes, is he going to wrinkle his nose at me? Because I felt like the wayward sister – the one who brings down the family's reputation.'

'He's working on that,' Mindi said. 'He grew up in a traditional family. It freaked him out a bit when I told him that you lived and worked in a pub.'

'Does he know about my role in the story classes?'

'Yes.'

'What was his reaction?'

'He was uncomfortable with it.'

'What a surprise.'

'The point is, he's coming around. He cares so much about me that he wants to be more accepting. It will just take him some time.'

'Why be with someone who's making the journey? You could be with someone who has already arrived.'

'His traditional values have a good side as well. He's very family oriented and respectful. Nikki, you go on about how narrow-minded everyone else is yet you think there's only one way to live and fall in love. Anybody who isn't like you is doing it wrong.'

'That's not true!' Nikki protested.

Mindi tossed the wipe into the bin and pushed past Nikki. She entered Nikki's bedroom and grabbed the letter from her dresser. She waved it at Nikki, who tried to snatch it back. 'What the hell, Mindi?' Nikki cried.

'I'm tossing this in the bin.'

'Give it back.'

'I don't know what it says or who it's from but it's clearly driving you crazy.'

'This has nothing to do with—'

'You're unsettled about something and I can tell that this letter is connected to it. Every time it catches your eye, you get that same pinched look you have on your face right now – like you're one step away from covering your ears and singing *la la la* until you're left alone. Read it or I'm throwing it away.'

Mindi tossed the letter on Nikki's bed and retreated into her own bedroom, shutting the door. Nikki was too taken aback to say anything. She sank back on her bed. Lights from a slowly passing car threw shadows across the ceiling. Mindi could be heard shuffling around her room. 'Min?'

'What?'

'Nothing,' she called back.

Silence from Mindi. Then: 'Idiot.' Nikki grinned and scooted towards the wall that they shared. She gave it a hard hit with her heel. Mindi responded by thumping back on the wall with her hand – just like they used to when they were children. Mindi's side of the wall remained silent for a few moments. 'Hey,' she said.

'Yeah?' Nikki asked.

'You're up later than I expected.' Mindi's syrupy tone suggested that she was not addressing Nikki. Next came a surreptitious giggle. Ranjit was on the phone. Nikki raised her foot, about to thump the wall one last time for good measure, but she decided against it. Instead she picked up the envelope on her desk, took in a deep breath and ripped it open.

Dear Nikki,

I can't expect you to read this letter without feeling hurt and disgusted with me. I lied to you. I had many opportunities to tell you about my marriage and my divorce, but I hid it from you because I was afraid of what it might say about me.

Everybody considers my marriage breakdown a failure and I've struggled to accept it myself – I've failed my family and I've failed as an adult.

I owe you an explanation and it's up to you whether you read it.

A few years ago, when I finished university and started working, I was expected to get married immediately – as the oldest son I was pressured by family to set an example. I would walk in the door after work and my parents would beckon me to the study to look at the top profiles they had shortlisted from the Indian matrimonial websites.

I put off meeting any of these women, wanting to live a free life before settling down. I figured I still had time but I fought constantly with my parents and I ended up moving into my own place. Then my mother was diagnosed with cancer. She went through exhausting tests and chemotherapy sessions that wore her down. The pressure began to mount again, from Dad, aunties and uncles, and even my younger siblings who just wanted something to celebrate at a dreary time. The message was clear: get married, and give your mother just a small sense of peace.

I met Suneet on the internet. She lived in London and we got to know each other through patchy Skype calls and email exchanges before I made the decision to visit the UK to meet her in person. I saw the trip as the first stage in the dating process; our families saw it as a confirmation of our engagement. I got swept up in all of it even though I was uncertain about how I felt. I told my family that I liked her and it was true. She is a pretty, intelligent and kind woman who cares very much about traditions and wanted an arranged marriage. There was no reason not to ask her to marry me, especially as my mother's health deteriorated – time was running out. In the lead-up to the wedding, I had moments of anxiety but I quelled them by reminding myself that we'd have time to get to know each other after marriage. This custom worked for our parents and it still works for thousands of Indian couples – why wouldn't it work for me? We were compatible enough. Most importantly, both our families were thrilled. Although my mother was still weak, my engagement put a spring in her step. My dad and I stopped arguing over everything. It was a peaceful time for our family, and after I had caused so much unhappiness I wanted badly to keep this peace.

As it turned out, Suneet and I weren't compatible in many other ways that I hadn't considered. There was little sexual chemistry between us, something I dismissed at first because it's not considered a valid reason for separation in our culture. Suneet also wanted children right away whereas I said we should wait. But Suneet felt pressured by relatives asking her parents when they were going to have grandkids, and I in turn resented Suneet for bowing to those pressures and accused her of risking our happiness just to satisfy our parents. And yet, as I said this to her, I realized I was also guilty of just that.

We grew restless with each other and argued over petty things. In the end, Suneet was the one who suggested divorce. She was weary and growing bitter, and she still had her best years ahead of her. I don't think I understood how much I had put her through until she said, 'You've already taken two years away from me. Don't waste any more of my time.' I knew that going back to her home a divorced woman would be shattering. Confronting both our parents with the truth was a ghastly experience. My mom had just begun a round of more successful radiation therapy and she seemed to be on the mend. Our announcement plunged her back into illness. She stayed in bed for a while and Dad didn't return my calls. Suneet went through the same at home.

I moved into a small flat-share during the divorce and I was contemplating moving back to California but the thought of facing my family was too much to deal with.

My dad finally returned one of my calls to inform me that my mother's remission was looking hopeful, and I went to the temple to give my thanks. That was the day I met you. But at Suneet's home, things went from bad to worse. Bitter, and suffering from a loss of face in the community, her dad launched a character assault on my family and me. He was heartbroken for his daughter – I understand that – but he went around saying horribly hurtful things about my siblings. These rumours travelled back to California through our family networks. It was his intention to ruin the family's reputation in the way that I had apparently ruined his daughter's chances for finding a suitable husband again. When he exhausted this tactic, he attempted to sue me for damages, claiming that I had caused irretrievable harm to the family by divorcing his daughter. Suneet did not participate in much of this, but she didn't stop him either. Everyone was hurting.

Those urgent calls that I had to answer – often when I was with you – were from my mother, Suneet's father, Suneet's father's lawyer (who turned out to be a real dud – an uncle with a law degree from a third-rate Indian university) and my siblings. There was always something going on, and it seemed to be my fault every time. I needed to placate everybody, which involved long conversations and negotiations. I was putting out spot fires that were more demanding that my full-time job. There was a tremendous amount of emotional blackmail.

I came close to telling my parents that I knew I was not in love with Suneet because I had experienced falling in love with you and I could see how different it was. But I didn't want to get you involved. I know it seemed like I was creating that distance from you because I wasn't interested, but it was the opposite – I was afraid that if we got closer, things would go disastrously wrong. I wanted to avoid you coming to my flat because I was nervous that someone would see us and accuse me of having an affair and that you would be dragged in.

Nikki, it was cowardice that kept me from finding the words to tell you the truth. I regret every second that I've spent without you. It was selfish and dishonest of me to lie and to disappear so many times without explanation. You were so open with me from the first day we met, and I could have repaid you by sharing all of this with you from the start. I'm so, so sorry Nikki. I don't expect you to ever want to see me again, but if you did, I'd do anything to gain your trust again.

Love,
Jason

Chapter Twenty-One

The morning air was crisp and a mild breeze made Nikki's hands tingle. On the train, she picked up a copy of yesterday's *Evening Standard* and busied herself with reading old news.

The shops were still closed by the time Nikki arrived at Notting Hill Gate station but a stream of tourists flowed towards the Portobello Road market. They stopped to pose for pictures in front of the pastel-painted homes.

Nikki headed in the opposite direction towards the cinema, which was still screening the French film that she and Jason had missed. She still had half an hour to kill before the show started so she carried on ambling. At a traffic light, a family of American tourists stopped to ask where Hyde Park was. She pointed in its direction but they wanted her to show it to them on a large, unfolded map. She was trying to see where they were on the map when a gust of wind hit the centre crease and ripped it. 'We'll figure it out,' the mother of the family said. She took the map back and folded it. 'We need this to last us the whole our whole trip,' she said.

'That's all right,' Nikki said. As the tourists walked away, Nikki overheard the woman telling her husband. 'We should ask a person who's from here.'

Nikki was dumbstruck by their rudeness. The husband turned around then and gave Nikki an apologetic nod. Nikki continued walking but she was half tempted to go after the woman and tell her that she was from here, thank you very much. She was so lost in a cloud of indignant thoughts that she overshot her mark and found herself on the end of the street, having passed Sally's Bookshop. She returned to it and lit a cigarette. Having her claim to Britain taken away from her by an ignorant tourist warranted a satisfying smoke.

Nikki peered into the bookshop's window, her eyes trained on the Sale bin at the back. Then suddenly, a face appeared in the window, and she jumped back, dropping her cigarette on the ground. It was the bookshop's cashier, the woman she'd spoken to last time she visited. The woman knocked excitedly on the window and gestured for Nikki to come inside. Nikki stubbed out her cigarette and went in.

'Sorry for scaring you like that,' the woman laughed.

Nikki smiled tightly. Now only two cigarettes remained in her pack and she was meant to quit after that. The one she had dropped was only half finished and as she thought of it lying on the pavement, a wave of grief washed over her.

'I just wanted to make sure that I didn't lose you,' the woman explained. 'You're Nikki, aren't you? I'm Hannah.' She disappeared suddenly behind the counter and popped up again, placing a book in front of Nikki. Beatrix Potter.

'Oh my goodness,' Nikki gasped. She reached for the book and hesitated, almost afraid to pick it up. Her fingers gingerly turned the cover. The first image was a portrait of Beatrix Potter. Her plump face was slightly angled and there was a tinge of mischief in her small, pursed lips. 'Where did you end up finding this?' she asked.

'Special order. It came all the way from India.'

There it was, a tea stain the size of a small leaf on the top corner of the cover. It was the very same copy that she had longed for in Delhi all those years ago. 'That's incredible,' she said. She plucked her debit card from her wallet and gave it to Hannah, who waved it away.

'The gentleman already paid for it,' she explained.

'Which gentleman?'

'The one who ordered this book. I asked him if he'd rather have it sent to his home or yours – do away with the middle man – but he insisted that we keep it in the shop window in case you walked past. I supposed he wanted to surprise you. I couldn't keep it in the window though because that meant it would be available for other customers to purchase, so I had it under the counter but I looked out for you and told the guys on the late afternoon shift to do the same but I think they used it as an excuse to lure every girl they fancied into the shop . . .'

Hannah's explanation faded into the distance. All Nikki could think of was the word "gentleman." It brought to mind a faceless benefactor in a top hat for some reason even though she was certain that it was Jason who had placed the order. He would have had to call every bookshop in Connaught Place in Delhi and she felt a little breathless at the thought.

'Thank you so much,' Nikki said. She clutched the book to her chest and walked outside in a bit of a daze. She passed the cinema, deciding to forgo the French film. Trees formed a cosy canopy on the street leading to the gardens. Nikki stepped between the shadows, finding patches of early morning light for momentary warmth. The din of traffic faded once she entered the gates of Hyde Park. Here, she walked for a while and found a bench opposite Kensington Palace. The book felt solid in her hands. Nikki ran her hand over the cover and brought the book to her nose to inhale its smell. She always had a small fear that it she ever found this book, it would bring some regret at how she had argued with Dad over it. But with her eyes shut, all she thought of was Jason – the navy jumper he had worn to their first date, the way her stomach flipped when she saw him walk into O'Reilly's. Nikki took time to examine each page – the letters, the sketchy doodles. Although the pages were smooth, these pieces felt textured and real, as if she were inside Beatrix Potter's mind. Jason had known just how much it meant to hold this very book in her hands.

In the park, tourists weaved purposefully between the more evenly paced joggers and dog walkers. What people wanted from London was all here – the lush green gardens, the majestic domes and church spires, the black cabs busily circling. It was regal and mysterious; she could understand anybody's impatience to be part of it. She was reminded of the widows.

They would have known little of this London before their journey to this country, and upon their arrival, they would have known even less. Britain equalled a better life and they would have clung to this knowledge even as this life confounded and remained foreign. Every day in this new country would have been an exercise in forgiveness.

Nikki picked up her phone and searched for Jason's number.

'I've got two cigarettes left and then I'm quitting for good,' she said. 'You're doing this with me, all right?'

She heard a prolonged sigh as if Jason had been holding his breath waiting for her to call. 'Save me one,' he said. Nikki told him where she was and she waited, watching a group of elderly cyclists rolling past slowly as they breathed in the crisp spring air. She couldn't wait to see him. She couldn't wait for them to begin again.

Chapter Twenty-Two

Kulwinder's new office gleamed. She sat in a chair with a headrest and wheels on its feet. A large window framed the summer sky in a perfect blue square. Kulwinder could not see the old building from here and she was surprised that she missed it. True, it had been cramped and mouldy and the building itself could use a few renovations, but at least she did not have to be next door to the men of the Association. They lingered as if her open door was an invitation to stare like she was a curious display – the woman who had rounded up all those old bibis to make demands at the Sikh Association meeting.

Not demands, Kulwinder reminded herself. Reasonable requests. Funding for a proper women's centre, one that would provide free services like legal advisers for victims of domestic violence and a dedicated fitness centre where women could exercise without being harassed. Still, Kulwinder chuckled at the memory of men's appalled expressions when she said, 'Take the time you need to need to consider our proposal, but I want to be present at every discussion from now on. No more impromptu decisions made in the men's cliques in the langar hall. Is that clear?' When nobody protested, she nodded and said, 'Good. We all agree, then.'

There was a light knocking sound. 'Come in,' Kulwinder said. The door remained shut. There was another louder knock. This was another thing to get used to in the new office – a more solid door blocked out the outside sounds but muffled her responses. 'Come in,' she shouted. The door opened.

'Nikki!' Kulwinder hurriedly closed the newspaper as the girl approached her desk. Kulwinder stood to hug her and noticed that her postman bag was missing. In its place was a backpack that bulged with books. 'You've been studying hard,' she commented.

'I have some catching up to do. University starts up in a few weeks and I had such a long time away.'

'I'm sure it will all come back to you.'

'I've got a few new things to learn. The course is slightly different.'

Nikki was so excited when she was offered one of the remaining spots in this program, a law degree with an emphasis on social justice. 'I want to help prevent what happened to girls like Maya,' she had said when she rang Kulwinder to tell her the news, which made Kulwinder's heart swell with pride. And then, in Nikki fashion, she had rattled on about women's rights, except this time Kulwinder paid attention. 'And there might be more unsolved cases like Gulshan's and Karina's killings. So few people questioned those girls' deaths that it made it okay to continue the violence. Who knows – we might have grounds to open investigations for Gulshan and to open up Karina's case again. I'm looking into ways to encourage conversations about honour crimes in communities like ours.' *Ours*. Kulwinder's throat tightened with emotion.

Nikki nodded at the newspaper. 'Anything new?' she asked.

'Nothing,' Kulwinder sighed.

'It'll take time,' Nikki said. 'I know it's hard to wait though.'

Jaggi was awaiting trial and that was all the information they had. She checked the paper habitually for updates, but with the passing of each day, she grappled with her disappointment. A part of her had hoped that he would be thrown straight into jail once Nikki had found the registration form among her belongings. Why did they need to ask him any more questions when the handwriting clearly matched? But the lawyers had explained something about due process of law and following procedures, which Kulwinder had to accept. At least she and Sarab had lawyers now

– Gupta and Co., Solicitors, had come forward with an offer to fight Maya's case for free. They assured Kulwinder that they had a good case, and they were confident about defeating Jaggi's defense team when the time came. Kulwinder was full of gratitude but she kept thinking there was a catch to this whole no fee agreement even though Mr Gupta himself explained it was an act of community service, so once a week, she walked to his office on the Broadway and delivered a box of ladoos to the receptionist.

Nikki pulled up a chair. 'This is a lovely office. Much bigger than the old one.'

Kulwinder looked around. 'Thank you,' she said with pride. She ran her fingers lightly over the smooth surface of her desk.

'I came here with some exciting news,' Nikki said.

'Your sister is engaged,' Kulwinder said.

'No, not yet,' Nikki said. 'She's seeing someone though.'

'Oh. A nice boy?'

'Yeah,' Nikki said. 'He's quite nice. She's happy around him.'

'Good,' Kulwinder said. She was mildly disappointed. It had been a long time since she'd attended a wedding. It would be nice to wear gold again. 'What was your news then?'

Nikki took in a breath. 'We're being published.'

Kulwinder stared at her and said nothing. Nikki had to be joking. 'The stories? *Those* ones?' She pointed at the photocopied collection on her desk with its flimsy spiral binding that had begun to uncoil from use. There were other copies floating around Southall and beyond, but this was the original.

'Those very ones – and possibly more. A company called Gemini Books wants to publish *Erotic Stories for Punjabi Widows*!' Nikki unzipped her bag and pulled out a thick stack of pages that she handed to Kulwinder. It was a publishing contract full of jargon and complicated sentences that Kulwinder did not understand but she made a show of arranging her glasses on her face and pointing to specific clauses as if she appreciated their inclusion.

'What language will they be published in?' Kulwinder asked.

'They're bilingual publishers and they're willing to have both Gurmukhi and English script. I told them that there are plenty more stories being written and they've offered us the opportunity to keep on publishing with them in a series.'

'This is wonderful news,' Kulwinder said. 'Will we be able to keep some copies here for people to borrow?'

'I'm sure we can. They can also buy the books. The profits could go into funding the women's centre.'

'Oh, Nikki,' Kulwinder said. 'This is even better news than an engagement.'

Nikki laughed. 'Glad to know it.'

'Speaking of the women's centre, have you given any more thought to my offer?' A week ago, Kulwinder had called Nikki to ask her if she would teach a few classes. Nikki had seemed hesitant. Her shifting body language told Kulwinder that she was probably going to say no.

'It's a great opportunity,' Nikki said. 'But I'm afraid that with all of my study commitments this year and living so far away, I won't be able to.'

'Where are you living?'

'Enfield,' Nikki said.

'With your mum?'

'Temporarily,' Nikki said. 'I'll probably share a flat with my friend Olive next year.'

'You'll need a job then,' Kulwinder reminded her. 'Rentals are expensive.' Nikki probably thought she was desperate but nowadays there was no shortage of people wanting to teach in the women's centre. Word had spread in the community and potential tutors called every day to inquire about vacancies.

'The widows want you back,' Kulwinder explained gently.

'I miss them,' Nikki said. 'I'm keeping in touch with them. I saw Arvinder, Manjeet and Preetam in the langar hall just now. And Sheena and I are having coffee later.'

'You could see them all the time. Sheena is going to teach the internet class. The others have enrolled.'

'I need to focus on my studies for now,' Nikki said. 'Honestly, I'd love to otherwise.'

Kulwinder understood. All of those books in Nikki's bag needed to be read and who knew how long that would take? Still, there were ways of reminding young people of their duties. Kulwinder winced and clutched at the fabric of her blouse in the middle of her chest.

'What's wrong?' Nikki asked.

'Oh me? Nothing,' Kulwinder said. She kept her features stretched with pain for a moment before relaxing. It was working. Nikki looked worried.

'Should I take you to a hospital?' Nikki asked.

'No, no,' Kulwinder said. 'It's just my acid reflux condition. I get these pains. They get worse as I get older.' Actually, the doctor had given her samples of a new medication that let her eat as much achar as she wanted – no consequent bloating or burping.

'I'm so sorry,' Nikki said.

'There are days when I just need to be at home,' Kulwinder said. 'Not worrying about how to staff my classes.'

'Have you got a class on Sundays?' Nikki asked.

'No, no, don't trouble yourself. You are very busy with your studies.'

'I could travel here on Sundays.'

Kulwinder knew the timetable by heart. No classes were allocated to Sundays because that day was usually dedicated to weddings and special prayer programs at the temple. 'We can't pay you to run a Sunday class.'

'So don't. I'll volunteer,' Nikki said. 'I'll come in on Sundays to run an English writing class or a conversation workshop. People can drop in if they want.'

'I couldn't ask you to do that,' Kulwinder said.

'I'll find the time,' Nikki said. 'I should be part of this place. You should be taking care of yourself.'

'It's just my stomach,' Kulwinder said.

'Yes, like my mother's migraines,' Nikki said wryly. 'Triggered during arguments and then mysteriously cured when she wins.'

Kulwinder gave Nikki a weak smile and a final wince for good measure.

After Nikki left, Kulwinder stood by the window. From up here, life in Southall shrank to miniatures – people and cars and trees she could collect in the palm of her hand. No wonder the men always seemed so high and mighty during meetings. They watched the world from this vantage point and it looked insignificant. Just look at that cluster of widows weaving through the parked cars like ghosts. They could be scrunched up pieces of paper. Kulwinder cast a weary glance over her office and made a decision. She would do the official paper work here but she would make it a point to spend most of her time on the ground with the women. She should start now.

As she moved away from the window to pick up her bag, she saw Nikki's tiny figure crossing the lot. A young man was waiting for her. It had to be Jason Bhamra. Kulwinder had heard from the widows that they were an item now. She saw them meeting, their limbs bumping in playful greeting. Nikki tossed her head back and let out a laugh as Jason whispered into her ear.

Kulwinder turned toward the temple and uttered a quick prayer in gratitude of pleasure. The sensation of contact, the anticipation of a kiss or brush of Sarab's hand across her bare thigh – such moments were miniscule but they amounted to a lifetime of happiness.

Acknowledgments

Gratitude, love and admiration for the following:

Anna Power, the first person to read this story and see its potential. From mentor to literary agent and friend, your dedication and enthusiasm keep me going.

The entire HarperCollins team for welcoming me so warmly and with such excitement. Martha Ashby and Rachel Kahan, your feedback and insights made editing a discovery rather than just a process. Kimberley Young, Hannah Gamon and Felicity Denham, I'm very lucky to have such passionate champions for this book.

Jaskiran Badh-Sidhu and her wonderful parents and grandmother, whose love and generosity made England feel like a second home. Without you, this book would not exist.

Prithi Rao, your comments on this manuscript were invaluable and your friendship even more so.

Mum and Dad, for encouraging me to pursue this crazy writing dream. My in-laws, the Howells for your love and support.

Paul, you are absolutely everything good, inspiring and true in this world. It would be a very unfunny life without you. I love you to bits.

About the author

About the book

Insights,
Interviews
& More . . .

About the author

Meet Balli Kaur Jaswal

Susan Gordon Brown

BALLI KAUR JASWAL was born in Singapore and grew up in Japan, Russia, and the Philippines. She studied creative writing at Hollins University in Virginia and was awarded the David T.K. Wong Creative Writing Fellowship at the University of East Anglia. Her first novel *Inheritance* was published by Sleepers Publishing in Australia in 2013 and won the *Sydney Morning Herald*'s Best Young Australian Novelist award. In 2014, she was the National Writer-in-Residence at Singapore's Nanyang Technological University, where she taught creative writing and worked on *Erotic Stories for Punjabi Widows.*

Reading Group Guide

1. "Her purpose came into sharp focus. 'Some people don't even know about this place'"—Nikki imagines herself saying—"'Let's change that.'" Why does Nikki—who has rejected Punjabi tradition and chosen a life independent of her parents' community—suddenly want to teach in Southall? Is her motivation selfless or self-serving?

2. The widows gossip that Kulwinder is stuck up and standoffish. Nikki feels scolded and humiliated by her. What do you make of Kulwinder at the start of the novel? At the end?

3. Stories of marriages—especially arranged ones—are a constant in this novel. Some women seem satisfied with their arranged matches, but Nikki utterly rejects the idea. What does the matchmaking of the younger generation—like Mindi and Jason—have in common with the stories from the widows' lives? How is it different?

4. "Nobody eavesdrops on old lady chatter. To them it's all one buzzing noise. They think we're discussing our knee pain and funeral plans," Arvinder tells Nikki. How do the ▸

widows use this kind of social invisibility to their advantage?

5. "We built Southall because we didn't know how to be British. . . . If you had any problems in this new country, your neighbors would rush to your side and bring you money, food, whatever you need. That's the beauty of being surrounded by your community." How does this view of Southall as a safe haven conflict with the younger women's view of it as a kind of prison? How would you feel living in a place like Southall? Are there similar immigrant communities where you live?

6. "That's the problem with having too much imagination, Nikki," Tarampal warns her. "Girls begin to desire too much." Do you agree? Why do you think Tarampal believes this? What do the other widows get from their erotic flights of imagination?

7. Karina's, Gulshan's, and Maya's stories give Nikki a glimpse into how things can go terribly wrong for women in the traditional, insular culture of Southall. Why do you think women like Kulwinder and Sheena choose to stay in that community even after seeing its dark side?

8. What did you think of Tarampal's storyline? Does her early life explain her later actions?
9. Which of the widows' erotic stories was your favorite, and why?
10. What do you think will happen to the novel's characters in the years after the story ends?

"Unlearning and Relearning": Talking to Writer Balli Kaur Jaswal About Her American Debut, *Erotic Stories for Punjabi Widows*

This interview was conducted by Pooja Makhijani, and originally appeared in *Brooklyn Magazine.*

Balli Kaur Jaswal—author of *Erotic Stories for Punjabi Widows,* her dark and funny U.S. debut—and my paths crossed in Singapore, as part of the country's small, tight-knit literary community. I was enchanted by *Inheritance,* her impressive debut novel that traverses the island-state's history from 1970 to 1990, the first English-language novel about Singapore's Punjabi-Sikh diaspora. The novel was published in Australia, where Jaswal lived and worked as a secondary-school English teacher, to great acclaim. She won the *Sydney Morning Herald*'s Best Young Novelist Award 2014. "Jaswal's story of one Punjabi family's efforts to contain the unspeakable is utterly engrossing and ambitious in scope," the judges wrote.

Her second novel, *Sugarbread,* was published in her home country and was a finalist for the 2015 Epigram Books Fiction Prize, the largest literary award in Singapore. In it, Jaswal draws readers into the world of ten-year-old Pin as she negotiates her Sikh faith and grapples with startling secrets.

In *Erotic Stories for Punjabi Widows,* law-school dropout Nikki hastily agrees to helm a writing workshop for women in a Southall gurdwara, which quickly turns into an erotic storytelling club, where otherwise silenced women share their tales about womanhood, sexuality, and the dark secrets within the community.

"I remember being absolutely thrilled by erotic stories when I was in middle school," Jaswal says. "Somebody would steal their mother's romance novel and we'd pass it around, giggling and asking questions and answering them with no real knowledge, of course. If I think about where the energy and electricity comes from in the widows' conversations in the novel, I'm certain it's from those early experiences."

I recently chatted with Jaswal via Google Hangouts and email about her genre-bending new book, fiction of the South Asian diaspora, and women's stories. ▸

"Unlearning and Relearning" ***(continued)***

Q: How did you come up with the scenario for Erotic Stories for Punjabi Widows*?*

A: When I lived in England, I visited some family friends in Southall pretty often. It was an intriguing place—on the western fringe of London, yet culturally much further removed from London. There was something very welcoming about this enclave of Punjabi immigrants, so I could see why it would appeal to new arrivals in a country that was hostile towards them, especially in the 1940s and 1950s. But I was definitely an outsider because I don't speak Punjabi and I'm not into Bollywood music and movies, and it was an alienating experience to be in a place where there seemed to be only one way to be an Indian woman. I wanted to write about this place, and to explore the idea of women defying expectations and rewriting their own narratives. I've always been interested in the taboos surrounding women's sexuality in South Asian communities as well, and how women who are silenced in the public sphere end up expressing themselves in private with other women in smaller, intimate groups. I've heard some older Punjabi women tell the filthiest jokes—only to their trusted female friends, sisters, or daughters, of course.

Q: A theme running through your novels is a concern with women's bodies, specifically how they are circumscribed by patriarchy and policed by society. Did you choose this subject matter or did it choose you?

A: The subject matter is certainly familiar from my own life. I was always made very aware by female family and community members that I'm a girl, and that girls sat a certain way, talked a certain way, etc. It seemed that women were put in charge of policing girls because we occupied the same spaces, but they answered to the men, and so much of their monitoring was about meeting the men's expectations of how their daughters or sisters or wives should behave. I didn't realize how strong a presence it had in my life until I started writing and then it was always there in my stories, this strong invisible force that keeps the female characters submissive and the male characters in control.

Q: Another theme in your work is that of secrets, stories, lies, and mythmaking. What about women claiming their own narratives is so compelling to you?

A: In traditional communities, there's a common narrative of the family being shamed because the girl/woman did something dishonorable, and women ▸

have such a massive responsibility to maintain the reputations of their families. It's terribly unfair that we have this responsibility, yet we can't tell our own stories. The stories that are told about women are usually from a male lens—the story of a woman who is sexually liberated becomes a cautionary tale about "loose" (promiscuous) women who bring shame upon their fathers and brothers. If we're going to be given this responsibility, then the men need to step back and let us tell our stories in a way that rings true to our experiences.

Q: You address womanhood from so many angles, and points of view. All three of your novels include the perspectives of women from different generations. Why is this important to you?

A: I'm interested in the way women in older generations oppress younger women, and I have no doubt that this is largely about doing men's dirty work for them. Men want their daughters/ sisters to behave a certain way but they're also afraid of their daughters or sisters, so they pressure their wives or mothers to do the disciplining for them. Comparing the way expectations of women have changed over generations also provides an interesting source of tension and conflict in the story. I'm also interested in how women from different generations define "oppression" according to the scale of their experience. In *Erotic Stories for Punjabi Widows*, Nikki considers her parents unbearably oppressive because they wanted her to finish her law degree, but for the widows—one of whom was married at ten, another who was abused by her husband because she craved sex—this wouldn't be oppression, it's a privilege. I didn't want to discount what Nikki experienced, because her struggles are real as well, but they are very modern struggles, and she does learn at one point that perhaps she doesn't have it so bad. What's important is that she stays true to herself, and again, it's an enormous privilege that she can even have a sense of self, unlike the women from the widows' generation, whose only identity was as wives and daughters.

Q: Like your previous novels,* Erotic Stories for Punjabi Widows *tells the stories of the Sikh diaspora; this novel also explores the connections between diasporas—in London, the United States, and Canada, for example. How do these varying diasporic geographies, histories, and identities influence your work?

A: I was conscious of mentioning other countries with Sikh diasporas because I wanted to add an element of universality to the story. Although Southall is unique, there are similar versions of thriving enclaves like it in other ▸

countries—Yuba City in California, I'm told by a friend from Southall, is very similar. That's why I made Jason's character American. I wanted him to be an outsider like Nikki so they'd have that in common, but also I wanted to show how the issues of being in the Indian diaspora are not limited to Southall or England. I thought it would be unfair to portray these as a strictly British-Indian set of problems. There are other elements of universality that I wove into the novel as well because they provide that sense of recognition to anyone who grew up Indian anywhere–the ice cream tubs used as storage containers for frozen dal or the morality tales of children causing their parents' health problems. I was probably aware as well that as a Singaporean writer taking on the British-Indian experience, I should weave some of my personal narrative into the story.

Q: This is a rather genre-bending novel—on the surface, it is a literary novel, but it also includes erotica (in the form of the widows' stories) as well as the elements of a thriller. How did you pull that off?

A: It was a process of unlearning and relearning. My two previous books were more solidly literary fiction and didn't have much intertextual stuff, so I had to really learn how to write in different genres and weave them all together in one novel. I read some erotica books and anthologies to have a sense of the language, and also discovered the wide range of subgenres within erotica. There was really a lot of trial and error, even in getting the humorous narrative tone right because it was a departure from my previous work, which was more serious. The mystery part was challenging; I spent more time trying to work out that plot line and the revelations were still a bit knotty right until the end of the editing process. It helped very much to be able to talk out the mystery and Nikki's discoveries with my editors—they were honest with me about what seemed too coincidental and they were good at asking questions that opened up more possibilities in my mind.

Q: What's next?

A: I'm working on a novel about three British-Indian sisters who go on a Sikh pilgrimage to India to reconnect with each other after their mother's death. All of those things I said above about religious hypocrisy apply to this novel, but I'm also excited to be writing a road trip story that features only women, because so many road trip stories are from the male perspective. Traveling and really just existing in India—especially Delhi and Punjab where the novel takes place—is an entirely different thing if ▸

"Unlearning and Relearning" ***(continued)***

you're a woman, so I'm focusing on how restricted, threatened, and vulnerable these three sisters feel and how their movements are policed by men. It's also lighthearted with dark elements, similar in tone to *Erotic Stories for Punjabi Widows.*